The Decline of Our Neighborhood

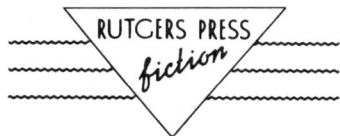

RUTGERS PRESS

fiction

The Decline
of Our
Neighborhood

STORIES BY
Robert
Wexelblatt

RUTGERS UNIVERSITY PRESS
New Brunswick, New Jersey

ACKNOWLEDGMENTS

"The Decline of Our Neighborhood" first appeared in *The Cream City Review*, 8, 1–2 (1983), 120–121

"Glnin" first appeared in *The Iowa Review*, 21, 3 (Fall 1991), 96–125

"Benton's Top Banana" first appeared in *Sou'wester*, 19, 1 (Summer 1991), 62–85

"Lucina and the Hermit" first appeared in *Four Quarters*, 33, 3 (Spring 1984), 6–25. Copyright La Salle University 1984.

"Baby in the Air" first appeared in *Sou'wester*, 20, 2 (Fall 1992), 62–80

Library of Congress Cataloging-in-Publication Data

Wexelblatt, Robert.
      The decline of our neighborhood / by Robert Wexelblatt.
         p. cm. — (Rutgers Press fiction)
      ISBN 0-8135-2015-0 — ISBN 0-8135-2016-9 (pbk.)
      I. Title. II. Series.
    PS3573.E968D4   1993
    813' .54—dc20   93-1114
                                                          CIP

British Cataloging-in-Publication information available

Contents

The Decline of Our Neighborhood

The Decline
of Our Neighborhood

*t*he old man and his dog were to be seen every morning heading
to and from the corner store at nine and every evening at five-
thirty. They had a way of moving together that could arrest an idle
gaze and turn it into an affectionate and melancholy gape. The old
man hobbled slowly with the help of a cane. The dog hobbled and
likewise required the aid of a cane. The old man shuffled and wheezed
and rested frequently at curbs and on garden walls. The dog shuffled
too and lay down, panting, at each curb, on each garden wall. The old
man would thrust out one leg, then wait while the other caught up with
it. The dog thrust out his left-front and right-rear legs, then vice versa.
The old man wore his cap the way the dog wore his leash. Hard-bitten
deliverymen were known to break down at the sight of the old man
hobbling along beside his dog. These tears were not inexplicable, nor
was the sentiment they revealed maudlin; for each deliveryman, no
matter how hard-bitten, saw himself in either the old man (it was
obvious that his pension didn't amount to much) or the dog. The two
were not only emblematic but lachrymariffic. When the two looked at
each other, rheumy eye to rheumy eye, or when the old man clutched
his little brown bag of cheap groceries in the wind, or when the dog,
shivering, collapsed at the old man's feet, or when the old man stood
stock-still beside the dog and put his gnarled old hand on the dog's
faithful head, trying to recall where he was—why then who wouldn't
weep?

The old man never pinched the cute girls walking home from high
school in their tight jeans and loose, bouncing curls. The dog never
barked at, let alone bit, the toddlers on their noisy plastic tricycles. The
old man did not whine and the dog did not grumble. Neither talked

with strangers and, to them, everyone was a stranger. Consequently, they were mute.

Occasionally, observing them from a distance, one might find oneself entertaining the thought of double euthanasia. From time to time, with horror and envy, one could imagine a grief far more profound than any one might hope to experience for oneself, like the secret griefs felt by the dispassionate in the dark corners of movie theaters. Of course one always dismissed such thoughts as quickly as possible.

The old man looked as if he might once have been a sailor; the dog looked as if he might once have been a puppy; but these looks were remote, sepia-tinted, vestigial. Youth was really inadmissible where the two of them were concerned. It was much easier, for instance, to think of them frozen in a snowbank in February. Horror was that much closer than joy. One wept at this image too. The more courageous their threadbare independence, the more one pitied them. That's how things are: the unapproachable move us far more than the importunate; we yearn to succor the self-sufficient even as we shrink from the helpless. Perhaps the old man was aware of this but he gave no sign. On the other hand, the dog gave every sign of advanced arthritis. He stood in need of a bath too, but how could such a decrepit old man, a semi-crippled pensioner, an old salt, give his dog a bath?

The old man wore the same peajacket, the identical wide trousers and peaked cap every day and at every season. This only added to his spectral, immutable appearance. You could tell that he was too warm in summer, too cold in winter, like his dog who, with his ragged off-white fur and brown patches, never changed either.

It was love, of course; at base it is always love that moves us most—particularly love in train with poverty, infirmity, loss, pain, loyalty, and, by way of caboose, death.

We attempted to imagine the old man in his room with the dog. We tried to conceive how they slept, how they voted, whether they were at all interested in baseball. We tried to conjure up a picture of them on vacation. We guessed roughly at the old man's bank account and where he might once have been born. It was inconceivable that he had ever been married, had ever fathered children. There was no virtuosity about their suffering; it was their gift for consolation that left us breathless. We knew that the old man purchased a newspaper every morning and every evening, but couldn't tell if he ever read them. The dog seemed, albeit from a distance, to have lost all his teeth as well as his interest in foreign relations. We couldn't picture the old man watching television, not with those eyes, not with all that dignity.

Suddenly, one day in March—that is, at the end of one of our bitter winters—we asked each other if anyone had seen hide or hair of them. No one had—not the storekeepers, not the deliveryman, not the cute high-school girls, and not the toddlers. We arranged, on the sly, to keep a lookout, not only at nine and five-thirty, but, by taking shifts, at noon and midnight too. Inquiries were discreetly lodged with real-estate agents and coroners. An ad was placed in the newspaper. An industrialist even hired a detective.

Did they die, starved in the winter? Worse, did only *one* of them die? Or did they become offended with us for some reason and simply move away under cover of late-winter darkness? What would we discover when the snowbanks dissolved on Easter Sunday?

Alas, we never found out. They were simply gone and we missed them terribly. We mourned and this mourning was all the deeper for being unmentionable between us. We fell mute in each other's company. We drove more rapidly too. There were accidents. The deliverymen became gradually more and more dry-eyed and mean-spirited; the toddlers evolved into vandals, and the high-school girls all became pregnant.

Glnin

1

*i*f Professor Alasdair Dundee, one of his many admirers in Glasgow, had not smuggled a bottle of genuine Laphroaig whiskey for him, Robert would probably not have slept through the noisy events of the night of November 23. Nevertheless, having polished off more than half the bottle by five P.M., he did. The Highland hangover with which he came to at ten the following morning did not make it easy for him to endure the pounding on his apartment door that awakened him, or the shouting of his surname as an imperative.

"Glnin! Glnin!"

"Shit," Robert grunted half aloud, as if addressing the ghost of Professor Dundee. It was a sort of pounding with which he was on terms of familiarity.

"Glnin!"

"Open up, please!"

Two voices. That cinched it. Rousing himself from the leather couch into which he had sunk so many hours before, Robert grumbled a reply.

"Get lost. I don't feel up to being arrested today."

There was a muffled conversation out in the hall. One of the goons laughed—most likely, Robert conjectured, exulting at the prospect of flattening the apartment door of Robert Glnin, a door he fancied must be famous in the service.

"Glnin! We aren't here to arrest you."

"That you, Spinkin? Since when do *you* make house calls?"

This Spinkin was at once Robert's favorite and least favorite secret police officer: favorite because he was well read, sophisticated, cultured; least favorite because, in addition to the requisite sadism, Spinkin was a pedantic bore.

"Yes, it's Spinkin." He sounded, one might have thought, just as irritated as Robert had, though he immediately mastered himself and added, with a hint of actual courtesy, "It's not an arrest. In fact, just the contrary."

Robert struggled to his feet, reeled toward the door. His mouth tasted of rotten oysters and the ash of newsprint. His eyes hurt around their entire circumference. He slipped on a bit of manuscript.

"What do you mean?" he asked suspiciously. "Not that I believe you, of course. I ask only out of intellectual curiosity. But what *is* the contrary of an arrest?"

An edgy laugh from Spinkin's partner.

"Won't you *please* open up?" Spinkin pleaded. Robert even detected a note of anxiety in his old interrogator. He sensed something like an advantage; after all, his door was still on its hinges and Spinkin himself had come to call.

"I *demand* to know what you consider the contrary of an arrest, Spinkin."

"You let us in, we'll tell you," offered the second voice, almost giggling.

Now here's something really odd, thought Robert. One of his subordinates would scarcely dare to say such a thing in such a place in Spinkin's presence. Also, there was something familiar about that second voice.

"Who's that?"

"Never mind," said Spinkin, clearly exasperated. "Just open up. Come on, *move* it, Glnin."

"Now, now, Captain," the other intervened. "Remember to whom it is that you are addressing yourself."

Robert, listening as hard as his headache allowed, thought he heard Spinkin growl at this bit of fancy grammar. Robert had to agree that it was out of place.

"Spinkin," he said, "I'm waiting."

"All right, all right. What is the contrary of an arrest? Well, surely, Mr. Glnin, you will recall the famous opening sentence of Franz Kafka's occasionally banned novel *The Trial?*"

"Oh Lord!" cried Robert. "You're not going to hand me one of your Kafka lectures, are you?"

"You want an answer or not?"

"I tell you there's no time for this," whispered the other voice and, at that instant, Robert recognized it. It was Minister Ferfatkin himself, chief of the whole rotten spiderweb. This must indeed be something special. Perhaps they meant to shoot him on the spot, with a silencer; or maybe they intended to hang him with his own belt after forcing him to write a suicide note renouncing all his works, confessing to being a spy, and who knows what besides. Robert became frightened. Best to stall, he figured.

"So what *about* the opening of *The Trial?*" he asked. "I'm curious."

"K. is suddenly found guilty on his thirtieth birthday. Thus, he is arrested. You, on the other hand, Mr. Glnin, have been suddenly found innocent," said Spinkin flatly.

"What are you talking about? And why is the Minister of the Interior out there with you?"

Confusion in the hall. Curses. Exhortations. Threats.

Ferfatkin answered. He sounded like olive oil running down a piece of silk. "Mr. Glnin, owing to the, so to speak, surprising events of last night and this morning—"

"What events?"

A pause. "You mean you don't know? You really don't? Is it possible?" And this time Ferfatkin laughed in earnest, on all cylinders. It was a laugh full of bitterness and hilarity, the way Macbeth might have laughed when Macduff told him his mother had had a Caesarian.

Spinkin went on for Ferfatkin. "Because of these events of which you are incomprehensibly ignorant, Mr. Glnin, you have been found *so* innocent that—but look, why don't you just open up? It's cold out here in the hall."

Robert, angry because they had frightened him, spoke from the heart. "What do I care if you're cold? You mules can freeze your asses off for all I care."

"Very well, Mr. Glnin," said Ferfatkin, who had evidently mastered himself. "Here's the story. The government is, so to say, in a state of crisis. Last night certain elements of the army joined the demonstrators who filled the center of the city. There was a little, well, shooting. At the moment there is, one might say, something of a standoff. Things are . . . fluid."

Robert suddenly recalled that he was indeed to have addressed a small rally outside the Cafe Magus the prior evening at seven. This was astonishing news.

"What you say is most heartening," he said. "But what do you want with me?"

"Damn it, Glnin," shouted Spinkin, losing all patience. "You've been elected president!"

"Just for the time being, of course," Ferfatkin added in a tone at once ominous and jovial.

"Huh?" Robert gasped as the nausea hit.

At that moment the telephone rang. It had not worked for three weeks, and Robert stared at it as he might at a resurrected corpse. He let it ring three times before picking it up.

"Hello?" he said unsteadily.

It was Pleyl, the poet and pamphleteer. He and Robert had been chums since way back in grammar school. What ideas hadn't they picked over in all those years? What books hadn't they dissected? And how much beer they had put away! Pleyl was also the organizer of the Magus rally which, apart from the shooting and Robert's failure to show up, had evidently succeeded pretty well.

"Robert! Thank heavens you're there! I thought for sure they'd come for you last night. I called, of course, but the line was still dead. Frankly, I assumed you were too." Pleyl was shouting over a noise like fighting children.

"Only dead drunk," Robert remarked with his habitual honesty. "Sorry."

"What a night, Robert!" Pleyl began at once to rhapsodize. He couldn't get it all out fast enough; it was the same as when he had told Robert about his first visit to a whorehouse. "Krillip was wounded—not too seriously, flesh wound in the thigh. The streets filled completely up. Lazlo, who stood in for you, was simply magnificent. He climbed up on the statue of Prince Frunzi and shouted at the riot police, d'après Mirabeau, 'You may tell your Master that we will not leave this square except at the point of the bayonet!' It was electrifying, Robert. Someone in the crowd yelled, 'That's right! And not even then!' After that all hell broke loose. I've got a million things to tell you."

"Glnin!"

"Mr. Glnin?"

"There are some people at the door," Robert explained to Pleyl.

"Who?" Pleyl asked nervously. "It's not the police, is it?"

"Well, yes, it is."

"My God, Robert! Don't let them in on any account. Barricade yourself. I can have some people over there in ten minutes."

"Well," said Robert, "you see they've just told me that I've been made President."

"What ?"

"Of the Republic, I think." Here Robert, understandably uncertain, called to the door. "President of the Republic, is it?"

"Yes," admitted Ferfatkin.

"Yes!" protested Spinkin.

"President of the Republic, Pleyl. By any chance do you know something about this?"

Pleyl, evidently dumbfounded, was silent for a moment.

"We'd heard rumors," he admitted. "But nobody credited them."

"Well, then, perhaps it's true?"

"Oh, Robert—"

Robert sighed, rubbed his forehead. "God, what a hangover I've got."

"Look," said Pleyl, suddenly as decisive as a boy playing soldiers, "don't move. Don't open that door. I'm coming myself."

"All right. I'll stay put. I'll only move at the point of a bayonet."

"Good," said Pleyl and, before hanging up, told Robert that he was with his Committee at the State television studio. "If your set's working, tune in," he suggested.

"Please, Mr. Glnin," begged the Minister of the Interior. "I have my orders. I'm to bring you to the Parliament building, you see, and right away. People are waiting for you right now. The nation is calling. And I'm not a well man, Mr. Glnin. I'm in the middle of an attack of shingles. I should be home soaking in the tub."

Robert went to the door. "You can stay in the hall, if you like, but be careful not to scratch; it only makes it worse, you know," he said in a friendly whisper. "As for me, I'm going to watch television."

As Ferfatkin whined and Spinkin blustered behind the door they did not dare to smash, Robert switched on the set and put on the kettle. He was annoyed that he had no coffee and would have to make do with some of the Iranian tea Cybele had left behind.

At length a picture materialized, as if reluctantly. It was blurred so that Robert had to concentrate to an unpleasant degree.

He saw a long table without a cloth; it looked rather like his mother's endlessly polished pre-war diningroom table. A young man sat on its further side and appeared to be speaking directly to the table, like an abashed child refusing to eat his peas. You could see his nose and the top of his head which, Robert couldn't help but reflect, was as thick with black hair as his own had been ten years before. Behind the young man stood two soldiers, at least as young. They wore full battle gear and held submachine guns. Farm boys, Robert judged, no more than halfway through their hitch. He could see that they were jumpy as hell; they kept looking left and right like body guards in a hostile crowd. And perhaps they were also excited about being on television, curious about the equipment. As the boy read his overwrought statement other people walked in from left and right. They marched back and forth across the screen, occasionally stopping to exchange papers or anxious whispers. Robert thought he recognized some of them but it was so much like looking through a February blizzard that he couldn't be certain. He tried to focus on what the boy was saying.

". . . found in voluntary associations are, we believe, those on which we shall build a future for our nation, or rather on which the nation may rediscover itself; for the nation is neither more nor less than the sum of all the individuals, high and low, who make it up at any historical moment, including, of course, these individuals' myriad links to the past—to ancestry, to history—from the ancient tribes, the dark ages, through the crucible of the Reformation and the riches of the Renaissance, right up to the terrible wars of our own century, and this latest dark age of inward slavery and wholesale alienation. The compulsion those of my generation have been under all our lives to form an inhuman community void of authentic human communion, the command to belong on penalty of persecution, to assent to every banal lie, every deceit, every false slogan and mindless directive, to sing on cue both figuratively and literally . . ."

The kettle began to boil, to sing both figuratively and literally.

"I'm about to have some tea now," Robert said to the door on his way to the kettle.

Ferfatkin tried a new tack. "So, Mr. Glnin, we may take it that your refusal to come to the Parliament building—indeed, to open this door—means that you decline election as President of the Republic? Is that not so?"

Robert poured the water into the teapot as he replied. "That is far from a simple deduction, Your Excellency. First of all, I haven't said yes and I haven't said no. Second of all, you've presented no proof of this putative election which, you must admit, appears improbable. You might be lying. After all, you're a government minister. Third, I'm puzzled by your confident use of the key word *election*. It's true that I slept soundly last night, but I don't recall any balloting either yesterday or the day before. In fact, I can't remember being nominated, speaking through a megaphone; I can't recall interviews by the foreign press, meeting with campaign workers, debating my opponents. Shall I go on?"

Spinkin, furious as ever, answered. "No doubt you *can* go on and on, Glnin. I've heard you do it often enough. You're no joy to interrogate, I can tell you, between your Oscar Wilde whimsy and your Aristotelian logic. But as it happens, this is a simple matter. You were elected by Parliament after your predecessor resigned and, to be candid, left town. If you don't want the job, say so. We're busy men."

"I appreciate that, but at the moment I prefer to drink my tea."

The phone rang again.

Annoyed, Robert answered with as much friendliness as the receptionist at the Writers' Union. "Glnin."

"Mr. Glnin?"

"You expected someone else?"

"Mr. Glnin, this is Cornelius Wertheim, Speaker of the House of Deputies. I'm calling from my office here in the Parliament building. Has the Minister of the Interior stopped by your place, by any chance?"

"He and his shingles are out in the hall right now."

"I see. And has he perhaps let drop something about an election?"

"Yes, something along those lines did come up."

"Well, Mr. Glnin, speaking for my colleagues as well as myself, I should like most earnestly to encourage you to accept the post. We are quite sincere. The vote was virtually unanimous."

There was a noise which might well have been a semi-distant explosion.

"So, I'm supposed to save your hides, eh?" said Robert.

There was a brief pause and a sound, as of Wertheim rising from under a large piece of furniture.

"Mr. Glnin, the situation is serious."

"Well, I'll certainly give it due consideration, Mr. Speaker."

"But—"

"Sorry. Frightfully busy at the moment. Goodbye, Mr. Speaker."

Robert had just poured out a cup of tea and was sniffing at it when Pleyl and his friends arrived, making a great racket out in the hall. It occurred to Robert that people naturally tend to carry the mood and even the noise-level of one situation into the next. Just as schoolchildren after a recess will continue shouting in the classroom, so, after the excitement of the television studio and the streets, Pleyl ran heavily up the stairs and spoke at the top of his lungs, as if to make himself heard over a bombardment.

"Robert! We're here!"

There was scuffling to be heard, like that of incompetent dancers.

"That's nice, Pleyl. But please don't yell so loudly. Mrs. Sturmzi is only hard-of-hearing, not deaf."

"Sorry. Look, we've taken these two into custody. You're quite safe now."

"They've got us at gunpoint, Mr. Glnin," Ferfatkin protested in a rather high-pitched version of his voice.

"Pleyl, in case you haven't met, allow me to introduce Minister of the Interior Ferfatkin and his colleague Captain Spinkin of the Spider-web."

"Robert," said Pleyl, "open up. You've got to come to the station right away."

"No," Ferfatkin objected, "you're wanted far more urgently at the Parliament building!"

"I think," said Robert aloud, but very much to himself, "it really is about time I woke up."

2

*b*ut, as we all know, Glnin was not dreaming, at least not in the oneiric sense. More likely, I am.

The 102nd aphorism of Klaren Verheim: "What a wonder is Art! When we become too placid, it braces our sleepiness with the tonic of chaos; when too disoriented, it alone can slake our thirst for order." Well, if so, bully for capital Art.

In his early essay "Art, Truth, and Corrosion," Robert Glnin himself wrote: "Two kinds of art, that of flesh and that of bone. That is to say, there is an art of surfaces and one of essences, actuality and reality, happenings and their clean structures. I confess to a preference for the skeletal sort because of my beliefs about the nature of truth, or, more accurately, what I would like to believe about the shape and feel of truth—that it is hard, articulated, angular, formal, unmitigated, unforgiving." The many citations of this passage end here, of course, as does Glnin's essay. In the holograph, however, Glnin added something: "But do I believe in my beliefs? That is quite another question."

I keep finding things like that. At first it was exhilarating, I admit, but now they are merely annoying. My fellowship proposal did not anticipate such perplexities. Bad enough that Glnin forces one to hop back and forth across the frontier between history and literature without all this unlooked-for skepticism, this fogginess of his corrosive truth-telling. A hero? An *homme moyen sensuel*? Father of fictions? Author of his country?

The word "history" derives from the Greek for inquiry, Professor Samartini was excessively fond of reminding us graduate students. But what *is* an inquiry exactly? I mean, once you discover some facts, how should you arrange them? And what of the facts you may not have discovered? Besides, into *what* do you inquire? Where do you stop? Is it necessarily less important to know how often a man brushed his teeth than his view of Hobbes or Marx? Moreover, only an inhuman inquiry would avoid all speculation. Is speculation history too? an inquiry? Can you see anything on earth without looking through our humid atmosphere? Are the structures of happenings ever completely naked?

There is no statue of Glnin in this city. He forbade it in his will. And yet you feel him everywhere, or at least the official story of Glnin. But there is a false note for me in the story which is owing to the national compulsion to make a myth out of it. Historians are of two minds about myths, as Glnin was about art. On the one hand, since they originally preceded history, myths are the strawmen of inquiry, that which the inquiry is to explode; on the other, myths are just as often the consequences of what historians themselves write. One has to approach myth cautiously, like a box which might contain either a bomb or a birthday present.

What have I invented? Practically nothing. For example, I found a telegram to Glnin from Alasdair Dundee announcing his arrival on November 23. The thin paper still bears the tan circular stain of a wet glass bottom. The prolix memoirs of Sergius Spinkin can be cited, *mutatis mutandis,* for the prolonged standoff outside Glnin's door on the morning of November 24—he even compares it to the opening scene of Kafka's *Metamorphosis.* The break with the actress Cybele Chatuchat, also her fondness for Iranian tea, Paul Krillip's minor flesh-wound, Lazlo Povric's public appropriation of Mirabeau, even Mrs. Sturmzi's partial hearing loss—all can be substantiated from the record, now that Glnin's private papers have been made available to scholars like me.

The discrepancies are really not factual, but personal. It is Glnin himself and not what happened to Glnin or what he did and said that puzzles me. Perhaps this is just a loss of confidence on my part; I mean a corrosion of faith in my discipline as the surest pathway to the truth. *Note Bene:* I know full well that the Objectivity of Truth is a kind of giant buffoon slain by hordes of earnestly bespectacled pygmies armed with quiversful of good, sharp arguments a century or more ago. Nevertheless, I feel a fondness for this dead giant, this punctured phantom, just as if he had once existed. The loss of belief in objective truth is a crisis faced by all young educated people, I think. In fact, it is an indispensable portion of their educations. Most simply give up on it, which is at least logically consistent, even if they persist in arguing as if it were knowable. As for me, though, I see objective truth as the unattainable after which one ought ceaselessly to strive, all the while being mindful that it is unattainable. It is this that makes my profession both tragic and comic—which is to say, fully human. Like Glnin.

"Among crows," says Verheim's 80th aphorism, "scavenging is the most respectable profession."

3

*i*n so far as it is possible for a woman with a serious headcold to blow her reddened nose in a sexy fashion, Cybele Chatuchat did so. Benedikt admired the short, almost refined noise she made, the tiny contractions of her bare toes, the gentle swell in the convexity of her abdomen, the slight roll to her hips, the way her long dusky hair fell forward from her shoulders and over her cheeks as though it had been carefully trained to do so. Benedikt loved to watch Cybele at such moments, adored her most when she performed the homeliest of tasks: brushing her teeth, combing her hair, bathing, dressing, undressing, sneezing. Like a falcon, he had a keen eye for any natural movement, and with Cybele such gestures were rare.

"Don't *look* at me," she said with a frown and a laugh. "I'm *frightful*."

Benedikt did not reply. He merely sat on her upholstered easy chair with his legs crossed at the knee and looked at Cybele on her outsized bed with its ten different-colored pillows.

When he arrived on the morning of November 24 the first thing he had done was to turn up the electric heat because of her cold and because he did not want her to put on too many clothes. Cybele was cheap about certain things.

"There's a revolution going on," Cybele had exclaimed at the door, her eyes shining, "and I've got a cold."

Benedikt, smiling as he saw to the heat, gave a mock-gallant answer. "The latter news is more weighty than the former," he said, and took off his brown fedora, grey overcoat, and yellow muffler.

"Where are you coming from?" asked Cybele, only brushing his freshly shaved cheek with her own. "The hospital?"

"Yes. As a matter of fact, I was there all night."

"Oh! Are there many casualties?"

"Many is a relative term. I'd say more than the government will admit, fewer than the opposition will claim."

A specialist in disorders of the skin, Benedikt practiced medicine with a degree of detachment that most of his patients felt as both unnerving and reassuring. Had they come to him with complaints about more vital or intimate organs, they would probably have found Benedikt's detachment repellent; but, as it was only their skins, his impersonal, clinical manner, his looking at their surfaces, so to speak, and never below, gave his patients confidence in him. He knew all about their pustules and rashes; only some of the women wished him to know about their lives and, excepting Cybele and three or four of her predecessors, Benedikt rejected these intimacies brusquely.

At the hospital on the night of November 23–24 he had been of real help to those bothered by tear gas and abrasions, and he had even worked for a while on a gunshot wound. At nine in the morning, when things had become quiet, he had walked home through the littered, dangerous streets, taken a shower, shaved, changed into a fresh suit, and come right to Cybele's.

"I'll make us some coffee," he said. Benedikt was dying for a cup of coffee.

"What do you think is going to happen, Benedikt?" Cybele asked anxiously.

He observed how her wet eyes implored, invited, complained all at once. She wore the white silk nightgown he had given her. It suited her well, even with a cold, he noted with satisfaction.

He shrugged.

"I've had the television on all morning. Students are giving unintelligible speeches, professors are making wild claims, colonels give assurances but look worried, union leaders make contradictory remarks. A man I know, Hrska, even claimed the President's fled the country."

"Anything's possible," Benedikt remarked indifferently and got to his feet with a weary sigh. "Where's the coffee?"

"I think in the refrigerator. Good stuff. Tula gave it to me. And there should be bread and preserves. Aunt Bemoise sent the preserves to me last week. Benedikt?"

He was already in the little kitchen, intent on the coffee—he was charmed by the rapidity of her imported coffee-maker—and didn't hear her. She took advantage of the moment to enjoy a really good blow.

"Benedikt?" she called again, using her diaphragm to project as she did on stage.

"What is it?"

"Don't you really care?"

"What about?"

"Revolution, politics, the fate of the nation?"

"No."

Cybele frowned and turned back to the television, which she had neglected to turn off, thus saving electricity.

"Oh!" she cried.

It was Robert, looking perfectly awful. He must have been in the thick of it all night, she supposed.

"These preserves are really excellent!" Benedikt called to her. "Brava, Aunt Bemoise!"

Robert was speaking in his customary manner, without any formality and with that unpleasant expression of his that challenged you to find fault with what he was saying. He looked straight at the camera, at Cybele. She caught a characteristic phrase: ". . . politicians who tell you that they, rather than you, are responsible for your happiness and that you are, thus, by definition, happy . . ."

She had not seen Robert for over two months. Before that, they had been together barely two weeks after he came out of detention. How horrible he had been then, cold and gloomy as a long November rain, sleeping half the time and grouchy the rest. It was, in fact, Robert's behavior, she believed, that had produced that attack of nervous eczema. Before she could concentrate on what he was saying, Benedikt was back, balancing a plate and two cups. He too looked at the set.

"Ah, your old boyfriend," he said. Cybele hid nothing from Benedikt, neither her skin nor her past. "Here, drink this. I made it good and strong."

"Shh, I want to hear," she said.

Robert was talking about truth-telling, his favorite subject, his idée fixe.

". . . to start with not a political question; for me, it is an artistic question. However, in a country where one is repeatedly arrested, boringly interrogated, ludicrously tried, and nastily imprisoned for telling even imaginary truths, art becomes political, so to speak, against its will. On the other hand, the peculiar prestige with the general population of our dissident film-makers, poets, dramatists, painters, and novelists—along with that of our nonconforming physicists, biologists, and mathematicians—derives from their own *non*political relationship to the truth. To me, it is a great irony that the politicization of the nonpolitical should be the final consequence of all this idiotic repression. And it would be a self-defeating irony too if the political goal of the dissident community were not what I hope it is: namely, to de-politicize speech-acts, at least to the degree of allowing people to think, feel, and say whatever they wish or must.

"But all this is rather parochial. Less so is my belief that liberty is a necessary, though by no means sufficient, condition of wealth. Wealth interests virtually everybody, even dissident artists and scientists. Now there are people, perhaps many people, who want to be free only so that they can be rich. If someone should convince them that they could be rich in another way, they'd give up their freedom quickly enough. Only then they'd end up both poor and enslaved. Free people work harder than slaves—and to far better effect . . . "

"This is boring," Benedikt complained. "And do stop rubbing your nose like that, Cybele. It's already raw."

"It's funny seeing Robert on television. It makes him look less skinny. Don't you think he's making sense?"

"Whenever I hear words like Freedom and Truth I begin to yawn. Can't help it; it's a reflex. Currency that's passed through too many hands and gotten thin and soiled."

"Robert's not really political, you know. It's as he said. He tried to keep out of it and couldn't. Still, after his second prison term he began to think about it more. In fact, I've just remembered something rather funny. An idea of his that we had a laugh over."

Benedikt put down his cup, moved to the edge of Cybele's bed, and began to rub her back through the cool white silk.

"What's that?" he asked.

"It was in January, I think, or February. Winter in any case. We'd gone up to Tastaya, to my place in the mountains. He'd only been out two or three days and wanted to get as far away from the city as possible. He said he couldn't stand to see cops on the corner or people cringing in front of traffic lights or to breathe the foul air. There was a tremendous snowstorm which made him happy. He sat by the window all afternoon just watching it come down and reciting poems about snow. The more the snow buried everything the jollier he got."

"This was before the eczema, I take it?"

"Oh *years* before. When we first—"

"Yes?"

"Well, Robert said he had had this idea for an absurdist novel.

Seeing him giving this speech reminded me of it. The novel was to be about a novelist—"

"So many of them are," sighed Benedikt.

"Yes, that's so. But this one was to be different. This novelist—a dissident, like Robert, and, like him, essentially nonpolitical—is suddenly made president of the country. Let's see. I remember he kept laughing the whole time he was telling me about it. Just a little lower, Benedikt. Yes, there. Let's see. The joke was that he's incompetent, of course. But he had this great reputation with everybody. Just as Robert does now."

"For what? Integrity?"

"Yes, I suppose. And that was the serious part, I mean why people *wanted* him to be president. He said that in a country where truth is outlawed, only outlaws tell the truth."

"As they see it," Benedikt remarked.

"Well, anyway, once he becomes president anybody can tell the truth, and everybody thinks they know what it is."

Benedikt cupped Cybele's round breasts. "*My* truths," he whispered in her ear.

4

*C*ybele's anecdote about Glnin's fanciful, but astoundingly prophetic idea for a novel—to be precise, an *absurdist* novel—is not itself fanciful. There is a half-page about it in his notebook from that period:

> A rakish fellow (perhaps an academic, seducer of students, maybe an artist, a writer) is unexpectedly made mayor (president?). There's been some sort of revolution. He has missed it (cf. the man who slept through the earthquake that destroyed his town). A dissident who suddenly finds himself with real power. He takes all bribes (none?). Is he any use? Clever, incompetent? Perhaps retrospective. Young enough for appetite, old enough for wisdom. K.'s story of the bad student who, on the day prizes are awarded, mishears and thinks that his name is being called.

I found this two days ago, or rather it was pointed out to me by a sixtyish man who is also working on the Glnin collection. I have seen him every day, clucking over the papers. I didn't like his looks, though ordinarily I am well disposed to the type of the elderly scholar, instinctively respectful, shabby old-fashioned suits and all. But he had the air of a fanatic ideologue about him—shining eyes, derisive mouth—and, in a sense, this impression is accurate. Also, he was unpleasantly insinuating, nodding at me in the reading room like an old homosexual. I might have guessed he is currently "between appointments." His name is Johannes Pilkrohmer and he has an idée fixe far narrower, far less noble than the one Cybele Chatuchat ascribed to Robert Glnin.

He accosted me at the door of the reading room as I was leaving for lunch. He put his hand on the door, virtually blocking my way.

"Obviously we are both interested in Glnin," he whispered with a smile more contemptuous than ingratiating, an expression which seemed to imply his superiority to the interest he was claiming we shared.

"Mrs. Gulwich informs me you are American?" He stated this as a question, as though the stern and punctilious librarian Mrs. Gulwich were not to be trusted in such matters.

"Yes," I said. "I'm here on a fellowship."

He looked envious. "Ah," he said. "Perhaps we could have lunch together? Discuss what we have found in this treasure-trove? Compare notes?"

I would have liked to avoid lunch with Pilkrohmer but could see no way out. As soon as I acceded, he insisted on a vegetarian restaurant which turned out to be five blocks away. Of course I paid. I had a fellowship.

Pilkrohmer's obsession led him to Glnin and not vice-versa. Fundamentally, I find his fixed idea silly and passé, though he presented it tricked out in highfalutin jargon, dropping names like rose petals.

"You see," he said across a spinach salad, "the whole world is a text or, more exactly, all that we humans do in and to the world. Nature is a constant; she is the sheet of paper on which we construct our lives, which, like all classical fictions, have a beginning, middle, and end. And, of course, these fictions can collide, collide all the time, in fact. But by virtue of this form alone—I mean this Aristotelian structure— the difference between a literary character and an historical personage is essentially moot. George Washington or Julien Sorel, Alexander of Macedon or Don Quixote de la Mancha—who, for that matter, is *also* an old Spanish gentleman by the name of Quijana."

"But with respect," I objected, familiar with this line of thinking from my sophomore year, "this is mere solipsism and game-playing, Mr. Pilkrohmer. If you're going to suggest that Robert Glnin is in some sense a *literary* character—"

Pilkrohmer began chuckling, looking at me as one might at a trained poodle standing up straight as a bank teller.

"No, no," he said with oily deprecation. "Nothing so simple. However, you must grant that a good deal of the allure of Glnin lies in his being the only example we have of a novelist catapulted overnight into the position of a head of state. Moreover, I do not think you can so easily distinguish between Glnin and one of his characters as you seem to suppose. Really, it *is* no easy matter—even for a brilliant young American with a generous fellowship."

It was at this moment that the check arrived.

"No," said Pilkrohmer once I had picked it up, "Glnin was in a metaphysically complicated position as, indeed, are we all. Here he was, really and truly President of the Republic, but did he cease for a moment to be an artist of the imagination? And is the world not, in some sense, really a text? Do we understand it any differently, with distinct tools? But come, let's go back. There's something I want very much to show you. It's in one of the notebooks I have been examining."

And that is how I came to see the passage I cited earlier.

"If you look closely enough," says Verheim's 44th aphorism, "all deception is self-deception."

5

*t*he excellent, utterly irreplaceable brains of Roman Propp and Carolus Peyser, both bearded third-year engineering students and the best of friends, mingled on the cobblestones under the equestrian statue of Prince Frunzi. The six drunken steelworkers who had clubbed them to death swaggered and staggered off in the direction of the Cafe Magus, the windows of which were already smashed, the slowest of its patrons streaming out the back way.

Karel wiped his mouth and asked his pal Viktor if he were certain that slaughtering intellectuals was really necessary. "They're only boys under those beards," he pointed out. "Poor bastards."

"It's a hard business, Karel, and no doubt about it, even if the eggheads've got it coming, which they do. That's why I'm drunk. Maybe you didn't drink enough? See there? You ought to grab a bottle or two out of that place," Viktor said, moving his burly shoulder forward in the direction of the Magus.

Across the square a few other steelworkers were still chasing people, but most just stood around under the sharp but pale November sun smoking and talking to one another. At the far end, near the National Museum, lay an overturned limousine and a burning tram. There were no police to be seen. Shouts and the sound of shattering glass came intermittently from the narrow streets that led off the square. Only a few of the injured lay about. Most had been dragged away.

An hour before these wolves had descended on the fold of Frunzi Square, Robert Glnin, dressed in his usual worsted trousers and outsized sweater, was signing a whole stack of executive orders in the ornate Office of the President, into which he had moved a cot. As he did so, he was also thinking of the interview he had scheduled that morning with Amanda Hare-Stephenson, the well-known English journalist and critic.

While he had never met Amanda, they had exchanged letters on two occasions. The first time was eight years earlier, when *The Last Two Positions of Gronsky,* smuggled out of the country by Professor Alasdair Dundee, had appeared in English translation. She had written him a fan letter and enclosed a draft of the splendid review that later appeared in the *Times Literary Supplement.* Robert had written back to thank her, saying, truthfully, that her own work was hardly unknown even in his country. Four years later, when he was in prison, it was Amanda Hare-Stephenson who had helped to organize the international protests that got him out—who knows?—a little sooner rather than later. After his release they had written back and forth more seriously, more politically; and, with his permission, Amanda had used passages from his letters in a long article about him for an American newsweekly. So, he owed her. Moreover, since he had seen her photograph, duty and inclination coincided in his decision to grant her his first foreign interview as President.

At ten o'clock Pleyl walked in. Robert, fond of living by a few metaphors, kept his office door open at all times.

"She's here," Pleyl said. "The Englishwoman."

"Good."

"You finished?"

"Not quite. I've put some aside anyway."

"What for?"

"Reconsideration."

"You want to reconsider something?"

"I *always* want to, don't you?"

"Robert, you're not revising a novel, you know. The syntax and diction needn't be altogether deathless. Decisiveness is—"

"Look, Pleyl, I went without sleep last night; the night before, the celebration went until three. Don't you think I might be allowed to go without a lecture this morning?"

Pleyl clicked the heels of his tennis shoes and gave a mock Prussian bow. "My apologies, Your Excellency."

"Cut the horseshit," said Robert brusquely. "The farce comes a little later, I hope."

"All right. So what is it you want to reconsider? I'll have to tell the others."

"Certain personnel matters."

"Oh?"

"Dismissals and arrests."

"The iron's only hot for a short while, Robert."

Glnin didn't answer. He didn't need to.

"All right," said Pleyl, "but I'm glad *I* don't have to interview you this morning." On his way out he added, "You've got exactly one half hour."

In the black and white photograph Glnin had seen of her—it was on the back of one of her collections—Amanda Hare-Stephenson was standing against a white background in a jet black dress with a long, full skirt, little epaulettes and a double row of buttons down the bodice, tightly belted at the waist. She wore her hair stylishly up and was looking straight into the camera as if she meant to yank the photographer right through the lens. When she came into Glnin's office she looked even better and much less intimidating. The first thing he noticed was that her hair was down and the thought flashed through his mind that her middle name was apt. He rose to greet her.

"Mr. President," she said and held out her hand. She spoke it formally, but smiled like an old, old friend.

"Amanda," Glnin said and enfolded her hand in both of his. "You'd better call me Robert. *Dear* Robert is how you began your last letter."

"Oh," she said, "before I forget. I've brought something for you." She was fumbling in her large shoulder bag.

"Your trip?" he asked.

"Uneventful. Here it is."

Amanda handed him a check for ten thousand pounds.

"What?"

"It's not a bribe," she laughed. "Don't look so horrified."

"Then?"

"Look closely. It's signed by your English publisher. They *owe* it to you, Robert."

"I see."

"There'll be more later."

Flabbergasted by the check and fuddled by her perfume, he offered Amanda a seat.

She doffed her overcoat. She was wearing a denim skirt, high brown boots, and a black turtleneck. He tried to think of adjectives to describe her hair.

"Well," she said, settling in. "Congratulations. I can't tell you how thrilled everybody is, how amazed."

"No more than yours truly."

"I guess we'd better get right at it, eh? I counted three ambassadors out there. At least there were three guys in three-piece suits."

Robert passed his hand down his sweater. "So far the new government's going casual," he said. "You see, you're just right, too."

She looked down. "Oh, my travelling outfit?"

"Among other things. Notice please that I am already flirting."

"Yes."

"Mind?"

"Not at all."

"Don't be so nonchalant. I'm sincerely flirting. Why, is it better for the interview if the subject flirts?"

"Oh, absolutely," she said, pulling out her little tape-recorder, pad, and pen.

"Smashing. Then I'll go on doing so. All right, first query?"

"There's a rumor that your government intends to dissolve the armed forces. True?"

Robert picked up the recorder and spoke directly into it. "Sugar dissolves in water. Ice dissolves in summer. What's the solvent for an armored division? Next."

"You'd rather not answer that one, I take it?"

"Not just at the moment, Amanda."

"Then you're not ruling it out?"

"Did I mention that I like your hair down like that?"

"So does my husband."

"Oops."

"What about subsidies to inefficient industries?"

"You know the story about the shepherd whose dog went lame?"

"No."

"The dog, being lame, couldn't keep up with the sheep. The shepherd happens to like his dog, so he hobbles all his sheep. That way the dog can keep up with them. Next?"

"Okay," she said slowly and with a fetchingly uncertain frown. "Elections?"

"In favor of them."

"When?"

"It'll take six months at least—and then, with any luck at all, I can be an ex-President. We're working on a new constitution already. Parties are popping up like fairy-rings all over the place. In a couple weeks or so I expect we'll be inundated with media consultants telling us all the most effective methods of fibbing."

"So you're not an idealist about democracy?"

"Idealism is anti-democratic, Amanda—or don't you have to read Plato at Oxbridge? Anyway, Pleyl told me you were divorced."

"He's misinformed. Separated."

"More like a shoulder, or more like a yolk and a white?"

"More like a fool and his money, actually."

It was at this moment that the noise from Frunzi Square reached the Office of the President.

"Another celebration?" Amanda suggested.

Before Robert could reply, Pleyl and Markovitz rushed in, both shouting.

"A riot's broken out!"

"Workers from Provice, the steel plant."

"They're clubbing everybody in sight."

24

"My God! What about the police?"

"Don't know," said Pleyl.

"I'll get on the phone," said Markovitz, already on his way.

Amanda, her blue eyes bright with Anglo-Saxon excitement, asked if she might stay.

"Better than going outside," said Robert, then turned to Pleyl. "Find Captain Spinkin. I want him here two minutes ago."

"But—"

"No questions, Pleyl." He pointed at the stack of unsigned orders. "You'll find him in his office, I'll bet. And tell him—or else. Got it?"

Pleyl nodded and shot out of the room. Glnin started rifling through the pile of papers, tossing the ones he didn't want over his shoulder.

Amanda carefully placed her tape-recorder on the corner of the desk and began to write.

Having found what he was looking for, Glnin got up and went to the elongated window behind his desk. He made a short, low noise.

Amanda looked up brightly from her notes. "Pardon me?"

"They're brutally murdering people out there, you see, and it's not really their fault. They've been lied to, of course, and then they are all too ready to hate intellectuals. It's obvious they feel threatened."

"*You're* an intellectual," said Amanda leadingly.

"I'm a writer, not an intellectual."

"Isn't that a distinction without a difference?"

"Not to me. I've always wanted to make books exactly the way those brutes make steel: mine the ore, purify it, smelt it, temper it, and then pound it into grand structures that weigh hundreds of tons but look weightless. I would have liked people to say of what I write, 'It's nothing for him to write,' but at the same time to know that it's back-breaking, soul-consuming—"

"Mr. President, you're having your first crisis—possibly your last—and here you are talking about writing."

Robert turned and smiled wearily at Amanda. "No. Merely flirting."

Amanda actually blushed, her cheeks turning just the color of an English primrose, at which point Pleyl arrived with Spinkin, the latter looking maliciously gleeful.

"This liberal bully's always threatening me with something," he said. "Ah, how do you do, Mademoiselle," he added, noticing Amanda.

Glnin resumed his seat behind the massive mahogany desk, beetled his brows, and picked up one of the two papers lying before him. When he spoke his voice was hard as Province steel.

"I'm going through this once, Captain, so listen closely, keep your mouth shut, and then do exactly as I tell you or I swear I'll sign this order for your arrest and will be the star witness at your trial, which I guarantee to be a quick one. Now, I want you to get me Ferfatkin and right away—I mean *right* away, within the hour. No arguments. I'm satisfied you know where he is. This government—*your* government, by the way—is going to survive this crisis, so don't for a moment bank on any other outcome. What happens to you will depend entirely on your behavior today. You understand me?"

Spinkin looked at Glnin fiercely, but with a kind of respect. "You surprise me," he said.

"No need to click your heels," Pleyl chimed in. "Just get them moving."

"One other thing," Glnin added.

"Yes?"

"Bring me a submachine gun when you get back with Ferfatkin. Loaded. One extra clip."

"What?" said Spinkin with exaggerated alarm. "But Mr. President, what about Gandhi and King and Thoreau?"

"Move it, Captain," Glnin said between clenched teeth.

And Spinkin did.

After he left, Glnin turned to Amanda and asked, "Do you know what Gandhi said about Hitler's persecution of the Jews?"

"No," she admitted.

"Gandhi recommended that the Jews commit mass suicide and thereby arouse the world's conscience."

"Robert," asked Pleyl in a rather subdued voice, "do you know how to use a submachine gun?"

"Really, Pleyl. My old drill sergeant made absolutely sure of it. Didn't yours?"

"But what are you really going to do?"

"At the moment, smoke one of my predecessor's first-class cigars. In addition, I'd like you to scare me up one of those trucks with loudspeakers we used to detest."

Markovitz dashed in, very upset indeed. "I've been screaming at the Commissioner of Police. It took me ten minutes just to get him to the phone, if you can believe it. He says his men are too *scared* to do anything!"

"He's lying," said Robert evenly, lighting up his cigar. "Please call him back and tell him the President *knows* he is lying and then hang up."

Markovitz left.

"Robert," said Amanda. "What *are* you going to do? Those workers could storm this building at any minute."

"Oh, they won't do that."

"Why not?"

"Not part of the plan. What nice earrings, Amanda. I just noticed when you turned your head like that."

"You're incorrigible, but thank you."

After a few moments of silence, Amanda asked Glnin if he would like to answer more questions.

"I'll answer one, and you needn't even ask it. While it's true I've only been in this ridiculously honorable position a few days, so far the chief difference I find between writing novels and being president is the number and variety of people who interrupt you. Otherwise, the similarities are remarkable. For example, both jobs call for a virtually infantile will to rearrange reality alongside an adult reverence for things as they are. Most governments, I suspect, begin with a lot of both, as do good novelists, with plenty of sharp pencils and fresh images. But the longer they're in power the less of both they retain. After a while, they become like aging writers who fall into sclerotic self-parody or those who find so-called new inspiration by succumbing to vulgar fantasy. Bad art and bad government, I suspect, bear the same relation to reality, which is the desire to evade it. Anyway, I was made president by a parliament which despises and fears me, that agrees with me about nothing—at least in private—and they did it under duress, simply to save their necks. I agreed because, strange to say, I actually *wanted* to save their necks. I'm acutely aware of what Socrates and Lord Acton had to say about this sort of situation; in fact, I find the phrase 'power corrupts' the only purely self-evident lesson of history. Easier to be one of the unacknowledged legislators of the world than to give a speech on the sewer system. And I know that I'm here to be compromised, that I'm being set up to disillusion and disappoint and can hardly fail to do so. Nevertheless, Amanda, nevertheless . . . "

"Nevertheless what?"

Glnin, who had begun pacing during his long speech, leaned back against the desk, rubbed his eyes, and looked hard at Amanda.

"Tell me," he said, "*is* power an aphrodisiac or not?"

While he was interviewing Amanda on this and related topics, Spinkin, carrying a gun, arrived with Ferfatkin, who looked both put out and frightened. Robert looked at him ferociously.

"And so," said Spinkin quite gaily at the door, "the whirligig of time brings in its revenges. In the present instance, Captain Spinkin brings in ex-Minister Ferfatkin as ordered, Sir." He gave a salute, put the gun on the desk, took an extra clip from his pocket, laid it down too, chuckled, and walked out.

"Ferfatkin," said Robert after resuming his official chair, "as you know, I'm a novelist. Consequently, I can see a plot when one pops up and bites me on the nose. Now, I have here an order for your immediate arrest, a pen, and a telephone. You can use the latter to call off your thugs and provocateurs, or I can use the former two. You already see that you can't trust even Spinkin, and he's an old hand capable of quoting Shakespeare. You've got one minute. And, by the way, allow me to introduce Amanda Hare-Stephenson of the United Kingdom."

Ferfatkin, still obviously stunned by Spinkin's betrayal, stared dumbly at the loaded machine gun. Robert picked it up and placed it out of sight on his side of the desk.

"Thirty seconds," he said.

"We only told them the truth," Ferfatkin said suddenly and defiantly.

"Oh?"

"That in two months you'd close the plant and they'd all be on the street."

"Fifteen seconds."

Ferfatkin made a cynical, hostile sort of sound, then went to the phone and began dialing. "This won't accomplish a damned thing, you know."

"This won't accomplish a damned thing, you know, *Mr. President!*" Robert thundered and pounded the desk with his fist, startling both Amanda and Ferfatkin. The tape-recorder fell to the carpet.

Ten minutes later, as Amanda watched from the roof of the Parliament building, a truck equipped with a loudspeaker pulled up next to the Frunzi statue, close by the bodies of Roman Propp and Carolus Peyser. Pleyl drove. Glnin climbed out with a microphone in one hand, the submachine gun in the other.

Karel, Viktor, along with most of the other steelworkers from Provice stood around drinking and smoking at the far end of the square, where there was more sun and no corpses. Others were desultorily looting, a few arguing or looking confused. All still held their clubs, their liquor, and their grudges.

"It's on?" Robert asked Pleyl, holding up the microphone.

"Yes," said Pleyl, nervously checking the switch. He had already refused to turn off the engine, just in case.

Glnin began forthrightly. "*Hey!*" he called into the microphone. "You murderers and dupes from Provice!" His words echoed off the baroque facades of Frunzi Square. A low rumble rose from the workers, as from an irritated rhinoceros.

"You can't hear me?" cried Robert yet louder. "Over here!" He raised the gun and actually squeezed off a short burst into the air.

Some of the workers ran for cover.

"I shot into the *air,* imbeciles," said Robert. "I want your attention, so try to concentrate, will you? At least *pretend* you're halfway sober and rational. This is Robert Glnin talking to you, not some fat colonel or lazy foreman."

A few men moved a little toward the truck.

"Jesus" said Karel to Viktor. "It *is* him."

"Yeah, and by himself it looks."

"Got to admire that."

"My old girlfriend—remember Trudi, the redhead?—she read one of his books once."

"No kidding?"

"Couldn't make it out, she said, but she liked it."

Robert now clambered up onto the hood of the truck, still holding the microphone, which had a nice long cord, and the gun as well. Up on her roof, Amanda tried at first to transcribe what he said, but then gave up and just took it in. It struck her that the words counted for less than something else—the music, so to speak.

"Look here!" Robert shouted, pointing downward. "Two young men dead. Two young men who stand for the future. Look hard, you who wanted to teach those damned intellectuals a lesson. You've broken their skulls; you've scattered their brains without which there *is* no future, not for you, not for any of us. Do you have any idea how foolish you've been? Agents of the old regime tell you that those smartasses up at the capital, those fairies at the University, are going to screw you out of your jobs. They give you a few drinks and off you go like a herd of elephants. I'm ashamed of you. You hear me? Ashamed!

"There's no place for violence in this country any more. No place for hatred and stupidity and blindness. Above all, there's no place for a herd of dupes who use clubs instead of brains. There's nothing wrong with your brains except lack of exercise. So *think*! Your factory *is* inefficient, and you know it. And you know *why,* too. And you certainly ought to be able to figure out that it can't go on that way either. How, then, are your jobs to be saved if not by those who can *make* it efficient—people with brains, workers who work, managers who manage—and students who study?

"All my life I've been opposed to violence and I'm just as opposed to it now that I'm your President. I would never order the police or the army to shoot you down—even though the imbeciles who did *this* surely deserve it. But I *do* mean to improve this country and that will call for sacrifices from everybody. A sacrifice means giving up something that's dear to you. So here's *my* first sacrifice. Much as I am revolted by violence, I will personally shoot any one of you who hasn't thrown down his club by the time I've counted to three." And with that, Robert threw down the microphone and pulled out his spare clip.

An hour later, back in his office, Robert downed a healthy dram of Laphroaig. He had prudently thought to bring what was left of the whiskey with him when he moved on the twenty-fourth. He needed it. Even the enthusiastic cheers he had received as he walked through the lobby and up the stairs and crossed the outer offices did not soothe him, lower his adrenalin, overcome his disgust with what he had done, or abate the fear still roiling up his stomach. Not even the English embrace of Amanda Hare-Stephenson helped much. However, Professor Dundee's scotch did; and, after a dinner of veal and broiled potatoes was brought up to them by Markovitz, Robert closed his office door for the first time in two days.

Amanda, showing the adaptability of her national character, was a good sport about the cot.

30

6

*V*erheim's 82nd aphorism, especially apt for historians: "It is easier to believe in the nobility of the past than in the free will of those who inhabited it."

Amanda Hare-Stephenson's feature article entitled "Glnin's Grand Coup de Théâtre" created what is called an immediate sensation. In retrospect, it is obvious that it could not have failed to do so, though, as Verheim suggests, one should beware of such suppositions. Life must be lived forward and in real time, not in fast reverse, so that truly it is only the past and the distant future that appear to us "inevitable."

Anyway, the article was reprinted all over the world and did more than anything else to give Glnin the peculiar international status he was to enjoy for the rest of his life—enjoy *and* loathe, I suspect, for years later he called this notoriety of the Frunzi Square incident "vulgar." In the same place, his private journal, he also analyzes with some amusement the singular effect of the incident on the foreign leaders he met in the months that followed. As he sees it, at one stroke (coup?) he had apparently contrived (de théâtre?) to unite in his own person the man of action and the man of peace, the intellectual and the swashbuckler, Hamlet and Fortinbras. You could say it was a magic that rapidly became myth, or, conversely, a bit of myth-making that made the name of Glnin political magic. What leader did not yearn to be photographed with the hero of Frunzi Square, the novelist-president who could also wield a submachine gun, at one bloodless but doughty stroke putting down a riot and inspiring the renewal of a nation? As Glnin himself notes, the irony of his "sacrifice"—which in a literal sense he never had to carry out, like Abraham—was suppressed. That part of the story became somehow commingled with the physical danger he faced down like a lion-tamer, and this was the very thing of which his fellow heads-of-state were most jealous, the secret of his aura. There was a deep need—one which the Hare-Stephenson article rather played up, in my opinion—to present Glnin as, above all, a *sufferer.* Why? Consider Verheim's incisive 67th aphorism: "A great leader must represent the suffering of his people; it is the only way he can bear their hopes."

Pilkrohmer, needless to say, has his own view of the Frunzi Square heroics. He talked to me about it the other day when I consented to buy him a beer.

"Of course a 'coup de théâtre' is precisely what it was," he said, wiping his lips. "In fact, a better illustration of my theory can scarcely be imagined. Consider what we know. First, we know that Glnin was not acting spontaneously, but rather carrying out a plan, albeit one he formulated with a kind of suddenness. But, as I see it, this is the suddenness which characterizes any inspired act of composition, or self-invention. Second, we know that there was an audience."

Here I objected. "But the square was cleared and the event wasn't even photographed, let alone televised."

"No, no," he said with that irritating, characteristic gesture of dismissal I so dislike. "The audience consisted, in the immediate sense, of only one person—namely, Amanda Hare-Stephenson. However, this Englishwoman was actually the conduit to a world-wide audience of billions."

"I still disagree. If Glnin were deliberately aiming at this audience of billions, he would certainly have arranged—as he might easily have done—for the great scene to be taped."

"That a lesser artist would certainly have done so, I grant. But Glnin was not a mediocre novelist, and like all true writers he believed in his soul that one mot juste is worth ten thousand pictures. Moreover, the absence of photographs or videotape left space for mystery, for imagination. One's imagination of Caesar crossing the Rubicon is a much grander affair than would be a snapshot of a short, bald, middle-aged man stepping daintily across a drainage ditch."

Well, Pilkrohmer's is one possibility, and probably it's wrong to have contempt for an idea merely because you can't stand the man who enunciates it. All the same, I cannot bring myself to accept what Pilkrohmer has to say, if only because he is so excessively sure of it.

A different train of thought was suggested to me yesterday when I at last succeeded in tracking down the obscure reference in Glnin's notebook entry about the prophetic absurdist novel. After asking Mrs. Gulwich for her advice (she suggested Kleist, Kipling, and Kierkegaard), I decided the "K." referred to was more probably Kafka—who owns the initial—but could think of no story of Kafka's about a poor student with bad hearing. And indeed there is none. However, such a story can be found in one of his letters—and not just any letter, but one in which he writes variations on the theme of the sacrifice of Abraham.

In one variant we have an Abraham who wishes to carry out the sacrifice properly and even has sufficient faith, but who "cannot imagine that he is the one meant. It is as if the best student were solemnly to receive a prize at the end of the year and in the expectant silence, the worst student, because he has misheard, comes forward from his dirty back bench and the whole class falls apart. And it is perhaps not that he has heard wrong, for his name was actually spoken, because it is the teacher's intention that the reward for the best is to be accompanied by the punishment for the worst."

So here is another Glninian perplexity, this time yoking the theme of Abraham's sacrifice to the author's summoning by history, to his ironic speech in Frunzi Square, even to the favorite author of the pedantic Captain Spinkin—once Glnin's interrogator, for a time his Minister of Education. It does make you think.

Perhaps in the end, and despite all the undoubted good he did, Glnin may indeed have come to regard the extraordinary turn in his life as more a punishment than a reward. Certainly he never wrote another novel and, as Verheim puts it in his 27th aphorism, "The world likes imagination more than imagination likes the world."

Benton's
Top Banana

*h*iram Conwell, forty years old and the soberest man in the lounge, sat with Joe Smedvig on his left and Cap Kristensen on his right, a trio of five-buck Cutty Sarks warming on the exiguous table in front of them. Joe was roaring, Cap simply red in the face. Hiram was intensely silent.

"Aw come on, Hi," said Joe with an encouraging elbow, "loosen *up.*"

On the tiny cafe stage, inside a spotlight, a sequined tank-top and pink spandex pants, under some dubious makeup and lots of teased brown hair, Katy Moffit was winding up her Ivan and Grushenka schtick.

"Okay, so one night Grushenka comes home after a hard day of shoveling the snow off of Red Square and finds Ivan in the john. 'Jesus,' she says, 'five hours I had to stand in line for the stuff and *that's* all you can think of to do with it?' "

Still incapable of articulation, Cap pounded the table twice, while Joe elevated to a yet higher register. "Come on, Hi, this is funny stuff," he wheezed. But Joe was wrong about Hiram. While he certainly looked as if he hadn't gotten the joke, his eyes were as bulbous and fixed as a frog's on a mayfly.

Katy shook herself like a go-go dancer by way of transition. "Okay, the other night I was out with this shrink. Nice dinner, good show, a few drinks, you know. So we go back to my place. Story of my life. Just when it's getting interesting, he says he can't get it up. Jesus, I say, you should advertise, Doc. You're a sure cure for penis envy."

There was a smattering of nervous laughter and from the bar an inebriated baritone boomed out, "Hey, honey! I got something *here* you could envy!"

Katy swivelled, pointing the microphone hecklerwards like a laser.

"Hey, big shot! If you weren't so drunk I'd come over and fling a whiskey in your face." Then she shifted her gaze to the crowd in front, to Hiram Conwell, in effect, and said in a softened, entre-nous tone, "Kind of like throwing shit at a pig, though. What's the point?"

"Wow, she's fast," whispered Cap admiringly over the laughter. "Havin a good time, Hi?"

"Yes, I am," reported Hiram with his customary sincerity, but without taking his gaze off Katy Moffit.

"So last week," Katy continued, "there's this convention of English professors in town. One of them gets busted on the Strip. Seems he solicited this undercover cop. Now, I know this cop—a size six and a real wit. He tears off his wig, cuffs the nimrod, and says, 'Sorry, prof, but I'm afraid this proposition's gonna end in a sentence.'"

Off to the left the drummer gave a ragged little roll. Hiram's heart beat raggedly too.

Still solicitous, Joe said, "I know she's pretty raunchy, but don't you think she's a *little* bit funny, Hi?"

"Yep," said Hiram.

A demijohn of a fellow in a string tie and a cowboy hat got up at a table nearby and yelled, "Hey there, pussy, ain't you got no shame? There's ladies present."

"Oh," Katy shot back, "I'm truly sorry, hick. I didn't know that was your wife with you. I thought you were here for the 4-H show."

"Shoot. I heard this woman hates men," whispered Cap in Hiram's ear, as if in fear of his third-grade teacher, Mrs. Quigley. "Damned lesbian feminist or something guy in the lobby said."

As if to confirm Cap's report, Katy looked contemptuously at her audience and wound the set up with a final joke.

"This pointy-headed truck driver in pointy boots says to me, 'You women's libbers, you're all full of shit. Women jes cain't do without men.' 'Hey, honey,' I say, 'a sperm bank and a five-watt vibrator would be huge improvements on you.' 'Yeah?' he says. 'Well, I say there're some things there ain't nothin but a man can do fer you.' 'Nah,' I say. 'If I want stains on my sheets I can always buy a cat.' Okay, that's it. Goodnight, and don't forget to check your cash in the casino."

With that, the crowd gave a low, unenthusiastic cheer, the combo broke into "Fine and Dandy," the waitresses fanned out from the bar, and Katy Moffit disappeared behind a frothy violet curtain.

HIRAM CONWELL HAD BEEN DRAGGED to Vegas by Joe and Cap like an eight hundred-weight of hay. For them, the consciousness of doing a good deed by their friend gently offset without at all marring the spice of vice in flying out to Vegas themselves, which they had done twice before and hoped to do regularly in the future. It was clear Hiram needed something; and, being unimaginative, forthright Hoosiers, Cap and Joe figured cheering up was it—getting out of himself, a change of scenery, a little fancy fun.

Two and a half years earlier Hiram's wife Hannah had died of cervical cancer. She was only thirty-six. The dying itself was about as awful as it gets. "Not a thing we can do for her, Hiram," said Doctor Hartwell solemnly toward the bitter end, "except to take away the pain." There was only the one child, Stephanie Marie. At only ten she took it better than Hiram, everybody noted. Positive-minded, optimistic, a precocious perfectionist, she threw herself into schoolwork, field hockey, cheerleading, and boys. She also took over most of her mother's chores—she cooked better than Hannah did—and kept herself busy and buoyant. With Hiram, things were different, when you looked closely. He just collapsed like a bridge washed out in the middle. That is, he was still connected to things—the Conwell Grain and Storage Company, the Rotary Club, the First Presbyterian Church, and the Ballywood Country Club, where he shot a handicap of seven and was the treasurer—but he simply wasn't connected to himself. Right at the center he had fallen into a swollen river of grief. Not that Hiram ever complained. He was a good stoical Hoosier, and he remained as community-minded as ever. But whether it was a meeting of the school board or negotiating a deal with a New Orleans shipper, everybody who really knew him could see that Hiram was just going through the motions.

After the decent interval of twelve months, a number of the matrons of Benton, mostly Hannah's old friends, interested themselves in finding Hiram a second wife. Dinner parties and barbecues were arranged with single women invariably seated next to him. Some of these were from as far off as Indianapolis, Elwood, and Muncie: divorced librarians, unwed college professors, hard-driving public defenders, soil geologists, legal secretaries. Heaven knew Hiram was amply eligible. He was a prosperous, good-looking, virtuous man, inheritor of both the finest house and the biggest business in town, with a sweet, over-achieving, low-maintenance daughter. But Hiram resisted these transparent schemes for his bliss. He was polite, of course, but nothing more. He himself never entertained, though Stephanie, thoughtful as ever, said she'd be glad to see to all the preparations. In fact, nobody was more worried about her father than Stephanie Marie.

"I don't know, Uncle Joe," she said to Joe Smedvig when she stopped by his hardware store one afternoon after cheerleading practice. "It's not like he's *depressed* exactly. I mean, you'd almost think he was the same as usual. But, you know, he just isn't always *there,* if you know what I mean. He watches too much TV, for one thing. He never used to watch much besides golf and basketball and Dan Rather. Now he'll watch almost *any*thing."

"Hm," said Joe. "Do you notice him sleeping more than he used to?" Only the week before, Joe had read an article about depression in *Reader's Digest.*

"No. Less, I think. He goes to bed at the same time he always did, but now he reads. I think he's up reading half the night, Uncle Joe. I saw his light still on when I was going, you know, to the bathroom." Stephanie blushed the blush of early puberty. "It was three a.m."

"Hm," Joe repeated, trying to remember more about the article.

The very next day he mentioned the Vegas idea to Cap Kristensen before the meeting at Ballywood. Cap liked the idea a lot and they contrived to go back to Hiram's house after the meeting to begin working on him, which they did over pieces of Stephanie's apple pie. Joe threw the girl a wink and said she'd be more than welcome to stay with Clara and the girls while they were gone.

"That'd be *great,* Dad," said Stephanie as she poured them some decaffeinated coffee. "Please say you'll go."

Hiram didn't like feeling trapped and said he'd have to think about it.

It took Stephanie all of three days to talk him into going. When Hiram came down to breakfast on the third morning, Stephanie leapt out at him from behind the refrigerator in her Shaker sweater and short pleated skirt, pom-poms at the ready. "Give me an L!" she pleaded. "Give me an A! . . ."

"All right, all right," said Hiram. "Give me a break—and a slice of that French toast."

THE CASINO WAS CRAWLING as usual when the three men split up at eight p.m. Upstairs they had agreed to set themselves a limit of two hundred dollars each. Cap was heading for the roulette wheel, Joe for the blackjack tables.

Cap wanted to know where Hiram was going. "Not the slots?" he said.

"Look," Joe chimed in with a glance at Cap, "maybe you'd better just stick with one of us, it being your first trip and all."

"Oh, I'll be around," said Hiram with a vague wave of his hand. "Probably just watching, actually."

Already that afternoon Hiram had spent more than five hundred. There was the assistant manager, then the manager, and finally somebody called the entertainment coordinator. When he got to the lounge Katy Moffit was feverishly delivering jokes that, had he or anyone else really been paying attention, would have been unfathomable. She looked more edgy and perturbed than the night before.

"I went out to eat with this real strict vegetarian the other night. He orders an omelet. 'Hey,' I say, 'you eat *eggs*?' 'Why not,' he says, 'I'm a bachelor and I went out with *you*, didn't I?' Now that's *weird*. Isn't that weird? Story of my life. Take my old boyfriend. Was he tough. *How* tough? He used Brillo as a loufa; he shaved with a McCullough; he used hairdressers as toothpicks. And speaking of hairdressers, the other day I'm getting my hair electrified and the roaches trimmed back when this old bat hobbles in and takes the chair next to me. Bruce asks her if she wants her usual set and blue rinse. 'Oh no,' she says. 'I want something really *radical*.' And she whips out this picture of Barbara Bush. 'I wanna look just like *that*,' she says."

Katy became more frantic at the silence behind the clinking glasses and indifferent conversations. Clearly it was an off night. Or she knew, Hiram mused.

"Okay," she said a little desperately, wanting either love or heckling, "these two hookers are standing on the corner when this hearse drives by. 'Hey!' one of them shouts to the driver. 'How's about a quickie?' 'Sorry,' the guy says, 'but I've got this big stiff in the rear.' 'Shit,' says the second hooker, 'not another one of *those*.'"

She looked out at them, squinting in the spotlight, suddenly fragile. Hiram watched closely from the bar. It was more than just an off night.

"Okay, this encyclopedia salesman goes up to a nudist colony—"

"Oh, put a sock in it, bimbo!" the drunk next to Hiram suddenly shouted, as if exasperated beyond endurance.

It took only a nudge of his shoulder for Hiram to knock the man off his stool. "Sorry," he said, and offered the man his hand.

"Mr. Seagram's revenge," said Katy. "Okay, that's it. I'm outta here. You suckers don't forget to leave your mad money in the casino and make the boss happy." She whirled and ran, like an embarrassed teenager.

Hiram caught up with her just after she went through the curtain. He touched her elbow. It was a squalid hallway with exposed pipes all over it and yellow walls.

"Hello," he said softly, as she spun around on him. Fear turned to a sly grin.

"Hey, it was you knocked that asshole flat, right?"

"You got the flowers?" he replied.

"Jesus, what *is* this? Prom night?"

"I know your late show's been cancelled."

"Long stem, yet. Any idea what I look like without this makeup?"

"I cancelled it. I want to take you out for supper."

"Supper? Oh, midwest, right? On the coasts we say dinner. So, who'd you have to pay off and where'd you get the chutzpah?"

"In Germany they say *Abendbrot* and in Italy I think it's *cena*. I don't know about Japan. What's *chutzpah?*"

"Why aren't you after the showgirls? All those legs and boobs that never quit."

"It's you I'm after," Hiram said quietly. "I like your *chutzpah.*"

"Little Miss Moffit sits on her toffit. Something special about me, or do you send fifty bucks worth of roses to all the lounge comics?"

Hiram smiled. "Curds and whey?" he suggested. "You must be hungry."

Katy looked suspicious but then laughed. "Okay, okay. What the hell. Let me change, straight arrow."

"Fifteen minutes?" he said with shy peremptoriness. "My name's Hiram and I'll be in the lobby."

"*Hi*ram? I thought only dead bankers were named Hiram. Well, I'm Katy and I bet you won't recognize me," she said.

But he did. He recognized her despite the plain white dress and combed-out hair—more auburn than brown—and the face gone real with no lipstick and only a touch of rouge, and a manner transformed from brash to uncertain. In fact, she looked exactly as he had expected.

He went right up to her. She smiled without much irony.

"In case you haven't noticed," she said, "I'm not in a real good mood tonight. Fair warning."

"Fair enough," said Hiram with a grin nobody in Benton had seen in three years.

DINNER LASTED PAST MIDNIGHT. Katy ate like a soldier in a fairy tale. Hiram ordered champagne.

Katy told Hiram about her failed marriage and Hiram told Katy about his reading.

"He was my first agent," she said. "I gave a hundred percent, he took ten."

"You know what bad faith is?" he asked.

Hiram talked about Hannah's death and Stephanie's resilience. Katy told Hiram about how tough it was for a female comic.

"It made a mockery of everything," he said. "But Stephanie's tougher than the mockery. Her defenses are so perfect they scare me. They're even more perfect than your jokes."

"If you do rough material you're unfeminine, right? And if you go ladylike, the rough stuff's right out. If you do feminist stuff the men are liable to throw things. In fact, if you joke about anybody but yourself, you're a bitch. If you just tell the truth, the men all squirm and the women all squeal."

"I didn't squirm," Hiram assured her, "not at the truth. I used to."

"You didn't?" she said. "Why not, straight arrow?"

"I like your hair that way," he said, "with the bangs."

After their late breakfast the next day Hiram astonished Cap and Joe by telling them he had an afternoon date. "A date!" they exclaimed. "Who with?" Hiram just drank up his coffee, looked at his watch and said he had to go rent a car. He drove Katy out to Hoover Dam and Lake Mead, which she had never seen. On the way they continued their parallel autobiographies which had suddenly intersected. When they arrived, Hiram insisted on walking to the middle of the dam.

"Look how big the sky is," said Katy, leaning back and looking up. She was afraid of heights—or, as she put it, "of depths."

"The sky's always that big," said Hiram, taking her arm. "It's the dam that's big."

"I think I hate my life," said Katy.

"I think I'm in love with you," Hiram replied.

"Fucking romantic."

"Class clown."

"Rotarian!"

"Will you marry me?"

"Probably not."

"*Pro*bably?"

"Probably *not*."

"I've been celibate for four years."

"I thought *everybody* in Indiana was celibate."

Hiram kissed Katy in the middle of the dam. She suggested a motel in Boulder City and when they got there, she kissed him back.

HIRAM WENT HOME WITH Cap Kristensen and Joe Smedvig, who kept their theories between themselves. For a month he courted Katy by letter and phone call, but mostly there were letters, often two or three a day. Initially brief, stilted, and sentimental, they soon turned into virtual essays, as if the act of writing to Katy were causing Hiram to make discoveries or to speak his mind.

"It seems to me," he wrote in one of them, "that our two worlds have at least this in common: both are hostile to the truth. You said yourself that even in a Las Vegas lounge your truths cause squirming and squealing. It's not much different here, really, except that you aren't here to tell these truths and I haven't the courage, the chutzpah. Nevertheless, wherever I look I see inward squirming, repressed squealing."

And in another: "You like to say I'm the heartland and you're just glitz, just showbiz. You want to make a sociological symbol out of my infatuation as a way of defending yourself against me, as if it were America's decadence and not my love for you that's at stake. Well, you don't really like decadence; moreover, you assume too much about both the heartland and your off-color jokes. What lies between the coasts, where people say supper instead of dinner, showbiz assumes is boring but real in order to console itself for being exciting but phony. That's what I think, at least. But it's too simple, Katy, like all prejudices. What I see on television is the boredom of unreality, what one of these writers I've been reading calls the Rotation Method. Entertainment is the murder of time. But time can murder back. Here it's the boredom of reality."

Once in a while Katy would answer in her headlong scrawl. "Can you really imagine me in Benton, Indiana? Wise up, pilgrim. You want a life of constant embarrassment or what? What happens the first time I tell a hooker joke over the corn muffins? What happens when I tell some Rotarian friend of yours to go fuck himself? And think of your perfect Stephanie Marie. Talk about your wicked stepmothers!"

Then Katy's contract ran out and her agent had trouble finding a new booking. She wrote Hiram and told him straight out.

"But I won't marry you. I might just come for a visit, but that's all, assuming you can square it with the Presbyterian elders and the Jay-cees. And if I *do* come, I'm leaving your number with my agent, so don't get the wrong idea. p.s. My real name's Brina Grossman and I was born in New Rochelle, New York, so don't tell me about prejudice."

On the Saturday that Hiram went to Indianapolis to pick up Katy, a day as crisp as the stubble in the cornfields, Stephanie had a hockey game. She was glad of the excuse and, no matter what he said, she thought her father was too. Hiram wanted to take them all out to supper at the country club that night, but Stephanie insisted, success-fully, on cooking a big meal so they could eat at home, just the three of them together.

"Use your imagination, Dad," she had argued. "If you were *me*, wouldn't *you* want to have a good chance to look her over without any distractions? And if you were *her*, wouldn't you want a quiet meal at home after all that travelling?"

"I don't think Katy's afraid of much," he said, "if that's what you're hinting."

Even if Stephanie had been less sensitive to the weather of her

42

father's moods, she could scarcely have failed to notice the change in him on his return from Nevada, but she had said nothing to him about it. She knew that Hiram's emotional and intellectual life had changed after her mother's death, had become somehow different, more private, more troubled. Of course she worried about him and she was curious and she wanted to see him happier; but something told her to stay clear, not to press too hard, not to make worries for him. Almost right from the start she had made up her mind that the best course for her was to reassure him about herself. His silent mourning for Hannah made her feel helpless but, paradoxically, it softened her own grief, as if to lose one's mother were nothing compared to losing one's wife. Between them everything went smoothly, but it was the frictionlessness of trains going in opposite directions on parallel tracks. That is, Hiram was a good parent, but Stephanie missed her father almost as much as her mother.

"Tell me all about her," she had asked eagerly when Hiram had, with touching awkwardness, broken the news of Katy's visit.

They were eating spaghetti with Stephanie's homemade tomato sauce, a tossed salad with fresh mushrooms, one of the loaves of whole wheat bread Stephanie had made the preceding Sunday after church, and there was iced tea, a misplaced November treat for Hiram.

"To begin with, what's she look like?" Stephanie wanted to know. "She must be, well, pretty cool, huh?"

"I don't know," said Hiram uncertainly. "She looks different when she's performing and when she's not. Comics have to look distinct because they're either brave or crazy. Katy's the brave kind. She teases her hair out and wears a lot of makeup and wears tight glittery clothes. Offstage she looks kind of sweet, vulnerable, soft."

"What *color* hair?" Stephanie insisted, a little exasperated by such a long, irrelevant answer.

"Light brown. Curly."

"Fat or thin or just right?" Stephanie teased.

"Finish your spaghetti, young lady," said Hiram like somebody named Hiram, just like a dead banker, a straight arrow.

"Come on, Dad. Tell me one of her jokes."

"You'll see her when she gets here. Maybe she'll tell you jokes then."

Stephanie took a hit of iced tea. "It's okay, Dad," she said in a low and daring voice. "I mean if she stays in your room."

"Thank you," said Hiram and got up to clear the table.

"So, SHOULD I CALL YOU Brina or Katy?" Stephanie asked.

Katy deftly turned the tables. "Which do you like better?"

Stephanie smiled and pressed on. "How'd you decide on Katy Moffit as a stage name?"

"How'd *you* get Marie for a *middle* name?"

Katy rolled over on Stephanie's bed and tickled her in the ribs. Stephanie squealed, but not at all like a female customer hearing a wicked truth, more like a child being tickled in the ribs.

They were in Stephanie's bedroom listening to the tapes of West Coast groups Katy had brought along as a present. Katy got up from the bed.

"Listen to this band," she said, putting a tape in the player. "All girls."

"What're they called?"

"Hot Pants," said Katy drily, and pushed the button. "Ever hear of them? No? First cut's called 'Tight Bra.' "

A rough bass line, messy drums, incompetent electric runs over three lost, shrill, frighteningly young voices:

> He says you're sweet
> he rubs your feet
> don't you compete
> don't you get beat
> He sticks his tongue
> right down your lung
> moves up your thighs
> check out his size
> Boys only want one thing
> Boys only want one thing

"Wow!" exclaimed Stephanie. "Judy's gonna *freak* over this."

"Hey," said Katy, falling back on the bed and rubbing her stomach, "that was one hell of a din- supper you made us." She looked down at her tummy. "Not much of a cook myself."

When she looked up Stephanie Marie was beaming at her.

ON SUNDAY EVENING they were all in the den watching Dan Rather's weekend replacement. "It's always some blonde on the weekends," Katy observed. The phone rang. Hiram picked it up and simultaneously clicked the set onto mute.

"Hello? . . . Oh, Margaret, yes . . . Fine, and George? . . . Oh, moved up to Thursday—"

"Hey, sweetie pie," Katy suddenly bawled, "you said fifty bucks and no interruptions."

Hiram grimaced and slipped his hand over the receiver. "How come . . . Oh, I see—"

"Ooh, *stop* that, you *fiend*!" giggled Katy, leaning toward the phone.

Hiram gave her a brave smile. Stephanie bunched up on the couch, convulsed.

JOE AND CLARA SMEDVIG CAME to their table at Ballywood. It was clear that Joe didn't recognize Katy, dazzling in her chiffon evening dress and her hair up. The dress was rather revealing, which Joe did recognize. Clara too. Hiram introduced her as Brina Grossman, from New Rochelle, New York.

"Can we set with you a spell ?" Joe asked, pulling out one of the extra chairs for Clara, who sat in it at once.

"Oh, please do, Mr. Smedvig," said Katy demurely.

"Oh, call me Joe."

"And call me Clara," said Clara, who liked to be friendly to strangers.

"Then call *me* Katy," said Katy.

"Katy?" said Clara. "Is that your nickname?"

"More like an alias," said Katy flatly, dabbing her lips daintily with the damask napkin.

"Say, Hi. Where'd you find this beautiful lady?" asked Joe.

"Well—" said Hiram.

"Actually, I was hitch-hiking outside this nudist colony," said Katy with a wink at Clara. "Amazing how many rides I was offered, but," here she put her hand on Hiram's arm, "I picked *this* one."

YOU CAN'T REALLY SEE Benton at its best in a November rain," said Hiram.

"No doubt July Fourth'd be better. Jaycees and the VFW. All the trees and drum majorettes in blossom. The Klan float white with all those sheets."

Hiram pointed. "There's the high school."

"Stephanie's in there now, poor kid. And *you* went there too, right?"

"Right."

"And Jughead and Betty and Moose and Veronica?"

Hiram slowed a bit. "You're trying way too hard, Katy," he said calmly.

"It's not Katy the foul-mouthed broad; at the moment, it's Brina the usurer's only daughter. But they both *hated* high school. Hey, you're the richest guy in town, aren't you?"

"Depends on the price of farmland, I guess."

"Okay, let's see Conwell Grain and Storage. You know I used to smoke pot and Kools. I used to drink Southern Comfort and Jack Daniels. I dropped acid, twice."

"How many abortions?" Hiram inquired coolly.

"Well, only one," Katy said apologetically. "But there was a miscarriage."

He slowed the Buick. "There. See those grain towers?"

"*Very* phallic," said Katy appreciatively. "A regular Pemberly."

"Pemberly?"

"Yeah, and you're a regular Darcy."

"Oh, yep. *I* read that. Jane Austen, right?"

"Very good. My favorite author," Katy said ironically. "She always winds up with terrific marriages in little villages between people who never work."

Hiram laughed. "Stephanie's crazy about you, you know."

"Hell, I could turn the kid into Cinderella in a flash. She already does all the cooking."

"Do you still hate your life?" he asked.

"Oh, which one?"

BOTH OF HIRAM'S PARENTS WERE DEAD. His father went early—gladly too, Hiram thought—in his fifties; his mother, just shy of seventy. As he lay beside the sleeping Katy, his hand on her hip, he began to think about them, about their lives in this town, this house, this bedroom, and about their deaths, especially his father's. It always pained Hiram to consider how his father would have adored his daughter, only child of an only child. He would visualize him and Stephanie together, cuddled on the porch swing, playing on the lawn, smiling clear across his own generation, the generation which, he now believed, had killed his father because it really was the sixties that did it, drove him to despair, not because he bullheadedly condemned the decade love-it-or-leave-it style, though he could bluster, but because he couldn't cope with the truths or the riots or the questions above all that made him squirm and lose that faith which was exactly the one Katy burlesqued and which he, Hiram, had tried hard to resurrect with Hannah, though it looked more like continuity, like rootedness, and then, after Hannah died, crashed down again and he, stoically, went on anyhow, thinking wrongness underlies everything anyway, like wiping out the Indians who weren't even Indians and then naming the state after their wrong name, like the mad farm programs or the national debt or the politicians with their cynical promises and everything else he saw on television. "Which are more important?" he'd quizzed Stephanie once, "the shows or the ads?" "The shows, Daddy," she said promptly. "It's the shows we want to watch, not the ads." "No, sweetheart. It's the ads. The shows are only there so the TV people can sell our eyes to the people who make the ads." And then he'd started reading books he'd only heard about in college from friends with other majors and one book would lead on to another, all of them pure acid eating down to the falseness right through the pieties, so that maybe it wasn't so surprising that he'd fall for Katy Moffit when he saw what he thought he saw in her and he thought maybe after all there was some *via media* between the loneliness that didn't even wait for Stephanie to go off to college and the wrongness of the continuity of pure inertial force which kept him rolling through middle age like a heavy train going downhill on smooth rails that didn't even need an engine.

He looked over at Katy, listened to the breathing that yielded a hint of her voice, and smiled to think what his parents might have made of all that bitter honesty, all that sweetness underneath it. The lion and the honeycomb. And he smiled also at her tests, her provocations, the improbability of things, at all the fun he was having. And then Hiram fell asleep. Smiling.

THURSDAY MORNING Hiram had to go to the office. "You sleep in," he whispered to Katy at seven o'clock.

"Sleep in what?" she mumbled querulously.

"Sleep *late*. I'll call around eleven. Okay? Okay, Katy?"

"Mmm."

She woke around ten to a silent house. In the kitchen there was coffee all made; a loaf of bread and a box of some sugarless cereal lay on the table beside a note: "*Gnädige* Brina—*Iss, iss, mein Kind! Liebe,* Stefi." Taking first-year German, Katy figured. What else? Kidding the Jewess maybe?

She looked out the window and saw not much sun, not much warmth in the grey Indiana sky.

After breakfast Katy put on Hiram's sweatpants and one of his heavy sweaters, found the vacuum, did the living room, which didn't really need it, and then washed the kitchen floor, which was likewise spotless.

"Good practice, just in case," she told herself.

At eleven sharp the phone rang.

"You okay? Have a good sleep?" Hiram asked.

"I'm fine, I slept *in*," said Katy. "In Indiana."

"Look, I'm going to be held up here a while. Lots of stuff 's piled up."

"That *my* fault?"

"Stop being so defensive."

"Stop being so apologetic."

"I just don't want you to be bored, okay?"

"It's okay. Reality doesn't bore me. Not yet, anyway."

There was a pause while Hiram took in the allusion. "Did Marvin call?" he asked. Marvin was Katy's agent.

"No. I'm not wanted."

"I wouldn't say that. Okay? There's plenty to eat in the fridge and I'll get home quick as I can. Okay?"

"Okay. Okay. Go and be prosperous. People are lining up for bread in Minsk. I can take care of myself."

For a while she sat at the kitchen table reading *The Joy of Cooking* and wondering, between dishes, what the hell she was doing in Benton, Indiana in November. Then she thought of Elizabeth Bennet's first vision of Pemberly and she went into Hiram's den and, with only a little trouble, found his copy and, with only a little more, the passage she had been trying to recall:

> Elizabeth was delighted. She had never seen a place for which nature had done more, or where natural beauty had been so little counteracted by an awkward taste. They were all of them warm in their admiration; and at that moment she felt that to be mistress of Pemberly might be something!

Katy laughed out loud at this sensible, middle-class, wholly English fairytale, but even more at herself for liking it. The whole point, she joked to herself, is that you have to know how good Darcy will be in bed. Just because she was a comedienne, Katy mistrusted happy endings.

At one o'clock Clara Smedvig, who, along with most of the local population could hardly stand it any more, phoned.

"Uh, hello Katy, is that *you*? Brina?"

"In the flesh, so to speak. Who's this?"

"It's Clara. Clara Smedvig. Remember? Joe and I sat with you and Hiram at Ballywood the other night?"

"Oh right. Clara. If you want Hiram, Clara, he's in the office and I think Stephanie Marie's in algebra or gym."

"No, it was *you* I wanted to talk to."

"Very nice of *you* to call, Clara. What can I do for you?"

"Well, it's a funny thing, actually. It's something Joe said last night."

"About *me*?"

"Well, maybe. He said—now please don't take offense—he said he thought he saw you out in Las Vegas."

"It's conceivable, Clara."

"Oh."

"Was he *in* Las Vegas?"

Clara's voice hardened a tick. "He said he thought he saw you *perform* there, telling jokes."

"Did he like the act?"

"Look, Katy. I was only wondering. You know. Actually, a *lot* of us were wondering, Benton being a small town and Hiram such an old friend," it was nearly too much for Clara, but she had Cecilia and Margaret right there to encourage her, "well, whether you and Hiram have made any, you know, *plans* or anything."

"Plans?"

"Yes, because," and here Clara spoke more firmly, more surely, "if you *have*, then maybe some of us could, you know, throw the two of you a party."

"Well, Clara, *I* like parties, but I'm not sure Hiram does. What do *you* think? I mean since he's your old friend and all."

Clara was silent a moment, staring at Cecilia and Margaret with a furrowed brow. "Well, I guess we'll see, then. Okay?"

Do they all end their sentences with "okay," Katy wondered. "Well, that'll be all right, then. And thank you for calling, Clara. I appreciate it. Really I do. Bye-bye now."

THOUGH KATY'S CHILI WAS like melted tires stewed in cayenne pepper and red kidney beans, and though the rice underneath it crunched, Hiram and Stephanie ate as much as they could. This only put Katy more out of temper than she had been to begin with.

"Come *on*," she said loudly, throwing down her fork. "This is swill! Admit it. Oh, the two of you!"

Stephanie, big-eyed, looked at Hiram who said, "It's not that bad; I've had worse."

"Christ!" said Katy. "Don't *pat*ronize me. Jesus, don't you ever get angry? All this goddamned perfection, it's like living on top of a wedding cake or something. I've never seen you really pissed, Hiram. Not once."

"Really, Katy," Stephanie ventured in a frightened voice, "it's okay."

"*Okay*? I'm getting fed up with that word. It's *not* okay. It's absolute shit." And Katy leapt to her feet, went to the stove, jerked up the pot, dumped the rest of the chili into the sink, then dropped the pot on top of it with a crash and a splash.

Hiram sat dumbfounded.

Stephanie burst into tears and ran from the kitchen.

Katy, breathing hard, looked seethingly at Hiram for about a second and then, to his astonishment, she likewise burst into tears and ran from the kitchen.

Hiram sat where he was for two or three minutes, then he got up and began cleaning the mess. "This encyclopedia salesman goes up to a nudist colony," he said to himself for some reason, perhaps because he was as perplexed as the salesman was about to be.

Ten minutes later, hoping things might have calmed down, he went upstairs, trying to decide which bedroom to go into first. He chose his own. It was dark. "Katy?" he said experimentally. "Katy?" Then he heard the laughter coming from Stephanie's room and went back down to the kitchen, poured himself some ferociously strong coffee, and sliced himself a big piece of his daughter's matchless apple pie.

"IT'S WHAT MARGARET called about on Sunday," Hiram had explained.

Katy and Stephanie Marie glanced up from a copy of *Spy*. Katy looked none too pleased.

"He does this often?" she asked.

"Oh, the school board's only once a month," said Stephanie. "But then there's the country club and the Rotary and—"

"God," exclaimed Katy with mock disgust. "What a joiner! It's like you were a Latin major in high school or something."

"How about renting a movie?" Hiram suggested.

"Or maybe we could watch a cooking show?" said Katy. "No, I think I'd rather come along. I've never been to a school board meeting."

"What?"

"How 'bout it, Stefi? Shall we—*gehen?*"

"*Jawohl!*"

"It *is* an open meeting, isn't it?" said Katy. "I mean you don't plan torture for these kids behind closed doors or anything, do you?"

"You'll only be bored," Hiram acquiesced.

And so they had all driven to the high school, with a stop for pretzels and potato chips.

Meetings of the Benton school board were held in the high school auditorium because there generally were a number of people who came to listen—principals, several teachers, numerous pairs of parents, the odd taxpayers with public spirit or axes they hoped to grind. The board was seated panel-like at a folding aluminum table with Alexander Hamilton Purdy, its chairman, in the middle.

Katy and Stephanie sat about halfway back in the hall, which put them behind the rest of the crowd. They munched their pretzels and potato chips just as if they had been at a movie.

Margaret Klopstock, who had been by Clara Smedvig's side that afternoon, sat next to Hiram and barely acknowledged his greeting. In fact, Hiram noticed that she looked even more sour than was customary.

Purdy called the meeting to order right on time. The board quickly accepted Mary Schiller's minutes, agreed to an elementary school principal's request to replace a reading teacher who had left to marry a shoe salesman in Elmyra, tabled Coach Stifter's request for a new scoreboard, discussed briefly the issue of how large a raise the town might manage for the teachers next year and decided they had better wait for the city treasurer's report in February. It all took less than twenty minutes.

"Well," said Purdy, "hearing no new business I suggest we adjourn all in favor?"

"*I* have some new business," said Margaret, looking all business.

"Margaret?" said the chairman wearily, as if he were accustomed to Margaret Klopstock having private agenda items and had hoped this might be a good month.

"Yes. It's about Dr. Keller's sex education classes at the high school."

"I thought," said Hiram, "we all agreed on that last year, Margaret."

"Well, *I* think we need to reconsider it and right away too. I believe we need to carefully consider the *effects* of that course which, judging by something I found my Judy listening to this very evening, may be a good deal less *benign* than we were led to believe." Margaret looked out in the direction of Katy and Stephanie when she said the word "benign."

"Listening to?" said Sam Aichinger at the end of the table. "Listening to what?"

"A tape. A *filthy* tape."

"I don't understand, Margaret," said Purdy.

"It was a rock group, so-called, and the lyrics were *utterly obscene*."

"Well, that may be, Margaret, but I don't see what that has to do with Keller's course," said Aichinger, who disliked Margaret more than sex education.

"The course creates a *climate*," Margaret began in response, but she was interrupted by a shout from the hall.

"Hey!"

"Pardon me," said Purdy, looking over his glasses.

Katy stood up. She was still wearing Hiram's heavy sweater over a pair of faded jeans. "Hi," she boomed. "I'd just like to say how impressed I am that you've got this course of Dr. Keller's. Stephanie Marie here tells me it's one swell course. She also tells me that she's the one who loaned Judy Klopstock the allegedly obscene cassette. I happen to know about the tape because I gave it to Stephanie."

Margaret Klopstock, just this side of infuriated, muttered something at Hiram, stood halfway up, and said, "Mr. Chairman, this woman can't speak here. She's got no standing, no right. She's not a parent or a taxpayer or a citizen or an employee of the school system. And if she's going to come to this town spreading smut—"

"Excuse *me*," said Katy, already at the aisle and marching down it.

Hiram broke into a broad grin and even nudged Margaret Klopstock, as if she were in on it, or perhaps perched precariously on a barstool.

"The lady's only partially correct," Katy went on, moving forward all the while like one of Patton's tanks across Normandy. "You see, Mr. Chairman, Chair*person,* Chair*thing,* I'm about to become Stephanie Marie Conwell's wicked stepmother and so I really think I might be allowed a word or two. So, if I can have your attention for a minute I'd like to tell you a little story about these two sex therapists who go into a gay bar . . ."

And then, for better or for worse, Katy went into her routine.

The Savior,
Ishl Teitelbaum

Adam Kurzweil
708 East Kingsley
Ann Arbor, Michigan

Dear Adam,

Well, well, well.

The law of proportionality requires that your five-page letter receive a nice long reply and I'm afraid that's just what you're going to get. It's your own fault, Adam. You've raised so many fundamental questions that I can't be brief. I don't know, maybe I ought to have just tossed your letter away. I suppose when you're denied tenure you're allowed to do things like that. From where I sit you're not just a voice from a life with which I'm finished, but one asking what that life's all about. Isn't that what all your questions amount to? To write back to you—I won't even say to *answer*—means looking over my shoulder deep and long, just like Lot's wife.

Mood is a fine word. It's the single syllable that does it, makes nebulousness sound concrete and vagueness plain. Fuck versus copulate, shit versus excrement. The fewer the syllables, the more Anglo-Saxon and the less Norman, the more vulgar and therefore the more honest. So before I really get going, let me say that I think I understand something about what you are pleased to call your "current mood." My own first year of grad school isn't exactly a vivid memory, but I can pretty well recall its mood.

A lot of it was due to a case of mental bends. I mean the transition came so suddenly, not only in the new expectations of the professors and the unexpected competitiveness of the other grinds, but most of all in oneself. The old not yet dead, the new yet to be born—that sort of thing. Oh well, historians love transitions.

In fact, I think you'll find that transition is not the exceptional state professors of history like to say it is. I can't remember reading a single book about a single historical period by a single historian that did not sooner or later proclaim the period to be "transitional"—and "highly interesting" for that reason. I used to find this funny and concluded that it was the interest of the historian that made the period transitional and not vice versa. How? Simply because interest made the fellow look closely and, looked at closely, every period *is* transitional. The concept *period* itself obviously suggests as much. Era, age, epoch—all of them imply the old before-and-after.

What's true of history is true for you and me, Adam. Of course there are quieter and more hectic periods of change in our lives. I confess a taste for the feverish ones. You once commented that I was the most popular teacher with underclassmen. Well, one of the reasons I liked teaching those frosh and sophs so much is that late adolescence has always seemed to me a heroic age, ontology-wise. Most of the older profs dodged the 100- and 200-level courses when they could. For this they gave sound reasons, such as that the material was too elementary, the classes too large, that only graduate seminars engaged their best energies. Popcorn. My suspicion is that they were bored by the students, or rather by the students' problems and difficulties and questions, which amounts to the same thing. Later, I came to realize my own taste for teaching such students—which, in my insecurity, I had imagined as due to my fear of a *real* challenge—lay in my sympathy with just these problems and difficulties and questions.

You were young yourself, you'll say. You're right. Still, it wasn't just my age. I knew twenty-five-year-old assistant professors who despised all undergraduates, even juniors and seniors, even the ones they were dating. No, the truth is not particularly flattering to me. The problems of adolescence didn't bore me simply because I had failed to resolve even one of them. I had the virtue of arrested development.

All this by way of prologue. I'll try to get on to your concerns instead of mine, but I'd like you to feel that yours and mine aren't all that different. The metamorphosis from the undergraduate who is studying what he loves to the graduate student in whom this love is mocked, who is being "professionalized" (amateur = lover) is not something original with you. The trick is having the knack of internal resistance, of course. It so often is. But on to other, less obviously personal and generic matters.

Some years back I came across a short story in a literary journal that had published a couple of my poems. These journals are read almost exclusively in bathrooms by their own contributors, or at least by those willing to look at others' work and not just to gaze beatifically on the transmutation of their own vagrant scribblings into the dignified finality of print. This story fascinated me, and it still does. The author's name, as you see, is given as "Hugo Ungenannt," an obvious pseudonym. I wrote to the editor to find out about the author. The editor was pleased by my inquiry, even delighted, but couldn't help. "It's very strange," she wrote back. "The story came in without a return envelope or a return address. Ordinarily, we would have just thrown it away, but one of the staff liked the title. The postmark, for what it's worth, was New York City."

The moment has come for you to read the xerox I've enclosed, assuming you didn't begin with it instead of me, a choice I would respect but not like.

The Savior, Ishl Teitelbaum
by Hugo Ungenannt

ONE SUFFOCATING August night in 1944 the Jews in Barrack 31 arranged themselves from one end of the airless hut to the other according to a hierarchy left over from their previous lives and settled themselves to listen to Rabbi Sholem Levanter, who began with the prayer thanking God for having brought them alive to the present day.

Everybody was expecting a stupendous debate. Some even claimed to have been sustained through the terrors of the last week by sheer anticipation. Lately the men had seen more and more people, women and children, running and staggering, goaded straight from the cattle cars toward the new gas chambers and the ovens. There were questions they wanted answered.

Rabbi Levanter, a scholar of such renown that his name had reached even the large hairy ears of Ishl Teitelbaum, was to debate Rudolf Sonnenschein, the famous Bundist pamphleteer from Lodz.

In no time Ishl had found himself pushed to the very end of the barrack, as far as possible from the two principals. A small space had been cleared for them by the door, which meant shoving everybody else even closer together than usual. Ishl crouched on the half meter of floor between the last bunks with his back right up against the rough laths of the furthest wall. "Who the hell do you think you are? Move back," the butcher Weiser had said to him. Weiser was the only man there who knew Ishl's name, but even he would not use it. Others simply said, "Out of the way, Jew." One scarecrow with spectacles produced an argument: "I was a professor of law; *I* ought to be able to hear every word. Make room."

All this reminded Ishl of how the guards had forbidden his work brigade to call the corpses corpses. "You gotta call 'em somethin', call 'em turds, you shits." In fact, Ishl was indifferent to where he sat. Even in his best days he had not been a brave man. Now, exacerbated by terror and hunger for months, neither his knees nor his bowels could be relied upon; indeed, absolutely nothing but food mattered to Ishl. That everyone could get worked up over some fancy debate amazed him. It also disgusted him a little; yet just because he was not up to sharing it, Ishl grudgingly admired the spirit of those around him and felt inferior to them. He was used to his position at the back and he accepted it readily. Only Ishl Teitelbaum, the tailor. To tell the truth, he had not been a very good tailor, yet he was a better tailor than he was a Jew, or a man. In his whole life no woman but his mother had ever looked on Ishl with anything but disdain. Well, at least he had no wife to dig up or child to watch being shunted off to the ovens, nobody to cling to as the Ukrainians tore at his fingers. He really was shit, always had been. How could shit care about this high-sounding debate filled with words he couldn't understand out of books he couldn't read?

The men quickly grew quiet. Even those whose whines and coughs always filled the close air of the barrack somehow found the strength to keep silent.

Rabbi Levanter went first. Of course Ishl could not see him with all the bodies in between, but he imagined the rabbi stroking a long grey beard as he talked—just as old rabbi Littauer used to do at home—even though he knew that all the people in the camp had been shaved as clean as turnips when they arrived.

Despite the rapt silence, not all of the rabbi's words could worm their way through the maze of bodies to Ishl. Nevertheless, his argument, despite many bewildering citations, was clear enough, even to Ishl.

". . . Did not the Lord, blessed be He, tell us this?" said the rabbi in a rising voice which under different circumstances might have been stirring. "'And a stranger shalt thou not wrong, neither shalt thou oppress him. Ye shall not afflict any widow, or fatherless child. If thou afflict them in any wise—mark you, in *any* wise—for if they cry at all to Me, I will surely hear their cry.' So I ask you, Jews, which of *you* can claim never to have offended, never to have afflicted in any wise? Maybe a neighbor came to you for the loan of five zlotys and you kept him waiting while you finished your soup, hoping all the while that he would go away. Or it could be you passed a poor widow's house with the unworthy reflection that while she well deserved her poverty, you did not deserve even your headache. . . ."

Exhausted and stifled by the foul air, Ishl had drowsed, but this final argument he heard. He was an ignorant wretch—who was Ishl Teitelbaum to criticize the great Rabbi Levanter?—nevertheless, disgust rose in him like heartburn. So this wise man wanted to compare the grudging of a loan of five zlotys to all *this*? He wished to *justify* all this with a complaint over a headache? Ishl respected the rabbi, yet the stupidity of this argument was too much for him. He groaned so loudly that the man nearest him turned around and gave Ishl a kick with a bottom of his foot. "Shut up back there," he snarled. "We're trying to hear the rabbi!" Ishl shut up.

Sonnenschein's style of speaking was just the opposite of the rabbi's. Levanter had spoken slowly and deliberately, his resonant voice flapping up like a pregnant pheasant with a rapturous hysteria whenever he invoked scripture, then falling to earth again with a solidity that conveyed certainty of its own wisdom, especially when he cited some learned commentator for support. But this Sonnenschein delivered every single word at the same ringing pitch, like some frantic tomcat caught in a trap, as if shrieking itself were a form of persuasion.

"We are not sinners!" were his first words. "We are not guilty! and this hell is no punishment—it's plain murder! Open your eyes, Rabbi! Our torturers and killers are no avenging angels; they're not even all Nazis. Our murder is a political act! Listen to me. It's *we* here on earth who make justice and injustice." Here Sonnenschein paused for breath. "By trade I'm a cobbler. I worked with my hands turning the skins of animals into something of use to human beings, and let me tell you that just like a shoe, man is man-made. God is silent, Rabbi, not because *we* are imperfect, but because *he* is—so imperfect that he doesn't even exist! The proof lies all about us. I tell you we're all sitting here at the farthest point of human history, and beyond the forces of history, beyond the doors of the gas chamber, there is nothing. . . ."

By now Ishl was not really paying attention. He fell from sleep to sleep and yet could not quite manage to climb all the way into the black bag of forgetfulness. If only there were more air, then he might have been able to sleep properly.

So Ishl heard how Sonnenschein wound up and also the coughing and arguments that immediately broke out up and down the barrack. Well, he thought, maybe there are historical forces, and maybe there are great men who can shape them, but they are surely killing me. Ishl had heard plenty from the Bolsheviks before; in his youth they were as common as red ants in July. At least then they promised all sorts of good things, like dumplings and coffee and feather beds—but here in Barrack 31 such dreams were out of place. Their tune was a different one. Sonnenschein's historical forces indeed ended at the doors of the gas chamber, with all his theories, and these doors would swallow everyone. Even Ishl Teitelbaum grasped that.

The Jews continued wheezing and buzzing and at last Ishl fell asleep.

THE GUARDS burst in before dawn. The exhausted Jews were all asleep, even the learned Levanter and the fiery Sonnenschein. The guards yelled. Some banged on pots while others waded into the barrack with their truncheons, beating the stupefied men to their feet. Howling orders this way and that, they marched the men outside, prodding them straight toward the gas chambers before anyone knew what was happening to them.

Ishl lay crumpled against the far wall, just where he had fallen asleep after Sonnenschein's rebuttal of Levanter. The better men went first; in fact, Ishl was the very last to be hounded out into the mildewed light. He staggered with terror, paralyzed by screams and frantic prayers. Somebody struck him a blow square in the center of his back and knocked him to the ground. Dark as it still was, he could see in front of him the bankers and butchers, the scholars and merchants, the doctors and musicians already disappearing into the blackness between the two big doors. His legs jerked uncontrollably and he wet his striped pajamas. Two guards yanked him to his feet with a curse.

Perhaps because, in his ignorance, he had a few moments earlier been dreaming he was in a high-ceilinged room in which dumplings were being served up to him by beautiful angels, Ishl opened his mouth to cry out. "Lord of the World!" he cried, or thought he cried. "Why don't you save us all?"

A voice answered him. "Ishl Teitelbaum! If you are able to accept this, it will be well; but if not, then I shall let the whole world lapse back into chaos."

Before he could make out where this ultimatum had come from, let alone think of a reply, the two guards hoisted Ishl like a sack of laundry and flung him into the darkness among the others. In less time that it would need to draw a breath, the iron doors slammed shut.

NOW, ADAM, LET ME GET professorial for a moment before I go all Talmudic on you. At the heart of your deepest question lies one posed long ago by Aristotle—*answered* by him too, of course; Aristotle being in this respect the opposite of Socrates, since he wanted to answer every question for himself. Aristotle put it a little differently from you, of course. He asked which is the more philosophical, history or poetry? By poetry he didn't merely mean the sort of lyrical lucubrations I engage in now and then, but all imaginative literature—*The Iliad, Oedipus Rex, Lady Chatterley's Lover.* Uncharacteristically, Aristotle gave a nearly Platonic answer. Poetry, he said, is more philosophical (i.e., better) because it deals with general cases, with instructive types, while history is limited to particulars, the individual and accidental. I guess Aristotle was distinguishing reality from actuality, which is a teacher's distinction. I'll be getting back to this eventually, but right now I'd rather concentrate on "Ishl" which I am hoping will fascinate you as it does me. I'm counting on you seeing at once why your letter sent me back to the story, for which I'm obliged to you since you've made me think about this tale and why I should be so attracted to it. It's true: you learn the most by teaching because of the responsibility of teaching.

Okay, here comes the Talmudic part. I want to look with you at a number of the possible views we can take of the story, views that are by no means mutually supportive but without quite being mutually exclusive either.

1. Ishl imagines the voice at the end. It is a case of aural hallucination brought on by such circumstances as the dimly heard debate, Ishl's groggy, dreamlike condition at dawn, his stark terror. The story implies that no one else hears the voice, so it is not booming down from heaven or anything like that. Though the words are so astonishing as to seem beyond the power of Ishl's mind to formulate, no one's mind should be underestimated, not even poor Ishl's. The story thus has a sort of clinical trick ending. O. Henry and the fifth-grader: "It was all a dream."

2. The voice is indeed the voice of God inwardly answering Ishl's cry, which itself may have been only inward ("or *thought* he cried"). If so, a number of ancillary possibilities arise. a) God is cruelly teasing Ishl, for the tailor gets no opportunity to reply, though God might

easily have arranged one. b) God *does* get a reply, and a positive one, but it too is unspoken; it is a bubble under the waves of Ishl's consciousness, no more than a spark's sudden leap between synapses. c) God and/or the author is being ironic in offering this choice to Ishl. Let the whole world lapse back into chaos? For a Jew in a Nazi death camp in 1944 hadn't the whole world *already* lapsed back into chaos?

3. Ishl did not imagine the voice *and* God did not answer him either. The story is nothing but a singularly unseemly fiction, a game played with the reader's mind. The author of this story really ought to be ashamed of himself.

4. Ishl is to be seen as a martyr whose martyrdom, like every martyrdom from the standpoint of the martyr, saves the world.

5. There is actually nothing in the story that proves the other prisoners didn't hear the same voice as Ishl, or even that each one of them did not put the same question to God. The title and point of view of the story cunningly force us to identify with Ishl Teitelbaum and so we make the assumption that the voice comes only to him. But perhaps Ishl is to be seen as one of millions of "saviors," one of millions of victims and martyrs on each of whom the continued existence of the world depends. Only these victims have the authority to reassure the Creator that his Creation remains good. Once again, in this view, the stability of the world would be only a perilous balancing act, a transition between existence and non-existence, rather as your heart is said to suspend its beating when you sneeze.

6. The voice at the end is real enough, but comes not from God but a loudspeaker or megaphone. The voice is only a sadistic trick of the bored guards who resent having to get up so early and wish to mock the Jews' faith prior to exterminating them. Suppose they had listened in on the Levanter/Sonnenschein debate? One can imagine a particularly sophisticated and vicious commandant doing such a thing, perhaps one who had been a Hebraic scholar at Heidelberg or Tübingen before the war.

7. The overriding truth about the story is just that it *is* a story. An author has imagined it, so it must be read as an internally consistent text. Like the Bundist's shoes, the story is man-made. So, for instance, Levanter and Sonnenschein are obvious emblems of the orthodox and secular arms of Jewry. The name Levanter suggests the eastern origins of the faith, the fierce religiosity of the desert-wandering Israelites,

while Sonnenschein's name calls up the bright promises of tolerance and assimilation streaming out of the Enlightenment. The two speakers appear to be opposites, but are they? If so there would have been no need to imagine an Ishl Teitelbaum, since between them Levanter and Sonnenschein would cover the whole interpretive terrain. But in one important respect the debaters are not opposites at all and so the author needed Ishl.

Levanter thinks the Nazi persecution is occurring inside a morally comprehensible universe and so concludes it must be a punishment of the Jews. This is not a novel line of thought; Levanter is not so very different from Jeremiah. The Bundist Sonnenschein *also* insists that the persecution is comprehensible. He thinks it's a manifestation of certain thoroughly analyzed forces of history in which he places his faith. Thus, the two debaters seem to have nothing in common, yet each claims to know the meaning of history.

So you see, Adam, I really haven't forgotten your preoccupations.

Now, the story makes clear that Ishl is neither pleased not persuaded by either debater. Is it possible that Ishl, who cares about "absolutely nothing but food," sees more clearly than these celebrities? But how is food actually treated here? Ishl's dream is about food, but not a pitiful half-bowl of watery lentils. The dream is ascribed to Ishl's "ignorance," which may not seem to be in Ishl's favor or that of the dream; but ignorance is not always a bad thing—remember what ignorance did for Socrates. Ishl's dream is of paradisal, of spiritual food: "dumplings . . . served up to him by beautiful angels." Only the savior can savor such food. If Ishl is the Chosen One it is because he alone acknowledges the incomprehensibility of it all, preserves the virtue of his ignorance and so does not distort his facts. He sees through Levanter's fanatical lack of proportion and Sonnenschein's rational yet vacant ideology. Perhaps your professors will disagree with me, but I should call Ishl Teitelbaum a first-rate historian.

For me it's significant that our author chose concealment. Hugo the Unnamed he styles himself. He takes no responsibility for his tale which he may well have written in fear and trembling, perhaps even against his will; for a writer cannot always write what he wants and so he may also write what he does not want. The author does not want to write the story because he feels deeply his lack of moral authority as one who was not *there*, who did not suffer, was not gassed. To such a person the writing of this story is actually a sin. Even if one supposes him actually to be thanking the poor despised Jew for his own life and that of our world, writing the story remains a sin. He does not have the right to thank Ishl Teitelbaum. Very well, so our author sends the thing off but doesn't wish to know its fate. He is indifferent as to whether or not it is published. In fact, he doesn't want to see it in print himself nor for many other people to see it. He mails it to an obscure literary journal (now defunct, incidentally).

But why send it at all if the story is a sin he is ashamed of committing? Well, it is one thing to be ashamed of having written a story and another to be ashamed of the story itself. You see, once written a story exists on its own, and once it exists on its own it is, so to speak, shameless. The story is what it is, and *there* it is, right on his desk. What to do with it? What would the author want except to be rid of it? His purpose is not to share it, certainly not to gain credit for having written it. He simply wants to be shut of the discreditable thing he has made. In the same way, Victor Frankenstein runs away from the monster he has so lovingly fashioned as soon as it flutters its eyelids: it wasn't what he had in mind, but he can't destroy it either. Simply to burn the manuscript would do no real good. Our author would remain responsible for the story; he would be responsible for its destruction and it is responsibility that he most wishes to avoid. So, out it goes and good riddance! Stuffed in its envelope, the story is launched into the postal system like a note in a bottle.

Yet our author *did* write it, and there's no escaping the feeling that he or she has identified with Ishl, the lowest of the low. The story has something of the fairy tale about it; I mean the revolutionary reversal by which the lowliest becomes the most exalted, the ugly duckling a swan, Cinderella a princess, better than ducks and ugly sisters. But in Ishl's case the exaltation is awfully ironic. Because of his prior lack of status ("a hierarchy left over from their *previous* lives" says the story), Ishl is the last to go into the gas chamber. All the "bankers and butchers" go before him, the whole social hierarchy. Naturally, the last Jew should be also the lowest; yet, paradoxically, this final victim is precious because he is unique. Only if *he* can assent to the evil of the world, the world (and is the world ever *completely* evil?) will be permitted to go on existing. Anyway, it's up to him and in this being "up to" lies Ishl's exaltation. He can save the world only by not being saved

himself. And Ishl is not unworthy. For instance, it's not his own sal-
vation alone that the asks for; he says, "Why don't You save us *all?*"—
a most comprehensive prayer. Well, saviors never do save themselves,
do they, Adam?

I hate to try your patience when it's your soul I'd aimed at, but I
need to hammer a little longer at making you see the story as a carefully
ordered text with a vexed relation to history and history's meaning.
I admit I hadn't really noticed all of them before studying it for your
sake, but the story weaves a number of suggestive patterns.

Take, for instance, the concept *spirit.* Early on we read that "Ishl
grudgingly admired the spirit" of those more interested in the debate
than he is. Lacking this spirit he feels inferior to the others and yet
their enthusiasm also "disgusted him a little." It seems to me this is a
very odd way of putting matters. Ishl can't pretend to be interested but,
humble as he is, admires an enthusiasm he doesn't *want* to share, since
it also disgusts him. In plainer words, no one is more honest than Ishl,
the one to whom the world has given nothing—which must be why he
ends up responsible for it. But after all, why is Ishl chosen to bear more
spiritual weight than Levanter or Sonnenschein, either of whom seems
so much better fitted for the job? Because, I think, Ishl's choice will
be freer than theirs. His mind is freer precisely because he is uninterested in the meaning of history, which I'm afraid always turns out to
be some grayhead's *theory,* Adam. Moreover, the world has no hold on
Ishl. The world can't argue that it ought to be preserved because it
has given him wealth, position, love, respect. Thus, lacking the spirit
of the others in Barrack 31, Ishl counts for more spiritually—a neat
paradox, but maybe no more than a literary one without implications
for earnest graduate students worried about whether history has any
meaning.

Here is another pattern. Did you notice the curious emphasis throughout the story on breathing, voices, and air? Does this suggest to you
the breath of life? I shouldn't need to tell somebody named Adam what
the connection is, that deep down spirit = breath. The August night
is "suffocating"; "whines and coughs" are suppressed during the debate
and resume after it; Ishl feels "stifled" by the "foul air"; Sonnenschein
breaks his screed to catch his "breath"; Ishl could sleep "if only there
were more air." And notice how the "suffocating night" of the opening
sentence is picked up and then nailed down with such finality in the

last: "In less time that it would need to draw a breath, the iron doors slammed shut." Does all this add up to a meaning? I leave it to you.

The diction of the story really is absorbing. I speak now as an amateur scribbler of verses. There are little ironies in the words, such as the tailor becoming "a sack of laundry." Then those "iron doors": Ishl is always furthest from the doors so that they can shut only after he is inside. What are those doors really, I wonder. The "furthest point of history"? Most curious of all are the particular words of the ultimatum. I mean, you're sure you know exactly what the voice is saying until you look closely at the pronouns. "If you are able to accept this..." Well, what is *this*? Ishl's own death? The Holocaust? All of human history? "...it will be well." What is *it*? Does *it* mean the world? Does *it* mean justice will prevail in the end, or that it won't? "I shall let the whole world lapse back into chaos." Is this the negative alternative or the positive one? Does it refer to the cosmic injustice that will follow a refusal by Ishl to accept a comparatively little local one? The voice certainly implies the cosmos came from a chaos, a nothingness of disorder as in Genesis, and that the universe is held together only by an act of will on the part of this "I". Well, who is *I*? Bishop Berkeley's Perceiving-God? Ishl himself, each person being a universe that dies with him or her? All of *us*, collectively? The voice doesn't say "the world" is at stake, notice, but "the *whole* world." Why? Is it to make the point that the world is not made up exclusively of death camps but also comprises pleasant suburbs on Long Island, villages in Uganda, amusement parks in Osaka? "Lapse"—oh, so the world *wants* to return to chaos. Just give it its head for a week or two. It's the Fourth Law, entropy: energy must be injected into any system just to keep it the way it is. Okay. Here I go again with my fixed idea. Even what we call stability is only a transition between creation and destruction. But between what two things is the story a transition, hm?

9. Have you ever noticed, Adam, that "learning the lessons of history" is a phrase that sets most historians' teeth on edge? It's a politician's cliché, isn't it? I also think the phrase smells a little of the old Aristotelian rivalry between history and poetry. Remember Aristotle judged poetry the better schoolmarm, but he spoke as if poetry were *about* the same things as history. Isn't this presuming a bit much? Most of your poets ands fabulists avoid history as if it were full of viscous cholesterol. They generally want to clear an aesthetic space around their work. At

most, they walk up to history as one does to an automatic teller; that is, when they need a little capital for a new investment, it's okay. But they don't like going inside; they know the bank is for the bankers.

"The Savior, Ishl Teitelbaum" is another case entirely, and this is why it so fascinates me, an historian, like you. This is why I forced the meal down your throat and am giving you this interminable commentary by way of dessert, goopy jello mold though it may be. I believe the story to be an unusual effort to *cope* with history, and not just one overwhelming episode either, but, to cite Sonnenschein's one quotable phrase, "the furthest point of history."

What did Aristotle mean by calling poetry more philosophical than history? What is it to present these general cases? Creon is all tryants? All heroes are Achilles? Clytemnestra all wives? Not so obvious as it appears. After all, literature is never made of abstractions, like philosophy. Somebody who knew even more about the matter than Aristotle put it this way: "Literature always depends on the old woman throwing coal in the stove." So, in literature, the general is not abstract, does not draw away from the humble world. The general has to be also an old lady with a scuttle. The general is only general because it *recurs,* and recurs in all its fleshy, bloody particularity.

Now, either the author of "Ishl Teitelbaum" understood all this about history and poetry and recurrence, about the old woman and the coal, or I'm a moron. The sheer nerve of this story! The chutzpah! No wonder its author is ashamed of himself. Look at the progression in it. The suffocating August night in 1944—well, that is precise, that is historical. Then the debate over the meaning of history—well, that too might be historical, might actually have taken place. All the same, without being aware of it, we are already moving to a different level, to theory, to ethics. In effect, the story is interpreting itself before the fact, which is too soon. Isn't this the stage you've reached too, Adam? Aren't your questions more or less the ones those Jews wanted answered, the ones Levanter and Sonnenschein are trying to lay to rest? But then the story moves on to a third plane—higher or lower I can't say, but certainly one we are wholly unprepared for. Ishl hears this voice. This is not historical but something else. Ungenannt. Unnamed.

Recurrence. "The Savior, Ishl Teitelbaum" is itself an instance of recurrence or, if you prefer, of parody or plagiarism. It has happened before; at least it has been told before. Asarah Haruge Malkat in Bet ha-Midrash, Midrash Ele Ezkera, etc. It is from the story of the Ten Martyrs, the ten great teachers publicly executed by the Romans in the bloody aftermath of the failed Bar Kokba rebellion in the year 135. It is the story of the martyrdom of Rabbi Ishmael, which is undoubtedly why Ishl is called Ishl. In this story you find not only similar and even identical details, but also the same progression from the historical to theory to the nameless.

Rabbi Ishmael and Rabbi Simeon are on their way to execution. Simeon's upset because he can't figure out why he's being executed. He knows the politics, of course, but that's not what's troubling him. Ishmael gives him an explanation which is essentially the same one given by Levanter, and Simeon accepts it at once. In other words, he accepts a purely ethical justification of the outrages of history. He sees no disproportion between the smallest failure of character and the punishment of torture and death. He is being killed for his little sins, which means we all merit anything that anybody does to us. He actually buys it. "You have consoled me," he says gratefully to Ishmael. And that's the last we hear of him. However, the story continues.

A Roman matron who has come for the entertainment is attracted by Ishmael, whose beauty my source compares to Joseph's—that is, the Joseph of the story of Potiphar's wife, since recurrence itself is full of recurrence. She offers to have his life spared if—well, you can guess. But Ishmael is an ethical hero with the whole universe neatly accounted for, like Levanter and Sonnenschein. "Shall I forfeit the bliss of eternal life for an hour of pleasures such as those!" he spits at her. That's solid revolutionary puritanism for you. Hell having no fury like this Roman matron, she orders the executioners to flay Ishmael on the spot, starting with his comely face. Notice, we are still inside the historical and its human interpretation. What's going on is what everybody can see. Atrocious but intelligible.

Now, it's to the last part of the old story I want you to pay particular attention, Adam. The executioners go to work on Ishmael's forehead. He screams—"a piercing scream that shook the earth," my source says—and cries out: "Lord of the world, will you not have mercy on me?" He gets an answer that, according to this source, is unequivocally from heaven, though there's no indication that anyone else hears it. The answer is virtually identical to the one Ishl gets: "If you accept the suffering to which you have been sentenced, it is well; if not, I shall let the world lapse back into chaos." Upon hearing (imagining?) this, Rabbi Ishmael willing accepts his martyrdom. The End.

I submit that this last stage in both stories is neither historical nor ethical, but that both stories are nevertheless, as I said before, attempts to *cope with* history. Cope, you understand, without submitting to an ideology. No ideology can survive that scream that shakes the earth, just as no ideology can satisfy Ishl's human hunger.

So, you're studying the Nazi period and, to your credit, can't do so with the "suspension of values" your professor is demanding of you. On the other hand, you're too good a scholar to wring the facts through the second-hand strainer of theory, pumping up old Vico or Spengler. Look, Adam, you too are at "the furthest point of history," not as a victim or a martyr fortunately, but as an historian, as an inquirer into the truth of the past. Not just the past, but its *truth,* mind you. I'm not handing you any clear answers to your questions, like Sonnenschein or Levanter, like Ishmael consoling Simeon. Anyway I don't have clear answers, and if I did I suspect you'd never have asked me such questions.

If you can remember back so far, you'll recall that I began this colossal letter by confessing that I never resolved the heroic questions of youth for myself and by asserting that my own life is as much in a state of transition as yours. So I've sent you a story and what I've written about it is equally for myself and for you. I believe the danger is not in the tensions you are feeling now so much as in the temptation to relax them, consoling or reconciling yourself prematurely to the confusion of our world and its atrocious history. Stay perplexed and uncomfortable, then, for as long as you can bear it.

Basta!

Yours down to my Reeboks,
Alexander Fernlicht

Lucina and the Hermit

1

*t*he famous courtesan Lucina lay in her boudoir idly pushing a needle in and out of a scarlet pincushion. Like a gust of wind, late morning light rushed past the heavy draperies, but Lucina still reclined lazily in her scented bed. The pincushion was a cunningly made gift; the bright silk surrounded a compartmented potpourri so that at every stroke of her needle Lucina was treated to a new and surprising fragrance. Each time she stuck in the pin, she held the cushion up to her charming nose and whispered "sandalwood from Samarkand."

The senator had said so many things just about her hips; it made her laugh to think of it. Long ago Lucina had learned never to laugh when senators were about, and particularly not at certain critical moments. That love was an illusion she did not doubt, but vulnerability was certainly genuine, and Lucina always respected the vulnerability of others. In fact, she accounted this her single virtue.

Lucina remembered that Feroni's new statue was to be unveiled that afternoon. The design was shamelessly unoriginal—even Lucina could tell where he had swiped it—and yet, thanks to the friendship of the wife of a highly placed gentleman, his proposal had been accepted with enthusiasm by the Commission. The model for the allegorical figure leading the people, fetchingly draped in a few classical rags, was Lucina herself. Feroni had been such a bore about it, really. He was just like all the artists she had known. What made them tedious was their exasperating single-mindedness. Lucina had no sympathy for such unity of purpose and regarded it as a form of vanity.

No, she would spend the whole afternoon in bed if she chose. At the unveiling there would be reporters and photographers, imbecile smiles, endless flatteries directed at Feroni, and a clump of indigestible speeches to endure. No, far better to stay put; besides, she lacked energy today. Nothing easier than to get herself forgiven.

Lucina set the pincushion aside and stretched first one way then another. Stretching her body felt so nice that she actually purred like a spoiled cat. Then, on a impulse, she pulled off her nightgown and looked at herself in the wide mirror fixed to the wall at the foot of her bed. She became intrigued by the idea of seeing exactly what her backside looked like—hips, thighs, and all—so she hoisted her buttocks up into the air, twisting her neck uncomfortably to get a really good view. Brushing the fine blond hair back from her eyes, Lucina looked and smiled.

2

*g*irondel burst into the white room. "Time to go out, Arnaud." "Damn," mumbled Arnaud. "Can't you see I'm studying?" His nose was indeed stuck in a book.

"Of course you're studying. When *aren't* you studying? But it's time to blow it off a bit, take a break, let it slide. There's something highly instructive I particularly need you to see."

"It's my one free afternoon," whined Arnaud.

"Well then, all the better!"

"You don't understand, do you? It's the only time I've got for my research."

"Research for what?"

"My special thesis, idiot. My honors thesis."

"Ah ha. I hope you haven't already told me what it's on. I have a bad memory for theses."

"It's on the history of political pedagogy."

Girondel laughed. "Really? But isn't that rather a contradiction in terms?"

"I could do without your flippancy just now. Go away."

"Arnaud, for a genius you're woefully deficient in irony."

"Irony's stagnating; it advances nothing."

"I'm no genius myself, to put it mildly, but I'm not so sure I agree with you there. You may be right that irony doesn't advance many things, but then you can hardly deny that many things conspire to advance irony."

"Very witty. Now run along and leave me with Cicero."

"With Cicero? Ugh! Never!"

"You absolutely refuse to leave me in peace?"

"Certainly. I'm here to drag you to a piece of political pedagogy, so it's right up your alley. Very serious. Anyway, I'm not leaving without you. So come on, I want you to see the new monument. The unveiling's at two in Rheinach Park. Surely your special thesis gives you an interest in such public monuments. Their whole purpose is to inculcate civic virtues in the general population. In short, political pedagogy. Besides, I want your opinion on Feroni's work. I'm supposed to begin studying with him this summer. Let's see if he's worth the tuition."

"You can have my opinion gratis and a priori: all monuments are bewilderments."

"Snob! Snob I say! You're insufferably pompous, Arnaud! You're a philistine! You're—"

"If you say so. But now that you know my opinion, you can go away."

Girondel struck a pose. "Oh, I know it all perfectly: 'the aesthetic is merely a snare for the senses, and while monumental statues may occasionally inspire, they inspire the wrong things.'"

"Exactly."

Girondel crossed his arms like the art student he was. "All the same, I'm not budging until you agree to come. Come on, Arnaud, it's only for an hour. It's beautiful out, whether you care or not. The sun shines just as brilliantly on the witless aesthete beguiled by externals as on the philosophical genius who penetrates so very deeply into the insides of things."

"I wish you'd cut out this genius-business, Girondel. It's tedious and I don't like it."

"Precisely why I harp on it. You're not easy to get a rise out of; praise is the only thing that works. Besides, you really *are* a genius. Klopstack himself says so. Apparently you're in line for a lectureship, you old *ornement de la université*!"

Arnaud looked up. "Oh, I'm an ornament, am I?"

"Heard him myself in the quad. He was chatting with the Chancellor no less. Couldn't say enough about you."

Arnaud's mind worked so rapidly that he could not prevent himself from imagining his first lecture, complete with illustrative anecdotes. "One hour, and that's all. Agreed?"

"Done!"

Arnaud got to his feet, smiling almost imperceptibly, which was about his limit for smiling.

3

*e*verybody presumed that the beautiful Lucina came from a poor family. This was not owing to any vulgarity in her address or commonness in her habits; it was simply prejudice. Courtesans are supposed to be the miraculously well-endowed daughters of poverty, rubies from the mud. Certainty of their obscure origins is an indispensable part of their charm and reinforces the sort of sociological probability with which the people in Lucina's circle never argued. In fact, in Lucina's case, everybody was wrong. She happened to be the only child of a proud and wealthy foreign nobleman and his devout and frail young bride. Things went well for the first six years of Lucina's life; that is, up until the duel. Lucina's father became embroiled in a lawsuit with a neighbor over four acres of beech wood at the edge of his estate. The neighbor, a self-made man whose irascibility matched his stubbornness, lost the suit and the same day sent Lucina's father a challenge which it was not in his character to refuse nor his destiny to survive. Upon her husband's death, Lucina's mother lost all interest in this world, even in her daughter. The woman grew thin, pale, fell into a religious imbecility and had to be placed by her relatives in a sanitarium. Lucina was packed off to a convent school. Fortunately, there was an adequate trust fund, fattened by the sale of the four acres of woodland to the nephew of the neighbor, who fled the country after the duel.

BETWEEN THE AGES OF EIGHT AND ELEVEN, Arnaud lived deep in the woods. He was an orphan. Both his parents had died in an automobile accident on the narrow road that twisted through the national forest. A symphony of just the sort his father, a musicologist of note, particularly disliked had come on the radio and, fiddling impatiently with the dial, he lost control of the car which collided with an oak tree. Arnaud, who had been asleep in the back seat of the roadster, was dazed by the collision and horrified by the mangled bodies of his parents. In confusion and terror, he wandered off into the forest and was found early the next morning by an old hermit. No doubt it was the trauma that kept Arnaud mute for the next three years. In any event, the hermit never made any effort either to rid himself of the boy or to induce him to speak.

AT THE CONVENT SCHOOL, Lucina grew to loathe discipline and spirituality, which her education taught her to regard as inseparable. Though an apt pupil, she was the wildest of the sisters' charges, by far the most intractable, disobedient, recalcitrant, skeptical, talented and high-spirited. She was, in fact, her teachers' despair, all the more so because of her intelligence. To make matters worse, her astounding beauty and precocious maturity infuriated the nuns and quite stunned her fellow students. Though she lorded it over the other girls, in whom envy and worship of her contended, the school was for Lucina a misery. Soon after her sixteenth birthday she ran away, crossing two frontiers for good measure. At the age of eighteen, and after a variety of adventures, she managed to contact the office of her trustee, only to learn that the year before he had run off with her trust fund and a tango dancer. Lucina was genuinely happy for the old gentleman and liked to think that he had profited by her example.

IT WAS ON A FINE OCTOBER DAY in his eleventh year that Arnaud dropped his axe and spoke up. He told the hermit, from whom he had learned more by his silence than he could have by asking childish questions, that it was now time for him to go back to the city in order to secure a formal education. The hermit—a stiff-necked and wise misanthrope—talked it all over with the boy, tried to dissuade him with calumnies of city life, but, in the end, consented. Together they walked out of the forest, the hermit in a thirty-year-old frock coat, Arnaud in patched overalls and a homespun shirt. With some difficulty they were able to discover a brother of Arnaud's father. This man was a well-off bachelor in the leather trade with no taste for music at all. He showed neither surprise nor pleasure at the sudden appearance of his nephew, for whom he had neglected to search, but, upon being convinced of the boy's identity, undertook to see to his education. At school, Arnaud's many peculiarities made him unpopular, but his intellect flourished and, on graduation day, he found himself the recipient of a scholarship. He returned to the forest in the early part of that summer to visit the hermit, but found the hovel abandoned. He dutifully stayed there for two days and nights in case the old man should come back, and then returned to the city to prepare for his matriculation at the university.

4

*g*irondel yanked Arnaud after him as he cut rudely through the crowd. Making their way to the front was easy because, apart from the displaced loafers and pensioners hovering resentfully around the outside of the assemblage, those gathered for the event were wealthy and important, and such people insist on maintaining a decent space around themselves.

"We can get a really good view from here," said Girondel when they had achieved a place satisfactory to him; that is, when they stood directly beneath the speakers' dais.

"I think you want people to have a good view of *you.*"

"What a mean-spirited accusation, Arnaud! But don't worry—I forgive you. I forgive you everything because you're a genius."

"You forgive altogether too much," mumbled Arnaud.

"Actually, the point of view's extremely important," Girondel explained carelessly, craning his neck this way and that. "Just like a woman, a statue has to be seen from every angle."

Arnaud looked at his friend's eager face. "Why, you're hoping for some sort of scandal, aren't you?"

"With any luck at all," whispered Girondel. "We haven't had a decent scandal for so many years that people are beginning to say the country's quite impervious. In my opinion, a nation without artistic scandals is washed up. A fellow might as well emigrate."

"But didn't the design have to be approved by an official commission?"

"Naturally."

"Then I don't see how there could be a scandal. Official commissions seldom approve scandalous monuments, which accounts for their unvarying tediousness."

"*Mon cher* Arnaud, only the *design* was approved—not the model."

"The model?"

"Feroni worked in secret. I only heard about it this morning."

"What?"

"Patience, *mon ami.* Be quiet and maybe you'll learn something."

Well-bred noises issued from the elegant crowd. Arnaud checked his watch. The canvas-covered monument reared up like a miniature mountain. A man in a blue shirt and matching overalls climbed onto the empty platform and did something cacophonous with the sound system.

At last, to the sound of three trumpets, the proceedings got under-way. Feroni, looking alternately earnest and beside himself with amuse-ment, marched on to the platform along with the five members of the commission and a government minister with his lady on his arm. They all took seats (it was obvious that they had rehearsed this part) except the chairman of the commission, who talked patriotically for ten minutes. He was followed by the government minister who spoke no less patri-otically for fifteen. Both orators alluded dutifully to the God-given talent of Signor Feroni and how equal it was to the spirit of the great events commemorated by his work. Each time his name was men-tioned, Feroni's face broke into indecipherable wrinkles and folds.

The crowd contained far more people accustomed to talking than to listening, so it was not very quiet during these proceedings. At length, though, the moment came for the actual unveiling of the statue itself, a privilege allotted to the wife of the government minister who was to pull a plush-covered cable for the purpose. Only then did it grow quiet. One could hear in the distance the murmuring of pensioners and the complaints of their pigeons.

A drum rolled somewhere behind the platform; the official's wife pulled the cable like a stevedore; the canvas dropped, and the monument stood exposed.

The gasps of the crowd—particularly the females—rippled outward but so near together that they sounded like a single gust of wind passing over the park. Girondel rubbernecked delightedly while Arnaud stared at the statue far more attentively than he ever had at Professor Klopstack.

5

*L*ucina was pacing from one end of her boudoir to the other in a pair of embroidered silk pajamas. Occasionally she addressed remarks to her English maid, Letty, who sat anxiously sewing at a little rosewood table near the large window. Letty was not yet accustomed to her mistress's penchant for passionate speculation and this sort of thing made her feel insecure in her position.

"Until recently, Letty, I've assumed that life is simply movement—random motion, rootless and, in the geometric sense, absolutely pointless. I mean quite *literally* without points, there being no halt to the perpetual movement of mind and body, no place to stop and consider, no anchorage, haven or harbor. You get the idea, don't you? Now, most people, I used to think, err in imagining their lives are actually a *series* of points which they can even anticipate. 'In just a few weeks I'll be married to dear Bertrand' or 'Alas, next month Aunt Emilia is coming to visit again' or 'Maybe tonight Gregory and I will do it in an altogether new and pleasing way.' Get the picture, child?"

At such moments Letty had learned the best thing was just to nod and get the lecture over with.

"Well, I've always believed these people have got it all wrong. Imagine if a person *moved* like that—physically I mean, from point to point. They'd look like an automaton, jerky and ungraceful. Quite a lot of people do, come to think of it. But in nature we see only spectra, Letty. In short, life isn't one damn thing *after* another; it's just one *long* damned thing. I tried to tell Feroni that nature has neither line nor color, that we just make them up arbitrarily, but the idiot only humored me."

At some moment in these harangues Lucina would abruptly leave off and either fall into grim pensiveness or change the subject—for example, by suddenly demanding of Letty how much last month's mercer's bill came to or how people in England keep their hair from curling in the incessant fog. Lucina's mind was one of those of which people justly say that it is always working. Misunderstood in the most condescending way, this shapeless and undisciplined mental vigor was supposed to be one of her particular attractions.

"Letty, I'm starting to believe that there may just be some other possibility I've overlooked. Or at least that there ought to be. Do you know why I believe that?"

This time Letty shook her head.

"Because I'm so frightfully *bored,* that's why! Take, for instance, a cork and an ocean liner. They're both moving on the sea, through the identical element, but the little cork's aimless and helpless, poor thing. It just keeps bobbing up and down until it gets water-logged or washes up on some beach. But the liner has a course to follow. It's fitted out with an engine and a rudder and a captain and an anchor. Letty, *I'm* a cork."

"Yes, ma'am," said Letty, who was only seventeen.

"Well, but give the cork its due. A cork's pretty resilient. A cork can have a lot of fun!" Lucina declaimed this vehemently, as though she were defending herself against an ocean liner. "Now tell me, Letty, what on earth is a cork to do when it becomes bored with all this bobbing?"

"Dunno, ma'am," said Letty, who felt a little as if she were back in school.

"Dunno either." Lucina shrugged and began to do a special exercise she performed for her chest. "Oh, by the way, on whose bill do we put tonight's party, Letty? I've forgotten again."

Letty considered for a moment, then proudly gave her answer. "Tonight's is on the Chairman of the Commission of Public Works, ma'am."

"You're invaluable, dear child," said Lucina, yawning and stretching. She relished calling her little maid "dear child" but wisely did not overdo it. The month before she herself had turned just twenty-one.

6

*d*uring the summer of his thirteenth year, Arnaud had earned a little cash by playing chess at the seaside resort where his uncle had dumped him with the family of an employee. One rainy day the father of this family, a bookkeeper who had engendered three daughters and liked having his boss's nephew about, taught Arnaud how to play and, within three days, was losing to the boy regularly and badly. The following morning the bookkeeper purchased ten inexpensive chess sets and a long folding table. These he placed on the public boardwalk beside a hand-painted sign challenging all comers to compete for a small stake against Arnaud, whom he reckoned could play up to ten games simultaneously. The bookkeeper divided the take evenly with Arnaud, once he had recovered his investment. Arnaud did as he was told, of course. At first it was fun, but he quickly wearied of chess and, in fact, had never played since that summer.

The night after the unveiling of Feroni's monument, Arnaud sat in his room not reading. Instead, he spent one hour thinking cunning thoughts and another writing verses. He then lay down on his cot, working out a couple loose ends. Here are the verses just as he wrote them:

The Hermit

The hermit bringeth joy to living things
for that viciousness is social and he,
of all folk, is least that. The dark hemlocks
bendeth to touch his brow; the grass stretcheth
to feel his foot; and beasts, that others bite,
curleth by his side in the frosty night.

The hermit eateth music and useth
no latrine, counteth time in melodies,
caring for neither minutes nor hours.
Grand polonaises and sad sarabandes
windeth their way through his golden colon,
emergeth no less sweet, and then roll on.

The hermit prayeth for that which he hath.
Fire he praiseth; he praiseth also soot
and mud and fear and agues and despair.
He blesseth headcolds, sumac, mosquitoes;
he blesseth winter, summer, spring, and fall
and praiseth pain when deepest in its thrall.

The hermit's wisdom seems stupidity
to most, his brain rusticated beyond
all civil use, his wit a stone's sermon
for dullness, one fallow weedy field his mind.
Yet troubled kings to the hermit hath sent
wise men to learn impregnable content.

At about midnight, Arnaud signed these verses with the florid name
Carolus Arnoldi, prepared the envelope then, as was his habit, went
straight to sleep.

7

Lucina slipped out from under the flaccid arm of the Commissioner—
or could it be Feroni?—and into her blue velvet Bessarabian robe.
She had already been lying awake for twenty minutes trying to recall .
all the things the hermit blessed or praised and could only remember
the seasons, the headcold, the sumac, and, of course, pain. She simply
had to have a look. It annoyed Lucina more that she couldn't recollect
all the beatitudes than that she was trying to do so.

An hour later, over breakfast, she contrived to ask Feroni (for it
turned out to be the sculptor, after all) if he knew anything of a certain
hermit living somewhere deep in the national forest.

Feroni went right on chewing his brioche and stroking the inside
of Lucina's left thigh, for she was seated close beside him at the table
with her robe a little open, a situation convenient for both eating and
caressing. He swallowed and replied that, indeed, many years before
he had heard stories of such a hermit, but believed them to be a good
deal short of true, merely so many folktales.

"Very likely," he went on, "once there really was a wise old hermit in those woods. There may even have been dozens of them. Once upon a time hermits were as thick as highwaymen in the forest, I guess. But all that's been over for a long time, my turnip. The last real hermit must have expired centuries ago. Why do you ask?"

Lucina picked up her coffee cup. "Why are *you* rubbing the inside of my thigh?"

Feroni laughed. "A fair question, pumpkin. I rub it because I am a sculptor!"

"Very well! Then I ask because I am—"

"A what, Lucina? Because you are an anthropologist or just a curious little cauliflower?"

"No. Because I am a *little tiny* cork!"

8

*a*rnaud had arranged to meet Girondel at the Bonaparte, a café near the university. He arrived early, sat down at one of the outdoor tables and ordered a beer, which he did not bother to drink. It was a bright day and beside him the plate-glass window of the café acted as a mirror. Arnaud observed with amusement how all the students passing by examined their reflections. He took note that these young people did not seem so much dressed as costumed. Even those engaged in lively conversations checked their neckerchiefs and pompadours as they talked and gesticulated, the men no less than the women. Apparently the window-mirror was irresistible. After five minutes even Arnaud was tempted to look at himself, but he refrained from doing so.

Girondel showed up ten minutes late. "I was talking to a girl," he explained as he flopped down, scraping his chair on the cement.

"An English girl?" Arnaud inquired.

"Yes! How did you—?"

"Very young?"

"Well, yes. It's really amazing. Somebody sent me her phone number. She—"

"Girondel, I have an important favor to ask of you."

Girondel raised an eyebrow. "A favor? You want a favor from *me*? This *is* quite a day. I'll order a double brandy!"

"Facetiousness noted."

"All right, I'm at your service. What can I do for you, *mon ami*?"

"The commission's very simple. I want you to say two things to two people."

"You mean deliver a message?"

"No, not exactly. I only want you to pronounce a couple of sentences to these people—not at all as messages, but merely as idle conversation. I leave the details to you, naturally. I'm sure you can manage it."

Girondel smiled, relishing the intrigue. "Do I know these two people, then?"

"Certainly. One is the English girl who detains you so pleasantly. The other is your new *cher maître*, Signor Feroni."

"Feroni?"

"He's not too eminent to be spoken to?"

"Of course not, but all the same—" Girondel was clearly nervous about playing any games with his new teacher. Arnaud noticed this and at once reassured his friend that there was reason to believe that Feroni would be highly interested to hear the aforementioned sentences. "Even from a vile student," he added.

"Really?" said Girondel, looking askance at his friend. "And how do you come to know so much about young English girls and the interests of eminent sculptors capable of making scandals?"

"Elementary," said Arnaud, "but how can I help injuring your estimation of my powers if I give away my little secrets? Let's just say I'm preparing a course."

"A course?"

"Why not? I'm a lecturer-elect, aren't I? In my opinion one should plot a course as one does a crime—in secret."

"I haven't the slightest idea what you're talking about, Arnaud."

"Bravo. That's just it."

"All right, then, what are these mysterious sentences?"

Arnaud sat up straight, all business. "To the English girl you're to say: 'I've heard that someone met an old hermit in the national forest.' "

Girondel repeated the sentence. "That's it?"

"That's all."

"Very well. It's easy enough to remember. And how about Feroni?"

To your *cher maître* you're to say: 'Last weekend a friend of mine was hiking in the national forest and he came across a hermit. He talked with the fellow for a while and seemed highly impressed.'"

"A hermit and a hermit? Oh, what a sly chap you are, Arnaud! What are you up to?"

Arnaud reflected for a moment. "An experiment on the difference between learning to have and learning to be," he said distractedly and pushed his untouched beer across the table.

9

It was six o'clock in the morning and, despite having spent most of the night with two senators, Lucina did not feel in the least sleepy. "I suppose there wasn't much exertion involved," she explained to herself while packing her knapsack. The truth was that Lucina was surprised by her energy. "There's no doubt I'm amazingly eager to get going," she thought, pulling the buckles tight. "Imagine—up to hear the dawn crack!"

Lucina was a naturally gifted shopper. Though she selected her clothing carefully, she did it with a rapidity that grisettes found breathtaking. Her taste was instinctively good and she had mastered the demanding discipline of not second-guessing herself, as so many fastidious women do. For example, the heather-green hiking shorts she had on were truly fetching—perhaps even excessively fetching after Letty had taken up the cuffs an extra half-inch. The boots she had selected, after only the most cursory glance at the two dozen styles laid before her, were at once sturdy and dainty, emphasizing the delectable parabolas of her calves rather than making her feet look like foundation stones. But now, looking in the mirror, she was faced with a dilemma. Should she wear her hair down and place her new plaid cap over it at a slight angle, or should she pin her tresses up beneath the cap to give herself a boyish look? It was a tricky question, but Lucina quickly settled it. After all, hadn't she purchased this pale blue sweater because of the way her hair looked against the wool?

And so Lucina was both packed and dressed before seven o'clock. She felt girlish, as light and fresh as the French piano music playing on her phonograph. She felt the pleasant superiority of the early riser; she felt the sun brightening her window was illuminating an innocent world. Lucina had eaten every scrap of her breakfast too, the prospect of fresh air having improved her usually sluggish morning appetite.

Letty stuck her tousled head in at the open door. "The car's here, ma'am."

"Thank you, Letty."

"Ma'am?"

"Yes?"

"When will you be back?"

"Back? Oh," she laughed, "any time between early afternoon and November." With that, Lucina slung her knapsack over her shoulder like an expert. "Never overplan, child," she added. "It's a capital error."

Letty looked perplexed and groggy. She would have liked to ask her mistress a hundred things about Girondel, who had visited her the night before and asked her to pose for him; but, before she could get out the first word, Lucina had pecked her on the cheek and vanished, knapsack and all.

Letty turned off the phonograph and began to gather up the empty breakfast tray; but then, after looking about her in a new way, she sat down on the edge of Lucina's bed, ran her fingers over the satin sheets, and even bounced up and down a few times. "*Pourquoi pas, hien?*" she asked herself aloud. Apart from *Bonjour, madame* and *Bon soir, monsieur* this was Letty's only French phrase.

10

*t*hanks to his excellent, though unwitting, sources of intelligence, Arnaud was able to calculate pretty exactly how many days he had to make repairs. Still, there were difficulties. One lay in finding furnishings that would look properly aged—a coffee pot, for example, and blankets. He devoted an entire afternoon to scouring the second-hand shops and flea markets. His quest was successful, resulting in an outfit not only authentic down to its fragrance, but cheap to boot.

Apart from food, the only new things he purchased were a briar pipe, a dozen boxes of matches, and half-a-pound of shag. He suspected the smoking paraphernalia might prove a useful prop. Though generally fussy about hygiene, Arnaud was prepared for any sacrifice. He gave up shaving for a week.

REMEMBERING HIS CHILDHOOD, Arnaud lost track of time. He was still chopping wood, had even taken off his shirt, when Lucina suddenly appeared. She was almost at his side. Her radiant hair (he hadn't even suspected it!) fell all over her shoulders, lit up by the noonday sun; there was a ruddiness in her cheeks as healthy and inviting as any apple's; her green eyes danced merrily, and her pink thighs shone between her abbreviated green shorts and well filled kneesocks. All these shapes and colors staggered him, but Arnaud recovered as quickly as he could, leaning on his axe to regain his equilibrium.

"How do you do," said Lucina boldly. "I'm here to find out what you've got to say."

"Is that so?" Arnaud answered, reaching for his shirt and wiping the sweat off his face.

Lucina looked him up and down. "You're a lot younger than you ought to be."

"That so," Arnaud managed to say as roughly as he could. The truth was that her appraisal had left him all but tongue-tied.

Lucina pouted with disappointment at this impolite and vapid repetition. It couldn't be called promising. But then she remembered the appropriate verses:

> . . . his brain rusticated beyond
> all civil use, his wit a stone's sermon
> for dullness . . .

"Let me put it this way," she said, slinging her knapsack on top of his pile of birch logs. "Recently I've begun to think I need teaching."

Arnaud managed a deep scowl, even though everything was going better than he had dared to hope. He drew himself up and spoke with thorough self-possession. "Madam, do not mock me. I am neither one of your side-show grotesques nor the stuff of childish tales. Nor yet again am I bait for your ambitious and condescending anthropologists. I am a simple man who lives as you see. What have I to teach you? I cannot suppose you desire to learn how to chop firewood?"

Even more surprised by his elaborate vocabulary and archaic sentence structure than his dignified manner, Lucina replied that, no, her interests ran to his views on grander or at least less practical matters, and added pertly that her curiosity was not so idle, seeing she had hiked alone for three hours through primary deciduous growth in order to satisfy it.

This was such a fine speech that Arnaud really couldn't help smiling; moreover, Lucina looked so very pretty delivering it that he barely kept from blushing. "Very well," he said. "You think you want to learn. How long have you got, then?"

"Depends."

"That so?"

She looked him right in the eye. *"That's so,"* she mocked.

ARNAUD TOOK HIS PIPE and his sock of shag from his trouser pockets. He was leaning up against an old willow tree by the stream while Lucina sat on the grassy bank. The afternoon had grown warm. "It's hot," said Lucina and pulled off her woolen sweater. The top three buttons of the silk blouse beneath it were undone, as if by negligence. She quickly took off her boots and socks then with an exhausted sigh leaned back against the bank, left leg extended, right bent. Arnaud steeled himself, fumbled in his shirt pocket for his matches, finally found them, lit his pipe deliberately, puffed out the smoke, and commenced his course in a cloud of blue smoke.

"Is it correct to say, then, that you wish me to be your *teacher*?"

Lucina dipped her feet into the water. "I said I wanted you to teach me, didn't I?"

"Madam, many people are able to teach us; only a few can be called our teachers."

Lucina smiled. At least this sounded like wisdom. "All right, then, consider yourself my teacher. Potentially. That's as official as I can make it." She spoke with a humorous smile and hardly a trace of irritation. The cool water felt so good.

"Very well. Now, to start with you must understand that because I am your teacher I know better what you want to learn than you do. And, because I am your teacher, I also know more about it than you do. Finally, because I am your teacher I respect not only your ignorance—which I must both cherish and cure—but also your . . ." Arnaud had nearly slipped and said "beauty."

"My what?" Lucina looked up wide-eyed, slowly reversing the respective positions of her two fine legs.

"I respect your *being*. I recognize it for what it is."

"You do all that because you're my teacher?"

"That and more. And yet I can do nothing for you that you will not do for yourself. As I am your teacher, that is the foundation of my respect for you."

Lucina, recalling her bitter days in the convent school and a few trying evenings with a professor of Greek, said that she had never known a teacher who showed any respect for students at all.

Arnaud relit his pipe and pretended to think over what she had said, as a kind of proof of his respect for her. "Madam, a teacher who does not teach out of respect for his student is not a teacher at all, though he may know how to read the stars and translate Chinese. Such a person interposes something between the student and the object of study—namely, himself. In fact, just because of his vanity and absence of respect he will not see any purpose to teaching *other* than interposing himself. It will be his opinion that the student is not capable of understanding the lesson, but only of understanding *him*. In this regard, as in many others, good teaching is no different from good cooking."

Surprised but not uninterested in this lengthy address, one which bespoke an unlooked-for depth of thought on the subject of teaching, Lucina asked, "And how exactly is teaching like cooking?"

"In that both have as their aim the nourishment of others. It is not enough for a cook to choose wholesome ingredients and refrain from drowning them in noxious sauces or scorching all the goodness out of them; a cook must also remember that when the meal is over the eater is to leave the table."

"I can see you don't think much of disciples."

"Certainly not. I am, after all, a hermit, and disciples are precisely those people of whom it is hardest to rid oneself. No, I hope you don't think much of discipleship either. It lacks weight. The disciple confuses the teacher with what is taught. It is as if a lover of music should wish to marry a violinist."

Lucina had an idea. "But one may also cook for oneself. Isn't that so?"

"Indeed."

"Can't one be one's *own* teacher, then?"

"For the instructed, madam, it is never otherwise," said Arnaud sententiously.

"For the instructed!" cried Lucina. "Oh, but who can instruct the instructed?"

Arnaud's pipe had gone out yet again. As he relit it he stared at the vicinity of Lucina's rib cage underneath the silken shirt with its three undone buttons. "First others, of course," he puffed and puffed, "and then themselves. A child cannot cook but must first be shown how to do so. After that it is chiefly a question of commitment."

Lucina clapped her hands together. "Ah, teacher, then how can you claim to respect me? You make me out to be an ignorant girl who has to be shown the way to her commitments."

Arnaud had no idea what to say to this. Though his heart was strong and glad, he felt himself tottering and so he took a step toward the water and looked down into the stream where the stones had been worn smooth beneath Lucina's feet. "This woman is a dream," he said to himself. "She is what is called a worthy adversary."

11

*L*etty squinted in the shifting light of the tallow candles she had lit in Lucina's boudoir as Girondel laid out his pastel sketches for her on the floor beside the bed. She pointed to one of them with her big toe.

"Why'd you draw my hip like that?"

"I draw what I see," said Girondel with a shrug.

"Really? So you see my hip as this great bluish bulge?"

"Bulge? It's an exceptionally pretty hip, Letty. Absolutely no kind of bulge at all."

"Oh, so you're saying you exaggerated it?"

"Well no. Actually I was working with the play of—"

Letty suddenly hopped up from the bed. "Quick! What time is it?"

"We're outside of time, my dear," Girdonel crooned.

"What time!"

Girondel rose slowly from the bed, walked yet more slowly to the bureau, gradually picked up his watch and looked at it as if it were inscrutable.

"What time!" Letty demanded. "Oh here, let me see."

Girondel pulled the watch away from her grasp. "Let's see now. In this room it is eternity, but as the world counts it's just eleven-thirty-six."

"Past eleven-thirty!" cried Letty. "Then you've got to go."

"Why, my sweet? I only just got here three hours ago."

In a panic, Letty was already smoothing the pillows with one hand and pulling the Bessarabian robe out from under Girdonel's trousers with the other. "Because."

"Because of what, dumpling?"

Letty straightened her back. "Because I'm expecting company," she said coolly.

Girondel laughed. "So, the pupil has big ideas."

"I may have big ideas but I don't have big blue hips, so I'll thank you to just get out and take that drawing with you. You can leave the other ones."

12

*i*t was morning and they had taken their coffee outside. Arnaud sat on his army surplus sleeping bag, which he had rolled up on the ground outside the small tent that served as his bedroom. Lucina had brought out the rush chair on which she perched in well-fitted jeans.

"But to live fully in each moment is beautiful," she was objecting.

"No doubt. But that kind of beauty is of little avail. Beautiful moments of that sort are only like diamonds."

"I'm extremely fond of diamonds!"

"You ought to get over them, then. Diamonds are dead, madam, deader than anything. Nothing leads up to or away from diamonds. To live one's life as if it were a necklace strung with diamonds is hardly to live at all. Water, on the other hand, is not only alive but of universal use. Water flows. It connects everything that lives, yet itself is always the same. Water spreads itself everywhere and yet is all compact of integrity. No one is able to hold it, and yet water is what we mostly are. It is water that holds us. Because it is alive, water is tougher than rocks. Water is capable of wearing away diamonds, given adequate time."

"One ought to be tough?"

"Only as tough as water, which is to say as gentle. One should not to be hard and brittle like a diamond."

Lucina mused. "Ice is a nickname for diamonds. Water freezes and then it's more brittle than diamonds. . . . But look, there's something I want to know. Why did you become a hermit, living out here all by yourself? Isn't *that* being more than a little like a diamond, a diamond in a frozen lake, not spreading anywhere?"

Arnaud put his cup on the ground, rested his arms on his knees, and looked hard at Lucina. He had not been mistaken in her. Feroni was indeed a master; whichever way you looked at her, Lucina was formidable.

"A hermit is like anyone else," he said, "except that he cannot bear vices."

"What've vices got to do with it?"

"All vices are social."

"That's a rather diamond-like saying," Lucina teased. "Was it other people's vices you couldn't stand or your own?"

"They are one and the same," said Arnaud, pressing his fingers together.

"That so?" said Lucina, then opened her mouth wide and laughed.

Her laughter always made Arnaud feel his vulnerability. He was simply overwhelmed by its music. If one really were to subsist on sounds, he thought, then Lucina's laughter would make a very tasty dish.

But he persevered. "The thing you most need to learn is how to stand."

"Really? I've been told by experts that my posture is impeccable."

Arnaud thought that this pertness of hers, her *absolute* pertness, was an unfair advantage, not unlike a woman's sanctioned tears; still, even when most frustrated, Lucina's eyes remained lovely and dry.

"Then your experts have been looking at the wrong thing," he said doggedly, summoning his self-discipline. "How one stands determines what one can resist, what one can bear. For example, you do not yet understand the art of standing *still.*"

"That's true," Lucina admitted with a frown. "Do you?"

Arnaud pointed to the hovel.

"All right. I'll grant that you've mastered how to stand still, but does that prove you also know how *not* to stand still?"

"There is no art in not standing still, madam. It is like the so-called art of concealment, which is not really an art either, but only a way of hiding within one's own skin, that bag inside which we all are born. Not concealment but revelation is the true art, and all great art is a genuine revelation. Speaking nobly and truthfully is an art. Devotion is an art. But bouncing from here to there, tossing out illusions at one moment and succumbing to them the next, or simply remaining mute— these are at best mere virtuosity. A true art demands the pain and discipline of childbirth."

Lucina had been attending very closely to what Arnaud said; she approved of some of it, and admitted it. "However," she added, "I don't at all agree that it's easy to remain silent. In my experience very few people know how to hold their tongues."

"Yes. Remaining quiet can also be a discipline, too."

"But you just said—"

"It is a *social* discipline, like duplicity or contract bridge. But silence is not an art, as it adds no life to the world. To refrain from trivial speech may be a sort of art, but only if the possibility of untrivial speech exists alongside it. Muteness is worthless except as a prelude to a well broken silence. To speak well one must speak *from* somewhere, however. And this brings us back to how one stands."

Lucina sighed and stretched. Listening even to such interesting talk was a strain for her; she was not accustomed to it, nor to standing still in order to listen.

"With me," she said softly, "nothing is ever easy until it's over. That's when I know I'll be able to do it."

This was such an artless and enchanting revelation that Arnaud had to get to his feet and force himself to yawn, an act which provoked a real yawn. He had not slept much or well since Lucina's arrival, and when he did sleep he was tormented by dreams.

"A thing is easy to do only if there's no resistance to doing it from the inside or the outside," he said. "In your case, the resistance is all from the inside."

"Yes, that's true," said Lucina, who also got to her feet. "My inside is stronger than everyone else's outside."

They were now standing quite close together. She was magnetic and, unconsciously, Arnaud touched Lucina's hand.

"What you must learn, madam, is that prohibitions can be meaningful and becoming as well as stuffy and priggish. Doing what is unlike oneself, for instance, is a violation which the soul will revenge."

"You really don't know anything about me?" Lucina asked archly, as always looking forthrightly into Arnaud's eyes.

Setting his feet firmly, Arnaud replied. "There are only two kinds of things one can know about other people." His heart was pounding so loudly that he feared it would betray him.

"Oh?"

"The things they try to tell us and those they tell us without trying. The second is, of course, the more significant."

Lucina looked down at her hand brushing against his. She made no effort to move hers either away or closer. "You know, when you say things like that you're insufferable!"

"You see," said Arnaud with a smile, fighting back the impulse to snatch her hand and raise it to his lips, "you are already learning something about standing. You're learning how to stand *me*!"

Lucina also smiled. She was enjoying herself tremendously.

13

*h*ere is how things stood when the rain began.

Lucina had been in the forest for five days. She adjusted easily to roughing it, even to going without make-up and letting her hair do as it wished. There were few times when she longed for Letty to bring her a little cold chicken, for her wide bed, her phonograph, the sunken bathtub, a massage and a proper pedicure. Arnaud had taken her on a hike up a small mountain from which she could look down at the forest. He had shown her a pond of clear water where she could bathe, a meadow with wild flowers and raspberries. At night they played gin rummy or canasta and continued their colossal conversation. It was inevitable that Lucina should think of her teacher as resembling the ocean liner; and yet she had suspicions about his navigation.

From the first day, when she had been taken aback by his youth, Lucina noticed that he was ill at ease with her. The contrast between his mental fluency and his almost virginal clumsiness amused her. With her experience, she had little difficulty in understanding it. In this instance, however, she found what was usually tedious to be touching and even something of a challenge. Certainly, she had no wish to seduce this man—what would be the point of it?—yet, at the same time, she could not prevent herself from doing a hundred things every day that increased his discomfort. Perhaps at first this was merely habit asserting itself. For her, flirting was a reflex; but soon Lucina found herself teasing him deliberately, as though carrying out an experiment. Besides, she knew every arrow in her quiver and she often had the sense that what was going on was a battle. But if it really was a battle she was engaged in with this exasperating man, she couldn't decide if winning would be preferable to losing. This was not the familiar sort of skirmish that always wound up in bed, but a struggle between equals who threw their minds and souls into it as well as their nervous systems. Such a battle, she discovered, is never boring, never wearying. On the contrary.

For his part, Arnaud's nervous system was sorely tested. At least a thousand times, with the vertiginous sensation of tottering on the edge of a cliff, he had been on the point of grabbing her, of rushing into the shack in the middle of the night, of suddenly dropping his head into her lap as they sat arguing on the bank of the stream. And on those agonizing occasions when Lucina went to bathe in the pond, he had to sprint through the woods until he fell exhausted. Yet Arnaud kept himself in check. He was an excellent capitalist of the spirit.

ALL DAY THE RAIN poured right through the trees, turning the place where Arnaud had pitched his tent into a mire. It was cozy enough inside the shack, and yet, in her green shorts, Lucina complained of a chill. The rain was regular rather than furious. It pattered down on the old roof shingles like French piano music and so steadily that it seemed it might go on forever.

While Arnaud set about building a fire, Lucina reclined on the cot and began to lay out the inchoate but mutinous ideas that had been taking shape in her mind.

"I think I'm beginning to grasp the way you think," she said, putting her hands behind her head. "It looks to me as if you want to divide existence into only two conditions, though you've got lots of names for them and this gives what you say an air of complication. On the one hand, you talk about people who are devoted, committed, grounded, anchored, faithful, serious, orderly, purposive, and bear-like; while, on the other, there are the people you call drifters, illusionists, mannequins, butterflies, stuffed heads, mockingbirds, floaters, and loose marbles. You then associate all kinds of states with one category or the other, such as pleasure, extroversion, triviality, meretriciousness, and weightlessness with the first; discipline, nobility, gravity, endurance, and conviction with the second."

Lucina lowered her voice as she delivered this last sentence, mocking the sober tone of Arnaud's lectures. For the sake of his dignity, he dropped a log, but he offered no defense.

"Now, teacher, what I find particularly significant, and more than a little questionable, is that you seem to think one condition can at best yield only joy, while the other provides number one, top quality, certifiable happiness. You distinguish the two—joy and happiness—by duration, intensity, and intrinsic quality, and then insist that one has nothing to do with the other. Joy and happiness, that is, are mutually exclusive."

"Is that so?"

"It most certainly is."

"I see," Arnaud mumbled as he leaned over to set the kindling.

"But all this philosophical boiling down and dividing up seems to me altogether too abstract and downright cruel. Yes, it *is* cruelty. If you'd seen more of the world you'd know that people move back and forth from one condition to the other so rapidly that you can't honestly fix them at any given moment, let alone sum up their lives. You'd realize that your kind of moralizing is unfair and willful. You'd appreciate that for most people joy and happiness are equally elusive, that one condition infects the other, that life's a spectrum and not a pair of poles. Take a snapshot of a swimmer and she looks like she's drowning."

"Oh?" croaked Arnaud, dropping another log.

"Yes! And stop patronizing me!" Lucina became more certain of her ideas as she spoke them and her own words made her feel angry. After all, dampness had never improved her temper.

With his back to Lucina, Arnaud sat himself down cross-legged before the fireplace in order to light the kindling. He swore that he would never think of patronizing her. In fact, he turned around for a moment and begged her to proceed with her interesting analysis of his views, but as he did so, he couldn't help noticing her dimpled knees and quickly turned back to concentrate on the fire.

"Well," said Lucina with a vehemence he could hear but the beginnings of a smile he was unable to see, "for example right now you're the paragon of the second category, anchored and bear-like and whatnot, right?"

"Let's say it's more a goal than an achievement."

"But underneath all that groundedness and order and contentment—none of which I question for a second—you're imaging something very different, aren't you?"

Arnaud sighed. "Anything we do in spite of ourselves is not ourselves, madam."

"Oh, this madam-business!" Lucina said so loudly that Arnaud glanced over his shoulder.

Lucina got up from the bed and began pacing in much the same way she would in her boudoir before Letty.

"A hermit? Fraud is more like it. I don't believe you're a hermit at all. I also don't believe you don't know my name. And I most *certainly* don't believe that those verses were written by anybody with the ridiculous name of Carolus Arnoldi!"

"What verses are those, madam?" said Arnaud to the rising flames.

Rising over the tapping of the rain and the roar of the fire Lucina's voice grew still louder. But, as she shouted at Arnaud's back, Lucina was quietly stepping out of the heather-green shorts, unbuttoning her silk blouse, unlacing her dainty and sturdy boots.

"So it's been one long argument, hasn't it, teacher? But I think you're finally beginning to learn a thing or two." She said this as angrily as if she were not becoming naked, as if she were not stifling an exultant laughter. "You thought of making me over, of dominating me by force of argument. You knew my weaknesses and exploited them when the truth is that you were in need of teaching yourself. With all your distinctions, teacher, you needed to learn that teaching isn't the same thing as instruction and that learning isn't the same thing as conversion. As for me, teacher, I've learned something too—only I'm still not sure it's what you meant to teach."

"And what is that?" Arnaud asked in a strangled voice, afraid to see her anger, and so staring at the orange and blue flames shooting up the flue.

"I'm learning the difference between being desired and being . . ."

"Being what, madam?"

Lucina, smiling not at all pertly now, but with precisely that serenity, wisdom, and resolution depicted by Feroni in his scandalous and truthful monument, put her hands gently on Arnaud's shoulders. "You know very well," she whispered into his left ear.

Arnaud shut his eyes and at last let himself feel the full warmth of the fire, of Lucina's tentative embrace, of her breath on his ear. The course was over, the crime executed, the king mated. But Arnaud no longer cared whose king, whose crime, whose course.

Baby
in the Air

O nly moments before I saw Helen Rushing for the first time I handed Phyllis Parsons a full-blown rose from my mother's bush because she had admired it so much. Phyllis lived across the long driveway that ran like a spine between the two rows of red brick semi-detached houses among which we were growing up. I cut the stem with a black-handled scout knife of which I was excessively proud and warned Phyllis to be careful of the thorns. Almost at once the rose began to fall apart. The petals tumbled over Phyllis's fingers. They didn't plummet and they didn't float but did something in between. "Oh!" cried Phyllis as if she had done something wrong and that was the instant when I glanced across the driveway and saw Helen bouncing down the steps that led into her aunt and uncle's yard.

She was between her two cousins Frank and Pete. Both boys were looking at her and making motions with their hands as if they wanted to support without actually touching her. It looked to me that they were afraid she might suddenly tumble down the steps which seemed silly because Helen moved lithely in her wide shorts, moved with certainty and grace. She had one of those slim athletic bodies common in girls of nine or ten. Even at a distance I could see that her face was not pretty, but it captivated me because it was an exactly feminized version of her cousin Frank's and Frank was just about my best friend. I stared at her. The nose had just the same slight hook to it. Like Frank's, her mouth was wide, with a thin lip on top and a drooping one underneath. Even the eyes seemed, at a distance, the identical deep brown. In fact, I couldn't have said where the difference lay, but there it was. And her curly hair was the same color as Frank's too, sandy but long, long even for a girl's. It leaped beside her head as she hopped energetically down the steps into the yard.

Six years before I had been sitting on the corresponding steps beside my own house with Georgie Gould, who lived next door at the time but had since moved to a suburb whose enormous distance delighted me. Georgie was two years older than I was and at least sixty pounds heavier. He had a cruel fleshy mouth, a double chin, and was a bit of a bully. That afternoon on the steps he told me that one day my mother was going to die because when people get old that's what happens to them. I ran inside and found my mother making beds and kept assuring her over and over about how young she looked until she found out why, then she made a funny story out of it to tell her friends on the telephone the next morning.

Things had happened on all the steps in our neighborhood, on every slab of pavement, in each little yard. For instance, in the yard at the bottom of the hill at the end of the driveway the Blessingtons' nasty little bitch Spicey had numerous times tried to bite me or my friends when we ventured into range to fetch whatever ball we'd been playing with. Spicey would have succeeded except that two of us held her off with long clothesline props used as lances. Spicey would bark furiously and Mrs. Blessington would chase us away and complain to our parents so that at first we were all happy when Spicey died. But we began to miss her the first time a ball fell in the yard and all you had to do was walk right in and pick it up.

Peter and Frank brought their cousin into the driveway and over to me and Phyllis and introduced her. Helen said "Hi." Her smile was nothing like Frank's. Her wide mouth opened and her eyes narrowed and made you want to grin back at her. I looked down, though, and kicked a deflated basketball across my yard. When I looked up Helen was shifting her weight from one foot to another. She looked eager to run. Phyllis showed her what was left of her rose.

It was about four o'clock on a Saturday afternoon and the driveway soon began to fill with children, all between eight and twelve years of age. Some had been to the movies or visiting grandparents. A few had been inside doing homework or had gone shopping with their parents. Joe Potlich had enjoyed a long bike ride with a girl he had a crush on and didn't mind bragging about it, despite the teasing from his younger sister Suzanne. Though no one said so, everybody was glad to be back in the driveway. While it was the fixed foot of all our compasses, it was a lively foot.

In the driveway we played football, stickball, halfball, hide-and-seek. Depending on the season, we staged our footraces there and built runs for our sleds. On its concrete the girls chalked hopscotch courts and jumped rope, though there was no shame in a boy's jumping or hopping with them, nor was it at all unusual for the girls to join in our games or races. Phyllis Parsons could cover the forty yards of the driveway nearly as fast as I could and a good two seconds faster than Pete Rushing. It was the driveway's configuration and eccentricities that shaped our play and often suggested our games and their fantastic ground rules. For example, there was an odd unisex game we called kickstone. It was played on the four broad squares of cement that made up the entrance to each house's garage. You had to throw the stone onto a square, then kick it from square to square while hopping on one foot. If the stone should land on a crack or go out of bounds, or if your raised foot touched down, you had to start all over again. Then there was wireball, a game with rules as complicated as canon law in the hands of a casuist. It arose from the fact of a double electric wire being strung ten feet over the driveway from the Blessingtons' to the Kramers', just above the hill that marked our territory's end. The great coup was to throw a ball so that it lodged between the two wires and another to knock it out while those below tried to catch both balls. Hedges, low fences, segments or indentations of cement, parked cars, fierce adult gardeners, stored awnings—all entailed rules, rules for overruling other rules, rules about how the rules could be amended. For example, the rules governing a simple game of handball depended on whose garage door you happened to be hitting the ball against, as some were smooth and others were slatted. For some games, hedges were out of bounds and not for others. The width and extent of the driveway itself determined many boundaries, but not those of wide-ranging games like hide-and-seek or baby-in-the-air, a local favorite for drowsy and humid afternoons or evenings of postprandial sluggishness when all fifteen of us were outside at once and on relatively amiable terms.

Billy Schmidt and I sat on the steps near my house whittling sticks with our scout knives. Kids were goofing around all over the driveway.

Helen and Phyllis started toward Phyllis's house, but Frank called them back.

"What's the matter?" Helen asked, only slowing up a bit and not stopping.

"I'd just like you to stay out here," said Frank lamely.

"Why?"

"I was only going to show Helen something," Phyllis explained.

Pete, two years older than his brother, pulled rank and gave his permission, though Helen didn't look as if she needed it. She had already turned her back on her cousins. "Come on," she was saying to Phyllis even as Pete allowed it was all right for her to go.

Frank's nose was out of joint. He furrowed his brow and whispered something at his brother, who just shrugged.

"Who's that?" Billy asked.

"Frank and Pete's cousin. Her name's Helen."

"I like her," Billy declared after a couple seconds of deliberation.

"Really?"

"Yeah. Why not?"

"Well, it's just that I've never heard you say you actually *liked* a girl before."

Billy looked up. "Not true. I like *lots* of girls," he said defensively, then resumed whittling and turned philosophical. "Girls are, you know, different. Or they *get* different. I mean Phyllis and Debbie aren't so different but my brother's girlfriend Sheila's pretty different. I mean *really* different."

"I know," I said. "The older they get the more different they are."

"Yeah. Kind of. It's not just boobs either."

"No," I agreed because it wasn't just that.

"Hey!" shouted Joe from the middle of the driveway. "How about a game of baby-in-the-air?" He was bouncing a brand new white pimple ball. The sound of a new ball on the cement was inviting and its whiteness seemed magically to focus everyone's attention.

Up and down the driveway things started to happen. When more than a dozen children are about to act in common but haven't quite decided to, they look and sound chaotic. "Baby-in-the-air!" shouted a few of the younger ones. I saw Phyllis and Helen stop near the rear door to Phyllis's house. They looked back and down into the driveway like two Eurydices. Phyllis loved baby-in-the-air and was probably saying so to Helen who, for her part, was in constant motion. She fidgeted like a filly outside the starting gate. Her body was electric.

Billy got up from the step beside me and ran over to Frank. Joe said loudly, "Come on, everybody." But Pete objected, "I don't know, Joe. It's getting pretty close to dinner." "Aw, we can finish the game *after* dinner," Joe argued back. "Yeah, it'll be like an intermission," added Sandy Rubin, who, like Phyllis and the rest of the girls, adored baby-in-the-air. I saw Billy and Frank walking down the driveway, just pulling apart from the uproar; they were still talking. Everybody seemed to be waiting for Pete's approval to organize the game. They tried to get him to say yes by telling him they needed him to give out the secret numbers. This was a not inconsiderable privilege, even for Pete, who was twelve.

Billy left Frank. He looked stunned. Pete said he still didn't think it was a good idea and that anyway he and Frank were supposed to stay with his cousin until they were called for dinner which would probably be in about five minutes.

Helen ran down the steps from Phyllis's house and said she'd love to play, if somebody would just explain the rules. Phyllis was right behind her. Billy walked straight by me. Up close he looked worse than stunned. He looked sick. "What's the matter, Billy?" I asked. "I'm going in," he mumbled. "But we're going to play baby-in-the-air," I said. "I don't feel like playing. Anyway, we're going to my grandparents' for dinner." A moment later I heard his screen door.

Pete gave in and ordered Frank to explain the game to Helen, but Phyllis was already doing that. I wanted to ask Frank what he had said to Billy, but it was too late. The kids were all lined up, Pete was giving out the numbers, and Frank was running down the driveway to take a long throw from Joe.

Baby-in-the-air was in several respects the ideal game for a neighborhood shaped and populated as ours was. It combined throwing, running, and catching with chance, secrecy, and spitefulness. The game required a space neither too confined nor too open, like our driveway, and a large number of players whose physical skills need not be decisive. It was a communal game, but not a bland one. It could even prove painful, though actually hurting anyone—especially a younger child or a girl—was deemed bad form, infinitely worse than simply losing. Here's how it worked.

A range of numbers would be chosen ten greater than the number of players; for example, one to twenty if ten kids played. One person would be chosen to assign a secret number to each player, ritually whispering into the ears of a line of children. He would reserve a number for himself, then try to forget everyone else's. All the players would then gather around in a circle as one threw the ball as high as he or she could—straight up, or it wouldn't count—while calling out a number. As soon as the ball started skyward and the number was called, everybody scattered. If the number were a blank, the player throwing the ball got a letter: b-a-b-y, etc. But if the number belonged to someone, that player would have to retrieve the ball. Here there were two possibilities. If he or she were able to catch the ball before it hit the ground, it could be thrown up again and another number called. Any such throw was unlikely to be caught as everybody would have run as far away as possible. When the ball was not caught on a fly, the player retrieving it would yell "Halt!" as soon as he or she got it. Everybody would then freeze where they were. The player with the ball picked a target—the nearest and least concealed player—and was allowed three giant steps in their direction. Then the target-player, still frozen, would be thrown at. If he or she flinched or were struck, that player would get the letter; otherwise the thrower would. The rules made it impermissible to leave the area of the driveway or the abutting yards; however, it was both allowable and advisable for those scattering to hide behind trees, hedges, fences, or trashcans.

Theoretically, the game continued until all but one player was eliminated by getting twelve letters. Watching the game was interesting enough so that those eliminated seldom became bored. In practice, daylight or parental patience never lasted long enough for anyone actually to win.

Baby-in-the-air always began in anxiety and mystery (would the number one called be blank? would it belong to somebody good at catching? should you run or hold back in case the toss were caught or the number yours?); but, once all the numbers' owners were known, it evolved toward teasing, vengeance, and spite.

"Sounds terrific," I heard Helen say to Phyllis just before she got in line to have a number assigned to her by Pete, who still seemed reluctant to have her play. As he leaned down to whisper he put his hand on her back.

It was disadvantageous to throw first. You might easily wear out your arm and call half-a-dozen blank numbers. Pete could hardly volunteer as he knew everyone's number while no one knew his. Frank and Joe were unwilling. They persisted in tossing the ball back and forth, pretending it was a hot potato. I was on the point of volunteering myself when Helen demanded the ball from Frank. "Let *me* go first," she insisted simply.

Frank looked first shamed, then dubious, but he obediently handed the ball to Helen. "Sure you understand the rules?" he couldn't help asking as he did so. But Helen took the ball and ignored the question.

The sky into which Helen was about to throw the ball was blue and cloudless, like the deep end of a pool. It would not be dark until at least seven-thirty or eight o'clock. Everyone watched Helen intently, feet set for a dash. She bent back so far her torso resembled a taut longbow. Her right hand grasped the white ball just at her shoulder, and she covered it with two fingers, like a boy. Just before she threw, her left arm rose perpendicular to the driveway and her face turned upwards so that her long hair hung straight down, partially interrupted by her narrow shoulders. She was smiling as though she could already see the ball flying up, the children running in all directions, and hear her voice echoing off the brick houses. She was all power and once again I thought of electricity.

"Seventeen!" she suddenly shouted as all that coiled energy released itself in sound and the flight of the ball up past the wires and higher than the roofs of all our homes.

Each child had already picked out a direction, a refuge, an object behind which to hide; and, though several had chosen identically, the effect was of an explosion. Children ran and howled like the fragments of a shell.

Seventeen was Sandy Rubin's number. Sandy had already run three steps toward the Murchisons' hedge before she realized it was hers; but even had she stayed put there was no chance of her being able to catch a ball thrown so high.

I ran parallel to Helen. She was very fast and ran joyfully, as much for the sheer love of moving her limbs as for the sake of the game. Her long legs gave her a stride that matched my own. I kept to the middle of the driveway, while she cut through several yards, easily hurdling low fences and flowerbeds; then, still running, she ducked behind Mrs. Barger's yew bushes just as Sandy desperately yelled "Halt!"

That is the moment I remember best, maybe the only moment I truly remember at all: Helen dashing behind the thick green yews then freezing as if metamorphosed into a statue of a sprinter just leaving the blocks, arms bent and ready to pump, legs caught in flight, face rejoicing.

Half-an-hour later Mrs. Rushing opened her kitchen door and called for Pete, Frank, and Helen. That halted the game, but everybody promised to continue it after dinner.

Before going home myself, I stopped at Billy's house. I wanted to ask him something, but no one answered the doorbell.

THE INQUISITOR: You like listening to music, don't you? You hardly mind that this music is actually a tangle of brambles and thorns like the ones that surround castles in fairy tales, that it cuts down your air so that breathing slowly becomes labored and your brain, short of oxygen, tumbles into miasmal vapors that make you feel almost bodiless, or that this quasi-incorporeal state is not remembrance, let alone transcendence, but merely nostalgia, which sounds like a disease and is. Oxygen-starved, you lose your critical faculties one by one and suppose that what appears before you is a real memory— that is, a memory of something real—much as you might, when asked for your social security number, see the actual nine digits parade in front of you. Music is seductive and because it can hardly be called false, you assume it is true. In fact, music can be neither true nor false any more than the weather can, and it is equally foolish to rely on either.

THE AUTHOR: I didn't call you out of the rubble to hear rhetorical questions, run-on sentences, prose-poems.

THE INQUISITOR: Why should I care about your motives? Here I am.

THE AUTHOR: That's better.

THE INQUISITOR: You seem to misunderstand the function of inquisitors, for whom the phrase "to put the question" calls up delicious images of the rack, voluptuous brandings, titillating screws and presses of all kinds, pits and pendula. We're sadists, not questers after the truth. For us, to question is to penetrate. All inquisitors wish for is stimulation; they already have the truth.

THE AUTHOR: I know. It's your truths I'm interested in.

THE INQUISITOR. And that's why you've dragged me out of the rubble, as you put it? For my wisdom?

THE AUTHOR: To be precise, I think you're as wise as a cynic can get.

THE INQUISITOR: And how wise does a cynic get?

THE AUTHOR: Exactly as wise as every other cynic.

THE INQUISITOR: That is itself a cynical saying, wouldn't you agree? Anyway, I'm certainly wise enough to know what you want with me here in the middle of your silly little story, during this intermission when baby is still in the air.

THE AUTHOR: How else could I go on? Or rather, I *could* go on; I could go on quite easily in fact, but—

THE INQUISITOR: But you suspect yourself. You vaguely sense that your story is like one of those vending machines in airports and university basements. You put in your money, select a button, push it; there's a brief metallic jangle and out pops something—or, even more often, nothing.

THE AUTHOR: Let's just say I'm dissatisfied. I feel like I've been writing only from the top of my cortex, from the thinnest cross-section on the very outside, as much as might be sliced off in a delicatessen.

THE INQUISITOR: You've put in the money, pushed the button, the machine has started to jangle, and now you want to pause because nothing interesting may pop out. If there's something further down in your cortex, I don't know what it is.

THE AUTHOR: I'd put it differently. I'd say it's like the moment when Helen Rushing's throw reached its apogee, when the new white ball went perfectly still in the blue air. My momentum's gone.

THE INQUISITOR: Very poetic, but that stillness is an excellent model for your illusions, which, because this is a short story and not a novel, I won't bother to enumerate. But do go on. I can see you're troubled. I know already, but tell me what stopped your vending machine *in medias crepitare.*

THE AUTHOR: I think it was the image of Helen Rushing in among the yew bushes, which is curious, because that's also what got me started.

THE INQUISITOR: You *think*? But it's obvious, since you wrote that this is "maybe the only moment I truly remember." If you were being honest there, then what do you suppose the *rest* of the story is? Isn't it what I've already said—a mechanical contraption, a vending machine? Let's see the candy bar.

THE AUTHOR: In my book, invention is different from memory. You're nothing if not critical, so doubtless you know that already as well.

THE INQUISITOR: It's not possible to be critical without also being cynical. You want one, you have to take both. For example, I assume you want readers to understand what you would call your literary subtleties, to listen for all the small tumblers clinking and turning inside the machine. But such readers cannot be naive, cannot surrender to your story. A vending machine appears magical only to small children, savages, and imbeciles.

THE AUTHOR: Perhaps it's the tumblers I want you to tell me about.

THE INQUISITOR: A fair request, almost fairly made, though you won't much care for what I have to say. Of course I know more about these tumblers than you do. You couldn't grasp the archaeology of your story unless you should also become critical; but at the moment you did so, you'd have to be aware of your frightful lack of innocence. Author that you are, until then—and you'll excuse me for this—you're a baby in the air.

THE AUTHOR: To be an adult on the ground is better?

THE INQUISITOR: It's more responsible, more stable, more dignified.

THE AUTHOR: All the virtues of government buildings.

THE INQUISITOR: Have you examined at all your fascination with Helen Rushing?

THE AUTHOR: Why do you assume it's fascination?

THE INQUISITOR: It's the only clear basis for the existence of the story.

THE AUTHOR: What about the unclear ones?

THE INQUISITOR: I'm coming to them. But first let's run through some of your sins against innocence, or just sense. First off, you've changed all the names. Second, you've eliminated all the adults. Third, you've pretended not to have an older sister—worse, you've made her into the older brother of Billy. Fourth, you've converted the driveway into Eden. And what you haven't shamelessly idealized you've sublimated.

THE AUTHOR: Such as?

THE INQUISITOR: For example, your dream of solidarity and peace among the children. You know as well as I do the ferociousness of children. Also, you've taken the repressive, dishonest, and insidious social, economic, political, and cultural conditions of thirty-five years ago and made of them a world indistinguishable from the mendacious sit-coms of the time. It's the sexless, senseless world of television, assuring viewers of its wholesomeness.

THE AUTHOR: Wholesome? If so, I regret it. But this is how I recall things. Children are unaware of the conditions you mention.

THE INQUISITOR: So much the worse for you and your readers, then. But go on, grit your teeth. There's more.

THE AUTHOR: I'm all ears.

THE INQUISITOR: Then let's get back to Helen. Who *is* she?

THE AUTHOR: An actual person. A girl of ten I saw only that one day when I was likewise ten.

THE INQUISITOR: You're sure of that, are you? You mean to memorialize this *actual* girl in your story? But it's obvious that she's entirely your fabrication. As you pointedly, though unconsciously, admit, she's the "exactly feminized version" of your best friend Frank. Don't you think that's an odd phrase, "exactly feminized"? Also, nobody else in the story seems to have noticed this astonishing similarity. Not even Billy Schmidt.

THE AUTHOR: Bad editing.

THE INQUISITOR: No, authorial vanity and displaced homoeroticism. Oh yes, I know you're no homosexual; however, on this afternoon you have imagined you were ten years old, thus in the very middle of that stage in which one's intimacy is normally given to a best friend of the same sex. Is this being unduly critical?

THE AUTHOR: No, only unduly cynical.

THE INQUISITOR: Pssh. Baby in the air. *Baby.* In the *air.*

THE AUTHOR: I live by routine. This routine roots me in the ground of every day. I write, or try to write, each morning. I ride my bicycle. I drink coffee at regular intervals. I listen to the news.

THE INQUISITOR: *Halb Kinderspielen, halb Gott im Herzen?* After all, what's routine but organized nothingness? And nothingness is your *real* theme in this story.

THE AUTHOR: Is that so?

THE INQUISITOR: Let's consider a few details. There are the yew bushes, Helen's metamorphosis into a statue, the deflated basketball, the bully's brutal introduction of mortality, the defunct bitch who is hated then mourned. I'd say your theme is *clumsily* obvious. Even in your first paragraph that rose disintegrates.

THE AUTHOR: You read carefully, it's true, though you're incomparably presumptuous. What makes you think I meant to conceal this theme?

THE INQUISITOR: You *didn't* mean to. That would have been a merely artistic failure. No, what you wanted was to *distance* yourself from your theme, which is a moral failure as well. Your work is like one long approach/avoidance attack; it is your supreme flaw as an author, though unfortunately far from your only one.

THE AUTHOR: Okay. Pour it on.

THE INQUISITOR: In the old days, when a ship was about to sink, the rule—and, by the way, your story stresses rules because rules are distillations of routine, or predictability, and they can even cover the nothingness of moral failure. Anyway, the rule was a simple one, a slogan: women and children first. Poe deduced that the death of a young woman would be the most poetic subject imaginable, and it is not quite superfluous that he insisted the young lady must be beautiful as well.

THE AUTHOR: Perhaps Poe was what he pretended to be, an aesthete.

THE INQUISITOR: On the contrary. The beauty Poe insists on is not an aesthetic ornament or romantic flourish but a material requirement. The beauty is sexual, a means of attracting the male, which in turn is the means by which the species is preserved. Women and children must be saved before men because women can breed and children represent genetic heritage. Biologically, life doesn't want very much from us men. The death of a young female, however, is an irretrievable loss.

THE AUTHOR: This is vulgar sociobiology, you know.

THE INQUISITOR: Excuse me, but it's your story we're discussing, not my vulgarity—*or* my vow of chastity, if that's what you'd like to take up.

THE AUTHOR: Look, the urge to write a story is mysterious to me, but it's nonetheless strict. This story has crystallized around a memory, a picture. This image, though powerful, insisted on being embedded in a narrative. It didn't want to be lyrical; however, the narrative at every point had to be related to the image—also to the title, the game. Perhaps the game is an emblem of some sort. *You've* certainly tried to make it an emblem for me and my predicament. Perhaps, as you say, I made the green blur I remembered into a line of yews and they were not yews but hemlocks or holly or even phlox. All this I grant. The story began as an attempt to recapture the past, as one might hold an old photograph for a long time, committing it also to memory, but as soon as I started to write, the story became something different. It became, as so many stories seem to do, a search for its own meaning. Do you follow me? The act of writing takes such nerve that it demands some sort of redemption. Writers love meaning more than critics, I've noticed. Perhaps this is because critics resent the grace they imagine writers can attain, the redemption by meaning found or made.

THE INQUISITOR: A pretty speech and a mean accusation; however, your story *is* succeeding in finding its meaning. It is becoming a vending machine.

THE AUTHOR: Not to me.

THE INQUISITOR: Oh, to *you* it can be whatever you like, even an involuted wild goose chase. To me, it's a vending machine. To you,

Helen and Phyllis may be real persons but to me they are as indistinct as their interchangeable namesakes in dusty pseudo-Greek pastorals, as diaphanous and evanescent as those ladies in Poe.

THE AUTHOR: Which only proves stories are not intended for cynics, who lack the grace to surrender to them.

THE INQUISITOR: You mean, who have surrendered to one too *many* of them. I know nobody is innocent, least of all authors. The pretence is an affront. Let me be frank. As a critic I despise the illusions of authors and as an inquisitor I will not serve madness.

THE AUTHOR: Well, I too have principles, of a sort. I believe that music *can* be either true or false, that all memory is *not* nostalgia, that to recall the past is not *always* merely to recreate it, and that human beings have as deep a tropism for stories as plants do for light.

THE INQUISITOR: Your story's about death.

THE AUTHOR: About the knowledge of death.

THE INQUISITOR: Whose death and whose knowledge? Helen's? Your mother's? Your own?

THE AUTHOR: I don't know yet.

THE INQUISITOR: Baby in the air. I'm returning to my rubble.

THE LAW WAS PROPITIATED to the degree that it permitted Helen to come outside after dinner, but only to watch the game. She sat on the topmost step looking down on us gladiators and resenting, I thought, the blue cardigan around her shoulders. Her chin rested on her knees. It was obviously bottling her up, this prohibition against playing. I felt she would not have hesitated to disobey except that all of us had heard her mother's stern and exasperated warning: "All *right*, Helen, but you're *not* to run around and play. You understand me?" We could tell that this was the last word of a long argument.

Sandy Rubin pointed out that the rules called for Helen's number to be officially a void, a blank. Frank looked at her murderously, but Sandy was constitutionally correct. The game resumed and we sailed on it into the darkening tide of the summer evening, our eyes adjusting so well to the failing light that if our parents looked out they must have been amazed that we could see at all.

Sandy called her own number and, rather easily putting aside her embarrassment, stoutly disputed the ruling that she get a letter. "But the number wasn't *blank!*" she objected like a crusading public defender, yet she lost her case all the same.

Frank passed up relatively easy shots at Phyllis, Joan, Fred, and me and chose instead to go after his brother, half hidden behind a trashcan. He threw hard and didn't even come close. The ball sailed into the Biancis' rose arbor. Had he thrown more slowly and with more control, he might have succeeded.

The game extended, elongated, became the longest game of baby-in-the-air we had ever played. The eliminations grew in number and some of the youngest children were called inside, stamping their feet on the way and groaning, "Aw, *Mom.*"

At last only Frank, Pete, and I remained, three shadows in the unlit arena. Helen was invisible or gone, but the ball seemed to emit a yellowish light.

Frank was furious. He called his brother's number over and over, throwing the ball as hard and high as he could. "Eighteen!" he'd grunt with the strain of his throw. I hung back, waiting for Pete to catch the ball, but Frank ran like a fiend down the driveway and into the dark. Pete, terribly self-possessed, would call my number or exasperate his brother by waiting for him to walk back. We were all good at catching, and the game turned into a stalemate.

Mr. Rushing appeared in the light of his kitchen door. "Frank! Pete! Time to come in, boys. Everybody's leaving!" He didn't sound angry that his sons had neglected their relatives, maybe a little sad, but it is hard to read the mood of a summons.

Pete said goodnight right away and headed inside, but Frank hung back, unwilling to walk beside his brother. I went up to him, my best friend. He was still holding on to the pimple ball. He took my hand

and pressed the ball down in it. The ball felt like a dead, curled-up frog. "Give this to Joey, will ya."

I was going to ask Frank right then. My mouth was open. But I couldn't find the question because I had already sensed the answer and didn't want to hear what I didn't want to believe and I wouldn't make Frank say. I was puzzled that he was so mad at his brother but I knew not to ask about that either or even what he had told Billy Schmidt. There wasn't much light but I could see that Frank was in no mood for any sort of conversation.

The sky deepened to blackish purple. My mother was still young and Helen was much younger. Helen was only my own age.

Frank turned away.

"Okay," I said just as if the world still made the same sense it had the day before. "Basketball tomorrow?"

"Nah, maybe," he mumbled, already heading toward the orange rectangle of the kitchen door out of which a slim black shape had been cut that might have been his cousin.

"Frank?"

He spun around on me, angry now. "What?"

"Never mind."

The Alpha Company Artists' Collaborative

1

i spent this morning looking at the snow again. Yesterday afternoon in the middle of the bingo game I saw it falling thickly through the thin drapes and I shuffled away on my cane, three-legged scarecrow, settled here on the verandah under this plaid blanket, listened to the snow descending, watched it soak up and transform the light. I liked how it molded to softly erect innocence the clipped hedges, buried with discretion the stupid geometrical garden, carpeted the parking lot so that the sole sound was an engine futilely racing, some nurse or orderly stuck fast and swearing. And when they found me later, full of patronizing reproaches, a clutch of mother hens, all they wanted to know was why, what was I watching, and I told them I was looking at the colors. Colors, they said, but it's snow, it's white, what colors. Imbeciles.

2

i have lived ninety-two years. I'm going on ninety-three. My lack of death is all the more surprising as I see death all around me. The people here are, at best, fractionally alive. This place is a waiting room built expressly for those who have divided their lives into quarters, eighths, thirty-seconds. Almost all of them used to be women because females outlive males. If women live longer it must be because they die more slowly. It follows that, at dying, I am as lethargic as a woman.

Two days ago Nurse Kolb told me I am famous. But she doesn't fool me. It's only that I've died so much more slowly than the rest. I am dying from the extremities, like a man succumbing to frostbite. First to go are the ear lobes, the tips of fingers and toes, the end of the nose; life retreats to the interior like a desperate tribe harassed by an imperial army, withdraws into the tangled jungle of vital organs, huddles around the last bit of fire and, knowing its doom, tells over its legends. Fame? Nothing more outward.

3

i saw Beaumarchais's head blown off. I got a good look because he was right beside me. His face was yanked upward like taffy. That look of displeased amazement I had seen so many times widened, lengthened, then became eternal. He did not die fractionally or from the extremities but from a mortar round. Sergeant Beaumarchais died astounded, looking down on me and on his crumpling torso. I thought he was going to tell me I had screwed up again, that my rifle wasn't clean, a button wasn't fastened, and that's why he was killed. Already the beach was dense with corpses, like droppings from a sick mammoth; the waves rolled with corpses, parts of corpses, green equipment, oil, blood, spoil, and spill. I wanted to crawl underneath the sand like a crab and pull the beach over me. Football players insist they never hear the crowd. Combat is the loudest silence. I saw everything but I never heard any yelling, howling, weeping, whistling, crackling, blasting, whining, every noise that could never be fashioned into music. Once Beaumarchais took off into the sky, I felt alone, alone for the first time since they'd issued me my uniform. The beach was crowded with men but there was no we. I pressed myself into the beach that heaved underneath me like a woman in her death throes, like a corpse still leaping with the superfluities of successive firing squads. Ancient history now.

I crawled forward. Why not? Every direction was equally bad. Winds rushed, pushed me downwards, reached underneath and grabbed my groin, rolled me over, sucked the breath out of my lungs. Like a rainfall by Seurat, glowing dimes of metal pattered. I pictured the bulbous-cheeked faces on old maps, hair streaming behind, strokes of air propelled from the puckered mouths, eyes fixed as if aiming at a birthday cake in one of the flat world's four corners. I couldn't actually see anybody, not since the moment when Beaumarchais's head took off for the firmament, and I hated the idea of being alone, being the only target. I was surprised to see my rifle in my hands. The sergeant had drilled us well. Despite everything, I still had my weapon and was moving forward. His warning "never lose your head" resonated ironically inside my helmet. Maybe everybody's dead, I thought. It seemed plausible.

Well, here I still am. In fact, all of us came through that landing, all of Beaumarchais's contemptible offspring. We all kept our heads.

4

Of course, I told Nurse Kolb, we were all in the war together. What other bond could have been so strong and lasted so long? Imagine that, she said.

Nurse Kolb has become attentive because I am now a famous man, a celebrated chip of flotsam from a golden argosy. Still, it's not respect I see in that new smile of hers. I observe the glint of dental work and in her voice I hear the insincerity of the cribside gurgle. I'd paint her as a smiling Fury, one of those euphemized Eumenides, just at the moment of transition. Now she even wants me to call her by her first name. It's Cecile, she says distinctly, Cecile Marie. Silly name for a Fury. She importunes me to remember. Look, I tell her, I won't do interviews. No graduate students or journalists. No critics or feature writers. No professors. She wants to hear about it just for herself, she assures me; she just wants to make a few notes of my memories. Well, perhaps she'll sell them. Movie rights. T-shirts. Until now, she confesses, she thought I was just a stupendously long-lived stockbroker, an old stick who'd been retired for most of her life, a wiseguy with some of his marbles and a quaint vocabulary, one cadaverous unit of resentful but resigned masculinity in this warehouse of querulous femininity. Art is the philosopher's stone. Fame is, anyway. I've gone from lead to gold. Ain't fame a bitch, we used to joke.

Pals, buddies, colleagues, it seems we have landed once again. The beachhead is secure. We have arrived and, but for my inexplicable longevity, our victory would be properly posthumous.

5

*O*ne should beware the pleasures of recollection. Memory is an unreliable seductress, wickedly clever with cosmetics. She favors a blemish-concealing base of nostalgia beneath crimson dabs of exaggeration. As if surprised, she looks out from under frondlike eyelashes. That said, I can't deny the joy I feel in remembering, though I will not divulge this to Cecile Marie Kolb, R. N. If you still have any memory at ninety-two your pleasures will all be mnemonic, and each and every pleasure will be genuine too, whether or not your recollections are.

Amazing to think that it took me years to get accustomed to the first-person singular, but if I am now systematically to recall what happened seventy years ago—a whole Biblical lifetime—I must resume the plural, for that was, in a sense, our goal. The plural is seductive too. Monks, tribes, teams, gangs, villagers, armies, regulars in bars—all know its allure. It is a thing about which men have always felt strongly, even religiously. The band of brothers. I do not include the many false *we's* of nations, political parties, committees, unions, boards, associations, clubs. These say *we* in pep talks, to deceive themselves, to manipulate others, to evade responsibility, to advance private interests. But to be able truly to say *we* is a condition one never forgets, about which sentiment inevitably turns lyrical. The true *we* proclaims responsibility of the purest sort and is the most human of pronouns. It connects us even to our ancestors, all the way back to the furry mammals picking nits off each other up in the treetops. The primal platoon is distilled into the solidarity, unanimity, and identity of this true *we*, knit in the common cause, warp and woof together. Perhaps the true *we* requires a common father as well, a potency to fear, hate, and envy, one whose death might seal the fraternity with a common triumph and a common guilt. That, I suppose, was the role of Sergeant Beaumarchais. We surely hated him enough. He was certainly dead enough.

6

*W*e could easily picture the bored non-com to whom the idea must have occurred. One sultry summer afternoon he is seated beside the screened window of a wooden office sparsely furnished by the lowest bidder. His regulation haircut does not betray the jitterbugging mind beneath; he is a virtuoso exacerbated by tedium. To him the war has brought no holiday, no breach in the flat walls of peace, only the tarpaper and lath routines of mindless tasks set by stupid masters. Perhaps it occurred to him as an astronomical game, the construction of a constellation. Chance has thrown onto his desk the dossiers of seven draftees, all art students. He pauses, smirks. No such coincidence has ever before turned up under his clerk's hand. He pauses. He fancies himself Zeus, laughs, hesitates, begins to cast at consequences. Drowsy flies bump against the screens. Somebody barks an order in the middle distance. Combat boots creak on loose plywood floors. He lights up a cigarette and wonders how loudly, over their beers that evening, his friend Corporal X. will laugh. He speculates on whether he might possibly get into trouble, decides he is transgressing no regulation and, in the end, types his bored irony into official language. Of the seven draftees he makes a military Pleiades, assigning them to the same company. He wipes his neck and smiles. The time passes.

7

*b*eaumarchais liked to call us by such epithets as the seven dwarfs, the seven wonders of the world, the seven sleepers. True enough, we were flamboyantly unmilitary. Our uniforms were seldom uniform, our marksmanship derisible, our marching only intermittently rhythmic. We were not at our best before at least ten in the morning and, from our sergeant's point of view, our best was by far the worst he had ever seen. He assured us we were his curse, his cross to bear. He took no pleasure in shouting at us because we were seven and seven made a sort of critical mass. Hard to intimidate, impossible to shame. Besides, we baffled him. We baffled him not only because we were young artists with the deeply subversive minds of our kind but for a far stranger reason. We exasperated and dumbfounded him because we liked being in the army, because he could see that we were happy.

Nurse Kolb claims to understand this, albeit in her own way. Of course, she says, just like the first year of nursing school. I mean you hate everything about it, the humiliation and the hours and the work and the teachers, but you like each other. Right? I mean, you're *part* of something.

Well, not quite. We didn't feel part of some great national effort, jolly cogs in the huge military machine. Our unity was not at all impersonal. We didn't even hate the enemy. We liked the army the way a couple who have become engaged in an inferior Chinese restaurant will feel affection for that restaurant no matter how bad the oyster sauce is. We liked the army because we liked each other; that is, because the army had brought us together under conditions of such intimacy. Together we marched, slept, ate; we shared the same latrine, got soaked by the same thunderstorms and berated by the same Beaumarchais. We were seven, a critical mass. One or two, even three, would certainly have been crushed, would have tried to hide, would have given in. But not seven. Oh no. We were too many and poor Beaumarchais was too pigheaded to think of his only solution, breaking us up. For some reason, he accepted us as a unit—the painters' platoon, the bohemian brigade, the daubers' division. The other recruits had lots of names for us too. As for ourselves, we talked. The army was even better than art school for talk. We talked endlessly about art. We talked whole paintings, frescoes, triptychs. We talked collages and landscapes and still lifes. We talked a mural around the whole barrack.

8

So eager is Nurse Kolb to learn that she forgets to patronize and humor me. She brings me not only articles cut from popular magazines but erudite essays out of scholarly journals. She has been to the library. I have a sort of power over you, don't I? Nurse Kolb looks at me as wide-eyed as Beaumarchais. The idea of being dominated by a patient has obviously not occurred to her. I ask if she chose to specialize in gerontological cases precisely to avoid such an eventuality. She is a little upset and so, going on ninety-three, I relent.

All this remembering has not made me more oblivious to my surroundings, just the contrary. Thinking about the war, the army, Beaumarchais, the smell of creosote in overheated barracks, recalling the faces of my six colleagues, their brushstrokes, dietary preferences, the timbre of their voices—all this has made me more attentive to the voices around me. I am a man with one foot in the grave who finds himself straining to catch details of the out-of-date gossip of peevish Mrs. Gregorian and envious Mrs. Narwash. Mrs. Abel's rambling tale of her scheming blond daughter-in-law enchants me for nearly an hour. All around me the resentments of lifetimes are being deposited, concentrated by the centrifuge of age. There are also those who have been born again thanks to forgetfulness. These have the knack of living completely in the present moment, like raccoons and toddlers. Their perspectiveless talk interests me as well. Mrs. Hamilton criticizes the green blouse of Mrs. Czerny. Mrs. Hemling is picky and objects to the limp celery at lunch. Mrs. McGovern gives out bulletins about the doings of her alimentary canal. The men, so few, are hardly different. In fact, from any distance they appear to belong to the same non-sex as the women. If they are distinguished at all it is only by an occasional flash of gallantry, a certain combativeness toward one another, and by their retreat into boyishness before an angry nurse.

What is lacking to us all, of course, is a future. The mind works differently when deprived of the future. Nevertheless, it works.

9

*V*ery well, I say to Nurse Kolb, I'll tell you how the Collaborative really came about. She leans forward on her chair like a crow on a wire.

The war ended. We were demobilized. Each of us was free to return to his art school if he wished. We sat gloomily on two facing benches in the bus terminal. One of us—I can't recall which, but it hardly matters—one of us began to speak. He got to his feet and walked up and down between the benches, formulating his ideas just as he spoke.

"In my opinion the artist who works alone is incomplete, eccentric, only partially human. All of us have been taught by teachers who put too high a premium on individuality, which they confused with mere novelty. They set up an idol for us to worship and called it originality. All of us have sat in large rooms with other students, looking at naked models or draped ones, at table with bowls of fruit and old green bottles. And the more the sketches of the students in the room differed from one another, the more pleased our instructors were. When they heard us arguing over this or that style, one or another theory, they were delighted with us. They despised community. For them, the history of art did not really begin until somebody signed his work. True?"

We all nodded. "Go on," we said, looking down at our olive duffel bags and shiny boots.

"But community, what of that? Quattrocento, the Dutch seventeenth century, the Refusés and Impressionists, Van Gogh and Gauguin, Braque and Picasso, mountain climbers roped together. Look, what is it that a painter does?"

"Sees," one of us said.

"Teaches seeing," another corrected.

"Translates seeing," proposed a third. It was a question that meant so much to us that we all wanted to answer.

"Well, what have we been doing for the last three years if not seeing *together*? And hasn't this seeing together improved each of us? Didn't the army succeed in this sense, that it called our individuality into question? Didn't it teach us to see, if not quite to march, in step?"

These were rhetorical questions, I explain to Nurse Kolb, who is looking puzzled. Do you mean, she asks, that all seven of you had become interchangeable, that you all painted identically?

Imbecile crow in a starched white uniform. Anything but, I said. Not only our styles but our favored subjects and media were as distinctive as ever.

Then I don't follow, she said.

I can see that. Don't feel too badly. Your learned professors in the subsidized journals, they didn't get it either.

Well, then?

Well then what?

Explain.

10

*Y*oung people believe excessively in individuality, yet they misunderstand it and do not pursue it as a goal. They do not pursue it as a goal because they believe they're already there. The truth is that individuality of any sort requires tremendous discipline and is a sort of fearful privilege. Any individual must be in constant tension, Nurse Kolb. And yet, as a rule, babies are more individuals than adolescents. Infants are incapable of anything but originality which is why Cézanne prayed to see with the eyes of the newlyborn. Now, your teenager has gone through years of careful conditioning aimed at making him conform, at overcoming the tiny measure of unruly infantile individuality with which he was born. Many two-year-olds are quite interesting painters, but by the age of six or seven they have become worthless. Even the most talented third-grader is no better than a third-rate realist. And why is that? It's because—

Of course Kolb interrupts me here, forgetting that I am going on ninety-three and might easily lose this train of thought forever. But, she says, you began by saying individuality is hard to come by and now you're saying we're born with it and all the hard work goes into getting it out of us. That's a contradiction.

So Nurse Kolb is suddenly a logician. Like all logicians she is not patient enough; she wants to stop everything at rush hour and rearrange the traffic into neat patterns.

The work of every stage of development, I say, lies in overcoming that stage. But with what? Or rather, to what? That's the question.

She shrugs her broad shoulders. I give up. Beats me.

To repeat the previous stage which will now have an entirely different significance. Really, these are rudimentary matters, Nurse Kolb.

Cecile. Cecile Marie.

Elementary spiritual truths, Cecile Marie. At our respective art schools we had been working at the re-evolution of our infantile individuality, overcoming years of careful socialization, recovering our lost freshness of vision. Then came the army, the war, three years of drilling, danger, and intimacy. We couldn't bear to part with one another. Individuality had simply lost its allure.

11

*W*e found a suitable space without much difficulty. This was during that hyacinthine urban interregnum between de-industrialization and gentrification. We leased the whole top floor of an old factory near the dockyards. It was so cheap that even our army pay more than sufficed to get us set up. The factory had once manufactured lady's underthings. It had high ceilings, skylights, and enormous long windows so there'd be lots of light for affixing all that lace, Nurse Kolb, all those tiny roses.

I'm not interested in the building, she said primly.

I know. I'm only reminiscing. I'm just getting in the mood. Before the verbs come the nouns, Nurse Kolb. First the setting and then the action.

Did I tell you that Mrs. Zelensky passed away last night?

Which one was she?

Mrs. Zelensky? Let's see. She was the one whose grandchildren broke the television last April. She always looked a little sour around the mouth—you know, disdainful—but she was really very sweet. An easy death, thank God. In her sleep.

Not what I'd prefer.

No. I can see that.

Can you? Really?

Go on, please. The old factory. You were all in this girdle factory. It was your studio.

Our *first* studio, yes. We stayed there about two years. It wasn't long before all those terrific old spaces were going for fifty bucks a square foot. There were poles and wide floorboards. It was quite perfect. Two cheap diners nearby. Three bars. Perfect. We bought seven mattresses, seven easels—

The seven dwarfs, she giggled. Nurse Kolb as Sergeant Beaumarchais.

Seven is a magical number, Cecile Marie. In Hebrew, for example, to be cursed is to fall under the spell of seven. There were seven against Thebes, seven last words—

Seven brides for seven brothers?

No brides.

You were all celibate? She was no longer mocking.

Yes and no, I said. We were against property and marriage seemed to us a form of property. You could say we were secular monks. Utopians.

Homosexuals you mean?

Certainly not.

Look, people are going to be terribly interested in this.

What people?

The people who read what I write about you.

I don't care.

They'll make things up, she cajoled.

You mean you will. Never mind. People always make things up anyway. Aren't they doing it already? Isn't your own imagination at work right now, Nurse Kolb? Aren't you thinking about those seven mattresses for seven strong young men, muscular veterans, about what yes and no might mean? Aren't you dreaming up orgies?

It pleased me to see that Nurse Kolb was blushing.

Our work was making art not love, I said sternly, mercifully. It's Mrs. Zelensky who died in bed. And she wasn't all that sweet. For example, did you know she used to call that sexpot Nurse Dasher by a not very sweet nickname?

Nurse Kolb couldn't help giggling. Oh, what was it?

Tight white.

12

*t*he junior high school glee club is paying its semi-annual visit of charity. The children look nearly as self-approving as their kapellemeister, Mr. Tomicelli. All the boys wear brown trousers, white shirts, blue ties. All the girls have on black skirts and white blouses. The trousers are not the same shade of brown, nor the skirts of black. The skirts are of different lengths, and the ties vary in color from deep sapphire to sky blue. The blouses are of many degrees of elegance and tightness. All the children sing with their eyes fixed on Tomicelli whose expansive gyrations under his loose suitcoat are more absorbing than the unfailingly upbeat repertoire.

The old women watch the children with smiles so frozen that their faces must ache. Some tap out the rhythms with arthritic fingers on metal wheelchair arms. A few even try to sing along.

Tomicelli's taste is so remote from the children's that they sing as indifferently as little parking meters. Their discipline is unnatural and unconvincing.

They belt out a clumsy medley of tunes that were popular half-a-century ago. This passes for thoughtfulness. I can still hear them as I make my way to the verandah. Nurse Kolb follows me, probably telling the others I must be feeling ill. Well, I am.

You don't like the music? she asks.

No, I tell her. It's fake. The music's fake, the harmony's fake.

But the children. They're so cute.

I use a phrase I haven't employed in years. Give me a break, I say.

The afternoon has turned windy. The trees bend and fallen leaves spiral from right to left. I can see the yellow schoolbus in the parking lot.

I'm sorry, I say.

You're in a bad mood? The children upset you?

Yes, that's it. I'm in a bad mood. The children upset me. I didn't care for their singing.

Nurse Kolb pulls the plaid blanket tight across my thighs. And yet, she says, a glee club's a little like the Collaborative, isn't it? I mean people working together to make art.

I trust that observation was aimed at changing the subject and not cheering me up, Nurse Kolb.

Why don't you like to call me Cecile?

Do you dislike your function?

What do you mean?

Nurse.

I'm more than a nurse.

Why more than? Why not *other* than? *less* than?

She paused, straightened up, clucked her tongue, pulled a chair up beside me. Tell me about how you worked, how you all, you know, collaborated.

Just what I was thinking about last night between naps, listening to the pipes gurgle and Mrs. Washburn snore. The scholars have got it all wrong. They haven't grasped the principle of our work, which isn't surprising. They want to see us as atoms in a molecule, planets around a sun.

Give me an example. I need something concrete.

I'll give you several. In fact, I'll give you all the examples I remembered last night. The principle should be clear from them.

Ah, exclaimed Nurse Kolb, as if to say "at last." Wait just a moment. I want to record your exact words. And she took out a little tape recorder, turned it on, said the date into it and my name, then steadied it on the arm of her chair. I could still hear the glee club faintly in the distance and wondered if it would get onto the tape. The air vibrated with their irregular harmonies and the windows rattled in the wind.

Example one. We would all paint the same thing. We would paint a bowl of peaches and plums, an identical view of the dockyards, the same drugged model—just as we did in school. And then, when we had all finished, there would be a vote on whose painting was not to be destroyed. Sometimes it would take several ballots to settle the issue. That was one method.

So six pictures were destroyed?

Yes. Painted over anyway. Canvases weren't cheap.

Did you argue about it?

There were discussions, of course, but nothing you could call an argument. We never argued. It was a rule, and all our rules were firm.

For instance you couldn't make a case for your own work, though you were free to vote for it.

Secret ballot?

Certainly not.

And who signed it, the one that wasn't destroyed?

We all did. On the back. We used our initials. We signed in alphabetical order. Didn't you know that?

No.

It was mentioned prominently in three of the articles you gave me.

I forgot.

I see. Well, another method we used was more elaborate. We'd all take turns on the same painting. Each of us would paint for exactly fifteen minutes and we'd continue the rotation until the picture was finished. This worked pretty well. The results were interesting. Then one day somebody suggested a division of space instead of time.

Space? How do you mean?

Simple. Say a canvas had 490 square inches to it. We would each paint seventy square inches. We ruled it off in advance.

Ingenious.

We often used chance too. We'd draw lots or spin a bottle or flip a coin to see who would do a particular painting or part of it.

Ah, aleatoric art. You see, I did read the articles. Kolb was proud of her new erudition.

Six of us would take vacations together and one would stay in the studio and do seven paintings while we were away at the seashore.

I see. What else?

For a time we'd each work on the subject we liked best—flowers, nudes, allegories, collages, nautical themes. Then we'd exchange subjects on a pre-arranged schedule.

Total cooperation. A fusion of interests.

Yes, but we had contests too. For instance. I remember someone talking about Velasquez and his elongated brushes which he'd wield like a fine swordsman. It was an exciting image, elegant and dashing. We had a contest to see who could manage the longest brush.

Extraordinary.

Also, we had a rule about self-portraits.

Which was?

That no one could paint his own, of course.

13

*d*r. Wishniak visited this morning. He pulled up a chair and smiled like an insurance salesman. We had a nearly sensible conversation for a change. It was mostly about bowel movements. The good doctor seems quite interested in mine, though I can't muster much curiosity about his. Nevertheless, he told me in some detail the history of his piles. "We doctors are not immune to all the ills flesh is heir to," he actually said. He enunciated this sentence solemnly, as though craving to display his culture and thus demonstrate the fellowship of pathology and art. This too is a curious effect of fame, I take it, for Dr. W. never spoke thus heretofore. He too wishes to establish a false solidarity. This fame of mine can only touch me slightly, like a puppy tugging on one's trouser leg, while to others it has transfigured me into an object whose very bowel movements are of significance. Nevertheless, when the time comes there won't be so much as a photograph of a lean and toothless codger in the Sunday supplement over the caption "last survivor." I've made sure of that.

Kolb tells me the scholars and journalists, the professors and graduate students do indeed telephone, do show up at the main office. I like to think they offer bribes. Imagine a professor of art, the sort who summers in Brittany, whose three-story house sports a small but carefully selected collection of sketches by the lesser Spanish masters. I'd like to see him try to slip a sawbuck to C. M. K., R.N.

14

*S*o what exactly do you tell them?

She is knitting. Wouldn't you like to know. Her voice is sly, almost flirtatious.

I can guess, I say. You tell them I'm a vegetating scraggle of brittle bones, a bag of dotless dice. Something to that effect.

The administration's only honoring your express wishes. Why? Change your mind?

Oh no. That's not a privilege one exercises after eighty. Too wearing. No, no. I'm content to be thought senile, and when I look at these liver spots I can believe it myself.

What's that you're reading?

I no longer read anything.

Then why that old book in your lap?

I'm *re*-reading this. It's called *The Monitor and the Merrimack*. It was my favorite book when I was about twelve. I still like it, as a matter of fact, but I don't know why so please don't ask.

Fine. Then I won't.

Nurse Kolb puts down her knitting and takes out her tape recorder. I notice that she's more comfortable with it now. She's become quite expert. The date has been put on the tape in advance.

Where did you all go after you lost that first studio by the docks? She holds the machine out toward me.

We went to our second studio, of course. Also our last. It was deep in the country, the hinterland, the sticks. Somebody inherited this old farmhouse, a ruin about fifty miles from pavement. So, *faute de mieux,* we fled civilization. No more chummy diners, no more bars with dollar pitchers of draft. We went on maneuvers, we bivouacked. We concentrated on work.

And did you take your seven little mattresses with you?

Still harping on those? Well, we took everything we could. Batteries, a refrigerator, cigar boxes. We bought a used bus and piled the stuff in it.

You were selling your work by then?

Oh yes. We sold moderately well. There was this downtown gallery that handled us. After the move we managed it all by mail. We thought it would be good for us, the change in scenery, the withdrawal from distractions. We hoped those of us who still suffered from nightmares about the war would be free of them. We looked forward to ordering things from L. L. Bean and Sears, Roebuck.

I take it from your tone that the move didn't turn out well?

At first we worked like mad. In the middle of nowhere we developed our technique to unprecedented heights.

New heights?

The ultimate. The apogee and zenith. We'd set up an easel, stretch a canvas, prepare a palette, lay out the brushes. Then we'd line up, seven in a row. One by one we'd pick a brush, apply a single stroke, go to the end of the line, and so on. We got to the point where we could finish an entire picture in a single day. The gallery owner complained that we were saturating the market.

Impressive.

Yes, yes, but we'd gone too far, you see. We'd overdone it. So, also one by one, we became discontent.

I noted how brief and pointed her questions had become. In what way? she asked like an experienced inquisitor.

We began to have doubts, Nurse Kolb. Doubts. Don't *you* ever have doubts? The Monitor and the Merrimack fought only one battle. They shot back and forth for an entire day and neither could sink the other.

There's a connection?

Maybe. I don't know. Maybe the men in those ironclads had their doubts too. Why not? Anyway, at dinner one night somebody said that maybe we weren't on the right track at all, that maybe what we were doing was just putting off our readjustment to civilian life, that we were trying artificially to preserve the camaraderie of our army days, that maybe the war had left us warped, if not as artists, then as men, and that maybe what we'd been doing was only militarizing our work and evading our responsibilities.

That's a lot of maybes.

Maybe. Anyhow, we agreed to sleep on it. At breakfast the next morning somebody said that maybe we were just overcompensating for the shame we felt.

Shame?

Shame about surviving, shame about the individuality we'd honed in art school. That morning was the first time we talked about Beaumarchais. In fact, that day the floodgates opened. Utopia can't endure doubt. It was everything, really. Property, credit, resentment, jealousy, ambition, vanity, privacy, disgust, fear. Everything, even money.

And women? A longing for women?

Yes, women too. But don't overestimate. All that was superficial. Underneath was the loss of faith. The war was finally over for us only when we lost our faith.

Faith? Faith in what?

In each other. In our work. In our system of defenses. All the things that had gotten us through the war. Who knows? It was a long time ago.

And so you—what? Split up? You started to work on your own like ordinary artists?

We weren't capable of being what you call ordinary artists; and even if we had been capable, it wouldn't have appealed to us. We all gave up painting. As you know, I wound up as a stockbroker. That was thanks to my brother-in-law. He was a good sort.

Was he a veteran too, your brother-in-law?

No. He wasn't a veteran or an artist. He was a good sort.

15

*t*his morning was so bright it almost hurt my eyes. I was sitting alone on the verandah when Mrs. Washburn was deposited beside me by Nurse Dasher, the one poor Mrs. Zelensky loved to call Tight White. Mrs. Washburn told me the whole tale of how she met her second husband, Dr. Washburn. It seems she was visiting friends in Boynton Beach and these friends introduced her to Washburn, a retired ophthalmologist from Muncie and a widower with this darling little mustache, just like Governor Dewey's. Mrs. Washburn grew so excited by her memories that she had to be taken to her room to recover herself.

I am not excited by my remembering but worn out. Nurse Kolb has squeezed me dry like a sponge and now the empty air is rushing in. It is not unlike lovemaking, this sense of vacancy and weightlessness. I felt so light this morning that I was afraid the force of the sunlight might be enough to carry me away. Now that I will not be talking to Kolb any more, now that she will no longer bathe me in the warm memory of the plural with its inspirations and guilts, my condition is hardly bearable.

Bingo.

Isaac Fehderflos

1

"**I**saac Fehderflos, the well-known violinist, will offer two recitals here next month. Mr. Fehderflos will be appearing, accompanied by Violet Halverson, on Friday and Saturday, June 12 and 13, at Rheinach Hall."

Never had I heard of the violinist Isaac Fehderflos, but then I am not musical. Indeed, I would not even have noticed an announcement such as the above in the Sunday *Tribune* except that it happens my own name is likewise Isaac Fehderflos. The notice leapt out at me from among the movie ads. It had the force of a cabbalistic incantation; there was my own name—a name I have always disliked and yet believed to be unique. So there was not only another Isaac Fehderflos in the world, but even a well-known one, a master of the violin.

I re-read the announcement, scrutinized and wondered at it. This discovery, the unexpected existence of another Isaac Fehderflos, made me feel as if the world had shifted so that everything stood in a slightly different place, an inch or two out of line.

I handed my wife the Arts section. "Read this," I said. She did.

"No, really," she murmured. "But it's so *fasc*inating. Don't you think you must be related?"

I looked at Janine to get my bearings. With her legs drawn up, she reclined on our camel-backed couch and I noticed how exactly the curve of the couch echoed the curve of Janine when she raised her head with a brightening glance, as though in anticipation of something new and wonderful. "Really, you *must* be related. It's too much of a coincidence."

"Related?"

"Well, I *mean*, Isaac, the same *name*?" Seeing my pout she began to tease me. "And *such* a name. *I*saac Fehderflos. It's not exactly John Smith, is it?"

The first time I saw Janine, which was over a punchbowl at a college mixer, she had laughed at my name. "*I*saac," she had giggled in disbelief. "But it's such an *old man's* name, isn't it?"

"Actually it means joke, sort of. And Isaac's quite a laughing matter, aren't you?" cracked my hearty roommate who positively luxuriated under the smooth and frictionless name of William Joseph Bryant—little Billy, happy Will, stolid Bill, dignified Sir William Bryant. "Fehderflos—now that's en*tire*ly serious," he added. A good thing I didn't have an axe on me at the time. But, despite my ridiculous name, Janine and I were married two years ago.

The truth is that I have always detested my name, though my reasons for doing so have changed with the years. When I was a child I feared the other kids' mocking nicknames—Izzie, Dental Floss. As an adolescent I despaired of fulfilling even one of my romantic fantasies under the indigestible bulk of the name Isaac Fehderflos. James Bond might well introduce himself at every opportunity with suave self-confidence, but Isaac Fehderflos would do almost anything to remain undercover. In college I actually thought of having my name legally changed. I confess that even the possibility of doing so excited me; it seemed to promise me the unearned boon of a fresh identity and novel activity—but then at eighteen who doesn't dream of creating himself anew? I was like a bald man contemplating a toupee; and, like most such men, I couldn't reconcile myself to the lie. Then too there was my father to think of, he who was as proud of our distinctive surname as I was ashamed of it. "Remember, Isaac," he liked to say, "it's up to you to carry on the family name. We're the final branch on the family tree. You're the last Fehderflos." This last sentence, customarily delivered with severe solemnity, made me want to laugh out loud. However, I loved my father so I didn't laugh. Anyway, it was this injunction of my father's that made me say to Janine that the violinist couldn't be any relative of mine.

"Oh come *on*, Isaac. What? Do you think it's not his *real* name? You think maybe he picked it for pro*fess*ional reasons? *I*saac *Feh*derflos?"

"I don't know. My father always said I'm the last Fehderflos, that the rest of the family died out."

"How does he know?"

"Why *shouldn't* he know? There were my grandparents, my father, then me. Did you notice any aunts or cousins at our wedding?"

"Hey, it's a big country," said Janine, "a big *world*. Maybe the violinist's from Europe? There could be another whole *line* of Fehderflosses somewhere, couldn't there? I mean there *must* be."

"Maybe. Another line, but not related," I insisted.

"Well, we should get tickets," Janine said with finality—for she did not like real disagreements, only teasing ones—and turned back to her beloved acrostic puzzle. No one could be more more fetching in a pair of jeans, or a pair of reading glasses.

When I met her Janine was a math major with 20/20 eyesight. The squinting began about six months before we were married, or a year after she became an actuary with the Prudential Insurance Company. I might as well admit that Janine's being a math major intimidated me from the first, that it made me wonder about as well as at her, wonder about where she put her emotions. Despite four years of college and a nice clean concentration in economics, I was crammed with prejudices about women. My mother died when I was four. No doubt this had something to do with my ideas. My father had even more to do with them, with everything.

My father, a man with a temperament serious to the point of gloom, made a saint of my mother, which is to say a mystery of perfection. It was all rather Victorian and not quite human, the angel in the house and so forth. I still haven't gotten used to conceiving of women as merely the females of my own species. "Your mother," my father once remarked when he saw me reading, "could say more by her silence than a talented author does in a thousand pages." This eloquent feminine silence was purely a mystery to me, and I took it as characteristic of females to communicate volumes with a glance, a smile, a shrug. I began to look for these tacit gestures in my classmates and women I saw on the street, tried to read the delectable, occult texts that I supposed all females were soulfully broadcasting. This sensitivity to girls and women did not, however, make me any less shy. In fact, if it weren't for Bill Bryant's humiliating introduction at the punchbowl

I would certainly never have met or talked to, let alone dated and married Janine.

We had a longish engagement, longer than I'd have liked, two full years. I proposed during Commencement Week and Janine gave me a sort of provisional acceptance, put me on lay-away, so to speak. The Prudential offer had come through and she wanted some time on her own. I took a job with a medium-sized bank, with prospects, and we lived ten miles apart, each in our own studio apartment.

Naturally, I assumed that my father would adore Janine—a paragon of that femininity he had taught me to rate so highly—just as I expected Janine to appreciate his solidity of character, which I so much respected and wished to emulate. But the relationship that developed between the two of them surprised me.

At first, Father was delighted with her, couldn't praise her enough, but then anything less than captivation would have struck me as monstrous. We visited him soon after our engagement. "Oh, but she's beautiful," he said, holding Janine's hand on that first visit. And later, taking me aside, he praised her grace, poise, intelligence. I beamed. After the wedding my father visited us, insisted on taking us out to dinner downtown, "a good seafood restaurant, so I can get a lobster," he had said frankly. Well, it was at that dinner—with Father looking infantile in his paper bib—that Janine let it drop that she wasn't in any rush to have children. Father turned all red; I thought he might be choking on a bit of shell.

Of course, I already knew Janine's views and more than approved them. To tell the truth, I felt more than a little frightened of having a child. As I saw it, Janine and I were only just getting started; we were still establishing our life together. She was happy with her work and I still hadn't gotten over my ecstasy about being her husband. What need was there to disturb all this with a baby, or to risk Janine in the uncertain combat of childbirth? To me, motherhood seemed a dangerous condition, possibly a lethal one. Father, however, was never the same about Janine after that dinner. He grew noticeably colder, even suspicious, asking me troubling and unpredictable questions about her cooking, how I felt about her working such late hours, whether it was too expensive for us to keep both cars. Janine's own parents simply did not enter into these dynamics. They lived far away, in Iowa, had three younger children to worry about, and appeared content to cross Janine "off their list of debits," as she herself rather coldly put it. For her part, Janine merely began to speak of my father with a little less deference, as if she wanted in this way to encourage me also to reconsider my excessive respect for him. Our conversation about the violinist Fehderflos was a good example. She disliked my citing Father as an authority, even an authority on the House of Fehderflos.

On the Tuesday after I had seen the announcement of the violin recital I was passing a record store on the way back from lunch and, on an impulse, decided to see if there might be any recordings by my namesake. I suppose I was hoping to find none. The existence of another Isaac Fehderflos disturbed me; just to think of it was uncanny. Besides, I didn't quite believe in this other Izzie, this Is-He. The notice in the newspaper might, after all, have been a mistake, even a prank. Or maybe there really was a violinist with a name something like my own, but the newspaper had spelled it wrong. True, if there turned out to be no recordings this would not prove no such person existed, but the existence of a recording would at least make his being a fact; it would confirm that I must adjust myself to a world with more than one Isaac Fehderflos in it.

It was midday and the shop was not busy, though it was noisy with rock music. A few well-dressed customers roamed the aisles; a young woman sat reading a novel by the cash register and another, dressed in a black jumpsuit, was removing compact discs from a carton and shelving them resentfully, untidily.

I found the comparatively tiny section marked "Classics." Naturally, the recordings were organized by composer rather than performer, and I hadn't time to look through them all. I remembered that there must be a catalogue and approached the woman in black unloading discs. Her hair was unnaturally black too.

"Excuse me, but do you have a catalogue I could look at?"

"What do you want?" she asked, not bothering to stop what she was doing.

"I'm looking for a recording by a particular artist, a violinist."

"We don't carry much classical stuff," she said dismissively.

"Yes. But could I see the catalogue anyway?"

"What's the *name?*" she demanded, but without much curiosity. She was still pulling out copies of various Grateful Dead discs. The carton was full of them. She lifted them out with both hands, like weeds.

"Fehderflos," I answered with some reluctance.

"What? That's the *name?*"

"What?"

"Fehder whatever?"

Did she perhaps think I had given my own name? "*Isaac* Fehderflos," I said pointedly. "He's a well-known violinist. Look, if I could just take a peek at your catalogue."

She grabbed the last of the discs. "All right. Ask over at the register." She stooped to pick up the empty carton and brushed by me.

I could find no recordings by Isaac Fehderflos in the entire Schwann catalogue. Nevertheless, I did not feel at ease, and when I got back to my office I phoned Rheinach Hall.

"Yes, sir. Two recitals. Nights of June 12th and 13th. Good seats still available. How many would you like?"

I had not been prepared for this and, before I realized what I was doing, asked for two orchestra seats for the 13th.

"That comes to 32 dollars," said the persistent voice of Rheinach Hall. "Now, if you'll just give me your name and credit card number, we'll hold them for you at the box office."

I found I was breathing hard and felt warm. "Fehderflos," I said sheepishly.

"Oh. Same as the performer? How nice. You must be a relative."

"No," I said. "No relation. It's just a coincidence. Here's my Mastercard number . . ."

As usual, I arrived home earlier than Janine. My father had been cagey to ask me about her late hours. I felt it would have been nice if she were waiting for me once in a while. Of course I didn't dare make an issue of this with Janine. It would have been irrational, as she'd be quick to point out. Not only did Janine tend to work late, but her office was a good deal further from home than mine, so that even if she left at five, she'd get home later than I did—even a good deal later, since the traffic was always tied up.

I decided to have a drink of whiskey and then see about dinner. The phone rang while I was pouring.

"Hello?"

"Hello," said an unfamiliar male voice. "I'd like to talk to Mr. Fehderflos, please." It was a voice one could call cultured, resonant and as practiced as a radio announcer's. It was a voice with lots of texture to it.

"*This* is Mr. Fehderflos."

"Fantastic. *Isaac* Fehderflos?"

"Yes?" I said suspiciously. It has been my experience that telemarketers favor the cocktail hour.

"Well, so am I," boomed this imposing voice with sudden warmth. "I mean my name is *also* Isaac Fehderflos." Sunshine flooded the wire.

"The violinist?"

There was a caesura for a vanity check, perhaps a private grin. "Then you already know about me?"

"Yes and no. I saw the announcement of your recitals in last Sunday's paper."

"Oh, then you *didn't* know until *then*."

"Afraid not." I thought I should excuse myself and added, "I'm not much for music."

"Oh, for a moment there I lost my head and thought I'd become famous." The tone was all charming self-deprecation, and he went on to use a phrase I'll bet he had used before. "Still clawing my way to obscurity actually."

"Well, it's quite a coincidence, isn't it?" I said to move off the sticky subject of his well-knownness.

"My thought exactly. Imagine."

"But how did you know about *me*? I'm a great deal less famous than you are. I don't play the violin or appear in newspapers." I felt strangely elated.

"Ah, but you *do* appear in the phone book."

"The phone book?"

"It may sound odd, but I read voraciously and travel almost continuously. It's become a habit of mine to look through local directories when I check into hotels. It's restful and somehow, well, *orienting*."

"So you look for more Isaac Fehderflosses all over the country?"

He laughed, though not quite heartily. "No, not for Isaacs, of course. I like to see if a town can boast of a John Milton, a Jane Austen, a Karl Marx, some Tartinis, a Bach family. In Troy, New York, for example, there's actually a Fritz Kreisler. However, I *do* look out for the name Fehderflos as well. Wouldn't you?"

"And is this the first time you've found one?"

"As a matter of fact it *is*. The *very* first. And for a second it was almost chilling to see my very own name in the book, but then quite the opposite. Tell me, do you have a middle name?"

"Never use it."

"I don't much care for mine either."

"What is it?" I asked, hoping for Frederick or Bertrand.

"Herman."

"You're kidding!"

"No! You don't really mean to say—but this is really *too* amazing."

"My wife's opinion exactly. When I showed her the recital notice she said we must be related." I found I was speaking faster and faster.

"Odd as it may seem, I don't think so."

"Neither do I, but you've got to admit—"

"Oh yes, it's a strange coincidence all right. But I'm the last of my family. My father died two years ago and he was an only child, like myself. He never mentioned any other branches of the family. In fact, he said we were all the Fehderflosses there were."

"Pretty much what I've been told too—by *my* father. All the same, don't you think there *could* be some connection?" Hearing my own argument from the violinist made me want to resist it. I could see its hollowness and, as usual, Janine's point seemed quite sensible to me.

"I suppose anything's possible, Isaac. May I call you Isaac?"

"Sure. What else?"

"Well, obviously we weren't the *only* Fehderflosses around, and whether or not we're related, I confess that I can't help but feel a closeness to you, a kinship. That's why I felt I had to call, I guess."

By then I could confess to the identical feelings, a sort of nominal brotherhood, and I expressed this in an apparent non-sequitur. "I got tickets to your recital," I said. "Bought them just this afternoon, in fact."

"Splendid," he said. "But look, I flew in to town early. I've got some other business to do and there's to be a master class at the university. That sort of thing. But I'm fairly free. Do you think we could maybe get together—you know, for lunch or something?"

"I can do better than that. How about coming to dinner, say this Friday?"

"Friday?"

"Saturday would do just as well."

"No. The sooner the better, Isaac. Friday'll be fine. It's really kind of you to ask."

"Great," I said, terribly keen to meet this other Isaac Fehderflos whose leading-man's voice had quickly grown on me. I was already convinced that we would become intimate friends. I wished to extend myself. "And what about, you know, your accompanist? The paper mentioned one. Would you care to bring her along?"

"You're very gracious. I'm sure Violet would *love* to come."

And so we fixed it all up for Friday at seven.

Janine was not delighted.

I committed the folly of telling her about the dinner invitation as she came through the door, before she had even taken off her shoes. Worse, I tried to explain matters the wrong way around. I started with Friday's dinner, intending to proceed through my phone conversation, the recital tickets, and wind up with the record store.

"Friday!" she cried, leaning fetchingly to one side to yank off her shoes. "But I'll be *work*ing all day, idiot. How am I going to get everything done in an hour? Weren't you *thinking*, Isaac? These people are mu*si*cians; they're cosmo*pol*itan, used to restaurants with *stars*. God!"

It was too true. I hadn't considered the logistics of the thing, which was thoughtless of me. Janine went about dinner parties the way surgeons go about bypasses, the way mothers-in-law go about weddings.

"I'll help," I said helplessly.

"Damn *right* you will." Her voice sounded choked. She vanished into the bedroom and shut the door.

Our apartment was not large, only a one-bedroom, though in a nice old building in a fairly good neighborhood. We were saving for our house. We both wanted a big one, so it would probably have to be about an hour outside the city, deep in exurbia, where the price would be right. Janine and I liked to talk about real estate, read the ads; we even visited a few open houses and, on a lark, one auction. I suppose the house took up the space my father wanted us to fill with children. No matter, since that is what the house itself was; I was sure that someday we would fill up the house with children. Of course we had to prepare the ground. As Janine liked to say, we had to be *ready*. Math classrooms are neat and orderly places where equations balance, where it is only reasonable to make plans.

While Janine took her shower I considered the small living room and tiny dining room where, in only a few days, we would entertain the well-known violinist Isaac Fehderflos and his accompanist, Violet. I was glad I remembered the accompanist. If they travelled together it was likely that they were married, or something like married. We had given dinners for other couples, once even for two other couples. We had enough room. We could easily make things in advance, and I could take off early on Friday. After all, Janine only wanted to make a good impression, and so did I. I prepared to propitiate her while I also prepared dinner.

I was cutting celery and carrots when Janine emerged in her long white robe, brushing out her damp brown hair. Apparently the equation had been balanced. She was smiling.

"We Isaac Fehderflosses are demanding as well as discriminating," I said, picking up what remained of my whiskey.

"Is that so?"

"Yes, indeed. We are cosmopolites and so we know a good thing when we see it."

"And have you seen something good *lately*, Mr. Fehderflos?"

I gulped down the scotch. "Let me put it this way. Would you consider going back into the bedroom? As all violinists know, practice makes perfect."

Janine turned her back, then looked seductively over her shoulder. "To Carnegie Hall?" she suggested.

It was about an hour later, over a microwaved lasagna, that I told Janine about our recital tickets, the disappointing absence of my namesake from the Schwann catalogue, and the interesting details of our phone conversation.

"I'm really *dying* to meet him," she confessed, "even if he *hasn't* recorded anything. How *old* do you suppose he is?"

"Haven't the vaguest, sweetie. Not very old, I guess."

"You know, if you could get home by five-thirty, we could do a roast."

"Just remember," I said, raising a matrimonial finger.

"Remember what?"

"That *I'm* the Isaac Herman Fehderflos who loves you."

Janine smiled at me with actuarial serenity.

2

*O*ver the next two days I was often tempted to phone my father to tell him about this other Isaac Herman Fehderflos, likewise an only son, also the last of his line. I'm not quite sure why I didn't. Perhaps I thought it would upset him in some way; he had always been so categorical about the unextended nature of our family, and there seemed to be a kind of pride in his assurance. Besides, as a rule we spoke only weekly, on Saturday afternoons, and I expected to learn more about the violinist over dinner on Friday. I could give my father a more complete account if I waited. And as I waited I found myself thinking often about the violinist, his accompanist, his nomadic life, his growing or stagnant reputation, that rather complex and commanding voice. Janine too was preoccupied by my namesake, so much so that the butterfly flutter of jealousy I had sensed almost with irony on Tuesday evening did not entirely go away. "I'm so eager to see what he *looks* like," she said putting on her silk blouse Wednesday morning, "aren't you?" How odd it felt to be jealous of this Isaac Herman Fehderflos whom neither of us had seen, who had dropped into our lives as unexpectedly as an unlooked-for legacy in a bad old novel.

I really did think of it as something of the kind—familial, yet out-of-the-blue. The violinist's conviction that we were not related troubled me just because I shared it. More exactly, I realized that the conviction we shared was not actually our own, but our fathers'. We had both inherited a sense of uniqueness from our fathers and, after all, both of them had chosen the identical name. It was a conundrum and I vacillated between thinking it all the strangest coincidence and the hypothesis—which *felt* logical, even if it wasn't—that we must be related in some way or other. I wondered how old *he* had been when *his* mother died.

On Thursday night something else, also peculiar and unprecedented, happened. The weather had turned sultry during the afternoon, a real foretaste of the dog days, and over dinner Janine worried that cooking a roast the next day would make the apartment stifling.

"So I've decided to change the menu," she concluded, gulped down her coffee, and made for the three cookbooks she had been given as wedding presents. They stood in pristine splendor at the far end of the counter.

"But sweetie," I said, "it's Thursday. When can we shop?"

"Umm," she murmured, her nose already deep in *The Joy of Cooking*, "no problem. I'm taking tomorrow off."

It was, I think, in February that Janine came down with some Asiatic flu. She staggered through the apartment that morning while outside treacherous streets lay quiet under a new eight-inch layer of snow, a day when the schools were closed and the sun glowed like a frozen heart. She went to work then.

"It's that important to you?"

Janine looked up distractedly. "It'll give me a chance to catch up on a *num*ber of things, Isaac. Hey, why not?"

"What things?"

"Oh, errands, you know, whatever. Why? Don't you think I'm en-*tit*led?"

"Only the other night you said—"

"Yes, I know. But things aren't all that busy at work just now so I figured what the hell. All *right*?"

Thus confronted, I used the old double affirmative. "Sure, sure," I said.

"This way you don't have to, you know, worry about getting home in time to put the roast on and—whatever."

"What a relief," I cracked, clearing the table and wondering why Janine kept saying whatever.

My facetiousness fell on stony ground. Janine had already curled up on the couch and was making notes for the bill of fare.

Friday turned out to be a scorcher, just as the weatherman said it would be, a steambath, an irrefutable argument for siestas and the global warming hypothesis. I was glad to stay at the dehumidified bank until five o'clock, watching wilted depositers and mortgage-seekers whine with pleasure as they came through the doors. In my chilled air and crisp business suit I had an edge, and I pushed my papers almost gaily, wielded my calculator with aplomb. If I was at all jumpy, as Ms. Cathcart suggested at around three, it was because of the prospect of the coming evening. Troy, New York had a Fritz Kreisler living in it, but only our city could, for the time being, boast two Isaac Herman Fehderflosses.

Shortly before quitting time, Janine phoned.

"Isaac, I don't want you to be surprised when you get home."

"What about?"

"Well, our guests came a little early. They're *here*."

"Already?"

"For a little while. We're having a fine time. Hurry home, okay?"

With a couple of Rolaids under my belt I did my utmost to follow Janine's injunction. I probably averaged eight instead of six miles per hour through the clotted Friday traffic, wishing I'd thought to ask why the musicians were something more than two hours early. It was unsettling. I even felt irrationally jealous, of Janine this time. After all, I was the one they were supposed to be coming to see, the other Isaac Fehderflos. It was *my* date. I sweltered in my Hyundai but didn't even loosen my tie. With the smoldering resentment of a peasant, I cursed Bermuda highs, myself for economizing on air conditioning, and several other drivers, so smug and temperate behind their ostentatiously closed windows. In a couple of years I'd buy a ponderous stationwagon to go with our roomy house, one with an industrial strength air conditioner in it. It will be full of children and bikes and Christmas trees, I mused.

Janine met me at the door smiling like brandnew bridgework and looking gorgeous in her simple white dress, her hair down but somehow different, curled.

"They're both *charming*," she whispered in my ear, almost as though she meant to warn me. The air around her shimmered with Shalimar.

It was only two steps into the living room. A tall tanned man with long blond hair pulled back into a short pony tail, dressed in a stylish suit with padded shoulders and a black open-necked shirt, stood waiting for me, keen-eyed. He looked as little like me as the comely blonde woman in a flowered frock seated on the couch. This lack of obvious resemblance was reassuring, even if he was magazine-handsome.

"Isaac Fehderflos, I presume," he said with a droll little grin and held out his long violinist's hand, fingers and all.

"Ditto," I replied.

"It's really wonderful to meet you, Isaac," he said with a convincing intimacy as we shook. Then he took a step back. "May I introduce Violet Halverson, an extraordinary pianist, soon to become famous the world over."

"Delighted," I said, still speaking one word at a time. I thought "delighted" sounded stilted. "Hi," I added.

"Isaac's only teasing me," said the attractive Violet as I took her pianist's hand in mine.

"Not at all!" he protested. "We signed a record contract just this afternoon. Remember that other business I mentioned, Isaac? The company reluctantly agreed to record me on condition of Violet's doing all of Ravel's solo stuff for them. Violet's *wicked* with the French, lighter than a soufflé."

Violet blushed.

"So it's a real *celebration*," Janine chimed in.

"Well, that's today's second big story."

"Congratulations to you both," I said. "How about drinks?"

"Janine's fixed us up nicely already," said Fehderflos, motioning to a something and tonic on the end table. It was sweating atop a rattan coaster, another unused wedding present.

"What would you like, Isaac?" asked my wife.

"A vodka and—" I began.

"Another—" he started to say.

There was a moment of silence and then we all chuckled.

"A real comedy of errors," said Janine with a delighted shrug.

"There's a Blaise Pascal in Syracuse," Isaac said.

"Oh, Isaac," said Violet.

"What?" asked Janine.

"Isaac here gets it, right?"

I turned to Janine. "He reads telephone directories," I explained.

"The boys from Syracuse?" Isaac prompted.

"Whatever," said Janine, blithely and yet again, then stepped into the kitchen to fetch more drinks.

"Feather moss?" asked Isaac.

"Pardon?" I had been looking after my wife's rear end and whatever.

"*Feather* moss. Did you ever get *that* one? You know, dental floss, feather head, Izzie . . . ?"

"Oh. No. I can't recall feather moss."

"Lucky you."

The violinist sat down on the loveseat, leaving Violet alone on the couch. I didn't want to squeeze next to my namesake, so I sat by the

144

soon-to-be-famous pianist. There was a faint but memorable aroma of nights in the gardens of Spain.

"You mentioned your father's death," I said, crossing my legs.

"Yes?"

"My condolences."

He nodded.

"What about your mother?"

"Died when I was just a little nipper of two."

"Did your father remarry?"

"No, though I rather wish he had."

"Neither did mine. So we were both raised by our fathers."

"Curiouser and curiouser," said Janine whirling in from the kitchen.

"It certainly is," Violet agreed.

Janine sat down beside the violinist and picked up her own drink. "Well, they don't *look* like each other, do they, Violet?"

"I think they're *both* handsome hunks," Violet replied and turned toward me and pulled a Mona Lisa. For a moment, it was Violet who resembled the fiddler.

"Isaac was telling me that they'll be recording this week—you know, before the recitals. He's invited me to come to a session."

"Nice, if you can get away. Sounds interesting," I added without sincerity.

"Oh it *is*, Isaac," said Isaac in his best baritone. "The equipment's fantastic. Besides, you get to hear all the flubs. Right, Vi?"

"We flub a good deal," Violet confirmed.

"Well, *I* do," said Isaac. "Pop strings like mad in last movements. It's the thing I'm best known for. Violet drops a note about once a decade, just to prove she's human."

"He's just teasing again," said Violet, touching my arm.

"I hope you all like salmon," said Janine tipsily.

"We're on excellent terms, salmon and I," quipped the fiddler.

Janine laughed. The violinist laughed. Violet confined herself to a grin.

"I'm curious about your age," I said.

"Twenty-eight last November. And yours?"

"Twenty-six."

"Well," said Violet, "*there's* a difference anyway." Then she asked me about my work and what I thought of selling Hawaii to the Japanese to pay off the national debt. "As I recall, they once expressed an interest in the property," she joked. I asked about how long she had studied the piano and where she had met Isaac.

"As long as I can remember and at the Curtis Institute," she replied. "Art's long, life's short," she added and asked if I'd get her another sherry.

Violet and I continued chatting while Isaac and Janine did the same, moving, after a few minutes, into the kitchen so Janine could put the meal together while they chewed the polyunsaturated fat.

"Violet, do you know where Isaac grew up?"

"New York."

"Ah."

"What is it?"

"That's where my father was born."

"What's your father like, Isaac? I *love* fathers."

I told her, at length. I talked about my father until the appetizers were on the table, taking time out only for another vodka and tonic. Violet said how refreshing it was to find a man who revered his father.

3

*a*ll four of us kept drinking right through Janine's triumphant and refreshingly cold cucumber soup, her acclaimed poached salmon, the tasty if somewhat overmoist lemon sponge cake and tart raspberry sorbet. We men, we Isaacs, faced each other across the tablecloth so I was beside Violet and she was opposite Janine, who was thus next to both Isaacs. There were questions I wanted to ask the violinist, lots of questions, but under the pleasant quilt of Violet's conversation, I lost these questions one at a time in the vodka fog. Isaac seemed content to go on talking with Janine. I wasn't sure what they were going on about, whether it was actuary or violinist stuff; I only had the rather sweet impression that we were all hitting it off and having a memorable evening.

The more I talked with Violet the more I wished to tell her. I wondered if Isaac might be annoyed by my attentions to his comely, francotropic accompanist and rather hoped he was. Violet could be quite fascinating, for example when contrasting Wagner to Debussy. Though I couldn't follow a quarter of what she said, she said all of it well. And she laughed at my jokes.

I offered them a ride to their hotel, but Isaac prudently and politely insisted on calling a cab, and we all kissed or hugged and said good night well past one in the morning.

Once they'd gone Janine gave a little "whew" of pleasure and said the dishes would keep until morning. This was pure afterglow, a tide to be taken at the flood. I wanted her and perhaps Janine wanted me too, wanted to touch base so to speak; nevertheless, we were both hard asleep in ten minutes flat.

I'm certain it was a night crammed with extremely rapid eye movements, but in the morning I couldn't recall a single image. Janine was hung over but pulled herself together sufficiently to tell me how wonderful Isaac and Violet were in her opinion and to say what a pity it was they'd be leaving in just a week.

"Are you going to go to that recording session?" I asked.

"You know, I think I *will*."

"Whatever," I mumbled into my black coffee.

I asked Janine what she figured their relationship was. She shrugged and said she thought she'd go back to bed for a little while.

I phoned my father early in the afternoon, as usual. "What're you up to, Dad?"

"Watching the ball game. Dodgers and Phillies. Contemplating my sins and reading *The National Review*. Good article on NATO."

"Sounds taxing."

"Later on Phil La Porte and I are going to a movie. Thought we'd catch the early bird at Roselli's. It'll make a nice evening. So, what's new with you? Any runs on the bank this week? Big-time defaults?"

"No, Dad. We're still holding on by our teeth."

"Good. It's gettting to be a real distinction, solvency."

"I *do* have something kind of special to tell you, though."

His voice tightened up at once. "Good news or bad?"

"Good, Dad, good. I met another Isaac Fehderflos this week. Another Isaac *Herman* Fehderflos."

"What?"

"You heard me. He's a musician, a violinist. He's playing a couple of recitals here this weekend."

"I don't like it, Isaac," he said rather harshly.

"What do you mean?"

"It sounds like a scam, some sort of con game. Somebody else claiming to have your name. Come *on.*"

"What're you talking about, Dad? Janine and I had him and his accompanist to dinner last night. They're *fine* people, really *nice.*"

His voice changed again, turned rather petulant and peevish. It was a tone I remembered well from ten years earlier. "Now you listen to me, Isaac. You listening? I don't want you to have *any*thing to do with these people."

"But, Dad—"

"*Lis*ten to me. *Nothing.* There *aren't* any other Fehderflosses so there's something fishy here. Didn't I always tell you you're the last of our family? Didn't I?"

I took a deep breath and leapt into it. "Seems you weren't *quite* right about that, Dad. I've met him. His name was in the paper. *Our* name, that is. He's going to make a record this week."

"You telling me I'm *wrong?* Well, well. Look, son, I don't care if this person makes *ten* records and *owns* a newspaper. You stay away from him. Understand?"

I was quiet, still a little weak from my insurrection.

"Isaac? You there?" It was the voice with which he used to call up the stairs when I'd shut the door of my room. It was not to be resisted.

"Look, Dad, do you *know* this man?"

His voice now rose to shrillness. "*Know* him? Of course I don' t know him. I only know he's bound to be trouble of some sort. He's an impostor. You stay away from him."

I paused three beats, the three on which I'd normally have said "Sure thing, Dad"—it takes no more to mark a belated adolescent rebellion—and then said, "Look, Dad. I've got to go."

"How's Janine?" he asked, obviously desperate to keep me on the line.

"She's fine too. So long. Okay?"

"Wait." His voice fell to a whisper. "Call me this week, Isaac. You'll do that ?"

"Okay, Dad. Bye."

"Goodbye, son." It sounded, I thought, almost like the hush of defeat. It was way out of proportion to the cause, but I felt a little as if I had made my old man hand over his sword.

"Bye, Dad—"

"Isaac, wait."

"What is it?"

"This man, this other Fehderflos—he doesn't, you know, claim to be a relative, does he?"

"*Could* he be?"

"No, absolutely not. I told you already. Only I want to know if he *claims* to be related to us."

"As a matter of fact he's sure we're *not* related."

My father was silent.

"He grew up in New York. That's really all I know."

"Remember what I said, Isaac. Stay away from him. Okay?"

"Good*bye*, Dad. Have a nice weekend."

"You'll call?"

"I'll call. Oh, and his mother died when he was two."

"Two?"

"Two years old."

"His father?"

"Died too. Recently."

"Umm."

"Bye, Dad. Okay?"

"Okay, okay."

The best likeness I have of my father catches a face etched by melancholy, by a sort of protective anxiety. He's now over fifty-five but was only about forty when the picture was taken. The lines on his face seem to me anticipatory, so to speak, just beginning to form, like the growing peevishness that would deepen them. It is a black and white picture, a little grainy, taken in the spare living room of my childhood, probably by a family friend named George who liked to experiment with photography. In the picture, my father is seated on the couch, head a little down, eyes staring at something inward, one arm raised in the air, as if resting on something out of the frame. The background is nebulous, but I know that the whitish blur is the picture of my dead mother on the mantelpiece. It is a worrier's face, almost the face of a suicide.

What I'm trying to explain is that the phone conversation I've just recorded was not all that exceptional, not quite strange enough for me to question or take seriously. In fact, my thought on hanging up was that it was predictable.

The ensuing work week was ordinary enough, except that I saw even less of Janine than usual. On Monday and Tuesday she was later getting home than ever. She explained that she was trying to work ahead so she could take off Wednesday and go to the recording session. "I'm *really* looking forward to it," she bubbled like a teenager.

Shortly after I arrived home on Wednesday, a day as fuggy as the inside of a Houston policeman's mouth, Janine phoned to say that she was going to grab a quick dinner with Isaac and Violet. They'd been hard at it all day, she said, as if she had performed too, and they were all famished. Hoped I didn't mind. Of course I should go ahead and eat the lamb chops, or whatever. Oh, and the session had been just *fa*bulous, really *fasc*inating.

It was all plausible and, well, whatever, but I couldn't shake the childish feeling of not being picked for the team, not being entrusted even with right field. I'd have liked to go to dinner too. And, in my disappointment, I admitted that I'd have particularly relished seeing Violet again, for I had been thinking more than a little about Violet since Sunday, such a sympathetic woman, with such good legs.

After dinner, in the same mood, I recalled my promise and telephoned my father.

"So, everything all right?" he asked.

"Oh fine, Dad. I'm only calling because I said I would. So, how was the movie?"

"What movie?"

"Nevermind."

"Oh, you mean the one I saw last Saturday with Phil? Not so hot. Too cynical or serious or something. How's Janine?"

"She's fine too," I said resentfully.

"Uh, and you haven't been hanging around with that musician?"

"No." It was no lie so far as I was concerned.

"That's good." I could hear the relief in his voice and the television in the background. He was probably into a movie, either a comedy or the kind he liked best, what he called a costume movie. "So, anything new at work?"

"Oh, same old stuff, Dad. Foreclosing on the widows and orphans."

"It's no joke, Isaac."

My father's politics were not so much conservative as anti-liberal. He used to get quite worked up over the news and make speeches at me. "Sorry, Dad. We're still building the American Dream."

"Um, all right. I'll let you go then. Call me Saturday?"

"Sure."

"No, better make it Sunday. Fred asked me to play a round at his club Saturday. Okay?"

"Sunday it is."

Janine came in at ten-thirty. She apologized but didn't feel like talking. I could see how exhausted she was. "I'm going in early tomorrow," she sighed, told me a little about the recording session—"so many takes!"—reported the name of the restaurant at which they'd eaten their unexpectedly lengthy meal, then hit the shower.

"How was Violet?" I asked casually as, pajamaless, we climbed into bed.

"She asked me a lot of questions, actually," Janine yawned. "All about *you*, too. You devil."

Then she tickled my ribs and turned out the light.

4

t hursday. Fresh images of Violet, like delicate aquarelles, have been installed in the stuffy museum of my mind. The fading music of her remembered voice, also watery and a little frail, not unlike one of her wispy French preludes, weaves through the chattering musak of my workday. If life, I reflect at two o'clock, is like banking, then where are my reserves? Janine comes home late again, hassled but blooming. Without willing it, I compare Janine's thick dark hair to Violet's fine, fair head, my wife's frank smile to Violet's elusive grin, Janine's quick gait to Violet's more stately glide, the clear timbre of Janine's voice to Violet's nuanced and cloudy tones. Suddenly longing to hear Violet play, I ask Janine about the recording session, but learn nothing.

Friday. Janine wakes up with cramps. "The big P," she reports glumly. "I'll go in late." I am sympathetic and bring her tea and toast. The weather has again turned sultry. As soon as I get to the office, sweaty,

I phone home, but Janine has gone. There is a brief rainstorm late in the morning and I wonder how Isaac and Violet are spending the day, waiting for the evening's recital. On an impulse, I telephone their hotel and experience the strangeness of asking for Isaac Fehderflos's room. There is no answer. I find that I am feeling nervous and unsettled, perhaps out of sympathy with my namesake. I recall the two months of clarinet lessons when I was eight and my half-hearted, spectacularly unsuccessful attempts to teach myself guitar during my teens, how I strummed and strummed up in my room and made my fingertips hurt, how the face of the last of the Fehderflosses was broken out. As usual, everyone is longing for the weekend, the only approved topic of conversation save for the tumble in real estate prices. The day ends with electrified air and nervous colleagues, an unfocused but persuasive feeling that things cannot go on this way. "Have a nice weekend, Mr. Fehderflos," says Dahlia and at once I regret my misplaced uniqueness. I am clumsy, unmusical, and graceless, every inch a dismal scientist. Janine is home when I arrive, dinner ready for the oven. She wants to go to a movie. I am prepared to sink into the clotted darkness too. The big P seems to be under control. The movie is a tearjerker. I begin to understand my father's affection for escapism and costumes. I too seek a refuge from my ordinariness. Janine is tearful and exhilarated and goes to bed as soon as we get home from the early show.

SATURDAY MORNING. Janine is dying to read the *Tribune's* review of last night's recital aloud over her blueberry bagel. I can see that she is excited. Actually, we're both excited but, unlike my wife, I am unsure what kind of review would please me most. I am initially inclined to judge the matter egoistically. For example, a rave could cost me even more of my self-esteem, diminish me; I'd be the I.F. who is *not* celebrated. A truly bad review, on the other hand, would shame me, shame me for my name's sake. By dint of a morally uplifting shrug of the shoulders, I achieve a more worthy equilibrium even as Janine is rifling the newspaper to find the article. I now think only good thoughts on behalf of those homeless and charming artistes who I assume are likewise searching through the *Tribune* in their luxurious but merely temporary quarters. At last, with a little whoop, Janine finds the notice. She begins to read it at once.

" 'Last night's audience at Rheinach Hall witnessed an extraordinary recital by Isaac Fehderflos (violin) and Violet Halverson (piano), two musicians on the rise who have paid their dues and will soon be releasing recordings on the Cecilia label.

" 'Mr. Fehderflos, whose playing was unfortunately marred by four excruciating errors, was even more a thing to behold than to hear. Imagine, if you will, a musician who is also a champion gymnast with the looks of a matinee idol. Imagine further that, in full pathos of the Brahms Third Sonata, he determines to execute a double back flip and a couple of Arabians while simultaneously carrying out a sort of universal seduction. This will give you some notion of Mr. Fehderflos's athletic and insinuating approach to performing on his instrument. He quite bewitched the audience in various selections. In the Prokofiev sonata, for example, he impersonated a piston at the start and wound up as something very like a corkscrew by the finale. Mr. Fehderflos's facial expressions are no less worthy of comment than his prodigious physical contortions. He is able to project everything from dignified piety (Bach), to sublimated fury (Beethoven), to central European anguish (Bartók) with his mobile countenance as well as with his torso, or even his much-abused violin. This reviewer must confess, though, to feeling a certain ambivalence toward this wholistic mode of performance wherein the entire being of the player is implicated, as tense as a gut string and, one supposes, as liable to snap. (A string did in fact break in the final movement of the Brahms.) Highly-strung indeed is Mr. Fehderflos. One is compelled either to admire the integrity of this artist who makes love to his music and his audience or to reprehend his counterfeiting of total musical submersion, whichever the case may be.' "

All this Janine does not read without pausing to comment; she comments after each sentence, as a matter of fact. I understand that she is responding on Isaac's behalf. We are both taking in the review with his eyes, so to speak.

"What the hell does *that* mean?" Janine cries after reading the reviewer's ambivalent confession of ambivalence. She is outraged by the implication that Isaac may be less than genuine in anything he does.

"Whichever the case may *be?*" she mockingly reiterates.

"Is there anything about Violet?" I ask, as if with reluctance.

Janine, anything but mollified, resumes her reading.

" 'The playing of Ms. Halverson was not only intelligent throughout but displayed a delicacy and lucidity of phrasing that compares with that of the greatest living interpreters of the modern French repertoire, which is, in fact, this performer's specialty. Particularly worthy of praise to this reviewer was how well Ms. Halverson managed her demanding task of accompanist; for in these affairs the piano is held to be the vase while the violin is the rose. No matter how gymnastic, pyrotechnic, or passionate her partner became, Ms. Halverson was able to support him with a tact so refined and a virtuosity so humble that I feel sure few in the distracted audience took proper note of her really admirable talent.' "

I am not at all displeased by the reviewer's treatment of Violet, not even by the perhaps too-clear preference. Boil it all down and it sounded a bit like Violet 7, Isaac 2. Judging by her startling remark after reading the above, however, Janine feels differently.

"What did she *do,* give him a blow job or what?"

An hour later, in her red sundress, my wife announced she was meeting her friend Doris at one of the more bombastic suburban shopping malls and was gone. I spent the afternoon riding my bike around the local reservoir and cooking spaghetti sauce, a Fehderflos specialty.

It was my mother's recipe, a magic formula. Thanksgiving of my freshman year I came home from college and of course Father and I got into a fight in about thirty seconds. I was now a guest and he wouldn't treat me as one; the argument must have had some such subtext. Instead of clomping off to my old room, which is what I'd have done only a few months before, I went to the kitchen and, for some reason, starting taking stuff down from the cabinets and cleaning the checked vinyl shelf paper. I found the thin bundle of 3 x 5 cards behind the cornstarch and an unopened bag of lentils. The rubberband had broken; it must have made a little unheard sound. I was enthralled by my discovery. This was not like seeing the little bit of jewelry or the curling old photographs. Here was a voice (the handwriting suggested a voice that was measured and calm) telling me how to nourish myself and others, patiently instructing me what to do with olive oil, ground meat, onions, garlic, tomato paste, with parsley, oregano, and sweet basil. And I could reproduce all this; I could do her work. I was reminded of the best scene in *Son of Frankenstein,* the one where the sane young doctor comes across his father's notes in the ruined castle and instantly forgets his hand-wringing fiancée. But these notes were healthy and maternal. This was a sauce she'd have made for me. I took myself into my father's study and apologized. I think we may have hugged, then I told him I wanted spaghetti for Thanksgiving dinner. He looked at me with big eyes. I showed him the card on which the thin blue lines had all but faded away.

"There's no family coming," he said despondently, "no Norman Rockwell. So, okay. You want spaghetti, we'll have spaghetti."

That Saturday I wanted spaghetti.

AFTER THE PASTA AND SALADS Janine and I dressed. I hadn't exactly gone to many recitals, though my father had dragged me to hear the symphony a couple of times. Should I put on a dark suit because I was in for high culture or a light one because it was June and warm, or maybe a sport jacket and slacks because, after all, it wasn't the symphony or the opera? I chose the middle road, selecting my tan suit and a striped tie, which Janine said made me look as cute and preppy as a new diplomat posted to some consulate in the torrid zone. As for Janine, she was splendidly decked out in a dress I couldn't remember seeing before and certainly would have if I had.

"That a new dress?" I asked foolishly.

"Picked it up today. You like?" And she spun around making a liquid sound one associates with senior proms.

"It's beautiful," I said. And it was.

SINCE I KNOW NOTHING ABOUT MUSIC I won't describe the recital except to say that the morning's review may have prejudiced me because I kept thinking now he's going to do a back flip and trying to make up my mind if what I was watching was a man moved to frenzy by what he was playing or just some highbrow con. Throughout the Brahms piece

I waited for a string to break, though none did. Hard as it was to take my eyes off my namesake, I observed Violet closely too. Actually, they made a perfect contrast as well as a perfect couple, like a salt and pepper shaker: over against his gyrations, her long straight back; beside his tortured face, her serene profile; next to his tight black tuxedo, the bottle green of her shoulderless gown. But I noticed with surprise that their hair was exactly the same color, albeit his flopped around while hers remained tidily coiffed. I hadn't remembered that.

Janine was obviously thrilled, entirely rapt. During the intermission she kept repeating "God, he's wonderful, really *won*derful" until I felt like saying, "Whatever."

As we settled in for the second half, Janine put her hand on my arm. "Now, Isaac, I hope you won't mind—"

"Mind what ?"

"Well, Violet invited me to come back to her dressing room after— you know, just for a look."

"And *I* can't come?" I said with a reflexive pout.

"Don't be *silly*. And look, we're going to go out for a drink after, just us girls, you know."

"A drink? You mean you're not coming home with me?"

"No. It's just girls. I just said."

"Why didn't you tell me?"

"I *am*."

"You know what I mean. Before."

"I didn't want you to make a fuss. You *know* you'd have made a fuss."

It was true; I would have. In fact, I was making one now. "Well, why shouldn't the two Isaacs join you?" I fussed.

"Well, I *asked*, of course, but Isaac's going out with some of the record company people. Business, I guess. You don't *really* mind, do you? I mean, I'll take a cab."

I minded quite a bit but I knew my lines and so I said I didn't.

WHEN THE THING WAS OVER the audience clapped thunderously. The same fellow I remember yelling "Bravo!" from the back of the Academy of Music when I was a kid must have had a ticket because there he was, ecstatically doing it again. The applause kept up until Violet and Isaac returned, suddenly informal, like actors bowing after a tragedy. The crowd cheered then hushed as the two of them took their places for an encore. They played "If I Fell" and then "Blackbird," two old Beatles tunes cleverly arranged as crowd-pleasers. The audience gasped audibly with delight, as if they had been holding their breath through each number.

Then, to yet more tumultuous raving, it was over.

"Goodbye," said Janine in the lobby. She pointed to a corridor. "I think that's where I'm supposed to go." She gave me a peck on the cheek.

I WOULD HAVE LIKED TO TALK with my father; but even as a younger man he'd go pale and grab at his heart if the phone rang after ten o'clock, and it was well past eleven when I got home. I wanted to hear his voice, take in its good architectural qualities, its solid foundation and careful brickwork. I felt troubled, maybe a little worse than troubled. I sat in the living room and by the light of one lamp dissected this feeling. What I found inside was not only resentment and envy because I'd been left out, which is what I'd felt on Wednesday. I discovered also some spiritual vertigo. Things seemed to be spinning out of control—Janine's hours, my emotions, the basis of my not-very-well-examined life. It was as if the appearance of this handsome, blond, nomadic, frenzied Isaac had called into question the other Isaac—that is, me—to whom I could attach only the dullest and most generic adjectives.

And now Janine was off having a drink with Violet, Violet with whom I had been flirting in my mind for a week. In what sense were Janine and I married, I asked myself. Up till then I had thought of marriage as a noun or at most a past participle, something you got or had, never as an active verb with one indirect object. But being married isn't like being grown-up or brown-eyed. You get married *to* somebody. Am I married to Janine, I wondered. I *want* to be, but *am* I?

I put on an old Billy Joel tape, which made me feel more at home after all the unfamiliar stuff I had heard in Rheinach Hall. I relaxed and began to think about things more randomly, the way you do when you're driving long distance: the thoughts have their own motor and you just direct them, the same way you point your car. I mused not only on Janine and marriage and odd coincidences but on uniqueness. I thought of it as a rather expensive privilege and wondered where its supply and demand curves might meet. My stomach was thinking simultaneously of a snack; it rumbled once and then the doorbell rang. Ours had a sort of final trump sound to it and I clutched my heart, just as my father would have done. It froze, then started to race. Ah, so *that's* why, I thought, calming down. I got up and flipped off the tape, thinking no doubt Janine forgot to put her keys in that tiny evening bag.

"Coming, sweetheart," I called reassuringly.

I opened the door and there stood Violet. She had changed into blue jeans and wore a loose blouse under a black tailored jacket. She looked like an undergraduate. She was alone. I checked.

"Where's Janine?" I asked, my mind now racing right alongside my semi-prophetic heart.

"May I come in?" she asked in a grave and measured tone, as though this were a condolence call.

"I'm sorry. Please, come on in." My own voice was a little too loud, fast, and high. I was scared but hadn't entirely forgotten my mental flirting. It would be fair to say I was confused.

Violet walked straight into the living room. I could see she was wearing cowboy boots. She looked around once, dropped her big leather bag on the floor and sat down on the couch.

"Can I get—" I began.

"No. Nothing, thanks."

She leaned down and took something out of the bag. It was a blue envelope. She placed it in her lap.

"Come, sit down, Isaac," she said strangely. Everything was happening very slowly; she spoke slowly. "Sit there, on the love seat," she said. "I have to talk to you." There was a peculiar sympathy, an intimacy about the way she was speaking to me.

"Something's happened to Janine," I said. This was not so much a question as a dead certainty.

"Janine's all right," said Violet sepulchrally.

I sat dutifully down on the love seat. "Janine's all right, *but*...?"

"Here. Read this first." She handed me what was in her lap.

The envelope had "Isaac" neatly printed in block letters, well centered—the fearsome finickiness of the math major, the actuary.

I only read about half of it, even though the letter couldn't be called long. In fact, it was more like a memo than a letter.

Dear Isaac,
There really isn't any way to say this gently. It's actually kind of funny, leaving one Isaac Fehderflos for another. But I expect you've noticed that of late things between us...

And so forth.

I was quiet for a while, just staring at Janine's signature. Then I looked up at Violet, who was looking at the wall.

"You here for her things?"

Violet turned her eyes on me, smiled faintly. "How about a drink?" she suggested.

"Okay. You want anything in particular?"

"Vodka, if you've got it. Neat."

I poured myself a scotch at least as long as Janine's letter.

"Isaac," she began after a long sip, "there's something else I want to tell you. It's a big something else."

It crossed my somewhat fuddled mind that Violet might be about to make a pass at me, that this was some sort of complex, kinky switcheroo. Do such things really happen to actuaries and economists who meet at college parties, I wondered.

"I'm all ears," I said feeling both queasy and numb.

"Isaac's my brother."

"Your brother?" Of *course*, I thought. That blond hair. "But your name?"

"Halverson was my ex's name. A Swedish cellist. I married him when I was all of eighteen. A stupid move, but I kept the name when we divorced a couple years later. I liked it better than—"

"So *you're* a Fehderflos too, then."

"Violet Dental Floss," she chuckled. "Isaac and I are fraternal twins. Two birds with one stone, so to speak, two eggs at once. It's about those eggs I want to tell you. I want you to know *whose* eggs they were and why all this happening. Isaac doesn't know I'm here. He didn't want you to know."

"Okay, so whose eggs were you?"

"Your *mother's*, Isaac."

"What! My *mother's*? You're saying—what? I mean, how can we all be Fehderflosses if my mother—I don't get it."

Violet polished off her vodka and asked for another. I think she just wanted not to tell me to my face because as soon as I got up she blurted it all out.

"Our fathers were brothers, Isaac. They never got along—different politics, different values, different everything. In fact they hated each other. But they loved the same woman. Our father—Isaac's and mine—met her at some socialist meeting in New York. Free love, the means of production, world revolution, strikes, oppression of the masses, the Rosenbergs and civil rights. Anyway, she got pregnant—with us. Father was glad to live with her, to support the family, everything. He loved her. Only, you see, he didn't believe in marriage. A worn-out bourgeois form, a legal slavery. It was a matter of principle for him. My own marriage was probably a form of rebellion against him, but I guess Father was *her* Swedish cellist. Anyway, on this point her views weren't at all the same as his. I'm piecing this together, Isaac, you understand? I'm guessing at what must have happened. Not at the *facts*; I know *them*, but at *motives*. I don't really know for sure."

I handed her the glass of vodka. "Go on," I said.

"All right. *Your* father—and he's the only one who can really explain anything now—your father, our uncle, was *there* all along, if you follow me. There and jealous as hell, I imagine. Anyway, he watched the relationship go sour, and it must have happened pretty fast. *He* was prepared to marry her. Only, you see, he didn't want *us*. Not that Father would've let him have us anyway."

"No, she'd *never* have left you," I objected, defending a woman I never knew.

"But she did, didn't she? When we were only two. I like to think she was desperate. Or maybe we were just too much for her. Apparently her health was never good, right? Look, I don't know. But she left us. She left our father and she married yours and she had you."

Violet was now looking me in the eye, looking at me like a cousin, a sister, holding nothing back, all mystery gone.

"So they just took off, your father, our mother." She paused, took a hit of vodka. "Who named you?" she asked suddenly.

"Who *named* me?"

"Who chose the name Isaac for you?"

"Wait," I said, suddenly furious with everybody. I went to the phone and dialed my father's number. It was past midnight. The phone rang three long times.

"Who is it?" came his terrified voice.

"Isaac."

"Isaac! What's the matter? You scared the hell out of me—"

"I want to know who named me."

"What?"

"I need to know who *named* me, Dad. You or mother."

"Isaac—" he pleaded.

"Just tell me, all right?" My voice was implacable.

"Isaac, I'm frightened," he whined.

"*Who!*"

"I did. It was—"

I hung up then disconnected the telephone.

"My father named me," I said to Violet.

"God," she sighed, falling back against the couch. "I *knew* it. How they must have *hated* each other!"

"He wanted to—?"

"To cancel us out of her life. Isaac anyway." Violet's eyes were watery now. "If you'd been a girl, he'd have called you Violet," she said, then gave up and started to weep.

I went to the couch and sat down beside her. I put my arm around her shoulders.

"It was his dying wish," she sobbed.

"Your father's?"

"He was dying in the hospital and whenever we went to see him he'd say it, over and over. Isaac and I argued about it."

"Revenge? He wanted revenge? Is that it?"

She nodded.

We both fell silent, but I went on holding Violet, telling myself, this is my sister and she doesn't hate me and I don't hate her. I have a sister.

Suddenly she laughed a little, put her hand up to her eyes. "I'm sorry," she said, clearing away the tears. Sorry for crying, sorry for me. Sorry.

I had an idea. "Are you hungry?" I asked.

She sniffed. "A little bit."

"Come into the kitchen with me."

We went into the kitchen. The light was bright. While I told Violet about the recipe, I boiled some spaghetti and warmed up what was left of our mother's thick red sauce.

Serenades
of Phantoms

*t*he police chief's arms flapped like the wings of a gull trying to lift too heavy a fish. His ankle was bad and he staggered melodramatically against the green wing chair by the side of the mayor's desk.

"Well I'll be damned," he said. "You're serious."

"Chief, I was thirty-six when I chased Big Jim Early out of this office. Early was fifty-five at the time and I was sure he'd been squatting here just about forever."

The chief was a man of quick perception. "And now *you're* fifty-five," he said, wincing because of his ankle and lowering himself into the wingchair.

"I've had five terms. Early only had *three.* Kids in their twenties think of me the way they do of traffic jams and business cycles. Inevitable but hardly indispensable."

The police chief chose not to say that, like everyone else, he too regarded the mayor as a fixture, a pillar every bit as solid as those holding up the portico down below. In the last two elections there hadn't even been an opponent. He was the fixed foot of the city's compass.

The mayor opened the box on his desk and took out one of his famous panatellas. He never chewed his cigars, never spoke with one vibrating in his mouth like a diving board. His panatellas were not props. He smoked them respectfully, taking the cigar out of his mouth after each puff and considering its length with a sort of religious gratitude reminiscent of the early history of the weed. People liked that the mayor respected his only known vice. Smoking humanized the ascetic workaholic, the practical puritan; his cigars offered reassurance to his constituents. It was generally known that the mayor permitted himself a cigar only when alone or in the company of his intimates. There were scores of big shots who yearned to be smoked at by him.

The mayor stroked the surface of his desk as he puffed away. The chief sat quietly, resting his ankle and recollecting images, as if he were at a memorial service. "Remember when you hired me?" he asked.

"Of course I do. You always remember the smart things you do."

The chief couldn't help smiling. "The interview was a little unusual."

The mayor chuckled amiably and examined his cigar. "Well, it told me what I needed to find out."

"What would you have done if I'd gone along?"

"Oh, had you arrested maybe, or just told you politely to catch a plane back to Cleveland."

"Barnes and I still laugh about it."

"An incalculable loss to the stage, Joe Barnes. When I asked him to pretend to slip me that payoff I thought he'd keel over. He loved every minute of it." The mayor fell silent and shook his head. "Oh, so many compromises, Chief. I'm pretty sick of it."

"With respect, Your Honor, I was under the impression you adored your job. I mean I always thought that was one of the reasons people voted for you—that you just loved it so much."

"A man happy in his work?"

"Something like that, I guess. Like the time you sank those foul shots on TV or when you filled sandbags during the flood. And how about when you took over that elementary school for a month?"

"I had my fun. And you're right, of course. The voters do like seeing that sort of thing." The mayor spoke wearily, which made him sound uncharacteristically cynical, even to himself.

"Then it was calculation?"

"That would be a one-quarter truth, Chief. In politics you should only tell *three*-quarter truths."

The police chief crossed his leg and rubbed his ankle. "You still play?"

"Basketball?"

"No, the flute."

"Oh, hardly at all. Kind of miss it, though."

"So. . . what'll you do? Take it up again? Go fishing? Play golf?"

"I haven't really thought," the mayor admitted. "In fact, I only just decided to quit. I mean here and now, while I've been talking to you."

"Is that a three-quarter or a one-quarter truth? Anyway, maybe you're just tired out?"

THE MAYOR TOOK his usual bus home. Half the passengers nodded or waved, some were self-consciously indifferent, a few went rigid.

"Hi there, Your Honor," said the driver, who relished the heraldic irony of the title. It was a sultry evening and the bus stank. "Air conditioning's on the fritz again."

The mayor shrugged as he dropped his token. "Budget's pretty tight, Roy," he said.

"It's not the budget," complained Mr. Fillmore. "It's the kids. Isn't it, Roy? I mean it was those little fuckers broke it, wasn't it?"

"YOU LIVE LIKE A MONK!" his mother had exclaimed the first time she saw his apartment. "A twin bed? Why not a king? You're the mayor, aren't you?" She died a few years later in Florida, still praying he'd marry or, at least, move to a two-bedroom with a dishwasher. Once he almost married and twice he nearly moved.

The mayor shuffled through his mail. Junk, a bill, invitations, half a dozen pleas and sups. Lately, the pleas and supplications had begun to rub him the wrong way. "Who am I?" he whined aloud. "Fucking Haroun al-Rashid?"

There was a letter from Wyoming. It had to be from Willy, his freshman roommate, trout fisherman and attorney-at-law. It had been a couple years since they had been in touch. Fifteen years earlier the mayor had visited Willy and Sarah for two weeks, just enough time for their daughter Lily (everyone called her Boxer) to contract a crush on him. Boxer and the mayor had corresponded faithfully for nearly a decade and then she had gone off to college and became definitively Lily.

Even before he opened Willy's letter the mayor resolved to visit Wyoming again. He grasped an image, half memory and half anticipation, of Willy showing him how to cast dry flies in a fast running brook the temperature of a vodka and tonic at an Ashburne House reception. The sky was a vast, smogless, unurban blue; the Grand Tetons swelled up like a Schumann finale in the distance. Wyoming! The name suddenly struck the mayor like a refreshing wave; it was a wild, flying, careening, bronco-busting participle. If a man were up to it, he could go wyoming.

Almost against his will the mayor put Willy's letter aside in favor of the sups and pleas. He chose first a cheap and crudely hand-printed envelope without a return address. Could be some crank or even a death threat.

> Dear Mr Mayer,
>
> I no your a good man. My mother always said you was. She's passed on now but was a good judge of charectar. So I am writting you about the electric. I am 3 munths behind because I got layed off from my job due to this coff which has gotten wicked bad lately, I got some medicine at the clinik and expect to be OK soon. But I need the electric for my baby. Please can you help me?

The mayor sank into his overstuffed easy chair and began to imagine his city. He pictured to himself the vast networks of power and sub-jugation, the fantastically reticulated systems for moving electricity, paper, voices, the infinitely complicated relationships between families, generations, coworkers, neighbors and enemies, the ways the past both undergirded and undermined the present, how the future nibbled at its edges. The city was a novel that not only refused to end but kept ramifying, redoubling, divagating, complicating.

Once the mayor had visited the University where some microbiologist placed him in front of a microscope and showed him yeast reproducing or crystals forming or some such sudden multiplication of forms and existence that seemed to him the emblem of his city's history. But the truth was that the city had ceased to burgeon, to cluster grapelike with accumulated civic sweetness and capital reserves. For years the mayor, like an inverted Sisyphus, had spent himself preventing it from rolling down a cliff. He pushed against its decaying school system, its potholed streets and littered parks, the leaky pipes, sordid public transport, evaporating tax base—the materialization of despair. "Par for the course" or "So what else is new?" his colleagues would reassure each other at their annual mayor's conventions. "So tell me something I don't already know."

He hated his city because he hated his job and he hated his job because it kept him in a state of perpetual anxiety, because the job had devoured his life which was because he loved his city and so loved his job. For such a knot there could be only one dénouement, a blow of the sword.

Willy's letter was importunate and beleaguered. In three months Lily was getting married. Could he see his way clear to coming? A formal invitation would follow, of course. It had been far too long since they'd seen each other. Age erodes the ephemeral and reveals the durable. Sarah sent her love. It would mean a lot to all of them. At the bottom Sarah had written "Please come!"

Dusk had fallen. The mayor sat in the semi-darkness and looked out the window at the city that was never really his, a jumble encrusted with the spores of two million human lives, also the lives of cats, dogs, rats, raccoons, skunks, possums, and roaches. The suburbs curled around it like soft violet snakes. The rising moon was the color of a rusty girder.

The mayor went to his bedroom closet, took out the oblong leather carrying case, unzipped it, removed the hard inner case, opened that as well and uncovered the three pieces of his flute. They glinted against the black velvet like silver trout in a deep shaded pool.

WYOMING LAY BELOW like a symphony. The mayor bit into another peppermint. The small plane was noisy and smelled of plastic and spilt beer. The Bighorn range billowed under the wing like a preposterous diapason.

"It's not quite a real place, you know," piped the leathery old woman across the aisle from him. Her high, vaguely British voice pierced right through the thrum of the engines. She leaned a little toward the mayor.

"Empty as a condor's nest. *Spiritually,* if you know what I mean."

"No, I'm afraid I don't."

The woman shot out a reptilian hand. "Harper," she squeaked in so clipped an accent that it sounded like a single syllable—harp with a little breathy tail. "And you're no Westerner, are you."

"Pleased to meet you," said the mayor with his easy politician's smile. "No. Not a Westerner. Pure city slicker."

"I knew it. Well, that's what the West's full of now—reformed slickers. Just look down there. Beautiful emptiness. None of those gridirons you see over Nebraska and Iowa. Gorgeous vacancy. Now that's just an invitation, isn't it? Myths, fables, tall tales. The place soaks them up the way an arroyo drinks rainwater. When you get into the low hills, the land's haunted, like all deserts and moors. Something that happened last week's the same as something a century old or something that never happened at all. Shootouts, rustling, massacres, lynchings, murders, stampedes, visions. History and news and fiction mean nothing down there because they're all just the same."

"You're from Wyoming?" asked the mayor, nonplussed by this speech.

"Born in Kenya. Only been in Wyoming the last fifty-two years. You like westerns?"

"You mean movies?"

"Movies, books."

"I watched them all the time when I was a kid."

"Well, that's something in your favor. The idyls of the West, scenarios of paradox and contradiction."

"I don't follow you," the mayor shouted across the aisle.

With some difficulty the old woman creaked a little closer and, seeing her effort, the mayor tried to meet her halfway. But for the engine noise, she might have whispered into his left ear.

"All the stories are paradoxes and every one of the heroes is contradictory. It's obvious. Only think of those movies from your childhood. The forces of civilization and culture—of Iowa and Philadelphia—they start out weak, while the wildness of the West shoots up their two-bit outpost of progress. Life's centered on the saloon, not the opera house or the church or the drygoods store. The lawless men triumph, even as they destroy each other, equalized by their revolvers. I admit their lawlessness is boyish, infantile, but I say it with respect."

"With respect? And the contradictory heroes?"

"The so-called hero, the one with the white hat and the fancy horse and the dessicated sidekick—he contradicts himself because he gets to be a hero only by wiping out what made him heroic in the first place. In the end he's merely a tool for the schoolmarms and store clerks. What do they always say? He brought us law and order, Lord be praised. But that law rules him out, doesn't it? And so when his work is done he looks around. He's flummoxed, so he runs for it. Rides further and further west, longing in his inarticulate way for that infantile freedom

168

he himself has just destroyed and which he will, it's understood, go on destroying until there isn't any West left at all."

The mayor rubbed his chin. "So in your view the *real* heroes would be the outlaws?"

The old woman beamed at him, her face shattering like safety glass. "Certainly the outlaws! All true Westerns, properly understood, are tragedies. They're growing-up stories and the happier their endings, the more tragic they are. In Fort Henderson today you can find six churches, two cineplexes, a K-Mart and a community college. Phew!"

"Civilization is fate," the mayor said with the sort of smile that accompanies dismissive clichés.

Harper sniffed loudly and settled back into her seat like a minister who has finished the sermon and is taking no backtalk.

An odd old lady with even odder ideas, said the mayor to himself, and wondered if the new Wild West were not really to be found in certain neighborhoods of cities like his. Nature red in tooth and claw where life is nasty, brutish, and, God knows, short. Boys with guns.

Later, when they had landed and he was helping Harper to her feet, she leaned close once again. Her breath was sweet. "Wyoming's not yet just another goddamn national park," she confided with a twinkle in her lizardy eye. The reassurance sounded almost like a threat.

LILY WAS WAITING for him at the tiny airport. The mayor had some difficulty recognizing her, though he would have been able to pick out little Boxer in a football crowd. Fortunately, she marched right up to him and gave him a hug.

He did not want to say anything foolish or banal, such as that she had certainly turned into a beautiful young woman or how much taller she was at twenty-four than she had been at eleven. But, as it was an occasion allowing only for triteness, he was left with nothing to say. As mayor, hackneyed phrases had bubbled out of his mouth like seafoam, but now he longed for something else. To be precise, what he longed for was a cigar. And so he simply smiled and let Lily prattle. Not to speak at all was a luxury of joblessness. He could afford to act strong and silent.

"Dad's still at work and Mom's got some meeting. I've been here a whole week just sitting on my can waiting to be thrown into the volcano, so I came for you. Actually, I was dying to come. I mean by myself. We'll have some time to talk. I'm *so* glad you came!"

"Oh, come here, Boxer," he said and gave her another hug. "Into the volcano?"

Lily laughed and submitted willingly to be hugged again. He could feel her bride's breasts and blushed. He would certainly not venture a cigar yet.

It was a long drive from Fort Henderson to Windy River. The mayor had abbreviated the distance in his memory, as if it were just a quick jaunt. He enjoyed the scenery: the round bales of hay like huge colons punctuating the rangeland, titanic boulders suggesting fabulous ambushes. He found himself regressing in this dreamlike landscape to the ground of many childish games of horses, guns, dust, sage, and cattle when he had played at what that philosophical harpy called contradictory heroism.

He could see that Lily was starved for intimacy, her college friends not yet gathered, her fiancé far away with his family in Buffalo. She had probably not been home for so many consecutive days in years, so they were both guests in Wyoming. Lily implied as much.

"I didn't want the wedding here, you know. I didn't want to hurt Mom and Dad, but I really didn't want it here."

"Why's that? Not ashamed, I hope."

"Ashamed? Of Windy River? Of *them*?"

"Coming from a small town maybe. People sometimes feel that they'll be measured by the size of their origins."

Boxer laughed wickedly at his pompousness. "It's men who are obsessed with size, in my experience."

The mayor was taken aback, so completely had Boxer become Lily.

"You don't understand," she was saying. "Just look out there."

Everybody was telling him to look. Fort Henderson's churches and K-Mart were already under the horizon.

"You think this is a place for getting married?"

"Why not? People get married everywhere."

"Mom and Dad did it back east. You were there. Best man, right?"

"Best man."

"Anyway, to me this place is *un*settling, and marriage ought to be a settling down. Wyoming's too open. In fact, I'll tell you a story about it."

The mayor figured he could take a chance. "Mind if I smoke while you tell it?"

"Smoke away, Your Honor, but open your window."

"Just as soon as I get it lit, Boxer. Go on."

"Okay. I was seven or eight when I went on my first overnight. I talked Mom and Dad into letting me go with Cal and Nan Ripley and their folks. A real outdoor family the Ripleys. We left at daybreak on a Saturday in June. It was just after school ended. The world was so endless it almost scared me. Going cross country on horseback isn't a lot like tooling up the road in a Buick. Know how in the city, wherever you go, even up a skyscraper, the scale of things stays pretty much the same? I mean you can get lost in a crowd, but you're never really *nothing* because everything around you's made by people and you're a person too, you know what I mean? It's not like that out there.

"Anyway, we were heading for Boon Lake which is up a way in the hills. We followed the river at first. Mr. Ripley had been a rodeo cowboy; he was a handy, wiry sort of man. About two hours into the ride he and Mrs. Ripley like, you know, they started in on each other. Oh, it was just a little sniping at first, but you could tell it was serious and that it wasn't unusual. I was too young to really pick up on what they were saying, but I understood the tone all right. It was nasty. Well, soon as they began, Cal and Nan totally stopped talking; they just froze up. The conversation got a little worse every mile and then a whole lot worse once we left the river and started climbing up into the hills. Finally Mrs. Ripley just gave this little yelp. I mean it was little but it was big at the same time. She spurred hard and started galloping on ahead. Cal wanted to go after her. He tried to get his horse to run but his father grabbed the bridle. He didn't say anything, just stopped the horse and looked at Cal. I was on the other side and I could see the way his father was looking at Cal. It was like a punch. Then Nan, who was a couple years older than Cal and me, rode over and whispered to me that it was all right, that their mother was just going on ahead to pick out our campsite up at the lake. I could tell Nan didn't really expect me to believe her, that she was just trying to be nice and calm me down. And sure enough, Mrs. Ripley wasn't at the lake when we got there. Mr. Ripley mumbled something about how she must've doubled back or something and we weren't allowed to say anything else about it. I felt scared. Cal was furious and soon as our tent was up Nan went in and buried her head in her arms so her father couldn't hear her." Lily stopped.

"So what happened to Mrs. Ripley?"

"Lots of people out here run off like Mrs. Ripley. I mean, she never came back at all. I'd feel better if the wedding were in the Bronx."

"Where do these people go?"

"To the outlaws," said Lily simply.

The mayor laughed. "Another man maybe—but *outlaws?*"

"The outlaws," Lily insisted. "The outlaws are all the people who run off. In the city people run away from each other too, but they don't become outlaws. They go to other people or other cities. Out here they just go."

"Are you teasing me, Boxer?"

"Did I ever tease you in my letters?"

"No. That was my job."

Lily looked over at the mayor and smiled. "When I was little I wanted to marry *you!* Anyway, Nan got married here and I don't think *that* worked out so well."

The rest of the way Lily filled him in, spoke gaily about her college life, her job with a computer company back east, and enumerated the manifold virtues of her fiancé.

As they drove into town the mayor found that he remembered almost everything he saw at exactly the instant he saw it, all the shops, the bank, the courthouse. He felt it was the same town and the same river, that nothing had changed in fifteen years.

Lily swung the car into a Mobil station. Two young men in jeans and a middle-aged one in overalls lounged in front of the garage. A Jeep was up on the lift, its underbelly exposed, the last of its oil dripping like life's blood into a rusty drum. The man in overalls pulled himself out of his beach chair and came over.

"Howdy there, Boxer," he said. "Filler up?"

"All the way, Mr. Sewall."

Lily introduced the mayor. Sewall rubbed his right hand on his overalls before thrusting it through the window and saying, "Mighty pleased." If they had met when he was last in Wyoming neither of them could recall it.

But the mayor was not thinking about Sewall; he was more intrigued by what he was able to catch of the conversation of the two young men by the garage. He could sense that it was about something serious, about death.

". . . Yeah, through the head . . . think. Didn't actually . . . myself."

"Old?"

"Fifty or . . . Bald, Johnny said . . . quite a fight . . . old guy like that."

"Shit, and . . . I guess?"

"Same as usual."

"Phil? We could . . ."

"Nah."

Lily started talking to Mr. Sewall, who was giving her change. "I suppose you heard they shot one of them yesterday?" he was saying.

"Yes," said Lily, not approving, not disapproving.

"Well, that sort of news gets around fast." Sewall himself didn't seem elated about what had happened. His voice was still as if he were describing a regrettable necessity, like putting down a lame horse.

"What was that all about?" the mayor asked as they pulled away from the station.

"Bunch of deputies tracked down some outlaws. There was a fight and they shot one. They got back yesterday."

The mayor, in whose city lethal shootings averaged roughly three score a year, was shocked.

"Outlaws *again*?"

"I *told* you. The people who run off." Boxer sounded impatient.

"Oh yes," mocked the mayor, "like that Mrs. Ripley."

"Look, you can ask Dad about it. Apparently things've gotten pretty bad the last few years. Gosh. I mean if they're sending out posses."

When they pulled onto the crushed rock of the driveway Sarah dashed from the back door of the big frame house to greet them.

"Welcome to Windy City!" she fairly whooped. "Come on and let me get a good look at you. "

The mayor got out of the car feeling boyish. Since his mother died nobody had asked to get a good look at him. He and Sarah considered one another. She had not only aged the full fifteen years but had put on at least a pound for each one of them. In Sarah's full face he could see how he too had altered. If she looked like a fertility goddess then he must resemble a weary ward heeler, a balding old pol redolent of cigar. Sarah embraced him anyway.

As soon as they were in the vestibule Sarah began apologizing. The mayor knew the drill. "The place is a mess," she said. "Meeting just broke up and I didn't have a minute to clear up."

"Looks fine to me, Sarah."

"Just what a house guest is expected to say. Everything gets so darned dusty in the summer. Lily, take those cups." Sarah fell lovingly upon her living room. "Willy called and said he'd be home in an hour or so."

"My old room?" asked the mayor, indicating his two bags.

"All ready for you," said Sarah, smoothing the cushions on the couch, fluffing the toss pillows. The mayor could tell that something was bothering her. It was as though she were hiding behind the house, behind plates and dust and cushions.

"I'll just take my stuff down then."

While the women fixed things to their satisfaction upstairs, the mayor lugged his bags down the short stairway into the guest room— a full apartment really, nearly as large as his home. Two high windows hung with gingham curtains looked out on Willy's sloped strawberry patch and a grove of aspens and pines. The room smelled pleasantly of cedar. A handmade quilt lay over the bed, intricate and colorful as a block party but more serene.

When he came back upstairs Sarah handed him a glass of iced tea. They all sat down at the kitchen table and he praised his accommodations, making a point of the quilt which he guessed was Sarah's work. He said it was far too fine to sleep under. Sarah ignored his hyperbole, as it deserved.

"Lily just told me you heard about the shooting," she said almost accusingly, as if he had not praised the quilt but stolen it.

"Well, yes, when we stopped for gas."

Sarah gave a curt nod. "Well, you might as well know that's what my meeting was all about. Some of us aren't all that happy about what's been going on, the direction in which things are moving."

"And Willy?"

"Willy doesn't say much. But then he's county attorney, isn't he?"

Boxer nudged the mayor. "That means he approves," she explained brightly as if answering a question in a course outside her major.

Sarah did not enjoy being humored by the bride-to-be and frowned. "You've gotten a little too fresh, young lady."

The mayor was quick to intervene. "Who are these outlaws? What do they do?"

"I suppose Willy'll tell you they're just criminals pure and simple. And they *do* act that way, I admit. No doubt they hate us—and with more and more reason, you ask me. Everybody's afraid to go up in the hills now. They just keep to themselves most of the time, though. It's generally food they're after. Mostly they just play their music, I guess."

"Music?"

"What's *this*?" Lily exclaimed.

Sarah got to her feet and started moving fretfully around her kitchen, straightening this and that, rubbing the counter with a sponge. "There've always been outlaws, of course. You know that, Boxer. Men who ran away from things, kids who got in trouble. More a bunch of pathetic wannabe mountain men than outlaws, really." She paused. "Once in a while a woman would disappear too, and maybe she'd go up into the hills. It's possible. But it was almost all men. Ranch hands, migrants, rowdies from the little towns. Not all that many, actually. Nothing the sheriff couldn't take care of." She looked right at the mayor. "It's commonplace out here. There's so much room. Want some more tea?"

"No. I'm fine. Please go on."

"Yeah, what about the *music*, Mom?"

"Well, all right. I didn't tell you about this, Boxer, because I didn't want to upset you. A couple years ago we had this orchestra visit town. It wasn't one of the famous ones, of course. A small one. Whaddyacallem? You know."

"A chamber orchestra?"

"That's it. No conductor. They were on this tour. Had their own bus and everything. Mixed group—lot of Europeans and Asians and some black people. Little of this, little of that spreading culture and good will. I guess they were working their way through the West. Government grant or something." She turned her back and started in on the sink. "Anyway, Willy was made chairman of the sponsoring committee and he put me in charge of finding accommodations for them all. I put about half up at the Bighorn Inn and found places for the rest with

175

local families. Maybe that was a mistake. I don't know." She sat back down, fingered her glass.

"I can't believe," said Boxer scornfully, "that folks around here would want to hear a *classical* concert."

"Are we all ducklings, Miss Swan," Sarah snapped.

Lily turned red, bit her lip, looked down into her lap. The stresses of the wedding were showing.

"As it happens, the high school auditorium was sold out. I don't say there mightn't have been a little pressure. I mean Charles Ives hasn't exactly pushed Johnny Cash off the Windy River charts, but it *was* going to be the event of the year. I mean people were getting duded up and the schools all did a week on music appreciation. The program was to start with Copland's *Billy the Kid,* which I think you'll agree would go over pretty well any place in Wyoming."

The last sentence was aimed at Lily who got up and went to the window. "Dad just pulled in," she said with ostentatious relief.

"Good," said Sarah harshly. "He can finish the story, then. Honestly, I'm sick of it. Sick *about* it, too. I feel like cooking something anyway. So, go on, the both of you."

They met Willy coming in the front door. He gave the mayor a hug just as the mayor had Boxer, declared himself ecstatic about the visit, apologized for having to be away when the mayor arrived, joked about his daughter being all grown up, wanted to hear all about the retirement and what was going on back east.

Lily, unable to get a word in, had to leave when her mother shouted for her. The two men went back outside after Willy had taken off his tie and jacket. The mayor noted with amusement that his roommate who had tried to outeast the easterners was wearing cowboy boots. The afternoon was warm, the air dry and sweet, the sky large and blue.

"Nice here," said the mayor. "Glad you came back, aren't you?"

"Wyoming's the navel of the universe," Willy assured him, "but I'm willing to allow there could be a few other bellybuttons. A man can get to feeling cut off. Out here the newspapers always put local news on the first couple pages and sometimes they never get around to the stuff you see on television. Boxer's come to the conclusion that her father's a hick," he said proudly. "College girl. Effete east-coast intellectual."

"Actually, I've been hearing some local news."

Willy asked if he'd care for some whiskey.

"No. I'd like a walk, though. The air's wonderful; I'd forgotten. How about we go over by the river? I'd like to hear a little more about what Sarah was telling me."

In five minutes they were sharing a boulder and the mayor found himself searching for trout in the shadowy water.

"Sarah doesn't know exactly what happened," said Willy. "I'm not sure I've got it all straight myself. There's this ranch about ten miles outside of town, the Colson spread, pretty big place. It was just Colson and his wife, a young couple with no kids, two hired hands out in a bunkhouse. Colson's wife agreed to put up a couple of the musicians. Germans or Austrians, I think. They pulled in on a Friday afternoon. The concert was set for Saturday night. Well, at about five Saturday morning one of the hired hands calls up MacKenzie, our sheriff. He's all excited, says Colson's been shot dead and the two musicians are gone. So's Colson's wife."

"What was her name?"

"Why?"

"Just wondering."

"Nan. Nan Colson."

"Used to be Nan Ripley?"

"Well how the hell did you know that?"

"Just a hunch," said the mayor drily and began to imagine it all in the way he used to summon up pictures of his city. He saw the woman— she'd still be in her twenties—and the two Germans, escapees from a rule-ridden yet intermittently crazy land, with their old violins and youthful fantasies of the Wild West exacerbated by the openness of the country, the smell of horses, the provocation of a woman wanting them there and the hostility of a man who didn't. Something like that. He imagined Nan brooding all those years on her vanished mother, her secret heroine.

"But then we discovered they were *all* gone," Willy was explaining.

"All who?"

"All the musicians. Whole damned orchestraful of them. The calls kept coming in all that morning. Only the tour manager was left. That fellow was no use at all. Kept going on about people applauding between movements. And things were missing everywhere. Food, horses, guns."

"You think they had it all planned?"

"I don't know. Doesn't seem likely it was spontaneous. Could be they were declaring war on us. We're not a very musical people."

"Sarah said something like that. She said they hated you."

"Well, maybe."

The two men were quiet for a while, looking at the fast low water, listening to it rush against the rocks.

"I heard them once," said Willy. "I was fishing up about forty miles outside Crichton, Crichton being a Texaco station with a post office in it. God's country. Skipper and Bud and me. We'd just turned in when we heard it. Faint, you know, far off, but I swear I recognized it. Brahms. We talked about doing something but decided to leave well enough alone. There've been three killings this year. I'm just as glad Lily's going to live back east."

"Hm," said the mayor, lighting up the last panatella in his pocket.

AS THE WEEK PASSED the household bustled more and more with wedding preparations and the mayor was often left on his own. He took walks by the river, even practiced a little on the flute he brought along at the last minute; he ate chicken fried steak, visited with Sewall, and took pipe-smoking lessons from old Mr. McClintock at the drug store who hated cigars and refused to carry them. In an evangelical spirit, McClintock related the history of the weed, sold him a good briar pipe and let the mayor try every brand of tobacco he had.

Boxer's fiancé and his parents arrived from Buffalo and took a suite at the Bighorn. They let it be known that this was a sort of hors d'oeuvre for the grand reception that would be held later on the shores of Lake Erie. They were, however, immensely impressed by the mayor. In fact, he was such a coup, he very nearly silenced them.

The wedding was an outdoor affair in sublime weather. Harper was there, reminding the mayor of the bad fairy in *Sleeping Beauty*, except that Harper was an invited and an honored guest who pronounced no audible curse. Willy explained that she was the widow of the biggest rancher in the county and had a whole heap of accomplishments behind her. "Strange woman, unpredictable. If we were back East I'd say she was eccentric." He lowered his voice and grinned. "Sarah calls her the Empress Dowager."

The mayor danced once with Boxer, twice with Sarah, and by special request with the mother of the groom, a woman so out of her element that she clung to him as if he were her best china. The mayor observed that the citizens of Windy River couldn't help being impressed by the way the Buffalo contingent was impressed by him. He understood their western sense of inferiority but regretted it.

The reception and party went on well into the June night around a striped canopy. A local band pounded out two-steps, popular ballads, dated rock tunes. The clear sky was riddled by a thousand times more stars than the mayor would have been able to see on even the clearest of city nights. The dazzling sky, the happy wedding, Harper, his impending future—it all made him restless and the mayor found a folding chair off by himself and smoked his new pipe to pacify himself.

Guests began to leave around nine and the band finally quit at ten o'clock. Boxer's brandnew husband, who already called his wife Lil, thanked the mayor excessively for the antique silver service he had bought for them. A businessman on the rise, he spoke deferentially to the mayor. This pleased Boxer, who was proud of both of them. She looked exhausted and luminous under the Chinese lanterns. It seemed obvious to the mayor that she was thinking not of her wedding night in Wyoming but of all the nights to come that would not be in Wyoming. According to her mother-in-law, "After the dears bask for a couple of weeks in Bermuda they'll settle down on the Upper East Side." The woman said this with her pinkie in the air, so to speak, and with all the heartiness of repressed envy.

The mayor kept a furtive eye on Harper all evening. She fascinated him as a gila monster might have done. He watched how the local people paid her court. He knew all about court-paying and yet this was nothing like what he had experienced at twenty years of official receptions. This wasn't democratic; it wasn't even modern. It was more like propitiation, as if Harper had fearful powers, as if she could command the moon.

With the band quiet and more than half the guests gone, the night grew almost silent, except for tired voices, insects, and the music of the spheres. As soon as he saw her approaching him, the mayor realized that he too was frightened of Harper.

Practically fleeing from her, he moved off into the dark at the side of Willy's house where the strawberries were. It was no use. Perhaps she could see in the dark. Her thin fingers seemed to curl and catch at his sleeve; and, though he couldn't see her face draw near his, the mayor felt it, cracked and dry as a dusty plain in Kenya.

"Listen," she whispered. "Can you hear them?"

The mayor did hear. It was faint and far off, just as Willy had said, but it was Mendelssohn.

"You take care of them, don't you?" he said. "You—"

But her hand tightened on his arm. "Shh," she said.

Branches
of Live Oak

*e*lizabeth's father, Professor Rudolf Sternheim, died on a Thursday in March shortly after four o'clock in the afternoon. A heart attack took him, his second, for which the professor may have had an instant to be grateful. Whenever he heard of somebody wasting away from cancer, Professor Sternheim would mumble Cicero's prayer that the lightning should get him before the doctors. He expired in his office just after adjourning his graduate seminar on Büchner and Kleist. A doctoral candidate looking for an answer found a body instead.

Though it was nearly April, Boston lay in the undiminished embrace of winter and Lizzie, no longer accustomed to such temperatures, felt chilled from the moment she arrived at Logan all the way through the hastily arranged funeral at Greenbaum's and the rather clumsy reception back at the small house in Brookline. It did not occur to her to turn up the thermostat, which her father never moved from sixty-two degrees. That he had decided to have his body cremated was no surprise. After the first attack, he had written her a circumstantial letter divulging all his wishes in the matter as well as the contents of his will. Nevertheless, to Lizzie the cremation felt like a second death, as if her father had been incompletely dead until consumed by that secret whoosh somewhere behind the dark walls of Greenbaum's Funeral Home. Now that he was absolutely not there, grief and jet lag caught up with her. When discreetly asked by the funeral director she could not say what to do with the ashes.

"I don't know. Don't you scatter them?"

"They *can* be scattered, if you wish." Greenbaum always favored the passive voice. "Where would you prefer?" The question sounded at once sympathetic and disapproving.

"Where?"

All mortician's decorum, Greenbaum knew better than to insist. "Many people choose the sea," he remarked as though idly. It was hardly even a suggestion. He was an experienced man.

"The sea?"

Her father was no yachtsman. As a matter of fact, he disliked even sitting on a beach. He considered sunbathing to be *stultifying*. Elizabeth could remember looking this word up when she was eight. Her landlubbing father had rented a house in Wellfleet for one half of her two-week summer sojourn. There they were on the sunny beach, she running between the sand and waves, he watching from a canvas chair when he sighed with resignation and groaned with unmistakable candor, "God, this is stultifying."

The reception was a small trial, more like an unsuccessful academic party. Lizzie felt fuddled; she ought to have ordered more liquor and less cheese. People nibbled a little and drank more, gossiped, joked, looked to see who else was there. Several persons made it a point to tell her their most glorious Sternheim stories—she should know the best of her father—then the crowd slowly departed with condoling faces as if to a dead march at the end of a play. The stories people told her were good ones, yet Elizabeth learned nothing from them. The stories answered no questions, though Lizzie could hardly have said what her questions were.

Her father had never called the cellar his study, certainly not his sanctum sanctorum. He would merely say, "I'm going downstairs for a while, Lizzie." After the final admiring colleague, the last respectful student and distant cousin had left her alone in the house, Elizabeth changed into a pair of jeans, found a bottle of beer, and ventured downstairs. The Sternheim basement had attained a certain fame, for it was well known that he worked there, spent his summers there, composed his lectures, wrote his books and graded his examinations there. It was thought to be the locus of his cheerful solitude, of his contented celibacy. In the course of years the word itself had become a metonym for his life's work, his whole mode of existence. "Why the basement?" some visitor would occasionally ask, rubbing his arms in the damp. Her father would reply with his little smile, "It's good practice," a typical irony, more ironic than ever, thought Lizzie, as in the end he elected the flames rather than the grave. After all, he had been the most jovial of underground men.

Elizabeth was thirty-one now, still unmarried, a lawyer laboring her way toward a partnership in a Los Angeles firm. It had been over two years since she had visited her father. He had been out to see her only once, a long weekend during which he had perversely run her off her feet, doing everything from Mexican food and the County Museum to Disneyland and Venice Beach, never hinting that he might be yearning for his cool basement, trotting out the word stultifying not even once. For three whole days he had been a good sport.

Looking at the family portraits above one of the six bookcases, Lizzie regretted that her mother and stepfather had not come east for the funeral, even felt a little resentment and self-pity. Hey, I could have used the support, she said to herself, but knew it was a cliché. Anyway, she understood. Her mother had her own talk show in Sacramento, a half-hour of women's chat after the noon news, and her stepfather, an obsessive golfer, disliked leaving the links. Besides, there had been so little contact between her parents since their early divorce that she had feared having to introduce them to one another at her dreaded graduation. Her father had been particularly uncomfortable on this occasion, alternately lockjawed and inappropriately jocose. She appreciated that he was not being completely facetious when he said he would be obliged if, when the time came, she would consider eloping.

So here she was, alone in the dank womb of her father's thought, as close as she could ever again come to the paternal mind or body. She remembered all sorts of scenes enacted on this set: how she would dance for him, interrupt his grading and beg to record the marks, learning to type on the IBM Selectric and, years later, a grave discussion about the nature of history and whether she ought to major in it. Her father had written his big book on Kleist down here; this was the floor he paced while composing the famous essay with the theory of metaphor that became eponymous. The place looked like a monk's scriptorium, full of books and pictures and files and dust—empty of the monk. But then she thought, maybe the basement really *was* the monk, that this room was her father's veritable corpse, already cold and buried. In the green cabinets she could find the tidy files of his memory. In the tracks worn through the carpet she could trace her father's life of willing renunciation, an exalted mental life whose inwardness was more majestic to him than the Atlantic Ocean. Here were his memorabilia and paraphernalia, pens and paperclips, framed pencil drawings and favorite prints. Every object poised at the ready. The typewriter held out its keys. A ream of paper offered its multiple virginity to the black fountain pen on the faded green blotter. The regiment of old LPs stood at attention under the high window like cavalry, not unaware of their obsolescence. The whole room had the sad air of an eager, neutered dog.

Elizabeth sat down at the desk. Across the blotter stood the old wooden lamp, to her right a legal pad, a bottle of liquid paper, a stapler, and a glass paper weight with nothing underneath it. Three files were heaped up to her left. She felt as if she had inserted herself into an old snapshot, a moth plucked from reality and impaled outside of time. Careful not to stain the blotter, she put down her beer.

The bottom file caught her attention because it was fat and old, worn soft and torn at the edges. Unlike the ones for Büchner and Kleist, it lacked a label. She drew it on to the blotter, switched on the lamp, took a look inside.

On top was a note handwritten on one of the University's yellow memorandum sheets. The handwriting was crisp but feminine.

10 AM

MDSR—

I was tempted to phone back last night but it was so late I didn't want to risk waking you. Whenever I call, early or late, you always claim you're up. I wonder: is it gallantry or insomnia?

Anyway, I had another of my embarrassing dreams. They're so predictable. Whenever I don't get to see you for two days the pattern's just the same and the dreams are so blunt. I'm blushing!

In this one you and I are sixteen-year-olds at a boarding school. Scene one. We're at some sort of meeting with school administrators and other students. The room has a vaulted ceiling, groined windows, plush cushions on turned chairs. That sort of place. I think the topic for discussion was whether to plant azaleas or rose bushes but you and I were more interested in watching each other. Everybody in the room could tell we were a couple, and every last one of them disapproved.

Scene two. It's lunch break and we rush back to my dorm room. There's hardly any time before the meeting is supposed to reconvene. My roommate (I think it was Rachel Hauser!) takes one look at us and heads for the cafeteria. We make love as frantically as sprinters (we're sixteen, remember) but one of the administrators pounds on the door about three minutes too soon, if you know what I mean. Time's up, he howls.

Scene three. We go back to the meeting without our lunch. The whole dour crowd is frowning at us. They've left only two chairs free, at opposite ends of the room. No cushions on them.

Except for Rachel, most of the people in this one were strangers, but one of the administrators was Joyce Rumboldt. Remember her? God, was she jealous of me. Did you know that?

Finally found Sylvie a dress for the prom last night, and she says she'll deign to wear it. Lord be praised.

Lunch? Missing you terribly.

L.

For about two decades Elizabeth had not troubled herself with speculations on the subject of her father and women. Between the divorce and her first year of high school he had occasionally dropped a name or two over the phone. And once, when she was visiting, a woman had stopped by, a colleague with a new baby. It could have been L. and Sylvie. In those years her mother would quiz her rather gracelessly when she got back from her visits. But eventually her father's silence and the evident absence of women from his life led Lizzie simply to assume there were none. It was actually more an image than a conclusion: the monkish professor pursuing the life of the mind. Her father had done nothing to disturb this cliché, everything to reinforce it. She recalled a remark he dropped when he had taken her with him to Montreal for a conference. He said the reason he did not travel more frequently was that it was no fun going alone. Lizzie had felt sorry for him but it pretty much settled the matter. No one, so far as she knew, thought differently. It was easy and even rather comforting to picture her father as an ineligible bachelor.

Lizzie grubbed through the file of notes from L. without really reading them. Some were only a sentence long and none had an actual date. About a third of the way down she came on a typed draft of an astonishing poem with about a dozen corrections in her father's handwriting.

> A trope: my head on your stomach.
> I am the baby we might have had,
> the phantom child with my toes, your eyes—

> your eyes condemned to traffic jams
> for my sake, inching home to your authentic
> family—the child gazing on the grass,
> skittish, quick to rush into your skirt
> just as I would like to hide in your womb.

Lizzie guzzled her tepid beer. No dates. So was this file the record of some brief furious affair long over, a precious episode her father had, in his meticulous *homme des lettres* way, preserved? But then why was the file lying on his desk, why would he have taken it out and left it there just before he died, and why should the papers on top not seem older, mustier? In fact, they smelled almost fresh. And why were there so many papers—letters, cards, at least a couple hundred items, all signed L.? Exasperated, not sure she wanted to see any more, Lizzie went on flipping pages until she stopped by more poetry in her father's writing.

> Dusk dropped. I picked the
> brown hair from the white linen.
> Quickly, the sun set.
>
> Absence and presence:
> two mysteries clasped tight in
> one hand. Empty rooms.

She counted the syllables. Haiku.

Elizabeth rubbed her eyes and, like a good attorney, set about formulating her hypothesis. She reviewed the faces of the brunettes at the funeral and the reception. But how could she be sure the love of her father's life had been there, that secrecy and renunciation of adultery had not carried even that far, all the way to Greenbaum's? L. was what Lizzie had thoughtlessly believed herself to be, the most important woman in her father's life, the chief mourner. It hurt Lizzie to think that just because she presumed she knew all there was to know about him, she scarcely knew her father at all. She had thought him solid and prosaic and mental, and all the while there had been this fervid romance that drove her father into verse. Lizzie felt frozen out and yet filled with admiration. L., with her authentic family, her unwitting husband, her Sylvie securely primping for the prom, had the discipline to love her father for years without imposing on his solitude. Stunned by the story she imagined, Lizzie felt bewildered by all the questions to which it was an unanticipated answer.

Her father was not what she had believed, what she had unthinkingly depended on believing. Here, in his subterranean cell, she found not only his brain but also his unsuspected heart, and when she came on a valentine poem he had written for L., Lizzie felt like doing what she had not done during the funeral.

Because you are a mountain I've learned the ropes
Because you are an ocean I can hold (and hold) my breath
Because you are the deepest sleep I've oiled my rusty dreaming
Because you are a giaconda smile I work on grinning back
Because you are breathtakingly sane I unpendulate my mood
    swings
Because you are a dark beech forest I like getting found and lost
Because you are better than three crutches I stand upright
Because you are a frank declarative I'm less of a whining
    interrogative
Because you are a home I scarcely need a house
Because you..........................I

Elizabeth, foolish little Lizzie who didn't even care where her daddy's ashes were scattered, who had unconsciously emulated a false idea of him in turning down three plausible suitors, felt herself fall like a silly pubescent into a pool of imagined romance; for at the level of passion all children understand their parents, though usually when it is too late. And as she sank deeper all she could think of was meeting L., silently handing over the secret dossier, then sitting beside this woman with whose grief she could only try to catch up, playing a long *duetto adagio* ending in a wordless communion that would somehow atone for everything yet imperil nothing.

Before going up to her old room that now seemed so ascetic and narrow, Lizzie phoned to reschedule her flight. Then she called Westwood and left a message on the receptionist's answering machine to say she would be delayed until the following week. She blamed what the partners would most readily understand, complications with probate. Thus lies do beget lies, she thought a little mordantly on her way to the bathroom.

With her usual quickness, Lizzie already had a notion of how she wished to proceed. Circumspection must be her motto; she must be discreet. There was L. to think of; in fact, Lizzie was thinking of little else. First, she must discover the woman's identity. The obvious clue lay in the frequency with which her notes mentioned lunch.

At ten o'clock the following morning she was at the University asking to see Professor Quant, chairman of the German department.

Quant, entirely bald and punctiliously dressed, stood not very much over five feet. He had made his name as a specialist on Andreas Gryphius but found his niche as a feisty administrator. By now, he was well settled into his fiefdom. At the reception he spoke to Lizzie briefly and conventionally, taking her hand in both of his, making it feel clumsy and mammoth.

Quant rose from behind his desk, perhaps on the toes of his wing-tips, as the secretary showed Lizzie into his trim, unbaroque office. A computer hummed at his elbow, half full of text.

"Ms. Sternheim." Quant came nimbly around the desk with an unnatural expression of surprise and warmth. Lizzie was not taken in; she knew academics well enough to gauge this one. In his field he would never admit surprise and in his office he would seldom exude warmth. "So good to see you again. Once more, our condolences," he said imperially.

Lizzie held out her suddenly elephantine hand. "Professor Quant."

He looked around as if unsure where the furniture had gotten to. "Please. Please take a seat." After an instant's hesitation he indicated the armchair across from his desk, not the one nearest it, probably the hot seat for tutorials, faculty evaluations, and conspiracies.

Once they were settled, Lizzie on the imitation Bauhaus, Quant on his upholstered throne, she waited for him to speak. This was by design; she must not appear eager, or even there for too specific a reason.

Impatient and perplexed by her silence, Quant finally spoke up. "If there was *anything* we could do for you here, you know you only needed to phone. We'd have been glad to save you the trouble of coming all the way down." The subtext was clear: had she not been so recently bereaved he would have demanded her business and checked his watch while doing so.

"You're very kind," Lizzie drawled. "It's just that I wanted to talk a little, you know, to a few of my father's colleagues. After all, it's pretty unlikely I'll get another chance and it was so hectic at the reception. You understand, don't you? I didn't get to see much of him these last few years . . ." and she trailed off.

Quant still looked puzzled. "I think he was as happy as ever. Always cheerful. You must know I cut his load back, of course; in fact, this semester there was only the one seminar. It's all right, by the way. I've got somebody who'll finish up and grade the papers. Anyway, you know your father always had an iron in the fire. I think he was working on a big review article. He was always being asked to do reviews."

"Oh, yes. He mentioned it, I think. But, you see, what I really want is some idea of what his life was like these last few years. I mean, for instance, who did he spend time with? Who were his closest friends? I'm sure they could tell me some things about him. He always wanted to know what I was doing and hardly ever talked about himself."

The computer's screen saver flashed on, a cartoon aquarium. Quant looked at it but struggled to be polite, bearing in mind that Sternheim's daughter might be distraught or just flaky. After all, he had heard that she lived in California. "I'm not surprised," he said. "Your father was a very modest man. It wouldn't be going too far to say that he was remarkably private. But I can tell you he got on well with every member of the department. Naturally, the younger people looked up to him. He was our grand old man. I myself often sought his advice."

Lizzie did not think this very likely but she smiled, crossed her legs, played a little with the hem of her skirt, and said nothing. Sure enough, Quant went on.

"Maybe you should talk to Professor Gardner. He's in the nineteenth century too; in fact, he's the one who's going to finish up the seminar. I think your father helped him out with his book on Stifter."

"Oh yes?" said Lizzie, implying that the list was not yet long enough.

"Let's see. Well, and maybe Professor Pirozzi."

"Professor Pirozzi?"

"In Anthropology, I believe."

"Really? My father never mentioned any anthropologists. Were they close, Professor Pirozzi and my father?"

"I think they had lunch together from time to time." Quant's tone was flat; it was impossible for Lizzie to tell if he meant to imply any-thing.

And is Professor Pirozzi female, perhaps named Lydia or Letitia or Lola, Lizzie would have liked to ask. Instead she inquired for Professor Gardner's office number and where the Anthropology department was located.

"Gardner's up in 311. Anthropology's in Hastings. You'll find it just across the way."

"Thank you. Is there a phone number, I mean for Anthropology or Professor . . . ?"

"Pirozzi?" Quant was already on his feet. "My secretary," he offered in an unmistakable tone of dismissal, "will be glad to look it up for you."

Lizzie did not press for a pronoun. She rose, thanked Quant, who quickly escorted her to the door, unnecessarily inquiring if she had received all the effects from her father's office.

As soon as the door closed behind her, Lizzie asked the secretary if she might look something up in the University Directory.

Associate Professor Pirozzi of the Anthropology faculty had the given name of Leda. On her way down the stairs Lizzie's memory bank printed out a long painting by Leonardo and a short poem by Yeats, residues from her undergraduate years. But there was also her father's odd love poem in which he imagined himself the child of Leda, hiding in her womb, perhaps inside an egg inside her womb. Could that be what men wanted, the secret of all their diving and delving? Lizzie recalled that Leda didn't have a single child; she had twins, two sets of twins in fact. Was this also significant to her father, a man who never took his literature lightly? A doubling of personality? A double life? A decade of duplicity? Lizzie already felt the dizziness provoked by her father's own complex writings and those of the writers he most loved. Anyway, Leda was a beautiful name, myth or no myth, twins or no twins.

Outside she found the temperature even lower and the campus nearly dark. A light rain congealed as much as it fell. Hastings Hall, a brownish neo-Gothic pile, appeared to absorb the light around it, though students scuttled colorfully in and out sporting Day-Glo raingear above their standard issue bluejeans and running shoes. Lizzie shivered and set out toward the place but stopped in mid-quad. "Thinking is what people do only when everything else fails." It was one of her father's favorite saws. "And too often not even then, " he liked to add.

Well, she thought, am I really up for this? I have Leda Pirozzi's number, but do I have her *number*?

Instead of making for the Anthropology department she walked half a block west and went into The Deck, a student restaurant with a dismal nautical decor. She took a booth and ordered a decaf from a pretty waitress who looked to be about fourteen. Perhaps, she mused sentimentally, it was here in this very booth that her father had eaten all those intimate lunches with Leda the anthropologist. She was surprised by how jealous she felt.

A scruffy, balding man of about forty reclined alone in the next booth. He sprawled with the ease of a regular or the apathy of a tramp. And he smelled. Lizzie could tell that he was looking her over. Just after her coffee arrived he swung his arm over the common back of their booths and tapped her shoulder.

"You're Sternheim's daughter, right?"

"Pardon me?"

"Caught you at the funeral."

"You were there?"

The impertinent man seemed amused by the implication that he had no right to attend her father's funeral. "Well, it was an SRO gig, wasn't it? I squeezed in way at the back with the rest of the plebes."

Lizzie prepared herself for one of the formulaic condolences she had received so many of in the last two days, but suspected it wouldn't be forthcoming from this sweatshirted boor.

"Okay if I join you?" he said instead.

"No, thank you," Lizzie said frostily, turned, and fastened her eyes on her coffee. She could feel his arm, unmoving and flabby, just behind her neck. She hoped that he would put it down, thereby covering his armpit.

The man was insistent and went on with a kind of Buddhist brutishness. "Every good bucket has a big handle so that if it gets too heavy two people can pick it up. In other words, better to mourn together than alone."

Lizzie did not reply.

"You *are* mourning, aren't you?"

Lizzie swung her head around like a gun. "Look, is there something you *want*?" She felt the condition of demi-orphanhood ought to exempt her from the insults of such jerks. And she knew her rights. She could threaten this guy with a charge of harassment, she could call a cop. But the truth was that Lizzie had all but forgotten she was a grown-up lawyer. Ever since touchdown in Boston she had been regressing. California was her proper habitat, the sunny home of independence and resolve, flashy with in-jokes, not lugubrious old New England with its mad Puritan ghosts and maddening academic pretensions, with its brainy elves like Quant who made her feel about twelve. So her father was not what he had appeared. So he was a swan and not a duckling, or vice versa. So he loved in secret, faithfully and illicitly, not wishing or knowing how to defend passion against convention. Such old-fashioned stuff. She had had to read *The Scarlet Letter* in high school. Why not just go home?

"Well, *are* you?" the man demanded with his infuriating lack of indirection, like somebody from the D.A.'s office. And he went on without waiting for her to reply. "You don't *want* to answer? Okay. All right. Fine. What is it to be in mourning, after all? To mourn is to pine, to grieve, to lament, to droop, but above all to *remember*. That's the word's root, you know, mourning means remembering. The mourner remembers and so to mourn means in general regretting the past and feeling damned lousy about the present. What is it you regret, Ms. Sternheim? Thinking back and all?"

"Look, why don't you just leave me alone?" said Lizzie.

"Maybe I want to remember *with* you? I'm in mourning too, you know, and maybe my mourning's worse than yours, maybe it's deeper, more tinged with regret."

As he spoke, he got up and moved right into Lizzie booth, pushing himself in across from her. Lizzie saw putty flesh, an unshaven chin under a derisive mouth.

She got up to leave but he stopped her with one sentence delivered in the kind of stage whisper that denotes sincerity.

"Rudolf used to say you kept him from feeling like a father."

"What do you mean by that?"

"*I* don't mean anything by it, sweetheart. It's what *he* said. What do you suppose he meant by it?"

Lizzie sat back down. Her companion summoned the young waitress with a seigniorial wave. The waitress appeared as quickly as if he were the proprietor.

"Ilana, my sweet, I think we could both do with a refill."

Ilana smiled and dashed off for the two pots—caffeine for the mysterious tramp, decaf for the displaced attorney—during which procedure Lizzie was treated to the following information.

"I gave her an A last year. But you're wondering about *me* no doubt. Oh, I'm nothing. Just one of those hangers-on around universities. You know, the semi-registered perpetual grad students who make occasional T.A.s, intermittent research assistants, part-time shelvers, textbook clerks, can and bottle collectors, T-shirt salesmen, tutors to the downwardly mobile, goof-offs and idlers. That sort of thing. Never quite ready to commit our ideas to paper, always rethinking and postponing, always looking up yet another source. Impossible to imagine writing the great work in *time,* so to speak. Ah, thanks so much, Ilana." Lizzie saw him wink at the grinning waitress. It struck her as a conspiratorial piece of nictation. Even his wink was repellent.

"How did you know my father?"

"Well, we were both seekers after truth, weren't we? I'd meet him now and then. We'd talk. I'd practice my German. You know."

"What's your name?"

"People call me Rank."

"Is that because you are, or because you don't have any?"

Rank fell back against the seat and laughed with unpleasant little wheezes. "Well," he huffed. "I can see what Rudolf meant when he said it was risky to argue with a daughter holding a J.D."

"He said that too?"

"Oh yeah. He liked to talk about you. Sometimes he talked about you as if he were almost afraid of you. Or awe-struck. Or distantly enamored."

"Yet he didn't feel like my father?"

"What he said was that you *kept* him from feeling like your father. It isn't quite the same thing, is it? I don't know. Maybe he had some Platonic idea of fatherhood."

Lizzie felt a need to defend herself. "Well, I didn't live with him so naturally he—"

"No, I really don't think that was it. Actually, I think he meant that you didn't *need* him enough, that you seemed to him, you know, kind of self-contained. Or maybe what he thought was that you needed him more than you knew but left him no way—"

"It's my fault I didn't need him enough to suit him?"

"I didn't say it was. Of course a need you don't acknowledge can look a whole lot like independence." Rank smiled at her like a judge sure of his sentence.

Not particularly eager to hear more of Rank's analysis of her needs, Lizzie changed direction in a way she certainly would not have had she not felt provoked. "Do you know Leda Pirozzi?"

"Oh, Professor Pirozzi? Only by reputation, which is impeccable. Obviously you know she was a friend of your dad's. Quite a lady, I hear."

"Yes?"

"Dignified, fiercely professional, worshipped by the heterosexual feministas. . . . But look, you haven't asked what it is I regret."

"Why should I?"

"Well I'm going to tell you anyway. The world's not a confessional so, for me, this isn't a chance to pass up. What I regret is that I constantly plagiarized your father, appropriated his sayings and ideas; and though I didn't do it without shame, I might as well have. Even more I regret that now there won't be any new Sternheimisms for me to lift. I regret that I let him down by not finishing my dissertation. I regret that I'm ashamed of myself and that I'm not more ashamed. I regret that your father knew perfectly well that I was stealing his ideas and that he didn't care in the least, that he only wanted to help me out. I regret that, to tell the truth, he actually laid these ideas out for me as somebody might food for a starving animal. In general, I'd say I regret that his compassion for me was indistinguishable from contempt."

"You wanted to *be* him? Is that it?"

Rank, wound up for a good spell of self-abasement, looked at her with a squint. "Okay. Why not? He had what I wanted."

"That could be a cause of admiration or emulation. It could have motivated you; it didn't need to make you envious."

Rank shrugged. "Envy has fewer syllables. Besides, it's more suitable for the untalented. I *did* admire him, of course. Hugely. My mourning's awfully complicated. In fact, I'm a highly complex fellow. Ilana over there can bear me out."

"No doubt," Lizzie said disgustedly.

Rank leaned forward. "More complex than your father anyway."

"Oh?"

"You bet. His inward life may have been infinitely rich and ramified, but the outward one was incredibly boring. I mean, everything settled, everything so secure. He taught, he wrote, he shat, and he slept. Thanks to you he didn't even have the complication of paternity to cope with. Thanks to your mother he didn't have to deal with marriage. *My* life, on the other hand, is nothing but distractions and anxieties. I have one more wife than he did and two more kids and none of them are shy about what they need. It's no wonder I couldn't *emulate* him, that I can't get anything done. If I wanted to be your father it was only because I wanted a piece of his security. Hell, with just half of it I'd be a full professor!"

"Was he always so serene?"

"Did he ever seem less than tediously serene to *you*?"

Lizzie considered. "But if his life was as completely inward as you say, then how could either of us know whether it was serene or not? He might have had all sorts of inward dramas and crises."

"I simply don't believe it, darling. Your daddy was one of those Olympian types, the kind who can separate their souls from their bodies. His sort's invariably serene, beyond humiliation. Humiliation's basically a bodily function. Tenure's one hell of a thing for the *vita contempliva*."

Lizzie sighed, weary of humoring this bloppy self-absorbed failure.

Rank greedily drank up his coffee. "Anyway, he was the nearest thing I still had to a thesis advisor, so what am I supposed to do now?"

"Try plagiarizing," Lizzie shrugged, then got up and left.

She no longer had any desire to go to the Anthropology department, and so she walked home in the rain.

Unlike the basement, which the night before had seem so animated, the living room looked lifeless. In the grey afternoon light, the maroon upholstery, the Bokhara carpet, the dark masculine drapes and dried flowers reminded her of her first acquaintance with death in the ghastly funeral parlor where her grandfather had been laid out. In the stillness of her father's living room, she remembered how the thick carpet in the funeral parlor had absorbed the little noise that people dared to make, how musty and ponderous the air was.

They'd never have spent time together in here, she thought. No, they'd have gone straight up to the bedroom or grabbed a snack in the kitchen, maybe they'd go downstairs so he could read her something.

Lizzie's domestic law course had been thorough. Because of a case she had been assigned to prepare, Frisch v. Frisch, she knew that in Massachusetts adultery was still a criminal offense, about the opposite of what it is in California. Frisch had brought charges against his wife and her lover to get out of paying alimony and win custody of the children. He won, too.

She tried to imagine her father working with two children under-foot. It had been difficult enough for him to function even during her two-week visits, though he tried gallantly to hide it. Perhaps, Lizzie thought with a little shock, it was she and not the beach that had been stultifying.

Now she tried to grasp not the happiness revealed by her father's poems and Leda's numberless and breathless notes, but rather the unhappiness, the sacrifices. They could not travel together or pass a quiet evening with friends, could not act honestly in public, smile at each other in a meeting. The two of them constituted a secret, there-fore there could be no secrets between them. Their decade or two of intimacy allowed of neither consequences nor let up; the relationship could feed only on itself, like the sun. Technically, they were criminals. For years they had skated over an abyss, arm in arm.

Lizzie went into the kitchen to look for her father's address book. He kept it next to the spices. Leda Pirozzi's name was in it—"L. Pirozzi," for safety's sake—with an address and two phone numbers.

Lizzie put the book back and headed for the basement where she spent the rest of the afternoon and half the evening reading through Leda's letters. They no longer seemed merely an agglomeration of notes discreetly dropped in a faculty mailbox, slipped under an office door, or surreptitiously mailed during family vacations; they were more like a rich epistolary novel. Characters danced in and out—eccentric professors, problematic students, obstreperous children, cross deans, impossible in-laws. Lizzie found philosophical passages about rapture, longing, guilt ("The responsibility's all mine. The put-up-or-stop-staring-at-me-that-way was my doing. Up at 3 a.m. again. Impossible to sleep until my imagination puts you inside me, where you belong. My subconscious is guilty too."). There were jokes, a good deal of gentle teasing, serious discussions of his ideas and hers. Leda reacted to the books he compelled her to read ("Don't you think your Kleist makes so much of the good of marriage just because he opted out if it, that he loves wedlock the way an atheist does Christmas?"). Many laid out secret plots to meet for movies or special afternoons. There was much about her two children ("Brian's sick again. He fell asleep with his little fist clutching my nightgown. I'm afraid you'll be risking another cold."). There were responses to her father's advice ("You genius! The role-reversal was a terrifying success. As a pre-teen I'm an anarchist, but as the mommy she's a fascist! Now we understand each other almost too well."). There were even a few passages about Lizzie herself, few but touching, and these she could not help scrutinizing minutely for they all showed Leda's concern for her welfare and suggested the extent of her father's worries on her behalf ("You worry too much. Lizzie's such a good judge of character I'm sure she'll see through her frater-nity hunk before Spring Break.").

Were Rank to pop in now, Lizzie could tell him what she regretted. She would be dying to tell him.

"Hello, is Professor Pirozzi there? I want to speak to her because she loved my father for twenty years and I didn't know." No, Lizzie could not bring herself to call. The better to procrastinate, she watched PBS unsuccessfully anatomize reality for an hour and then NBC trium-phantly ignore it for another.

Saturday was blustery but bright enough to hint at something softer. She got up early, resolved to accomplish all the chores she had been putting off. She phoned the local Century 21 office, then walked out in the wind to buy a few groceries. The real estate agent was there by ten and by eleven they had settled on both an asking and a taking price. After lunch she drove to the local dealer and sold her father's Saab. She charmed the sales manager into agreeing to pick the heap up early Monday morning and personally delivering Lizzie to the airport. It was a good day's work, yet Lizzie felt anything but satisfied and not even remotely tired. There was still a day and a half to get through. She had been an idiot to stay.

So jumpy was she by four o'clock that she phoned her office, fig-uring somebody was bound to be in who could at least give her her messages. Only the answering machine answered, a vocal whore wel-coming all. Lizzie was surprised by her disappointment and decided that what she really needed was to talk to somebody, somebody in L.A., city of license and free-floating enlightenment, where all secrets are public and only tourists get hung up. She tried Jodie. Then Cecilia.

She tried Jake and Marty's number. Machines and more machines. Why is it that everyone in L.A. is always somewhere else, she wondered. Sprawling city of answering machines and car phones.

As the sun took off for the Golden State the air in the kitchen turned briefly purple. Feeling like a child about to play a prank, Lizzie reached around the oregano for her father's address book. Dialing on the wall phone seemed quaint. Her father had not bothered to hook it up to the answering machine she sent him two birthdays ago. She had not come across the box anywhere so maybe he gave it away, maybe he gave it to Rank to help with his complicated life. After all, her father had always been there when she called him.

Lizzie's stomach ached and she gulped. The phone was really ringing. Someone was saying hello. "Professor Pirozzi?"

"Yes?" Even from this single syllable, Leda's voice struck Lizzie as queenly; it was deep and capable of guile, the sound of still waters that run deep.

She galloped through her message in what she hoped was a brisk and lawyerly fashion. "This is Rudolf Sternheim's daughter, Professor Pirozzi. It's Elizabeth. I'd like very much to meet with you, if that's at all possible. I have a flight on Monday and there's something I'd like to give you, something I think you should have."

The measured reply came slowly. "It was terrible about your father, Elizabeth. I'm sorry that I couldn't come back for the reception. You know that your father was a wonderful man. Please accept my condolences."

Did Lizzie imagine a stammer, holes over depths patched by this clutching at cliché? Condolences, she thought, and replied cheekily. "I'll accept yours if you'll accept mine."

During the awful pause that followed something or other happened. Lizzie, concentrating, heard what might have been a stifled gasp but could have been just the breeze of a wayward electron.

"I'm terribly sorry again, but I won't be able to see you. Before Monday." Leda sounded more determined than regretful. "Family plans," she added pointedly, perhaps more as a reminder of her situation than to soothe Lizzie's feelings.

Lizzie found herself begging. "We could meet at The Deck tomorrow, say for brunch?"

Silence again. Lizzie began to realize how painful this must be for

Leda but also how fruitless for her. She was tugging at a tree with real roots. Who can yank up a tree?

"No, I'm sorry. It's just not possible."

"But I really do have something to give you. Something my father kept—"

Leda, sounding more desperate, interrupted. "Couldn't you just send it? I mean to my office?"

"You know what it is?"

"It doesn't matter. I'm in the Anthropology department."

"I know. Hastings as in battle of."

"That's it. Look, Lizzie, I'm really sorry. I *have* to go now. You understand?"

And that was that. Leda had called her Lizzie which meant that she knew, knew Lizzie knew, but would not see her. No, Lizzie was certain. Not ever. Never.

Sunday was distended and pointless. Lizzie felt trapped on the wrong coast, beside the wrong ocean. She bought the *Times* at the corner spa, couldn't bear to read it, then, out of an urge to etch her loneliness even deeper, walked down to the University and continued all the way to the Charles. The sky was still grey but the air had turned temperate. A pale yellow fuzzed the branches of the maples. She concentrated on trees, old Eastern trees, the many-armed beeches, the high fluted oaks. Once, when she was nearly hysterical over some examination, her father had told her the cure. "Go and look at a tree," he had advised.

On Sunday night Lizzie wrote a brief note to Leda, opened the flue, and burned the ragged folder and all its contents that had once been trees.

The Saab dealer showed up promptly at seven. He talked enthusiastically about his trip to California. Traffic was light until they hit the tunnel where an accident stopped them dead for twenty minutes so that Lizzie only just made her plane. By eight-thirty she was up in the air.

Ölmaler of Mactan

I. Serfdom

"*Y*ou're dripping!"

O'Malley turned his head slowly until his chin touched the inside of his right shoulder. The maddened electric eel shot from the base of his skull all the way to his bicep then slithered nastily back again. He squinted down, gritted his yellowing teeth, and replied murderously.

"Sorry, Mrs. Bernoulli, but that's what the drop-cloth you're standing on's for. The cloth catches the drips and later, when I'm done, I take it away and your floor stays clean. Got it?"

He did not need to look down to know that the old woman was rubbing her hands together like a fretful vulture. Worry, worry. In less than an hour he had identified the definitive Bernoulli gesture.

"How long till this smell goes away?" she now demanded, as if at her age she had had no experience of the properties of fresh paint. Perhaps her sensorium had so shrivelled that bad smells and worse anxieties constituted her chief ties to the world. O'Malley pitied and detested her. To him she was a daughter of Pharaoh, Hansel's witch, a withered mother superior, a helpless crone, somebody's ex-muse.

"The smell'll be gone by tomorrow," he assured her with almost the last of his patience, mentally inviting her to go sip weak tea and just leave him to finish the wretched job in peace. But she lingered by the foot of the ladder, threatening to topple it, unwilling to leave him, scrutinizing each stroke of his brush. Woman, what have I to do with thee? O'Malley laughed to himself. Here was the attentive critic for whom he had yearned, the one who missed nothing, and all he could dream of was dumping a bucket of autumn white onto her brittle cranium. Still, it was only the head of a wizened and lonesome widow who meant to get her eight dollars' worth out of every hour.

"You're going pretty slow," she whined as if he were a taxi.

O'Malley simply ignored her, climbed down, walked the ladder over three steps, scaled it, resumed painting the wall. *What It's Like To Be Me,* he thought. An excellent title for the chef d'oeuvre he could only paint in his mind. The familiar sensations of applying paint synesthesially hammered him down like a spike into the dark corporeal flats where all his work began, for his brain was ever the servant of his hand. How many critics would know that? Yes, *What It's Like To Be Me* would be a most fitting title suggesting the most intimate autobiographical elements of his complex design—the fogged-in willow outside his bedroom window when he was an ambition-besotted romantic of sixteen, the body of his first woman pulling a slip over her head, the railroad ride from Bern to Copenhagen—but also firmly tying the work to tradition. How many paintings, books, or poems could, without violence to their intent, have adopted the same name? What could any sincere artist do but try to tell the generations about himself? *To Be Me: What It Was Like.* And the generations sometimes even paid attention, for a moment or two.

But there was no money. No money and so no painting—no paint, no food, no rent, no canvas. No canvas and so the Bernoulli kitchen wall instead.

"I have another little job for you," Mrs. Bernoulli declared even before the first coat was finished. She had been waiting to tell him and for good reason.

When her grandson the dentist had come two weeks before, removing from the attic all he wanted, he warned her about the strain, how the ceiling could collapse at any time, pinning her in her bed. He had not offered, of course, to do anything about it himself. He had gums to probe and a weak back from leaning over mouths. Don't be so cheap, granny, he advised. Hire some lummox.

The attic was attained by means of a narrow collapsable stairway built for sylphs. In it stood a dozen large bags of cement. Mrs. Bernoulli had no idea how they came to be there. At some epoch in the attic's eventless history water had gotten to these bags and now each weighed well over a hundred pounds.

"You find them yet?" she called fretfully up the stairs. O'Malley was always on high, always being yelled at. Hunched over in the creosoted dark, he admitted he had found the bags.

"Good. Did I mention I'd like them put outside? On the curb?"

O'Malley summoned up a couple lines of verse. ". . . This time last year I was fifty-four,/And this time next year I shall be sixty-two." The shoe fit, and he strained away the whole afternoon under hundred-weights of cement, negotiating the three flights to the curb, sweating as the autumn white dried in the kitchen out of which no snack issued. Mrs. Bernoulli found her place on the large imaginary canvas, decapitated in one of the bottomless holes of O'Malley's private Malebolge. The stairs were steep, the eel darted all over his torso, the paint dried relentlessly upon the crude topography of the kitchen's four plaster continents steeped in redolent tides of Bernoullian cuisine.

For this he was to be grateful, grateful to Mrs. Bernoulli, grateful to Pomerantz who thought himself a great patron and benefactor because he had had two large pictures and three drawings cheap, because he used O'Malley for every slavishness from gardener to electrician to plumber to caretaker to dog-walker and gave him a meal or two, grateful because now he had found O'Malley day-labor for a month doing construction, cleaning out basements, painting slums for his friend the slumlord, repairing bathrooms, and now this last cement straw for a stinking eight dollars an hour? Enough. Basta!

His true surname was not O'Malley, a hod-carrier's name, but Ölmaler, painter in oils, no doubt misconstrued by some uniformed lout at Ellis Island.

Seizing his fate by its throat, so to speak, O'Malley threw down the last bag of cement and vowed to paint or die.

2. Xenia

She sat huddled in the corner beside the broken television set, shivering in nothing but a ripped grey sweatshirt. Her brown-green eyes regarded him with something between a plea and an apology, an unbearable gaze just because there was no reproach in it. With her little hands between her bare knees she looked pitifully young and fragile. In fact, every week she looked younger and more fragile so that by now it had become unseemly for her to remain. O'Malley, taking all this harder than he wished to show, tried not to look at her as he came in the door. He was determined not to be the first to speak; yet, despite everything, he was reassured by her presence and, wishing to show her this, gave a nod in her direction on his way to run himself a hot bath. Of course the minute he had some sort of firm idea he would tell her; but it was a day for vows and on the way home he swore that, if she were still there, he would make no more empty promises, no more shameful displays such as on the night he had completely broken down and then, because he couldn't weep forever, resented her for seeing his tears and runny nose. A miracle that she was still there at all, yet no reproach could sting worse than this suicidal fidelity of hers.

No sooner had the word entered his head than O'Malley saw that it was suicidal indeed. She was dwindling, no doubt about it. Already she looked like a tubercular child from a daguerrotype, she who only a decade ago had been so powerful and shapely, worthy to bathe in a corruscating pool for Monet. Look at her now.

O'Malley's heart grew heavier as he stripped off his clothes, grunting at his own stiffness and guilt. Her question floated in the room like a strong aroma, like the steam rising reproachfully from the tub.

"What can I do?" he said at last, breathed it out as he lowered himself into the hot water.

"You could paint."

Xenia hadn't actually said this sentence, of course. She hadn't said a word in over a week. Perhaps it was O'Malley's convolutions speaking.

O'Malley settled in the tub and sighed, looked up at the paint flaking off the ceiling, touched the grime caked on the side of the tub, looked down at his fifty-five-year-old feet.

"I'm unutterably grateful to you," he said aloud. His chest rose as he spoke, his speaking making his chest buoyant. "And I'm frightened for you. I know you're dying and that it's my fault. Who else's fault could it be? Your death lies inside the dark wings of my failure, if that doesn't sound overly poetical. You were always so beautiful—never more so than when you started to grow younger and thinner. I thought I was the cause of it in some other way, that maybe you'd become a twenty-year-old sexpot because of my lecherous old imagination. I didn't understand, did I? I was a pig and you forgave me that. Maybe you even blame yourself. Is that it? You think maybe you didn't inspire me sufficiently? Not so, Xenia. Even now, even now. I'm plenty inspired, but I'm broke, kid. Maybe we're not conventional enough or too conventional, but nobody's buying and, anyway, what's there to sell? Pomerantz had the last two canvases and now I have to hew wood and carry water. It's the way of the world. Why don't you leave me?"

"I can't."

As a shadow is to a body, so this was to her voice. His eyes had closed as he spoke and now her voice was at O'Malley's ear, ghostly and insubstantial, a wisp of smoke. Within or without, it scarcely mattered.

The idea that Xenia could die and he go on living was intolerable to him.

"I don't think you understand," hummed Xenia's small voice as plaintively as a streetlamp. "I'd leave if I could." Buzz, buzz.

Every moment is part of both history and eternity and this was one of them. Eternity is history and then some. O'Malley exhaled and sank like a lost sailor, let the grey water swamp his chest, swallow his neck, cover up his mouth. He looked around at the misty mirror over the sink, took in the faded blue towel that hung stiffly from its plastic rack, settled on the depressingly white porcelain fixture whose open seat was exactly at his eye level. Every moment is part of eternity, but one moment in particular.

"*Pingero ergo sum,*" he bubbled into the water. And not the kitchen walls of widows either.

"In eternity you may find yourself on a dusty noonday plain or in a moonlit clearing and all the women with whom you've slept and even those with whom you've only imagined fornicating may come running from the woods or down from the hills maddened and giggling, naked and inflamed, and tear you to pieces with their long hands and white teeth and, as in that nightmare when you found the basketball under your arm was your own head, decapitate you, throwing your head into the river and your head will shoot the rapids alongside pine forests and float under the verdigris bridges of ancient cities and under the gushing waste pipes of demonic factories until it reaches the sea into which all rivers flow, even all the rivers of forgetfulness and then perhaps then it will begin at last to sink . . ."

Thus Xenia's sing-song voice persisted in its lullaby until, at the last moment, O'Malley shook himself awake, tore himself loose from the tepid, hardening water, and bellowed the name of his pitiable vanishing muse.

3. Kathleen

a chill and rainy Tuesday morning in November with a sky so low and steely it would make even the suburban industrial zone in which O'Malley rents his studio feel cozy if only the place had proper heat. The cars on the turnpike, which he can easily see from the window behind his bed, have their headlights on as they doggedly burn up the sunlight compacted and stored for them during the Age of Dinosaurs. Pomerantz will be driving to his downtown office, his mind musing on the national debt or his last vacation in Aruba, on the level of his satisfaction with his knockout of a second wife Female (pronounced fee-*mal*-ay) and what to buy her next; or perhaps he is considering the harmonization of idealism with materialism he deems, with particularly annoying self-satisfaction, his specialty, a harmonization wholly personal and not in the least philosophical of which his relation to O'Malley is, from Pomerantz's own point of view, the supreme illustration.

O'Malley, on the other hand, considers only materialism. His rent is due in ten days' time and he is well shy of the sum. There isn't much to eat and his skeletal easel leans neglected in the corner. The air is as grey as Xenia's sweatshirt which now lies like a mechanic's soiled rag on the grey cement floor under the eloquently empty easel.

The urge to paint is hard upon O'Malley, strong as ever it was, perhaps even stronger. Yet because he cannot paint, the world is grey, stale, flat, and decidedly unprofitable. If to paint is to be, then O'Malley can hardly be said to exist, just as Xenia's existence is indisputably dubious in the light of this iron morning. His senses are dulled, his head a bag of hardened cement. If he were not so morose, he would be sickened by his self-pity.

Kathleen's car pulls up punctually at nine o'clock. He watches her step out of the silver Honda in her bright green overcoat. Kathleen favors shades of green because, O'Malley deduces, she has been told that green sets off her clear white skin and dark hair and is the color of the Old Sod to boot. Kathleen manages the office of the Age of Gold Travel Agency which occupies the first floor of the converted machine shop whose top level constitutes O'Malley's studio and semi-legal domicile. The location is unprepossessing for a business; however, the Age of Gold conducts its global affairs electronically: by telephone, by telex, by fax, by computer network. In practically no time at all Kathleen can put her finger on Tahiti or Tegucigalpa, Christchurch or Kharkov. O'Malley is duly impressed by this power but also frightened of it, as if the world were covered by an invisible web spun by the spiderwoman Kathleen sitting at the center contemplating death and disaster. Fortyish, tough, a svelte lesbian with no need to dwell on her preferences, let alone apologize for them, unsentimental as a black widow, as she needed to be. The Age of Gold Travel Agency's clientele is restricted to persons over seventy to whom it offers luxury tours and cruises. In the natural course of things many customers lose their memories, sicken, or simply die during their peregrinations, a contingency on which, O'Malley would not be surprised to learn, many count.

One afternoon Kathleen invited O'Malley down for a drink and expatiated on the difficulties of her trade.

"You know, the real problem isn't finding clients but tour guides. They burn out at an awfully stiff clip. None of them's ever stayed on after a single Magellan, for example."

"A Magellan?"

"Our sixty-day deluxe around-the-world cruise. To tell the truth, even a week's junket to London is too much for most of the twerps. The Agency's policy is to hire laid-off teachers, new college graduates, second-rate professors on sabbatical, that sort of person. They know a thing or two, are easy to train, and see a chance for cheap travel. They *come* cheap, but you wouldn't believe the whining messages I get from them as soon as they have to cope with an Alzheimer's lost in Istanbul or a heart attack in Douala or a broken hip in Tsinan."

"I can imagine," said O'Malley. "Of course Magellan himself, as I recall, didn't make it all the way around either."

"Really? I didn't know that." Kathleen laughed like someone with a good head for business. To her the clients were just fares, berths, seat and stateroom numbers, pathologies. Hearing her laugh was like grabbing a fistful of broken glass. O'Malley had shuddered and was impressed.

But, like so many men deeply affected by their mothers bending over skinned knees, O'Malley had the lifelong habit of taking wounds to women. In his forlorn and thus irrational state he convinced himself that Kathleen had enough of the woman about her that he could confide in her. Anyway, she would certainly offer him a cup of coffee.

"Haven't seen *you* around for a bit—just hold on," murmured Kathleen with her hand over the mouthpiece, then resumed in a voice of such professional suavity and opulence that O'Malley felt dirty and wretched before it, truly a serf in the Presence. "Certainly we understand, Mr. Demetriu. Your reservations will be cancelled at once and your refund will be in tomorrow's mail, don't worry about a thing." O'Malley noted the rather magisterial use of the passive voice, grammatically irresponsible but, in the mouth of the Countess Kathleen, sparkling with the brasswork of bureaucratic reassurance. "And may I offer you our condolences on your terribly sad loss? We deeply regret that you and Mrs. Demetriu will not be able to join us after all; however, if you should care to rebook at a later date, we are always at your service. As you may not be aware, we offer several tours especially designed for the recently bereaved. Yes, sir, that's right. Many of our clients have told us these journeys provided enormous solace to them. Yes? Yes, of course. Yes again, Mr. Demetriu. Yes, but of course men are always very much in demand. Yes. Very well, then, we'll look forward to hearing from you whenever you like, sir. Goodbye now, and once again, our condolences."

Kathleen hung up on the bereaved Mr. Demetriu and, resuming her normal voice, the brittle one, explained the obvious to O'Malley.

"Happens all the time, naturally. We never make any difficulties about refunds. They tell their friends."

"And how long before the survivors rebook?"

Kathleen gave a cynical little smile and sat back in her revolving chair. "Oh, about a week, usually—just as soon as the children are gone."

"How about a cup of coffee?"

"Oops, sorry. All out. I can offer you some herbal tea, though."

"Very appropriate. Paint is just pain with some tea afterwards."

Kathleen leapt from her machine-clogged workstation and hopped to it. "Oh dear," she said with glassy irony, "we aren't in very fine fettle this morning, are we?"

"Kathleen," said O'Malley, "how long would you say we've known each other?"

"Known? I wouldn't say we know all that much about each other."

"Just the essentials?"

"That you paint and I'm sapphic?"

"Oh, more than that, surely."

"Like what?"

"Well, for example, I know that for you time's money."

Kathleen settled the water on the hotplate and chuckled. "While for you, I suppose, money's time?"

O'Malley held out his empty palms. "So it is for all of us imbecile artists."

"You mean the true artists, the unsuccessful ones."

"I also know you enjoy finishing my thoughts for me."

"Apple cinnamon okay?"

"In my picture I'll immortalize you as Eve, handing out the forbidden apple cinnamon."

"I'd rather be Lilith. She was probably more interested in Eve than Adam."

Grey light streamed in the window but was overwhelmed by fluorescence. The telephone rang and Kathleen answered it. The water boiled.

As O'Malley poured the water over the aromatic teabag in a cup with "I ♣ Q" on it, he briefly speculated on the problems that would have arisen had Eve actually been homosexual and decided they would not have been appreciably worse than the ones that arose anyway. He understood Kathleen's aggressive banter in his own fashion; that is, as defensive aggression, each snappy riposte a little pre-emptive strike. With women, he figured, she would be altogether different. What he wanted was that Kathleen should be that way with him this morning, when he lacked the heart for playing Beatrice and Benedick or even Pat and Mike. Or did he truly want her sympathy at all? Playing for compassion is a weakness that, in natures like his, invariably revenges itself later on. No, he really wanted Kathleen's advice. Such a strapping, high-colored, clear-headed woman, a first-class businessperson, might actually have a useful idea. To hell with sympathy then.

As O'Malley paced to and fro trying to present his plight without whining, to lay out the facts without liquefying, Kathleen gradually moved her buttocks forward on her chair until they were about as much off as on. Rhythmically rotating the seat in an arc of 20°, she lay her hands on her knees with her elbows out, like a football coach about to explain the counter draw to a large and thick offensive guard. Sure enough, even before O'Malley had finished a story that, after all, didn't have much to it, Kathleen interrupted, inspired by the muse of liquidity perhaps, visibly warming to her idea even before she had begun to explain it.

"Look, O'Malley," she said with unconcealed excitement, herself looking beatifically beyond him toward the grey plateglass window, "how serious are you about this paint or die thing? I mean, do you *mean* it or is it just romantic popcorn and good posture?"

"Let me put it this way. I'm not going to clean any more stables for Pomerantz and his circle of plutocrats. I don't have any money, so in due time I'll be evicted and homeless. I won't go to my sister who, last time we were in touch, was moving to Alabama and told me I could move to Hell. But yes, the long and short is if I can't paint I don't want to live."

Thrilled, Kathleen moved a perilous three or four inches further forward on her seat. A ripple of excitement passed through her imposing green frame, as if the idea that had her in its fist were shaking.

4. Female

*M*aybe she was getting her period or coming down with a cold. It wasn't as though the cause didn't matter.

Female lay in bed feeling definitely out of sorts, even humiliated and alarmed, and this was because she believed in the mystery of dreams.

It was already nine o'clock and Ezra was long gone, of course. What was it he had said the other evening? That he loved letting her sleep, relished watching her in the morning because then he could see her truest face. No doubt Ezra believed that would please her, that bit about her truest face especially, but it didn't, not at all. The idea that her truest face lay naked and open to him when she could do nothing about it and, worse yet, when she herself would never be able to see it . . . But of course she could ask Ezra to take a Polaroid of her one morning. Would it be the same, though? And was it vanity or curiosity that made her want to see how he saw? What she examined in the bathroom mirror each morning was not, in her opinion, beautiful. No make-up, no nothing, just her, just a blank truth that would grow worse every year until Ezra found himself, as rich men do, another and younger female. And then what about these horrible dreams?

Female stretched her limbs and looked up into the gathered silk of the sumptuous four-poster, a shining sky of robin's-egg blue, such a long twenty years away from the mildewed ticking in the five-room house in the fetid flats outside of Mobile. But she was smart and good-looking and she got away, all this way away. Scholarship student, beauty queen, executive secretary; up, up and away and now she was Mrs. Pomerantz and mistress of a big house in cool, efficient Yankeeland, hooray. She was a happy, loved second wife, and maybe Ezra's last, if she could keep her looks and her wits. No, what do dreams mean beside such a solid bed? In fact, wasn't the dreadful dream already decomposing, already quite gone?

Female was indeed a beauty queen—"simply gorgeous," as Ezra's sister Phoebe perpetually put it, with that heavy stress on the *gorge*. "How's that *gorge*ous wife of yours!" She stood naked in the bathroom, still pleasantly humid from Ezra's morning shower, not unlike Mobile in late June, brushed her teeth, looked herself over in the wide mirror. Well, thirty and no sagging yet. Nipples still pinkish, flesh firm even on the upper thighs, knees smooth, complexion clear. Not so bad, after all. She gave herself a little smile before pushing her long blonde hair under the showercap, less narcissist than treasurer.

It was in the shower that the dream returned, or part of it, the part that took place in the shower. The third such dream this week! The dream was an outrage and Female felt the worst sort of indignation, the kind without any precise object. Pointless to blame *him*, however irresistible.

On her way to the kitchen she had to confront one of the pictures she used just to dislike but now found personally offensive. It was a big one of a white woman on a vast green plush couch, faceless, elongated like a piece of taffy. On the one extended arm the woman wore a vulgar red bracelet and her purple-gloved hand sharply outlined

210

in black—the hand of a two-bit Storyville whore—hung down into the very center of the picture, a fetish, a totem.

A curse on O'Malley and his lousy pictures, she said to herself, and resolved yet again to talk Ezra into getting the things off her walls. She despised O'Malley as worthless, aging, balding, coarse, unfashionable, parasitic, ungrateful, and judgmental. Anyway, he *looked* judgmental.

So why should she dream of coupling with him not only in her own shower stall but in all sorts of other places, in all sorts of ways? The dreams were so crude and explicit that, try as she might, Female couldn't convert them into some symbolic code for anything else. The only thing cryptic about them was their existence, a problem which her smattering of Freud could do nothing to alleviate.

What made them all the more exasperating was that in each of the dreams she should be the aggressor. For example, in the first she found herself seated in an expensive restaurant, the saloon of an old-fashioned hotel, the kind with terraces, mirrored columns, ormolu fixtures, and a string trio on a white dais. She was languishing at a table with six elderly women, all dowdy with lorgnettes and long strings of pearls. They seemed to be planning the complicated wedding of one of their daughters—perhaps Female was even the very daughter—when O'Malley swung into view, cutting among the long white tablecloths like a pirate ship in a polite marina. In the dream she rose up from the table and blocked his way, actually pushed her body up against his—oh, Female remembered it all too well—and whispered in his ear the suggestion that they repair to her room upstairs. She had even used the word *repair,* for the dream had a Victorian decor, not excluding her own complicated underthings. The bed was high and absurdly soft and none too wide, piled up with pillows and bolsters. He had made her howl.

The second dream began in an airport and moved to a motel; last night's started out on a beach and featured underwater scenes, something torrid in a cabana, and the aforementioned episode in her own shower. The consistent motifs were the crowd of unfamiliar, repellent people, her boredom and inanition, O'Malley's sudden appearance, her immediate and quite unlimited shamelessness in seducing him. And throughout each dream, each episode, each fabulous coital moment, he had remained silent, a tacit and virtually serene observer, detached and appraising.

To despise a man in daylight and consciousness and fornicate with him in the darkness when her imagination, like her face, could not be ordered was infuriating enough without having Ezra burble so uxoriously of truest selves.

No wonder Female tore so angrily at her bagel.

5. Letter

*t*he nerve. That's what gets me, his *gall.*"

"I think you should just take those pictures down and burn them, really I do."

"No, I mean it's really too much. It's blackmail. That's what it comes down to. It's as if he's saying we owe him a living and we'd better ante up or else. And even if we do. I mean it's in*sult*ing, as if all we cared about were money. Haven't I done more than right by him? Haven't I been his goddamned *pat*ron—his friend and confidant? Or so I thought. Hell, if I hadn't bought those two canvases he'd have starved months ago. Starved. And then I found him all those jobs. You know what I had to go through to talk Smyrnotte into letting him work on those apartments. And Smyrnotte's not somebody you like to owe a favor to, believe me. Ferocious. And he didn't much care for the way he talked to him either. Naturally, O'Malley doesn't understand how you should talk to a man like Smyrnotte. He's a baby, really. And now *this.*"

"You're right, honeybunch. He *is* a baby, a spoiled one. But he's also an ingrate and a lunatic. I've always tried to tell you—"

"A lunatic? You think so? Well, this sure as hell is a lunatic proposition. What really gets me is the way he tries to make it sound so businesslike. What a tone! Trading in *fu*tures, for God's sake. What's *he* know about futures or trading?"

"Nothing at all. Not the tiniest little thing."

"You know, I'm wondering who else got this letter. I mean I'm just wondering."

"I don't see it particularly matters. *No*body's going to fall for a crazy line like that."

"Don't be too sure, Female. Some collectors are pretty eccentric, and a lot of them are just greedy bastards."

"Fools, you mean."

"Some of them might not find it all that foolish."

"Oh come on, honey. I know how kind you've been to him, how encouraging, but face it. The man's a total failure. It's not like he's one of those intense and promising geniuses of twenty-one with lots of hair. I mean the man's past *fifty*. If he was ever going to make it, don't you think he'd have done it by now?"

"You really don't like his pictures?"

"Hate 'em."

"I didn't know. I'm really sorry. You never said. What was it? Didn't want to hurt my feelings?"

"He was your friend before you met me, Ezra."

"I just don't like to think we have any secrets, darling. Besides, this house is yours as much as it's mine. If you hated O'Malley's pictures you—"

"Now, now. A second wife needs to be even more tactful than a first one."

"Tact's one thing but . . . So, you never liked *him* either?"

"You couldn't tell?"

"Well, no."

"Of course I was always *polite.*"

"Look, I want to make a phone call."

"About this deranged letter of his?"

"I want to call Simon. I'm sure he'd have gotten one too. I just want to see what *he* thinks about it. I don't know, I don't want to be unfair or hasty. O'Malley's an artist, dear, somebody long on idealism and short on the material side of things. I mean Van Gogh never sold anything at all and then he went and blew his brains out in that cornfield, didn't he?"

"Don't be absurd, sweetie. O'Malley's no Van Gogh."

"What is it about him you don't like exactly?"

"Oh."

"No, I'd really like to know."

"Pretty much everything, I guess."

"You've got to understand. O'Malley was one of my projects, someone it gave me pleasure to help out. Besides, he represented something to me, the artistic side of myself, I guess. And I admired him, even looked up to him in a way as a sort of impractical older brother. We used to have these endless talks at his studio, oh three, four hours sometimes. I liked hearing him talk about things. You know once he went on for two hours straight about cars from the 40s. He had this book of photographs—the grills, the fenders. I learned from O'Malley. Artists teach us how to look at things."

"Even cars?"

"Yes, cars. And women! Could O'Malley ever talk about women."

"Their grills and fenders?"

"You really hate him?"

"Frankly, honey, I don't care enough to hate him."

Ezra huffed a bit and went off to his den to phone Simon, a sixtyish periodontist whom Female respected, thought a man who combined wit and a kind of gravity. Her own feelings were in disarray. She was irritated by her part in this conversation, knowing that she had not only failed to express the truth but had displeased Ezra too. As soon as he was out of the dining room, where she sat over her cold coffee, Female realized that he had wanted her to defend O'Malley, to be his advocate. Ezra thought in cliches: artists are visionaries but babies about money, while women are soft and need coddling but should always be sources of comfort and nurture. His shallowness was rather touching, really.

Ezra had left the astonishing letter itself on the table. He had read it to her aloud—indeed, at the top of his lungs—but now, sitting under the crystal chandelier in a privacy at the edges of which nipped her inadmissible and almost nightly dreams, she read it for herself.

At once she was startled to see that it was actually a form letter. She imagined O'Malley—a big man with a big fist—scribbling in Ezra's name after the *Dear.*

Dear Ezra,

As you have shown some prior interest in my work and as I am unwilling to persist in living without producing more of it, I am offering you the following proposition.

You are, of course, familiar with the trade in futures. This is such a proposition. If you and a sufficient number of other subscribers will deposit to my account the sum of $6000.00 as a tax-free gift, I will undertake to produce as many paintings as I can, consistent with my own standards of excellence, over the next two years. At the end of that time, always assuming an adequate response to this offer, I shall divide all the completed works on an equitable basis among the subscribers and commit suicide. If there should be an insufficient response, I will of course return the money of those who do subscribe. It might almost go without saying that, in such an event, I will simply do away with myself sooner rather than later. To arrive at the sum of $6000.00 I have calculated my needs most carefully. My budget includes no extravagances.

This is a straightforward business proposition whose advantages I should like briefly to highlight. First, works of art are commodities whose value is subject to supply and demand. However, in certain respects, art is a special case. For example, too great a scarcity may actually depress rather than increase prices. The work of an artist who produces too few first-class pieces is unlikely ever to earn top dollar simply because not enough of it will appear in distinguished collections. Curators and collectors are human beings and, as such, are profoundly influenced by the judgments of others. What several collections have, others will, in due course, crave also. Though I have produced a considerable body of work in various styles, I am now at the height of what I may with confidence call my final period, the products of which, if only there are enough of them, I believe will someday be the most valued of my oeuvre. Consequently, the potential return to you on the relatively small investment I am requesting stands to be considerable.

Second, it is not at all uncommon that the work of an artist should rise steeply in price upon his death for the simple reason that the world is assured there will be no more of it. I need hardly stress, moreover, the effects on prices of the work of an artist the manner of whose demise attracts notoriety.

I will be expecting your reply by February 1 at the latest. With thanks for your consideration, I assure you I am,

Most Earnestly,
D. O'Malley

Female put down the letter and experienced a sudden and unambiguous impulse to comfort and to nurture D. O'Malley. It was quite a sharp pang. As this pang originated somewhere near her lower colon, she quickly convinced herself it must be gas.

6. Simon

*h*e removed from the bottom drawer of his bureau a large formal photograph of his dead wife. He had commissioned one of his grateful patients, a well-known society photographer, to take this picture for him shortly after his wife left the hospital for the last time and came home to die. Fortunately for Dr. Solomon, who had difficulty in asking the favor, the photographer was also familiar with the nineteenth-century custom of memorial photography and did not hesitate to agree. "After what you've done to save my poor teeth," he had said, "anything." And so they had arranged matters that, as soon as Cecilia breathed her last, Simon would call the photographer's answering machine, leaving a coded message: "That time of year thou mayst in me behold." Cecilia died within two days, at 6:15, her normal dinner time, and she was memorialized at 9:30. Without too much difficulty, Simon had dressed her in the gown she had worn at their daughter's wedding two years before. The undressing at 10 had proved a wrestlers' agon.

The photographer was all discretion of course, and this photograph was a secret. Simon seldom looked at it, but was glad of its existence. He had several albums full of family pictures which he looked over from time to time and willingly opened up for friends, albums that his children and grandson sweetly pored over whenever they visited, but this one picture was just for his eyes. It seemed to give his happy married life a kind of completeness that didn't so much satisfy him as allow him to proceed through his widowhood with a certain unalterable equanimity. His many friends, all good twentieth-century folk, would have been shocked to know of the existence of such a thing, though little more than a lifetime ago such photographs were commonplace. It is because death has changed, thought Simon. Death too has its history. Why shouldn't it?

Dr. Solomon proved as popular as a widower as he had always been while married: well off, cheerful, polite, witty, solid, with two successful children at opposite ends of the country. He was likable through and through. As is so often the case, what attracted people about Dr. Solomon was a quality more felt than named. This was his air of judiciousness, of genuine wisdom, like his namesake's. One of his old friends even called him Solomon the Wise from time to time and in a manner less mocking than ironically deferential.

The truth was that Simon was indeed the unusually thoughtful man he appeared to be, one whose detailed knowledge of the afflictions of the human gum did not corrupt his broad and humane view of life. He bore his sorrows inwardly and maintained a keen interest in everything around him. He was a talented amateur of many disciplines and people who met him at dinner parties, of which he went to several dozen a year, were frequently surprised by how much this aged dentist knew about their own fields, for he made it a rule never to speak of his own.

It was at a dinner party thrown by his young colleague Bernoulli that Simon Solomon met Ezra Pomerantz, with whom he had a brief conversation about painting, about which Simon knew roughly a thousand times more than Ezra. This conversation led Ezra to inveigle Simon into visiting his great friend O'Malley's studio. Here, to the latter's surprise, he found some excellent work by an artist of true spirit. That very afternoon he actually purchased a comparatively small painting, a wintry, dusky cityscape in shades of blue with characteristic slashes of red and purple. O'Malley had managed a particularly inspired treatment of the streetlamps. Somehow he had contrived to show that they had only just come on, making his picture a perfect portrait not only of a specific place but of a precise and poetic time. The picture appealed deeply to Simon as if it were the likeness of some remote yet sharp memory of his own, the moment when he had first grasped to the fullest what is dusk, what is winter, what is city.

What prompted Simon to take out the memorial photograph of his dead wife—of his wife dead—was O'Malley's letter. Unlike Ezra Pomerantz, whose phone call he had dismissed brusquely, Simon understood O'Malley's proposition was no confidence trick, that the death of the body alone closed out a wife's calendar of pain, an artist's futile days.

"Are you so sure we *don't* owe him a living?" he had said taking up Pomerantz's asinine cliché. "After all, it's through artists that we speak to one another. That's worth a great deal." As if Pomerantz would understand the paradox of the artist's altruistic selfishness, that it is through this almost childish insistence on doing exactly as he chooses that the species addresses itself to each individual and the generations discover a common tongue. That O'Malley's appeal was framed in such clumsy terms only proved the gap between his condition and the ruthless economy in which he needed to participate if he were to execute his purpose. Of course one could agree that it was a crudely romantic gesture, not especially becoming in a man of O'Malley's years. And yet, thought Simon as he sat on his bed and held tight his own memento mori, a man of O'Malley's age could pretty well calculate how few years were left.

"I'll tell you," Simon had said sharply, "if I had his talent and were in his fix, I believe I'd do exactly the same. He'll certainly get my six thousand, Mr. Pomerantz. You will, of course, do as you think best. Good night."

7. Posing

*i*n so far as the stiffness of his years permitted, O'Malley bounced out of bed at seven these early spring days. No more hiding among the bedclothes for him, no more hibernation. It was astonishing how quickly the long-buried rhythms of his salad days reasserted themselves. He had even resumed listening to the news on the radio over breakfast and dinner, half-hour-length arms of planetary concern embracing the capacious waist of private labors that he often danced joyously into the decreasingly dark evenings. Winter had come, but spring wasn't far behind. So what if there were more hairs stuck in his brush or his back ached all the time. His body felt well used. A freshening wind had blown the stale air out of his soul:

> Make me thy lyre, even as the forest is:
> What if my leaves are falling like its own!

At around ten on most weekdays—though to him all days were now gloriously interchangeable—he would go down the stairs to drink a cup of coffee with the Countess Kathleen, his redeemer. O'Malley's somewhat extravagant gratitude moved Kathleen less than the success of her plan. We always feel warmly towards those we have helped, especially if the help is effective and costs us little, and so Kathleen now looked on her neighbor as a friend. She became less defensive with him and more confiding and found she enjoyed his company. She even tried to express an interest in his work, though both quickly learned this was a pointless civility. Kathleen didn't care at all about painting. Her cultural tastes ran to bestselling novels, salacious biographies, the popular music of her college days, and televised sports. She often talked about football, once she discovered that O'Malley, though not a fan, had been a player in college.

"That's actually how I became a painter," he told her one morning. "Because of football."

"Really?"

"Well, I'd always loved to draw. Football got me my scholarship and the coach told me I could major in any damned thing I wanted just so long as I didn't miss practice or lose my eligibility. I took a lot of ribbing about it. Linemen aren't supposed to be artists, are they. Yep, lots of jokes about life class."

"Life class? What's that?"

"The one where you draw the models. Mostly women, mostly nude."

"And I wasted my time with sociology!"

"That's what half the team majored in."

"Now don't be nasty."

O'Malley was with Kathleen when Female pulled up in her red BMW. Kathleen, who faced the window, saw her first.

"My God!" she cried. "What's this?"

O'Malley turned.

"This is the second wife of one of my subscribers."

"Yum."

Though she was not in her finery, only jeans, a sweater, an open leather jacket, Female did indeed look as appetizing as, say, a shrimp cocktail.

"I wasn't expecting to be checked up on," said O'Malley as he went to the window and motioned for Female to come in.

"Female Pomerantz, Kathleen Reilly."

Female advanced through the cluttered office like a trim thirty-foot yacht, leaving a fragrant wake of shampoo and Shalimar. She hove to beside O'Malley.

"Pleased to meet you," she said quickly.

Kathleen, already on her feet, stepped forward and held out her hand.

Female took it but without either alacrity or interest.

"Here to see me?" O'Malley asked. "It's my coffee break."

"Artists get coffee breaks?"

"Good ones do."

"Boastful ones anyway," Kathleen quipped. Female ignored her.

"I was just on my way back up," said O'Malley uncertainly. "Did you want to—"

"Fine," said Female with finality, then turned to Kathleen. "Goodbye. So nice to have met you," she said chillingly.

"I love your accent," Kathleen added almost desperately.

"Thank you," said Female, her back already turned.

Kathleen went after her. "Such an unusual name, Female."

"My mother was confused."

"Pardon me?"

Female turned on Kathleen. "On the birth certificate. She wrote down my sex where she was supposed to write my name."

More embarrassed than amused, O'Malley ushered Female toward the stairway and threw a rueful look back at the nonplussed Kathleen.

"Sorry if I seemed rude to your friend. I don't like lesbians," said Female unapologetically on the stairs.

"How'd you know?" O'Malley asked foolishly and was answered with the silence he deserved.

The door was tricky and O'Malley had to bull it open. Xenia sat cross-legged, contented, and invisible in the middle of the bed, nearly of an age with Female by now, all her fine curves restored, an elusive pinkness just dusted over all four cheeks. Her eyes were closed. She was deep in her afternoon meditation.

Female entered slowly, placing rather than stepping with her new boots. "It was different when I was here with Ezra," she said when she reached the middle of the studio. She put her hands on her hips and revolved her torso, looking around, doing an exercise.

"I wasn't working then," O'Malley explained.

"You mean you weren't painting. Ezra found you plenty of work."

O'Malley went to his easel, nervously rearranged his brushes. "That wasn't work. That's what any dunderhead can do."

Female was challenging. "So what was it then?"

220

"Breadwinning." O'Malley shrugged toward the canvas on his easel. "This is work."

"You think Ezra's a dunderhead?"

"Not a very fair question. Besides, Ezra wins a *lot* of bread, doesn't he?"

"Oh yes, quite a lot. Which is why I'm here. Ezra wants some of the bread he's given you to take the form of a portrait of me."

"He never mentioned it."

"Because I told him not to."

"Then you prefer not to be painted? I mean by me?"

"I haven't decided. I'm here to decide. Look, can I sit down?"

O'Malley rushed to his one proper chair, a big ugly club in yellow leather, smeared and maculate with old paint. It faced his easel. He quickly cleared off the three shirts, two books, and the cigar box that prevented Female from sitting, then he gave a mock flourish and bowed.

O'Malley could hardly help being aware that Female detested him. He had felt it the first time he met her, back in his days of bondage. Pomerantz had asked him over to work on the upstairs plumbing just after they returned from the three-week honeymoon. Female took one look at him kneeling and grunting under the bathroom sink, said she hoped he'd be finished soon, then commanded Pomerantz to take her to the mall. O'Malley's feelings about her were hardly positive. The fact was Female intimidated him. She was too good looking. Hers was not the kind of beauty he loved, only the sort other men might collect. Pomerantz, for instance. It was just the same as with paintings. There are always pictures an artist admires but will walk miles to avoid looking at, pictures that are, so to speak, bad for his talent, pictures that will sleekly condescend only to be appreciated—or rather, appraised.

"I'd like to know how you'd paint me."

"Oh, in my late manner." Half evasion, half joke.

"I mean how would you *pose* me. Would you, for instance, stretch me out like that poor faceless creature on our living room wall?"

O'Malley rubbed his chin, noting that he had neglected to shave that morning, and tried overcompensating for his fear of Female.

"That wasn't a portrait, actually. No, if I were to do a portrait of you—and I haven't said I would—I'd naturally aim at capturing your character. I'd want to do what no photograph could."

Female blushed, she supposed at his impertinence. Save for the complete absence of eroticism, this scene was growing to resemble one of her persistent dreams. She felt aggressive and humiliated at once. But she was there for a reason.

"Tell me, would capturing my character require me to take my clothes off?"

O'Malley hadn't expected to hear such a thing and, for a moment, thought he must have affronted her. The truth was that he was dying for her to go away and leave him in peace.

"No, no of course not. In fact, the clothes would be an essential feature."

Female sensed that her advantage lay in sexual threat and couldn't resist pressing it. "Then you don't believe my character is well expressed through my body?" She waved her hand from her breast down to her knee.

"Excuse me. I'm afraid I don't understand. I've been painting more or less non-stop for over a month. Sometimes I become a little detached from things, a little disoriented. What is it we're actually talking about?"

"You don't seem particularly detached to me, O'Malley. It's quite simple. We're discussing whether you'll paint my portrait, which is what my husband wants. It's understood that neither you nor I have agreed to anything as yet." At which point Female uncrossed and recrossed her scissorlike legs. "I'd just like to know how you'd go about a portrait *if* you were to do it and *if* I wanted it done, that's all. I hope you'll be quite frank with me. I can see how very busy you are and wouldn't like to waste your time. I know how precious it is."

O'Malley scratched his head, fondled his bald patch. "Oh, what the hell," he said like the condemned man he was. "I'd *love* to paint you in the nude. Anyway, isn't that what Ezra is hoping for?"

"No."

"No?"

"Certainly not."

"Well then."

Female paused a moment, looked around, and then, almost to her surprise, replied, "But it is what *I* was hoping for."

Quite suddenly Female looked to O'Malley like some impenetrable metaphysical poem, whereas he had always taken her for an idiotic catalogue of overpriced fashions. "You'd pose for me then?"

"Yes."

"But if Ezra—"

"No need for Ezra to know."

O'Malley was overwhelmed. "You'd keep it a secret?"

"It would be a surprise for him. For his birthday, let's say, or maybe Thanksgiving."

O'Malley began to laugh so hard that he staggered against his poor easel.

An instant later Female also laughed and then everything loosened up like a magician's false knot. Over on the bed, Xenia blinked and stretched.

"Come on, O'Malley. Tell me your theory about sex and painting. Ezra tells me you've got one. You can give me a lecture while I get out of these things."

O'Malley gulped and chuckled at the same time, chuckled at the sheer nonsense of the cosmos and at Ezra Pomerantz. "All right," he said. "My theory is very elementary, or you might say elemental. For me, sexuality and painting are inconceivable except in terms of each other. To a painter flesh is canvas and pigment, and vice versa; even landscapes—trees, lakes—are flesh. That Freudian crap about art being sublimation is, in my opinion, standing things on their head—"

"What are you staring at, O'Malley?"

"I mean it's just the other way around. Art takes the sublime, the idea, and incarnates it. The painter is, in the deepest sense, a carnal creature."

"The deepest sense? Penis as paintbrush? I'm getting the picture. Have you got a blanket or something? It's a little chilly."

O'Malley tore the blanket from his bed, only slightly disturbing Xenia who merely rocked to and fro like a buoy on a tidal swell. He then resumed his position by the easel, a lecturer at his podium.

"It's not altogether simple, though. Sexually, painting and painters are of two types. Masturbatory and coital."

"For example?"

"Oh, Mondrian and Monet or Manet and Modigliani."

"Most alliterative. How about Picabia and Picasso?"

"Brava! Excellent! I'm impressed. The distinction lies, of course, in

the painter's orientation toward the subject. Take a peach, for instance. The masturbatory painter never seeks to bite into it. He doesn't
want to penetrate the peach, which is not to say he's merely superficial
or purely mental. On the contrary, certain masturbatory painters can
achieve amazing revelations."

"A peach by Cézanne?"

"Why not? The gratification is his and then ours, but it's not the juicy
satisfaction we get out of Chardin or Van Gogh. Now Vermeer you can't
really tell about. Who wouldn't kill for such balance! But take a really
whole-hearted coital painter like Turner. Turner could screw an entire
ocean!"

Female, well wrapped up, was enjoying herself tremendously. Already she felt that she could see better, think more clearly, breathe
deeper, as though her dreams of O'Malley had woven a screen between
her and the world.

"And O'Malley? Which one is he?" she asked pertly.

"It appears we're going to find out."

8. Masterpieces

*L*ook at it, Xenia, just look. A canvas like this, what would you say
it's like?"

"An empty swimming pool into which you're about to dive. The
emptiness of the universe a second before everything begins. A new-
born about to draw her first breath. A white whale."

"I can't remember being this happy."

"Uh huh."

"You too?"

"Mmm hmm. Now, suppose we get started with the charcoal."

"I'm a little scared. It *is* scary, making that dive."

"If you dive properly the water always turns up."

"I know, but look—my hand's actually shaking."

"And you're thinking of hanging yourself?"

"To tell you the truth, doing this painting and hanging myself aren't
all that different."

"Is that a pun?"

"No, I didn't mean it that way. I mean, when you come to execute your crowning work, should you know it? Is that healthy? It's not the sweating blood I'm afraid of, Xenia. It's something else. I don't know what."

"All right. Sit down and steady your nerves. You need to relax, breathe deeply. Look, I'll tell you a story."

"A story?"

"The story of Master Barrildo de Huesca, which may even inspire you. Unfortunately, as the story's so old, there's some confusion about it. I'm familiar with two versions, but there are many more."

O'Malley drew back from the vast, newly stretched canvas that awaited *What It's Like To Be Me* (alternatively, the more valedictory *To Be Me: What It Was Like*), retreated all the way to the club chair. Xenia, looking decidedly ripe, even middle-aged, composed herself on the bed in lotus position and began her tale.

"One Sunday morning in the year 1521, the painter Don Barrildo, the pride and also the bane of the town of Huesca, an artist at once revered for his transcendent treatment of religious subjects yet reviled for his libertinism, walked down the nave of the cathedral just as the priest was about to start the Offertorium. All the good Catholics of Huesca, their reales clutched in their hands, turned to look at Barrildo. The priest himself fell silent. Barrildo marched directly up to the altar where, as nobody failed to note, he did not kneel. On the contrary, he pulled himself up as straight as a cedar tree, looked beyond the great altar-piece which he had himself executed a decade before and pronounced a terrible vow. In his own style, which was blunt to the point of rudeness, he said, 'I am going to paint the greatest picture in the Old World or the New. I hereby swear it.'

"What prompted Don Barrildo to such a rash and arrogant oath can only be guessed at. Perhaps he wanted to prove himself to his muse, O'Malley, or maybe it was a deliberate act of sacrilege, a personal protest against the vile atrocities of the Holy Office, as the Inquisition was then at its height. Perhaps he only wanted to scandalize his fellow citizens of Huesca of whom he is supposed to have had a low opinion. Barrildo is also said to have offended the Dominicans more than once by contrasting the high culture of the Moors and Jews with the low one of the Christians. Maybe his was a purely personal vow, something between him and God, a vow made to provoke himself into an act to which he didn't feel equal and Barrildo made it as public as possible so as to engage his own pride, which is said to have been fierce even by Spanish standards.

"In any case, once he had made his extraordinary pronouncement, Don Barrildo turned on his heel and left the church. There was much whispering among the congregants and more than one voice was raised against Barrildo there and then, but the priest held up his hand and silenced everyone. 'Vengeance is mine, saith the Lord. God forbid that anything should distract you, my dear children, from the holy sacrament you are about to receive.' The people dutifully lowered their heads and said 'Amen.' The offertory baskets were passed around and the mass went forward. But there was uneasiness in the town from that day and people remembered what the priest had said. Barrildo was, as I mentioned, the town's chief glory and for the sake of his talent a good deal had been swept under the rug, including an affair that landed a young noblewoman in a convent. But this vow of his in the cathedral was something else again, a provocation so brazen that people became frightened of Barrildo as they might of a demon or, for that matter, an angel. As for Don Barrildo, he responded in kind and soon stopped coming into town altogether.

"Barrildo had an old housekeeper named Jacinta. Some of the ignorant peasants considered her a witch, but she was really just an old gossip. It was this Jacinta who kept the people of Huesca informed about what Don Barrildo was up to, which may have proved his undoing.

"'The Master has set up a canvas as high as the walls of Don Alonso Fuentes's castle in Merida,' she would say; and, as nobody in Huesca had ever been to Merida to see this castle of Don Alonso's, her hyperbole seemed the more impressive. 'Just think! The Master is painting everything on the earth,' Jacinta would boast to her cronies at the marketplace, 'all the pigs and lions and gryffins, and every kind of tree you ever heard of, and also more people of every estate than there are in all of Aragon and Castile!' And more than half the people more than half believed her. Each week Jacinta would add something to the fabulous canvas—sea monsters, the nine ranks of angels in heaven, the Holy Family, all the popes from Saint Peter himself down to Leo X, the pit of Pandemonium, Balaam's ass.

"With nothing but Jacinta's tall tales to go on, the notion soon got about the Don Barrildo had finally overreached himself, had gone beyond what was properly human, that his great painting was nothing short of an attempt to rival the work of the Creator Himself. The fearsome word 'heresy' began to be heard in the streets of Huesca and again the people trembled to recall the priest's words about God's vengeance. Whenever Barrildo was mentioned, people crossed themselves.

"In the tavern one marketday, the miller Longo, who had been drinking more than a little, at last said aloud what was troubling so many minds, namely that when it arrived the vengeance of God might not be so discriminating as to fall exclusively on the head of Don Barrildo but might well consume all of Huesca.

"News of what the miller had said reached Jacinta, who was terrified by it. According to most versions of the story, she ran home to Barrildo to tell him what was being said about him, but he just laughed at her. It is very probable, incidentally, that Jacinta had never even seen Barrildo's masterpiece and that all her extravagant stories had been made up out of whole cloth. It was Don Barrildo's custom to keep his studio under lock and key; he was never known to show a single picture until it was completed. One can imagine the hysterical Jacinta shouting through the locked door at her master, pounding on the door even, as he laughed and went on with his work.

"What happened next is not quite definite. According to the official version recorded by the Bishop of Zaragosa, Don Barrildo's house and everything in it, including the painter himself, was consumed by a fire of divine origin, so that whatever Barrildo's masterpiece really was nobody ever saw it."

"And what's the *other* version?" mocked O'Malley, deeply attracted by this fairy tale and chiefly by the heroic character of Don Barrildo, whom he saw as a sort of artistic Don Juan Tenorio.

"The other version," said Xcnia with her eyes cast down, "is that Don Barrildo hanged himself after setting fire to his house."

"That's a bit more interesting," said O'Malley. "Did he do it before or after finishing his picture?"

"How could anybody know that?" said Xenia teasingly. "As I said, there are all sorts of rumors and legends that attach themselves to a story like this."

"Such as?"

"Oh, you can pretty well imagine, I guess. There's the obvious explanation that the superstitious people of Huesca, perhaps egged on by the local clergy, burned the house down themselves. Another view is that there never was any painting at all, that Don Barrildo, overwhelmed by the task he had set himself, was incapable of even starting on it and so he destroyed himself out of sheer frustration and self-loathing."

"And you think this story is inspiring?"

"There's another opinion too."

"Oh?"

"Of course. There are always more versions of a story like Don Barrildo's. In this view Barrildo indeed finished his great painting, rolled up the vast canvas, stowed it in a wagon, and one night escaped from Huesca after setting fire to his own house."

"In that case, what became of the masterpiece? I've never even heard of this Master Barrildo de Huesca."

Xenia looked straight at O'Malley, smiling like La Giaconda. "How about picking up that charcoal ? We don't have forever, you know."

9. Midnight

*i*n the middle of December Dr. Solomon's family more or less compelled him to celebrate his seventieth birthday. They simply showed up, unannounced, at his office, one at a time, son, daughter, son-in-law and grandson, nephew and nephew's wife, like so many bright scarves turned out of a magician's sleeve. Simon thought he had endured it fairly well. At least he did not have to dissimulate too much; the surprise and pleasure he felt at seeing everyone were authentic enough. And he made the customary deprecating sounds when everybody assured him, also one at a time, that he didn't look sixty. His own quite objective opinion was that he looked about sixty-one. But surprises of this sort—which really ought to be happy endings—leave too much time to be filled by anticlimax. The burden inevitably falls on the surprised one to maintain the energy level, to keep up his grinning and draw out his joy, everyone else feeling they have done their share—or, as his son used to say, shot their wad.

The kids really had seen to everything. They had arranged with Mrs. Kisleff, his faithful receptionist, to reschedule all his appointments for the following two days, made dinner reservations at Pigalle no less, and invited three of his oldest pals. Above all, they gave him the gift of themselves for an exhausting four-day weekend during which they freely interrogated him about such dispiriting matters as retirement and what plans he had laid for his imminent decrepitude. By Sunday he was not displeased to see them go, the dears.

It was this on the whole lugubrious celebration that led Simon to entertain for the first time the notion of some sort of "extended vacation," so often a euphemism for interminable unemployment. The idea of travelling appealed to him, and not only because it meant liberation from the anxieties of his children. He and Cecilia had taken some very satisfactory, if brief, trips to Europe, through the national parks with the kids, to some island or other in the Caribbean, even to Washington for the cherry blossoms. However, they had never been on a cruise. Cecilia, having crossed a choppy Channel in her teens, remained terrified of seasickness ever after. To Simon, on the other hand, an aficionado of Melville and Conrad, the images conjured up by the word involved a ship in the Pacific, entailed that dreamy iconographic come-on from a song of his distant youth: I'd like to get you on a slow boat to China. The operant word was slow.

So, when his young colleague Dr. Bernoulli began to brag one day in the manner of the generous son about the cruise on which he intended to send his mother for *her* seventieth birthday, when he extolled the meticulous arrangements of this grand tour especially designed for well fixed Americans of a certain age, Simon allowed himself to dwell on some rather enticing images. He even asked Bernoulli to lend him the brochure.

There was something familiar about the address on this document which Simon could not immediately place. It bothered him. As a library might file away a request for a book and inform the applicant of its availability well after he has forgotten asking for it, so Simon's mind made the connection two days later in the middle of a delicate gum graft. When he got home, he found O'Malley's letter and checked the return address against the brochure. And this is how he came to visit O'Malley, about whom he had thought only at long intervals over the previous year.

Simon had never seriously credited O'Malley's intention to commit suicide, though he was scarcely the man to hold the threat against a talented and sympathetic artist. Nevertheless, this coincidence affected him strangely, as if it were a reminder of some obligation he had been neglecting. Who knows, he said to himself. Maybe he *was* serious. And if that's the case, surely it's my duty to prevent it. Though it was irrational to think that O'Malley meant what he had written, much less that fate had laid on him the task of forestalling it, Simon was unable to shake the feeling, especially after he re-read the absurd letter. The two years of the contract were nearly up. Simon, with his literary turn of mind, found himself musing about Cinderella and the miller's daughter in *Rumpelstiltskin,* those two bargainers with forbidden powers. He thought also of Faustus and the expiration of his blood contract, the gaping of that terrible trapdoor in the middle of the stage, the tremendous final speech:

> Stand still, you ever-moving spheres of heaven,
> That time may cease and midnight never come . . .
> O I'll leap up to my God! Who pulls me down?
> See, see, where Christ's blood streams in the firmament!
> . . .
> O soul, be changed into little water drops
> And fall into the ocean, ne'er be found.

Simon actually went and looked it up.

On the following Monday Simon cleared his schedule and shortly after nine o'clock parked his Buick in the slush in front of O'Malley's building, likewise the office of the Golden Age Travel Agency, which could scarcely have inspired the confidence expressed by Bernoulli. He went straight upstairs.

O'Malley, in a bulky blue sweater, a pair of chinos, laceless desert boots, and a three-day beard, opened the door after some delay and squinted suspiciously at Simon, who had to introduce himself.

"I'm Simon Solomon, remember? Ezra Pomerantz brought me here once? I bought a picture. I'm one of your backers."

O'Malley straightened his back and drew his hand across his mouth. "What is it? You want to see if I'm really going to do it, is that it?"

Simon answered slowly and with a broad smile, as one might talk to a growling dog. "Mr. O'Malley, believe me, just the contrary."

"What the hell," said O'Malley and threw open the door.

The studio was a shambles. Xenia, invisible and looking old, sat on one of the two wooden chairs at O'Malley's narrow table, wrapped in a shawl like Whistler's mother, peering out the dirty window toward the turnpike. The easel was empty but there were canvases everywhere, at least two dozen of them and of every size, all leaning against walls or flat on the floor with only their backs showing. Simon's attention was drawn to one on account of its colossal size. It had the longest wall all to itself.

"Gracious," he said, "that one's enormous."

O'Malley didn't respond. He seemed spent, exhausted. In fact, he collapsed into the yellow club chair.

Simon whistled in admiration. "You did all these in two years?"

"One year and ten months. Haven't touched a brush in three weeks."

Simon knew better than to ask to see any of the pictures. They were backside out for a reason. O'Malley's condition was evidently precarious. He looked wretched.

"You all right?" Simon asked.

"I've got a cold."

Simon walked up and down in front of O'Malley, holding his shoulders. "It's cold in here."

O'Malley looked up. "I'm going to, you know."

Simon thought for a moment. "Mr. O'Malley, may I ask you something?"

O'Malley shrugged his permission.

"Do you still want to paint? I'm asking this because your letter made it clear that two years ago you wanted nothing more than to paint. Now, I can see that you've been working at an astonishing rate all this time. Couldn't it be that you're just tired out, that you need a rest?"

"No. I'm finished. Nothing left at all. I'm like one of those salmon who fight their way up the dams to spawn and then die not the little but the great big death. You understand?"

"So then, you *want* to kill yourself?"

"I'm saying it doesn't matter."

"Yes, but do you want to be *dead*, Mr. O'Malley? Seeing no more green fields, hearing no more string quartets or dirty jokes?"

O'Malley shrugged. "Anyway, a promise is a promise."

"Don't be flippant," said Simon sternly. "I'm not a young man to be talked to flippantly about death. And neither, with respect, are you."

O'Malley sat up a little straighter and began to examine Simon. "What are you doing here? Come to pick out your pictures or what?"

"Have I asked to see them?"

"So?"

"I don't know why I'm here exactly. Or rather, I'm here because of a coincidence."

To Simon's surprise, O'Malley perked up. "Coincidence! Oh yes, they're queer things, aren't they? Always seem to mean something. Since there's no meaning without form, whenever we stumble over something with form we look for a meaning in it. You've noticed that?"

Simon nodded.

"Here's one for you. I just found out my sister's living on the same block in Alabama where Pomerantz's wife grew up. Very strange, but does it signify anything?"

"I don't see why it should. But you're right, of course. Coincidence is, well, it's literary. When we encounter a coincidence it makes us look at the world as if it were a book, for a moment or two anyway. And then everything dissolves back into ordinary confusion or routine—too little order or too much. Modern people are inclined to believe in routine more than coincidence, which may be what makes them modern."

"You're a philosopher?"

Simon smiled. "Close enough, I guess. A dentist."

"Here," said O'Malley getting to his feet. "I'm being rude. Please sit down."

"Oh no—"

"No, I insist." And O'Malley rushed across the room to get one of his wooden chairs; fortunately, it was the one without Xenia on it.

"To be honest," he said, throwing a leg over the chair, "I don't know what to do with myself." His tone was now nearly confidential but also wholly self-absorbed. "I mean I'm cleaned out. Occupation's gone, not to mention the cash. And all this stuff's bespoke. I've been sitting here for days, sneezing, eating, crapping, inert as a slag heap. Do I have to die, just because I don't feel like living?"

This time Simon shrugged. "If the world's a book," he said musingly, "then we die when we're meant to, and also how we're meant to. Your letter now, that was certainly a plot. You wanted desperately to paint, so you invented a story—not entirely original perhaps, but not unimpressive either. However, maybe your plot was part of some other story. Have you considered that?"

"Wheels within wheels? I don't believe it's proper for a dentist to be a mystic. You've gone and upset my prejudices, and before lunch too."

There was a knock at the door. Shave and a haircut, two bits.

"What time is it?" asked O'Malley.

Simon looked at his watch. "Ten past ten."

O'Malley got up and headed for the door. "Then that'll be Kathleen. Wonderful woman. She runs the place downstairs."

"You don't say. But that's my coincidence. I was thinking of signing up for one of their cruises."

"Kathleen'll be delighted. Business's been a little off lately."

Kathleen came in bearing a steaming cup.

"Cuppa joe, Joe?" she said in a chirpy, nurse-like voice.

"I've got a guest, Kathy. Dr. Solomon, the famous mystical dentist and connoisseur."

Simon got to his feet.

"A dentist? Nice to meet you anyway," said Kathleen rudely.

"A pleasure, anyway," answered Simon and shook her hand almost as firmly as she shook his.

"I think you might talk him into an ocean voyage," O'Malley said.

"No way. At the Golden Age rules is rules. You've got to be at least seventy to get on our cruises and this dentist can't be over forty."

Simon laughed. "Seventy on the nose and proud of it."

"No, I don't believe it!"

"Where do I sign."

O'Malley took the coffee from Kathleen and offered it to Simon, who shook his head. O'Malley drank greedily.

"Well," said Kathleen with a sigh.

O'Malley gulped. "Dr. Solomon's a backer, a man of discernment as well as occult wisdom. As you can see, he's to be respected. Kathleen here's a woman of spirit, Doctor. She's the one who suggested that letter."

"I see," said Simon, raising his eyebrows.

"Oh, but he's serious," said Kathleen. "You can see that, just look at him. A perfect garret-starver. Won't let me do a thing for him."

O'Malley, offended by this third-person status, shuffled toward the window, flopped on his bed.

"Has he let you see any of them?" Kathleen whispered.

Simon shook his head.

"Me either." She pulled a long face. "Look," she said aloud, "I've got to get right back. It's just that O'Malley usually comes down for a cup at ten."

"You see, Doctor, routine," said O'Malley from the bed. "The turnpike out there's a monument to it, all those Pomerantzy ruts."

"If it's all right, I'll stop by in a few minutes and we'll talk seriously about that cruise," said Simon.

"At your service if you're not lying shamelessly about your age," said Kathleen, waved, and left.

O'Malley, still supine, surprised Simon. "Could I ask you to look at one of these pictures, Doctor?" His tone was grave.

"I'd be privileged."

"If you could just give me a hand?"

And so Simon Solomon was the first to see *What It Was Like To Be Me*, O'Malley's massive chef d'oeuvre, which was completely fitting as he was shortly to become its owner.

An hour later Simon signed up for the deluxe Magellan around-the-world cruise for superannuated singles. Between them he and Kathleen decided that O'Malley would make a superb tour guide.

10. Magellan

C rowlike, Mrs. Bernoulli perched on her usual deck chair and cawed away to Mrs. Wisnewski about the food, the humidity, about O'Malley and her pidgin-spouting steward, even about her son whom she had idiotically let talk her into this nightmare. Mrs. Wisnewski tried to cheer her companion up with a few ineffectual phrases. "Oh," she said, "you're exaggerating, my dear" and "I thought the veal rather good." However, before long she succumbed to the dreary insight that here was another of those old women whose chief pleasure lay in complaints into which they poured the residue of their vitality. As she had not come halfway around the world to waste her time with such women but precisely to get away from them, Mrs. Wisnewski quickly excused herself and headed for the pool.

Simon Solomon was enjoying his regular morning stroll around the deck with Mr. and Mrs. Chen, two retired academics of boundless charm. Their friendship had begun the first night of the cruise when the three found themselves seated at the same table and Simon had humorously pardoned them for being married. Rules were not always rules for the Golden Age Travel Agency, it seemed, and Simon was delighted with the result. Mr. Chen had been a professor of physics, Mrs. Chen a lecturer in East Asian history.

"With the two of you I feel like Mark Twain with Rudyard Kipling," Simon was saying.

"And how's that, Simon?" asked Mrs. Chen.

"You know everything and I know the rest."

Not the least cause of Simon's delight with the Chens was that he felt able to take them into his confidence on the major topic of shipboard conversation, which was the peculiar incompetence of the tour guide.

The Chens were fascinated by his story and, together, they secretly undertook to assist O'Malley without offending him. In a marvelously unobtrusive and gallant fashion Mr. Chen would propitiate the perpetually dissatisfied females like Mrs. Bernoulli, while Simon himself quietly took over the formulation of O'Malley's daily schedule. For her part, Mrs. Chen tirelessly tutored him on their ports of call. Along with their shared secret, these obligations and little acts of charity bound Simon to the Chens in an unexpected intimacy that became the least mentionable yet most obvious joy of the cruise. In a perverse way, worrying over O'Malley provided a métier for these reluctantly retired parents, teachers, and givers of care.

O'Malley was feeling under the weather that morning. Though the voyage had given him a tan, toned up his muscles, and fed him better than he had ever been fed, he had never completely recovered from his cold. His morale was ill too; he could not convince himself that he had actually escaped anything. Naturally, he ascribed his malaise to not painting—to not even desiring to paint, actually. It made him feel like a cold furnace, a farm overgrown, a machine slowly oxidizing in desuetude. Besides, he knew he was on board under a whole series of false pretenses, dependent on Kathleen, Simon, the Chens, that he was bumbling and feckless. He liked to think sometimes of Female, whose beauty had turned out to be more than merely epidermal, and he could always cheer himself up with the image of Ezra Pomerantz tearing open the brown paper in which he had wrapped that magnificent naked maja. But whenever his gloom began to lift like the morning mists over the green islands through which they were then steaming, there was Xenia.

She had grown so ancient that he could barely recognize in her the companion of the last two years. She was wizened and apparently bitter or senile, for she had not said a word to him since they had first weighed anchor.

That morning her silence exasperated him to such a degree that after breakfast he returned to his cabin to have things out with her before she simply evaporated.

"Talk to me, Xenia!" he demanded, peremptorily flopping on his bed.

She sat still, as always, only blinking from time to time.

"Come on. Tell me things. Tell me why you grew younger and why you've grown so old. Tell me what happened to the masterpiece of Don Barrildo de Huesca. Tell me what's happening to you."

Xenia turned her glaucous gaze on him.

"You tell me something first."

O'Malley was overjoyed just to hear her voice, which was still the same, still as sweet.

"Anything," he promised.

"Where are we?"

"Near some island. I think it's Cebu."

She nodded twice. "In that case, I'll tell you what I can."

"What do you mean?"

"Whither thou goest, O'Malley. I grew younger because you had so much to paint and couldn't. You understand?"

O'Malley thought hard. "So now," he said slowly, the idea forming as he spoke, "you're growing old because I can paint but have nothing left to paint? Is that it?"

"More or less, my dear. Neither of us ever cared for sentimentality, so let me just say clearly that we're going to die."

236

"If I die—you do too?"

Xenia nodded once. "Whither," she whispered. "As for Don Barrildo's masterpiece, I doubt if it ever existed. I only told you that story so that your own masterpiece would exist."

"You made it all up?"

"Maybe some of it. I can't remember now."

"But why put the story in Spain all those years ago?"

"Why not? It was a fine century for painting and a good country too. Besides, it was a clue to another story."

O'Malley recalled what Simon had said about stories within stories and began to comprehend.

"So...my contract was...genuine?"

"Fate, like all artists, is amazingly easy to tempt, O'Malley. Now leave me alone. I'm tired out from all this talking."

"I've always loved you best," said O'Malley unsentimentally then climbed up on deck and looked out at the Pacific Ocean which, that morning at least, appeared true to its name. All oceans are really one, he thought, and the world is round. And when he saw the Chens and Simon Solomon coming his way, O'Malley was glad.

The fatal heart attack struck during the night. In the morning it was discovered that O'Malley had left an undated note on the chair in his room. The envelope had Simon's name on it. O'Malley's note requested that in the event of his dying during the voyage he receive a sea burial.

Simon saw to all the arrangements, even sending the requisite wire to Kathleen. The Chens were most helpful and stood on either side of their friend at the ceremony. The Captain officiated, but Simon delivered the eulogy.

Just after the body splashed into the sea, just before the crowd dispersed, Simon turned to Mrs. Chen with a question.

"By any chance do you know the name of that little island over there?"

A B O U T   T H E   A U T H O R

Robert Wexelblatt has published poems, essays, and stories in a wide variety of journals in the United States, including *San José Studies, Sou'wester, The Midwest Quarterly, Poetry Northwest, South Dakota Review, American Literature, Descant, The Kansas Quarterly,* and *The Iowa Review.* His work has received numerous awards, among them *The Kansas Quarterly*/Kansas Arts Commission First Prize Award for Fiction, *San José Studies* Annual Awards for Fiction and Best Essay, Theodore Christian Hoepfner Prizes for Best Essay and Best Story, the *Arizona Quarterly* Award for Best Essay. He is Professor of Humanities in the College of General Studies, Boston University, where he has also been recognized for his excellence as a teacher with the Metcalf Cup and Prize, and a graduate of the University of Pennsylvania, the University of Michigan, and Brandeis University, from which he holds the Ph.D. This is his third book.